MW00932592

WE ARE AKAN

Our People and Our Kingdom in the Rainforest
— GHANA, 1807 —

DOROTHY BROWN SOPER

Illustrations by James Cloutier

LUMINARE PRESS

WWW.LUMINAREPRESS.COM

We Are Akan
Copyright © 2020 Dorothy Brown Soper

All rights reserved. No part of this book may be used or reproduced, transmitted,
or stored in an information retrieval system in any form or by any means, graphic,
electronic, or mechanical without written permission of the publisher.
The exception is for the use of brief quotations in a book review.

Printed in the United States of America

Cover Design: Claire Flint Last

Cover illustrations by James Cloutier show a strip of *kente* cloth and the
celebration of the *Odwira* festival in Kumasi, the capital of the Asante Kingdom. The
king displays the Golden Stool, the kingdom's symbol. This illustration was inspired by
a drawing of the 1817 *Odwira* festival in Kumasi by T.E. Bowdich and included in
Mission from Cape Coast Castle to Ashantee, originally published in 1819 and
republished in 1966 by Frank Cass and Company, London.

Luminare Press
442 Charnelton St.
Eugene, OR 97401
www.luminarepress.com

LCCN: 2019919041
ISBN: 978-1-64388-068-6

For my grandsons,
Eli, Tommy, and Jordan

TABLE OF CONTENTS

Part One:
OUR TOWN

Part Two:
THE ASANTE KINGDOM

Part Three:
THE COAST

VEGETATION ZONES IN THE ASANTE KINGDOM

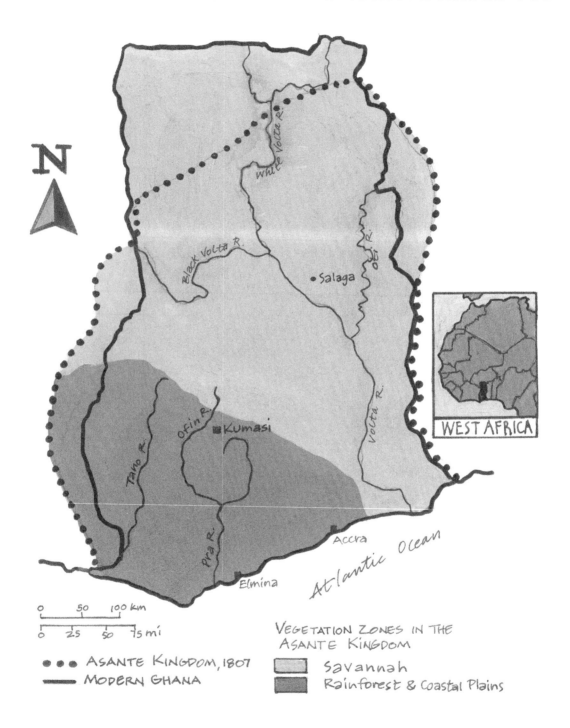

THE ASANTE KINGDOM IN 1807

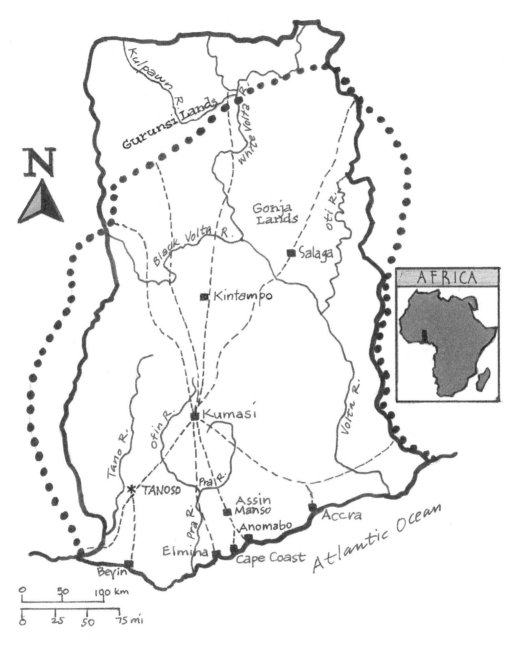

Kulpawn R.

Gurunsi Lands

White Volta R.

Oti R.

Gonja Lands

Salaga

Black Volta R.

Kintampo

AFRICA

N

Tano R.

Ofin R.

Kumasi

Volta R.

* TANOSO

Pra R.

Assin Manso

Pra R.

Anomabo

Accra

Elmina

Cape Coast

Atlantic Ocean

Beyin

| 0 | 50 | 100 km |
| 0 | 25 | 50 | 75 mi |

• • • ASANTE KINGDOM, 1807 ━━ MODERN GHANA
- - - - THE GREAT-ROADS
* Fictional town of TANOSO

2

Part One:

OUR TOWN

The chief's home in Tanoso

— CHAPTER 1 —

Into the Forest

As dawn broke, Nana and his son, Kwame, followed the footpath downhill from their home. Elder Kofi waited at the low log fence that marked the boundary between town and forest.

"*Maakye* – Good morning," they greeted him.

"*Yaa*," Elder Kofi replied, smiling. "I'm happy to see you. Will we find duikers this morning?"

"I hope so," Nana answered with enthusiasm.

"I'm ready to hunt," Elder Kofi affirmed. "I want to eat duiker meat tonight. Let's go!"

Leaves of the tall trees ahead glistened with dew that soon rained on them. "Stars are falling. I'm getting wet," Kwame said with pleasure, though shivering. His shoulders and feet were bare and he wore only a cloth tied around his waist.

"It's always wet in the forest," Nana reminded Kwame. "Can you keep up with us?"

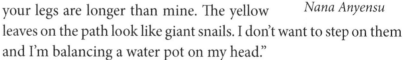

Papa, Tanosohene
Nana Anyensu

"It's hard, Papa. You're wearing sandals and I'm barefoot, and your legs are longer than mine. The yellow leaves on the path look like giant snails. I don't want to step on them and I'm balancing a water pot on my head."

"We'll slow down, Kwame. Elder Kofi and I have light loads. I'm carrying only my spear and a machete. We don't need to hurry."

"Papa, when we get to the rocks, I want to step off of the path to pee and I'm hungry. We didn't eat much breakfast." Nana agreed.

At the bottom of the slope, Kwame put the water pot and a smoked fish that he carried wrapped in a leaf on top of a flat rock and stepped off of the path. Two small monkeys sprinted across the rock, grabbed the fish, and scaled a nearby tree.

Elder Kofi

"Stop! Don't steal my fish!" Kwame yelled at the monkeys, but it was too late. "Papa, look what happened," Kwame said when he returned to the path. "The monkeys are hungry, just like me."

"I'm sorry. We weren't watching," Nana sympathized. "Asare and Baako will have bananas for us at the stream. We'll eat soon."

"Elder Kofi, why didn't Kwaku come with you?" Kwame asked. "He wants to learn to hunt, like me."

"My son's going to his mother's farm this morning to harvest plantains for the market. He wanted to come. He wants to know how to throw a spear and hunt."

"I'll see him in the marketplace later," Kwame replied. "I'll tell him what happened."

Kwame

"Let's be off," Nana said. "Here, Kwame, your hands are free now, take my machete. Lead the way and chop bushes along the path."

Kwame reluctantly accepted his father's machete. "I'm watching for leopards, Papa. I'm scared of them. Elder Kofi, why didn't you bring your gun?"

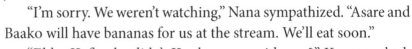

"I don't need it today," Elder Kofi replied. "My spear and a bow and arrows are enough. Why are you thinking about leopards?"

"Grannie told us a story about them. She said they're dangerous."

"Leopards are gone now," Nana said. "When we Akans got guns, we killed too many of them. Every chief wanted a leopard skin. I'd like them to come back."

Kwaku

"Are leopards the only animals that hunters shoot with a gun?" Kwame asked.

"Hunters shoot crocodiles," Elder Kofi confirmed. "They're always dangerous but they stay near rivers."

"Asare will look for duikers in the forest today," Nana said. "They're small and hunters can get close to them. Guns are too powerful for small animals, and ammunition is expensive."

Beyond the rocks, the path curved through a grove of oil palm trees and again to enter a thicket of bamboo. Balancing the water pot carefully, Kwame swung the machete to trim bushes on both sides of the path. "This is easier than weeding, Papa, but the bushes aren't overgrown."

"Bushes grow fast, Kwame. Watch for spider webs. Chop them. Don't walk through webs."

The path soon wound around thick tree trunks where little light reached the ground. Listening carefully to the forest noises, Nana asked, "What do you hear, Kwame?"

"All kinds of insects. They're always loud. Bush babies crying and some hissing. Maybe porcupines. What about puff adders? They hiss and they're deadly."

Spearing the cobra

"We won't see puff adders. They like more daylight. Do you hear grunting? What's doing that?" Nana laid his hand on his son's shoulder, as the group stopped to listen.

"Grasscutters? They're good to eat, Papa. Asare could hunt them."

"We hear grasscutters or hogs. Most likely grasscutters," Nana replied. "They're out at dawn near water. I won't ask Asare to hunt them though. Duiker meat is better.

"Today I want to find a good staging area to hunt duikers. Elder Kofi wants a duiker for tonight and I'll ask Asare to kill one for me tomorrow morning, for *Adaepa*. We'll have a crowd at our home and, as the chief, I have to serve the best food. Let's continue."

"Do duikers make noise? I've never heard them." Kwame said as he strained to listen.

"They make quiet sounds, like whimpers, except for a distress call that has a high pitch," Elder Kofi explained.

"Some hunters imitate the call to attract duikers that will come to see what's wrong. I don't do that because the call scares other animals away. It's good that we hear steady noises. There's no disturbance."

Kwame stopped suddenly and stiffened. "Papa, look, a cobra!" he whispered and pointed the machete at the snake ahead and to the side of the path.

The cobra raised its head and spread its hood.

"Back away!" Nana said in a calm voice. "It's warning us. Get behind me." Kwame moved quickly.

Nana stood still for a clear view of the snake. Gripping his spear

Forest cobra

firmly, he drew his arm back and threw the spear with all of his strength. It hit the ground hard in front of the cobra that spun around and slithered away.

"I couldn't get close enough hit it, but it won't bother us now," Nana said. "I'm glad you saw it, Kwame."

"When the cobra stood up, it surprised me. I'm always careful when I walk to the stream." Kwame shuddered. Kwame and many other children followed the path every day to collect water.

"You know how to be safe on the path, Kwame. I want you to teach the other children who walk here. Come in a group, walk fast, and make noise. You'll scare most animals. If you see a snake, stay away from it. If we keep the path clear, children should be safe. They have to work. We have to have water."

Nana, Elder Kofi, and Kwame entered an open area, once cleared for a farm but now lying fallow. The path straightened. With fewer trees, there was more light.

"The forest is alive, Kwame," Nana said. "I hope you'll grow up to love it as I do. *Nyame* created it and our ancestors have cared for it. If we honor the spirits of the earth and forest, we can raise our crops, eat some of the animals, and build with the wood. Foreign people are afraid of the forest, so we're safe here. Only the leopards are missing and only the crocodiles threaten us. We're in a clearing now. Give me my machete. We'll walk faster."

"I've been wondering about something, Papa. I know that Asare and Baako belong to you. They're *nnonko*. Baako's my friend. What will happen to him and the other *nnonko* children when they grow up?"

"I'm glad that you and Baako are friends, Kwame. *Nnonko* children like Baako learn to speak Twi and how to be Akan. If they're healthy and work hard, our families will adopt them."

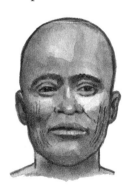

Asare

"Baako has a scar like me, and he speaks Twi, like me. I want him to be free, like me," Kwame explained.

"I've thought about that seriously," Papa replied. "I'm impressed with Baako's work and he's smart and healthy. I'll probably adopt him. He would be free then."

"That's good. When would you adopt him? Does he know?"

"When you and Baako are a little older. Baako's parents know. They might have told him.

"If I adopt Baako, Kwame, you must never reveal his origin. In my oath to become the chief, I promised to protect my people in this way. Our first king gave us this law. Baako would belong to my clan and after many years, no one will remember that he was once an *odonko*. All free people in the forest are Akan. Do you understand?"

"I understand, Papa. Baako would be an Akan who speaks Twi and Nankane. What will happen to his real mama and papa? Will they ever be free?"

"Baako would see them in the *nnonko* village and work with them on my farm. Asare's my foreman and Baako's mother works in our home. I trust them and depend on them, but they'll never be free. Asare has the long scars of the Gurunsi people on his face. If he and Anyetata travel outside of my district, they'll be captured and forced to work for someone else."

Baako

"Where do *nnonko* come from?" Kwame asked.

"Long ago, before we had a kingdom, Akans fought each other. Victorious chiefs kept their prisoners of war as *nnonko* or sold them to the whites on the coast. Now that we have a kingdom, Akans usually don't fight each other. Our kings, the Asantehenes, have been strong. They've kept peace among us most of the time and defeated kingdoms in the savannah. Those kings have to give the Asantehene prisoners and other items to pay their taxes. The savannah kings capture people from weaker groups outside of their kingdoms.

"The Asantehene keeps some of these prisoners and gives others to his army commanders and chiefs to reward them. He sells some inside the kingdom and others to the whites. These prisoners become our *nnonko*.

"Asare was captured with his parents and grandparents when he was young. The Asantehene gave his family to my uncle, who was the chief then. Asare and I grew up together. I inherited my *nnonko* from my uncle. Now Asare translates Nankane for me because I can't speak the Gurunsi language."

"That's a sad story, Papa. If you adopt Baako, I'll never tell anyone that he was an *odonko*. He'll be Akan just like me."

"You understand." Nana smiled at his son. "Look, I see the termite mound ahead."

CHAPTER 2

The Hunt and the Mine

Baako and Asare

"We'll see duikers this morning," Asare told his son in Nankane. "They drink from the river near the new mine."

"Papa, I'm hungry. I want to eat bananas."

"We'll wait for Nana, Elder Kofi, and Kwame. They'll be hungry too," Asare explained. "I'm glad that you're coming with us."

"When Kwame and I are older, will we be able to hunt by ourselves? Will I be free to hunt with Kwame?"

"If you stay healthy and if Nana is satisfied with your work, he'll adopt you. Then you'll be free."

"I want to be free, Papa, but will I see you and Mama if I'm free?"

"We'll always be here," Asare assured his son. "You'll be able to visit us in our village. You'll work in Nana's fields with Kwame and Kwaku like you do now and I'll see you there. Akans don't work in the mines so you won't have to do that anymore."

"That's good," Baako replied. "I don't like that work.

"No one does. It's dangerous," Asare said as he stooped to drink from the stream. "The water tastes good and it's warmer than the air. It feels good to splash it on my face."

Asare continued, "I hope that Akan families will adopt your brothers and sisters and other children from our village, too. I think that will happen because Nana wants more free people in his district. I want my family to stay together even if only some are free."

"I remember the savannah and my parents and grandparents and I miss them," Asare explained. "They're gone now but I would like to see the savannah again. That was my home and your mother's, too, but we'll never be free to go back. We will always stay with our children."

"I'm glad about that. Papa, I'm working on throwing a spear so I can hunt. I've been practicing."

"You're doing well. I want to work with you more before the rains start. I'll ask Nana if Kwame can join us."

"And Kwaku," Baako added. "He's my friend, too."

"Yes, Kwaku. He may be the chief someday. If he is, he won't be allowed to hunt but he has to know how to throw a spear. Chiefs fight in wars. I hear footsteps."

NANA, ELDER KOFI, AND KWAME APPROACHED THE STREAM. KWAME SMILED WHEN he saw the bananas. "*Mema mo akye* – Good morning to you both," Nana said softly.

"*Yaa*, Nana. *Yaa*, Elder Kofi," Asare and Baako replied as each knelt on one knee, bowed his head, and extended his right hand to Nana. "Are you well?" they asked.

"We are well," Nana replied as he touched their hands lightly. "Stand now."

Kwame and Baako looked at each other but said nothing. Kwame set his water pot on the ground. The boys ate bananas and drank from the stream while their fathers and Elder Kofi talked.

"I'll inspect the new mine this morning and look at the soil that you've dug out," Nana told Asare, "but first Elder Kofi wants you to look for duikers. He wants to eat one tonight. Have you seen any?"

"Near the new mine," Asare replied. "They drink from the river. I've killed a few. There are too many duikers now. They're eating your crops. The *nnonko* working in the mine have seen a crocodile in the river. It's looking for duikers, too."

"That's serious. We didn't bring a gun," Nana replied.

"You can sit on the log pile next to the mine. You'll be safe," Asare assured Nana. "I can kill a crocodile with a spear. I've never used a gun. I brought two spears to be sure. Let's go. I'll carry my spears and yours, Nana, and a machete. Baako and Kwame can carry machetes."

"I'll eat a banana first," Nana said as he considered the plan's safety. After eating, he drank from the stream. A chief shouldn't take unnecessary risks, but Nana knew that Elder Kofi and Asare were good hunters, and that Asare would not risk anyone's life. As a chief, he didn't hunt but often helped search for a safe staging area as he was doing now.

Nana stood up saying, "I'm ready. We'll go." The group crossed the stream on a sandbar and followed the path deeper into the forest.

To protect the others, Asare led, setting a fast pace. Nana and Elder Kofi walked behind him, pleased to be moving once more. Kwame was next in line, chopping bushes, and relieved not to be balancing a water pot. Baako was last. He looked for snakes in the trees.

Without talking, the group walked steadily. Everyone stopped when Asare held up his right arm and pointed to a narrower path on the left. "We'll take this," he said. "We built it when we dug the new mine. We cleared a large space but left some bushes next to the river. We'll walk slowly because the light won't be as good, but we don't have far to go."

They soon entered the large clearing. The pit was covered with logs and more logs were stacked behind it, away from the river and next to piles of soil and rock dug out of the mine. Men crushed the rock and women sifted it and the soil to search for gold.

"I see that much work is going on here," Elder Kofi observed. "You don't want a crocodile nearby."

"Sit on the log pile and I'll go into the forest to look for duikers and drive them to the river," Asare said.

Nana agreed and cautioned the boys. "If you see a crocodile, you'll be scared but stay on the log pile and try to be quiet. A crocodile can drag a live duiker into the water fast or take one that's been killed. There's no stopping it."

Asare gave Nana's spear back to him while keeping his own two and a machete. "I'll leave now," he said. "Call me if you need me. I'll stay nearby."

"Climb to the top of the pile," Nana directed the others. "Baako, stay next to Elder Kofi and hold his spear. Elder Kofi will stand. The rest of us will sit."

"If duikers come into the clearing, I'll use my bow and arrows," Elder Kofi told the boys. "If the crocodile crawls up on the bank, I'll use my spear. I think that I can kill one with a spear. I never have but I have a good aim and I'm strong. You'll see what hunters must do." Elder Kofi took an arrow from his quiver and readied his bow.

Speaking softly, Nana complimented the boys. "Kwame and Baako, you're brave to come with us. How do you feel?"

The boys felt shy to answer. Kwame spoke first. "I'm not sure how I feel. I want to see duikers but I'm afraid of the crocodile."

"I'm afraid, too," Baako confided to Nana. "I don't know what a crocodile will do."

"Kwame and Baako, you should be afraid of crocodiles. We're safe on the log pile. A crocodile can't reach us here. Let's watch for duikers."

The air was still and cool. Heavy with dew, leaves on the trees barely moved. The group saw the wide river well because the early morning light wasn't blocked by trees. The water was almost covered with leaves. Everyone listened to the gently flowing river and familiar forest sounds.

Kwame watched leaves float slowly down the river. They didn't look like snails anymore. They looked like boats. Nudging Baako, he asked, "Where do you think the leaves are going? Will we see them again?"

"They'll float by town," Baako whispered. "Maybe they'll go all of the way to the ocean. I wish we could do that."

"Me, too," Kwame agreed. "Baako, do you work in the mine?"

"Sometimes I have to go down into the pit and shovel dirt into a basket. Papa sends me and other boys when the pit is narrow. We fit. I don't like to do that. I like to work on farms."

"It's good that we can work together on Papa's farms," Kwame replied. "I hope that we'll hunt together sometime, too."

Staring intently at the river, Nana pointed to the near bank and said to the boys, "Look at the two circles shining in the water. Do you see them? What do you think they are?"

The boys looked carefully and Kwame answered fearfully, "Papa, I see the eyes of a crocodile. It's waiting for duikers."

"You're right. What should we do?"

"I want to ask my papa but he's not here," Baako answered.

"He would know," Nana said, "but since he isn't here, let's decide."

"If duikers come to the bank, the crocodile will go after them," Baako said.

"It's fast," Nana added. "I wonder if there are other crocodiles in the river."

"Crocodiles don't live by themselves, do they?" Kwame asked.

"Some do but I don't know about this one."

"If this one is fast, Papa, it will snatch a duiker and disappear into the river before Elder Kofi can do anything."

"If there are two duikers, I would kill the other one," Elder Kofi speculated. "If there's time, I'll try to kill the crocodile first. Baako, if it climbs out of the river, be ready to hand me my spear."

"I'll be ready," Baako assured him.

Nana cautioned the boys, "If we see a crocodile, you'll be scared but stay quiet. You'll think better. We're safe here. Do you know that some people believe duikers have the power to disappear if they're threatened?"

"I didn't know that," Kwame answered. "Will they disappear if they see us or a crocodile?"

"What would scare duikers besides hunters and crocodiles?" Baako asked.

"Pythons," Nana replied. The boys shuddered.

Soon the group heard Asare approaching while uttering a low sound. "He's found something. Let's get ready," Elder Kofi said as he braced himself, readied an arrow, and drew his bow string taut.

Three duikers entered the clearing, walking slowly and gracefully toward the river. Elder Kofi released his arrow and made a direct hit. One duiker fell. The boys smiled to each other.

At that moment the crocodile stood and hissed. The other duikers turned and uttered a high pitched distress call while running toward the log pile.

Elder Kofi gasped, put his bow and arrow down, and took his spear from Baako. The boys stood holding on to each other, and yelled, "Ahhhhhhh!"

Elder Kofi breathed deeply, raised his arm, took aim, and with his full strength threw his spear. It sank deep into the crocodile's skull behind its eyes. The beast stood still in the river, frozen in place. Elder Kofi picked up his bow again and reached for an arrow. At that moment a second spear pierced the crocodile's skull. The huge beast tossed its head from side to side.

One duiker fell.

"I'm here," Asare called, holding his remaining spear high as he raced across the clearing and climbed onto the log pile. He took a wide stance, drew his spear back, and hurled it with great force. The third spear found its mark, too, in the crocodile's skull.

The group watched and waited in silence. With three spears in its skull, the crocodile turned and sank into the water, ignoring the fallen duiker and disappearing from view.

"Crocodiles take a long time to die," Asare said. "We're safe now. We can climb down."

As a chief, Nana knew how to control his emotions, but he felt enormous relief. He raised his arms in the air and exclaimed with enthusiasm, "We killed the crocodile! I thank my ancestors. I thank the spirit of our great Tano River, Elder Kofi, and Asare. We are blessed."

The boys could barely believe what they had seen. Encouraged by Nana's words, they jumped up and down shouting, "We did it! We did it! The crocodile's gone!"

When Kwame and Baako were quiet once more, Elder Kofi said to them, "The crocodile was fierce, but try not to yell when you're hunting. That scares animals and other hunters, too. Though today, the crocodile didn't hear you in time."

Elder Kofi turned to Asare. "Your spears made the difference."

Asare lowered his head with modesty and replied, "I followed the duikers to the clearing and saw the crocodile. I had to throw my spears. Miners will be safe now."

Kwame looked at the fallen duiker. "I don't think that duikers have any magic but they can make a lot of noise and run fast," he said. "What will happen to the crocodile?"

"The *nnonko* will look for it later," Asare explained. "We'll collect the spears and take the carcass to our village. Akans don't eat crocodile meat, but we do. We'll have a feast tonight and smoke the rest of the meat for later."

"Asare pointed to the duiker, saying, "Elder Kofi, here is your duiker for tonight and, Nana, you'll have the grasscutter that I found in a pit trap. I'll look for more duikers here in the morning. We'll have plantains, cassava, and one or two duikers ready for *Adaepa* in the morning."

"That's good, Asare. The *nnonko* will have the most meat tonight though. You've earned it and you've found an excellent place to hunt," Nana said.

"I'll come back here to look for more duikers," Elder Kofi said.

"What do you boys think about learning to throw spears from Asare?" Nana asked. "He knows how!"

"Yes!" the boys said together.

"Kwaku, too," Baako added. "We want him to learn with us!"

"He's ready," Elder Kofi agreed.

"The three of you together," Nana said. "We'll find a time."

"Kwame," Nana continued. "I want you and Baako to give the duiker and grasscutter to Baako's mother. She'll find an *odonko* to dress them and take the meat into town.

"Baako," Nana added, "from your village walk with Kwame to the stream and bring a machete. Kwame, it's still early, you'll probably see other children at the stream or on the path. Make noise!" Kwame smiled.

"Be quick, Baako," Asare urged. "We'll need you to help harvest cassava and plantains today, and we may need you at the mine. When you get back, ask in the village where most *nnonko* are working and join them. I'll get my machete and the grasscutter now."

Nana continued, "Kwame, tell your mother and Grannie that I'll be back after the market closes. Asare, Elder Kofi, and I will look at this new mine. I want to see how much soil the *nnonko* have dug out. We'll go to other mines later.

"Listen to the parrots everyone," Nana said as he looked up into the trees again and spread his arms. "They're ready for the new day and so are we!"

CHAPTER 3

Morning Chores

Cooking at the hearth

We Are Akan

Madam Ama awoke early and dressed quickly while gazing fondly at her daughter, Akua, and her second son, Yaw Mensah, snug in cloths and asleep on mats in her hut. Wrapping a cloth around her chest, she placed another over her head and shoulders, and slipped on her sandals. Bracing herself against the cool outside air, she stepped through the doorway into the small courtyard of the home that she shared with her husband, Nana, and their three children.

Mama,
Madam Ama

After walking across a second and larger courtyard, Madam Ama left through the front entrance, and continued on the road down the hill to a public latrine. A guard at the chief's home, always called the palace, stood across the road. He waved to her and she waved back.

Madam Ama soon returned to the smaller space that she called the family courtyard. It was a private space with two large shade trees, a hearth, many stools to sit on, and surrounded by sleeping and storage huts.

With smoldering embers, Madam Ama built a fire in the hearth and then washed her hands with water from a small gourd. She poured water from a water pot into a cauldron and added corn paste to prepare porridge over the fire. Porridge and bananas would provide a hearty breakfast for her family.

A crowing rooster woke Akua and Yaw Mensah. Smelling the corn porridge that they loved, they dressed quickly and ran to the hearth.

Yaw Mensah

"Good morning," Madam Ama said with affection as she hugged both children. "I'm happy to see you. Bring stools and sit by the hearth."

"It's cold, Mama," Yaw Mensah said.

"Take my extra cloth," Mama offered. "Wrap it around your shoulders. Akua, there's a cloth for you in a storage hut. It's cool now, but the sun will soon warm the air.

"Eat your porridge. I'll sprinkle peanuts on top. They're always good. Have a banana, too. Nana and Kwame left early. Kwame will bring more water when he comes home, and Grannie will be here soon."

Akua

When Kwame and Baako entered the *nnonko* village, Kwame greeted Baako's mother, Anyetata, politely and she returned his greeting with a friendly smile. Like her husband, Asare, she knew Nana's family well and spoke Twi. The boys gave her the meat and explained what Nana wanted her to do. She nodded.

When Baako told his mother about the crocodile, she was pleased but asked about everyone's safety. "We were brave," Baako assured her.

Anyetata knew that Asare would need help to bring the crocodile's carcass to their village and dress it, prepare some of the meat for the night's meal, and smoke the rest. Handling such a beast was the work of many. "I'll let everyone know," she said.

Kwame was surprised when Anyetata asked, "Have you tasted crocodile meat?"

"No, I haven't," Kwame replied.

"We'll save some for you," she offered. "You'll like it."

"*Medaase* – Thank you," Kwame replied, feeling pleased, yet concerned about how it would taste.

"Let's go," Kwame urged Baako. "I have to help Mama at the market and she wants more water. Don't forget your machete. Cut off a bamboo stick for me to break up spider webs." The boys set off quickly.

With more daylight, Kwame and Baako saw the true colors and shape of the forest. The red clay soil was flooring for massive brown tree trunks that were often hosts to green vines. The tall trees reached heights that were out of sight and bore crowns that formed a protective shield above. The forest always looked green even though the leaves of some trees turned yellow in the dry season and fell to cover paths, streams, and the river. The boys followed the curving red path dotted with yellow leaves as insects buzzed around their ears and parrots squawked overhead. Baako chopped back bushes and Kwame poked spider webs.

"Has Asare started teaching you to throw spears?" Kwame asked.

"I've started and it's hard. You'll see."

"How far can you throw a spear?"

"Not far," Baako answered. "It's hard to hit a target, even one that's still. You have to aim carefully and throw hard. I want to get stronger. I don't know if I'll ever be fast enough to hit animals. They move."

"Elder Kofi and Asare are strong and they know how to aim," Kwame said. "I hope that we can do that someday and kill crocodiles." Baako nodded.

When the boys neared the stream, Baako set aside his machete. "Let's get wet," he said. "The water's warm."

The boys threw their cloths on bushes, jumped into the stream, churned the water with their hands, and kicked to splash each other. "The water feels good," Kwame shouted. Soon they were drenched.

"Let's swim like crocodiles," Baako proposed, as he lay face down, beating the water with his arms and legs.

"You're not a good crocodile," Kwame objected. "You're too noisy. You'll scare the duikers. Look, move quietly like this, like a fish." Putting his face in the water, Kwame crawled along the muddy bottom of the stream on his hands and knees without splashing and soon climbed onto the opposite bank. "See, I'm quiet. I'll get more to eat than you."

"You're right. Crocodiles are quiet. That's why they're so dangerous. You don't know when they're coming after you," Baako said.

"They're always here. You have to watch for them. I'm getting out now. Mama's waiting for me."

"You're on land. You're a duiker. I'm coming after you," Baako cried out as he crawled onto the bank.

"Catch me," Kwame yelled, running toward the tall, reddish termite mound that rose ahead to the side of the path, seeming to guard the stream. Hiding behind the mound, Kwame peered around it to see Baako struggling to crawl on land. "Duikers can outrun a crocodile. We know that," Kwame said, smiling.

"Ahh, you're right. It's hard to crawl if you're a rock. I can't do this any more. You got away," Baako admitted. "Next time I'll catch you while you're still in the water."

"I'll get my cloth and go upstream to find clear water for Mama," Kwame said.

"The air will dry me," Baako replied. "I'm going now."

"See you tomorrow," Kwame called to his friend. "Bring me crocodile meat sometime. I want to try it."

Baako smiled and waved, crossed the stream, picked up his cloth and machete, and disappeared down the path.

KWAME RETRIEVED HIS WATER POT, CROSSED THE STREAM, PICKED UP HIS CLOTH AND bamboo stick, and walked a short distance upstream to find clear water. Returning to the path, he heard voices. Children from town saw him and called out, "Kwame, Kwame, scare away the snakes for us! Scare away the monkeys!"

"Oh, you little ones," Kwame answered as he smiled and waved. "Don't be afraid. No snakes or monkeys are here. Break off some leaves and come quickly."

"This is the best place," Kwame explained as he waded upstream once more. "The water's moving and it's clear. I'll push the leaves away. Don't play in the water or it will be too muddy."

Kwame helped the younger children fill their water pots. For each child he knelt next to the water, dipped the pot to let water fill it slowly, and then placed it on a cushion of leaves on the child's head. "Keep your back straight, look ahead, and balance your pot carefully. It's heavy and you'll get wet, but you shouldn't spill much. You can all do this."

Bringing water home

The children smiled with their eyes. "*Medaase* – Thank you, Kwame," they said.

"What about spiders?" one child asked. "They're always here and I don't like them."

Kwame looked at the children standing tall. "I'll walk first in line and greet the spiders," he said as he picked up his bamboo twig.

"Let's march. One, two, three, four. We look like ants. We'll scare spiders and snakes. Let's march," he said again, "and count together and make a lot of noise."

"Five, six, seven, eight," the children shouted, now feeling braver and walking faster.

Kwame led the counting until they reached the log fence. "We're home," he shouted.

Children hurried into town and scattered. "See you at the market," Kwame called to them and waved as he returned home with water and news to share.

ENTERING THE FAMILY COURTYARD, KWAME SMELLED CORN PORRIDGE AND SMILED. HE SAW everyone in his family, except his father, sitting on stools around the hearth, eating breakfast.

"*Mema mo akye* – Good morning, everyone," Kwame said and everyone replied.

"Put the water over there," Madam Ama instructed, pointing to a storage hut. "We'll use it tonight. Pull up a stool and sit down. I'm sorry that we had to start breakfast without you. I'll dish up your porridge now."

Kwame followed his mother's instructions and soon joined his family at the hearth. The morning air was still cool and he welcomed the warmth of the fire.

"*Maakye* – Good morning, Grannie. I hope that you are well," Kwame greeted his grand-mother individually to show his respect. Grannie was Nana's mother and held the title of Queen Mother.

"*Yaa*, Kwame," she replied. "Yes, I'm well and I'll go to the market with everyone today. I want to visit with my friends and see what traders brought from the coast. They should have the smoked fish that I love."

"Fish tastes good," Madam Ama said, "but food from the forest like our giant snails and duiker meat are better than fish in peanut soup."

"Oh, my dear," Queen Mother laughed. "You're right when we think of soup, but for lunch, nothing tastes better than smoked fish and fried plantains. They're crunchy and easy to eat."

Kwame finished his porridge. Children were not expected to talk at a meal, but this morning was different. "Please, I want to talk," he said.

"Go ahead, Kwame," his mother replied.

"At the river, Elder Kofi killed a duiker and he and Asare killed a crocodile that was big and scary."

Madam Ama gasped. "That was an adventure, Kwame. Crocodiles are dangerous. How did Elder Kofi and Asare kill it?"

"With three spears. Elder Kofi threw one and Asare threw two. The crocodile went back into the river to die and Asare said that the *nnonko* will find it and the spears. Papa, Baako, and I watched from a log pile next to the mine. It was exciting."

Madam Ama sighed. "Crocodiles are horrible. I'm glad that we don't see them often."

"Let us praise our ancestors," the Queen Mother said in a low voice. "They took care of you."

"*Nnonko* eat crocodiles," Kwame continued. "Asare said they would take it to their village."

"Yes, the *nnonko* will be happy. Will we get a duiker tomorrow for *Adaepa*?" Madam Ama asked.

"Mama, tomorrow morning Asare will hunt for duikers and bring you one or two. For tonight an *odonko* will bring a grasscutter that was in a pit trap for us and the duiker that Elder Kofi killed. Papa will be home after the market closes. He said to tell you that he's going with Elder Kofi and Asare to inspect mines."

Grannie,
the Queen Mother

"Kwame, were you scared when you saw the crocodile?" Akua wanted to know.

"Yes, I was scared. Baako and I were supposed to be quiet but we yelled. We couldn't stop. Next time we'll be braver but the crocodile was fierce. The duikers were scared, too. They made a lot of noise. Two of them got away from the crocodile."

"I want to see a crocodile," Yaw Mensah said. "Can I go hunting with you next time?"

"You can't go yet, Yaw. You're too little. Maybe when you're older and can run fast," Kwame answered.

"I want to go, too," Akua added.

"Wait until I can throw a spear. Papa said that Asare will teach Kwaku, Baako, and me."

"I want to throw a spear, too," Akua said.

"Girls don't throw spears, Akua, you know that," Kwame answered. Akua frowned.

"We saw a cobra," Kwame continued. "Papa threw his spear to scare it. It was too far away for him to kill it. He said that when we go to the stream we should be in a group and make a lot of noise to scare snakes away."

"He's right," the Queen Mother agreed. "I don't know anyone who's been bitten by a cobra but be careful when you see a snake."

"My son, Kwame, you had adventures this morning. I'm glad that you're safe at home now. Everyone finish breakfast and clean up. It's market day."

— CHAPTER 4 —

Market Day

"It's market day!" Madam Ama reminded everyone. "My children, sweep both courtyards. Be sure to get all of the leaves. I don't want snakes hiding here. Let the chickens out. Collect any eggs you find."

Yaw Mensah sweeping the family courtyard

Akua and Yaw Mensah finished eating and took their gourds to the storage shed to wash and put away. Picking up brooms, they walked to corners of the family courtyard. "Come on, Kwame," Akua called out. "We need your help!"

Walking to a far corner where the gate was open, Yaw Mensah repeated, "Kwame, we need your help!" as he waved to children passing by.

"I'm coming," Kwame replied, gulping down the last of his porridge. He washed the gourds, put them away, picked up a broom, and walked to a third corner. "Let's sweep fast. I want to leave for the market," he said.

"Don't make dust fly," Akua warned. "I don't want dust in my eyes."

Yaw Mensah, Akua, and Kwame stooped and swept.

"I'll be back soon," the Queen Mother promised as she stood to return to her home next to the palace. Walking through the main courtyard that she knew well from her childhood, she thought of her senior brother who was the chief before Nana and who had designed and built the palace. She remembered watching *nnonko* construct the wood framework for the double walls of the huts and pour a mixture of clay soil, twigs, small leaves, and water to fill the openings and plaster the walls.

The huts had solid wood doors that were often a step above the ground but no windows. The interiors stayed dry in the rainy season while fresh air entered through the opening between the top of the walls and the roof. The steep, tiered roofs made of palm fronds rose high to crown the huts and shed the rain.

The main courtyard was usually busy. The Queen Mother remembered watching her brother meet with elders in the open, three-walled council room. She thought of her mother, the Queen Mother before her, joining ceremonies and telling stories to children in their family. The beautiful tree that her brother had planted still provided welcoming shade. The Queen Mother had loved playing games with her friends under the tree, the girls chasing each other until they all became dizzy and fell to the ground laughing. Thinking of her family and friends, the Queen Mother smiled with deep pleasure. She knew her brother would be pleased and proud to see the palace now.

On market days the courtyard was quiet. On other days visitors often came to the palace to talk to Nana in the council room or to wait for him in the shade of the tree. Nana's sleeping hut opened to this courtyard, as did the hut where the sacred stools of the grandfather chiefs were kept and three other huts used for storage or lodging guests.

Throughout the rainy season, Madam Ama and her sisters worked hard with their children and *nnonko* on a vegetable farm. At times their senior brother, Elder Kwasi, joined them. Madam Ama and her family were pleased with their abundant harvest this dry season.

As the children swept, Madam Ama packed three baskets at a storage shelter in the family courtyard. In two baskets she started with banana leaves to use to display vegetables and wrap them for customers. Next came peppers, onions, tomatoes, garden eggs, okra, and finally a new crop, carrots, that she planned to give away in the market today. She devoted the third basket to kola nuts, the fruit of the wild kola trees that grew on her family's farm. Long distance traders bought kola nuts in forest markets to resell to traders traveling to the savannah.

Cloths to spread on the ground, an empty water pot, gourds to drink from, a hand scale, and gold weights filled the tops of the baskets. Madam Ama hoped that some customers would buy with gold dust, which was scarce and highly desirable. She traded much of her harvest for food and a few other items, and some customers paid in cowrie shells.

"Grannie's back. It's time to leave," Madam Ama instructed her children. She, Kwame, and Akua each carried a large basket as a head load. Kwame brought a machete.

Yaw Mensah was pleased to carry a bucket of giant forest snails. "Look at them," he exclaimed. "They're bigger than Papa's hands. We'll sell them fast!" Due to her high status, the Queen Mother carried nothing.

The group left the palace through the front entrance to join the town's wide and well-traveled main road dotted with tall, bushy trees that often drew people together to enjoy shade and a cooling breeze. There was a drainage ditch on each side of the main road and beyond, huts that lined family courtyards.

Huts were all built in the same style with a wood frame, plastered exterior walls, a steep roof and a solid door, but no windows. The town, called Tanoso after the nearby Tano River, was built on a hill with the chief's palace at the highest point and the marketplace at the lowest point, next to the river.

The Queen Mother, Madam Ama, and the children walked downhill toward the marketplace and the river. The women greeted everyone saying, "*Maakye* – Good morning," over and over.

Friends and family members replied, "*Yaa*," and asked, "How are you? How is Nana? How are your children?"

"Our family is well," the Queen Mother and Madam Ama replied many times.

Walking to the marketplace in Tanoso

At the bottom of the hill, the family joined one of the great-roads that united the kingdom. Here the road was called the Tano Road, named after the river, like the town. There were eight great-roads fanning out from Kumasi, the capital city, like rays of light reaching all parts of the kingdom.

The great-roads were wide, nearly straight, built to support trade, government business, and the quick passage of the army. The roads were constructed, maintained, and guarded by local chiefs, like Nana, but paid for by the king. The Tano Road bordered the marketplace to provide easy access for traders and shoppers alike.

Children of all ages went to the market with their families. Most walked but the very young rode, tied to their mothers' backs. Older children wanted to play but couldn't with bundles on their heads or in their hands. "Come see me at the river," they cried out from one family to another. Many were cousins or best friends.

After a short walk, Madam Ama and her group left the Tano Road to enter the marketplace that fit neatly between the great-road and the river and was bordered by trees on the other two sides. They looked for the manager.

"*Maakye*," they greeted her.

"*Yaa*, Queen Mother," the manager replied with a curtsy. Turning to Madam Ama, she said, "*Yaa*, Madam Ama. Do you want your usual place?"

"Oh, yes. Everyone knows to find me there," Madam Ama answered.

"Please go ahead and have a good day," the manager replied and waved them on.

The morning sun shone brightly. The market sounds were low-pitched and pleasant: traders talking, children playing, and the river flowing. Local and long-distance traders unwrapped bundles and emptied baskets of crops, meat, fish, cloth, pottery, and other products that they had made, raised, gathered, purchased, hunted, or traded for. Traders filled stalls or spread their goods on the ground. A few women dug fire pits to cook food to sell.

With Kwame and Akua's help, Madam Ama set up her trading stall. "Kwame, cut the grass," she instructed, "and then cut some palm fronds and small branches and add them to the roof. I see some holes. Akua, take out the cloths to spread on the ground and help me empty the baskets. Then go to the river to fetch drinking water. Check with the guard before you get close to the water."

When Kwame returned with new fronds to add to the roof, he gave Yaw Mensah extra ones to play with. Yaw was happy.

Akua made an attractive display of her mother's vegetables. She alternated red tomatoes and peppers with green okra and the pale white garden eggs, all displayed on banana leaves. Once finished, she said, "Mama, your vegetables are so pretty."

"I agree," Madam Ama replied smiling. "Now add the carrots in the front where everyone will see them. I'll tell people to try them."

"Who'll buy your crops, today?" Kwame asked.

"Many people. My sisters and I have the best vegetables and no one else has carrots. We're willing to trade for cloth, peanuts, shea butter, oranges, and pineapples. Not everyone will do that. Long-distance traders from Kumasi or the coast are good customers. They need food and buy with gold dust. We like to sell to them."

Akua was pleased that she could help in the market. She was eight, old enough to work, but she also wanted to play. She knew that Kwame would look for their cousin, Kwaku, but he, too, had to work first. "Mama, how can we help you now?" Akua asked.

"You've already had a busy morning, but I need your help to do some trading," Madam Ama replied. "Find the traders with crops from the savannah. I need a large basket of peanuts and some shea butter. I like the pale kind of shea butter to rub on our skin when the Harmattan wind comes. It's pure. If it's yellow, there's something added to it. The traders will be men."

"Oh, Mama," Akua said, "they're strangers."

"Don't worry," Madam Ama reassured Akua. "We don't know them, but they're forest people like us. They aren't from the savannah. They buy from the savannah traders that the Asantehene allows to come to Kumasi. The traders will speak Twi, like we do, just a different kind. If you speak slowly, they will, too, and you'll understand each other.

"They'll want kola nuts to sell to the savannah traders in Kumasi," Mama explained. "Kwame, take the kola nuts. Put that basket in a larger one and trade the kolas for the larger basket of peanuts.

"Akua, take three snails. They're giants. Some traders will want snails to eat tonight. See how much shea butter you can trade them for. Respect the traders, but try to get a good price."

"Come on, Akua, let's get ready," Kwame urged. He picked up the basket of kola nuts, placed it inside a larger basket, and put both baskets on his head. "I'm ready. Let's go," he said.

Akua selected three snails, wrapped them in banana leaves, and put them in a gourd that she balanced on her head. She felt inspired to be a good trader and also wanted to see if there were new items in the market.

Madam Ama encouraged both children. "Good luck and good trading," she said. "You can play in the river when you come back."

Turning to Yaw Mensah, Madam Ama explained, "I need your help, too. Stack the banana leaves for me. Your cousins will come soon to take you to Auntie Abena's stall. You can all play in the river later."

Yaw Mensah set to work immediately. "Watch me," he said.

The Queen Mother waved good-bye as she began a walk through the market to join friends and see the goods for sale. She planned to return with food for lunch.

CHAPTER 5

Shopping

The marketplace in Tanoso

WALKING ALONG THE CROWDED AISLES OF THE MARKETPLACE, KWAME AND AKUA greeted everyone. Akua curtsied and Kwame bowed his head slightly when they met an elder. The two admired the forest crops that they knew well, including yellow papayas that were plump and ripe. "I love papayas. I hope that Mama will trade for some," Kwame said.

They were curious about food from the coast, especially the pineapples. A trader offered them pieces of pineapple saying, "Eat some. You'll like them."

"*Medaase* – Thank you. Pineapples are juicy," Akua replied.

Kwame nodded because his mouth was too full for him to talk. "*Medaase*, they're delicious," he said after swallowing. He took a second handful.

"The smoked fish looks good," Akua observed. "Grannie will be happy to see it, but I don't like the smell."

"Do you see the salt?" Kwame asked Akua as he pointed to it. "I like the way it smells. It makes me feel hungry. People say that the water in the ocean has salt in it. That's strange. The river doesn't taste salty and it's going to the ocean. Why does the ocean have salt? I'm going to ask."

Kwame greeted a salt trader, "*Maakye* – Good morning, sir."

"*Yaa*, young man. How can I help you?"

"Where does this salt come from?"

"I bought it from Fante people on the coast."

"Where do they get it?"

The trader smiled. "Ocean water is salty. The Fante build dams to hold the water on land until it evaporates and leaves salt. It takes a long time, but they get enough salt to sell to traders like me."

"Why do people want salt?"

"We preserve food with it and it makes food taste better."

"Can you drink the water in the ocean?"

"Oh, no. It's too salty."

"River water goes to the ocean and it isn't salty. I drink it."

"It's a little salty. Rivers bring both water and salt to the ocean. The salt stays when the water evaporates. That leaves a lot of salt," the trader explained.

"I have a question for you," Kwame said. "I've heard that if you go to the coast, you might see an *oburoni* – a white person. Have you ever seen one?"

"Oh, yes, but only from far away. I don't trade with them."

"Would an *oburoni* drink salt water? Maybe they like it."

"I don't think so. I've tried it and it's awful."

"What does an *oburoni* look like?" Kwame asked.

"They look like us, only they have a lot of hair on their face and their skin is pale. They don't go far from their castles. The Fante say that an *oburoni* will get sick if he leaves his castle."

"That's interesting, sir. Thank you for the information," Kwame said as he turned to walk away.

Kwame caught up with Akua. "Look at the beautiful beads, Kwame," she said. "The Fante make them. I love the bright colors and designs. Some are round and some are square. Some are little balls. You can string them any way that you want. My beads don't have so many colors.

"May I pick them up?" Akua asked the seller.

"Certainly," the seller replied. "These beads are well made and they're not expensive. Bring your mother to see them. The ones that come from the whites cost much more. I have a few of them, too. Your mother might want to see them."

"I'll ask my mother to come some time," Akua replied. "She's busy at her stall now. *Medaase.*"

Kwame and Akua continued walking and admiring goods from the savannah: colorful baskets, leather hats and belts, long cotton shirts for men, cloth for women to wear, and peanuts.

They greeted the peanut traders, who returned their greeting in the Twi spoken in Kumasi. The accent sounded unusual to Kwame and Akua and made them smile, but they didn't say anything. They understood what the traders were saying.

Kwame selected the trader with the most peanuts, greeted him, and explained, "My sister and I want to trade kola nuts for peanuts." Kwame set his baskets on the ground and picked up a handful of kolas. "These kola nuts grow on my mother's farm. We helped gather the pods and took out the nuts. We soaked them and peeled them. They're firm and beautiful. Just hold them."

"May I taste one?" the trader asked.

"Of course," Kwame replied.

The trader took one, put it on the ground, chopped it open with a machete, and put half of the nut into his mouth. He sucked on it and let red saliva run down his chin, making the other traders and the children laugh.

The trader soon spit out the nut and wiped his mouth with his hand. "Ah," he said, "I've learned to like kolas. I'd like to keep this one in my mouth, but then I couldn't talk.

We forest people are lucky to have kolas here at home. These are good ones. Savannah traders will buy them. What's your price, young man?"

"Oh, sir," Kwame responded quickly. "My family works hard to gather kola nuts. Ours are large. One of them fills the palm of my hand and one kola nut is all that you need to stay alive in the savannah for a whole morning. People say that when you chew kolas, you don't need food or water." The trader nodded, smiling.

"Peanuts are small and have a soft shell that you can crack with your fingers," Kwame continued. "You can eat many peanuts faster than you can eat a single kola. I want to trade my medium basket of kolas for a large basket of peanuts."

"Young man, young man," the trader replied, "we forest people love to sell kolas and eat peanut soup. Peanuts are small but delicious. Peanut soup with fufu, that's a meal for a chief!

"I tasted one of your kola nuts," the trader continued. "You were wise to wait for me so that I could see that it was juicy and had a strong flesh. I liked it. I'll accept your offer. But first, I want you and your sister to eat a few of my peanuts. Then you'll know if you're making a good trade."

Kwame and Akua shelled and ate several peanuts and agreed that they were good. "We have a deal," Kwame said.

"Then you may pour your kolas into my bag and I'll fill your large basket with peanuts," the trader said. "I'll add two small leather pouches to our deal. One is red and the other green and each has a leather string so you can wear it around your waist. These are made by savannah people from the hides of cattle. We don't have cattle in the forest. Keep something precious in them."

"*Medaase*," Akua said. "The pouches are beautiful. They're like the ones that Papa has on his war smock, only his are old. These are prettier. When I'm not wearing my beads, I'll keep them in a pouch." Akua took both and tucked them into her cloth saying, "Kwame, I'll keep yours for you."

"*Medaase*," Kwame repeated to the trader. "Before we go, I have a question for you. You're selling peanuts from the savannah and you sell kola nuts to people who live in the savannah. Have you ever been to the savannah?"

"Young man, I'm from Kumasi. I've never been out of the forest. It's difficult for an Akan to go to the savannah. It's hot and dry and there aren't many trees or rivers. You have to walk a long way between towns. Savannah people ride horses. We don't have horses and I don't know the languages of the savannah people.

"The king allows traders from the savannah to travel on a great-road to Kumasi to sell their products there, but they can't go any other place. I buy peanuts from them and sell the peanuts in forest markets."

"Thank you for the information, sir. I was just wondering. Now, would you please help me lift this basket of peanuts? It's heavy."

"Indeed, I will."

"*Medaase*," Kwame and Akua replied as they left. Kwame balanced the basket of peanuts on his head and carried the empty basket. Akua balanced the small gourd of snails on her head. They were pleased with their work and hoped that Mama would be happy with the peanuts.

"There's one more thing that I want to know," Kwame said. "Kola nut trees grow in the forest. Why don't Akans eat kola nuts?"

"I don't like them," Akua answered. "Have you ever tried one?"

"Yes, I don't like them either, but I know that there's nothing wrong with them. Maybe Baako knows about them. I'll ask him."

AKUA TOOK THE LEAD CONFIDENTLY AS SHE AND KWAME LOOKED FOR TRADERS WITH shea butter. "Walk fast, Akua," Kwame coaxed. "This basket of peanuts is heavy and it's hard to balance if you walk slowly."

"I'll try but the aisle is crowded and we have to greet people. Use your hand to balance the basket. I see shea butter." Akua and Kwame approached a trader who had arranged small balls of yellow shea butter in circles on banana leaves spread on the ground.

Akua stopped, curtsied, and greeted the trader, "*Maakye*, sir." Kwame stood nearby balancing the basket of peanuts on his head.

"*Yaa*, my daughter," the trader replied smiling. "How can I help you?"

"Oh, sir, I want shea butter for my mother. She likes the kind that smells good. She wants it to be soft, too, to rub on our skin and shaped into a ball that fits in her hand."

"I have the beautiful shea butter that you see here," the trader said. "It's soft and oily, good for your skin, and the best for cooking. You live in the forest so you may not know how it's made. May I tell you?"

"Thank you, but I don't have time, now. Your shea butter is yellow. My mother likes the kind that is the color of an elephant tusk. Why is yours so yellow?"

"When the nuts of the shea tree are being made into butter, the root of the borututu tree is added and that makes the butter yellow. The color doesn't change the butter. It makes it prettier."

"I see," Akua said, "but I want to look more since my mother doesn't want the yellow kind. Please excuse me. Kwame, let's walk on."

"All right, Akua, but I'm going to put this basket down the next time you stop. I don't want it to fall."

They soon reached a display of pale shea butter shaped into small balls and stacked in pyramids on banana leaves. "Let's stop here, Kwame. This shea butter looks good," Akua said.

"*Maakye*, sir," Akua greeted the merchant as she curtsied.

"*Yaa*, daughter. Are you looking for shea butter?"

"Yes, sir. I want some that's the color of an elephant tusk and smells sweet. We want it to rub on our skin."

"Mine is pure shea butter. Smell it," the trader said as he picked up a ball and extended his open hand to Akua. "It smells as sweet as a banana. It's good for your skin."

"Sir," Akua continued, "I have three giant forest snails to trade."

"Ah, yes," replied the trader. "I'll offer you three balls of shea butter for three snails. That's a bargain because women and girls in the savannah spend a long time making shea butter."

"Yes, sir, *medaase*," Akua agreed, and took the three snails out of the gourd and placed them on a banana leaf to let them crawl to show that they were alive. "I didn't make these snails, I only found them," Akua said, smiling. "They're valuable because you can eat them. You can't eat shea butter."

"That's true," the trader said, also smiling. "The snails are giants and they look delicious. We'll eat them tonight." He wrapped the shea butter in a banana leaf and placed it in the empty gourd. "Enjoy the shea butter and give my greetings to your mother. Tell her that you're a careful trader."

"*Medaase*, sir," Akua replied as she curtsied once more and turned to Kwame. "We can go now," she said, placing the gourd on her head.

Akua and Kwame quickly found their way through the crowded market aisles to Mama's stall. "Wonderful, wonderful," Mama exclaimed seeing the peanuts and shea butter. "The fragrance is perfect," she said of the shea butter. "*Medaase*, Akua. This is the best kind!

"*Medaase*, Kwame, for the peanuts. They smell good, too. You're good traders. You must be tired now and it's getting hot. Go to the river. Yaw Mensah is still with Auntie Abena."

"Yes, yes!" Akua and Kwame answered together. They put the baskets, the gourd, and the leather pouches in the shelter and left quickly. Before going close to the river's inlet where children played, they checked to see that a guard was still watching for crocodiles.

— CHAPTER 6 —

Playing, Lunch, and Visitors

Akua and Kwame joined other children who were chasing each other, running up and down the riverbank, and digging their toes into the mud. Once close to the water, they threw their cloths aside and waded in, stepping carefully over small pebbles, feeling with their toes for a muddy place to jump. The water was warm but still a welcome change from the hotter air.

"Kwame, come over here," Akua shouted. She had found a place where they could dive under the water and walk along the bottom on their hands. They saw old logs and large rocks. They scraped the bottom, pretending to be monsters churning up the mud, and looked for pebbles and sticks that they could use to scare each other. They crawled around the base of a big rock and then climbed on it to use it as a slide, disappearing into the water with a splash.

"I'm the spirit of a waterfall!" Akua yelled as she slid down the rock head first into the water.

Kwame followed her, feet first and shouting, "I'm a river spirit!" They came up quickly, stood, and began splashing water. Other children joined them and they saw their cousin, Kwaku.

"Hello, hello, Kwaku," they called out. "Come over here!"

Kwaku saw them and he, too, climbed up the big rock and slid down shouting, "I'm the spirit of a fish that jumps over rocks!" He disappeared under the water and when he stood, he shouted, "Here I am. I'll do that again!"

"I'm coming after you," Kwame said as he chased Kwaku up the rock. The two boys slid down together. They laughed when they stood and turned to climb the rock again while other boys followed them. Soon there was a chain of climbers and sliders.

Nearer the bank Akua found friends. Some put their faces under the water to blow bubbles. Akua stretched out and tried to stay on top of the water. She knew that people who lived next to the ocean did this. She lay down, first on her back and then on her stomach, kicked her feet, paddled with her arms, and sank. She kept trying and kept sinking. "Someday," she thought, "I'll find out how to stay on top of the water."

Akua saw girls playing *Ampe* on the bank and climbed out of the water. "Can I play?" she asked as she tied on her cloth.

"Yes, come on!" the leader shouted.

Playing Ampe

The girls formed a line in front of the leader. Everyone clapped as the leader faced each girl individually, clapping and jumping. After two jumps the leader and the girl she faced put one leg forward. The leader won and moved on if they put opposite legs forward.

Akua saw that this leader was strong. She jumped fast. Clap, clap, jump, and kick. Clap, clap, jump, and kick. The leader won again and again. Everyone laughed and cheered as they tried to keep up.

Watching the leader carefully, Akua saw her pattern. She kicked first her right leg then her left leg twice and then her right again. When she stood in front of Akua, the two clapped and jumped, and then kicked forward their legs that faced each other, the leader's right and Akua's left. Akua won. The other girls cheered as Akua stepped forward to be the leader.

Clap and clap and jump, kick; clap and clap and jump, kick; Akua continued winning. She kicked her leg at the last possible moment so that her opponent saw no clues but she followed a pattern, left-left, right-right-right, left-left, right-right-right. She hoped that she was too fast for anyone to notice her pattern. She jumped faster and faster, tiring the other players.

With so much kicking, players began to fall, grabbing one another, making everyone laugh. Akua jumped and clapped until she, too, fell. Her friends pulled her up, but she was too tired to continue. "That was fun," she said. "One of you can take my place. I'm going now."

AKUA SAW KWAME AND KWAKU CLIMB ONTO THE BANK AND PICK UP THEIR CLOTHS. "I'm over here," she called to them. "It's time to go back. Kwaku, come with us."

The three walked slowly to join Madam Ama, the Queen Mother, and Yaw Mensah. When Madam Ama saw them, she waved. "Hello, everyone. It's good to see you, Kwaku! Lunch is ready."

Kwaku greeted the women politely. Everyone sat in a circle, each using a portion of a banana leaf as a plate. They picked up smoked fish and fried plantains with their fingers and drank water from small gourds. No one talked.

As they rested after eating, Akua said, "Grannie, I love this food. I know it's your favorite lunch."

"I love it, too," Yaw Mensah added. The Queen Mother smiled but quickly turned serious and spoke to the older boys.

"Soon Nana and some of the elders will go to Kumasi to celebrate the *Odwira*, our yam harvest, that marks the beginning of a new year. Chiefs have to go to pledge their loyalty to the king. Kwaku and Kwame, you are eleven and twelve years old, and you need to learn about our kingdom. It's time for you to go with Nana. I'll talk to him, but I wanted to tell you first."

"Oh, yes," Kwame said with enthusiasm.

"I want to go," Kwaku replied.

Madam Ama had other thoughts. "Kumasi is big and many foreigners are there. It's crowded for the *Odwira* festival, and people fire guns in the air for the celebration. There is so much noise and smoke. I went when I was a little older than you are. I was frightened, but I know that you must see Kumasi."

"The best part about the *Odwira* in Kumasi is seeing the big, beautiful umbrellas that shade the chiefs," the Queen Mother said with enthusiasm. "The umbrellas come in many colors and are very fancy. The bearers twirl them to move the air. They look like giant cloths waving in the wind. I went to an *Odwira* in Kumasi long ago, and I'll always remember the umbrellas."

"They're like Nana's umbrella but there are so many in Kumasi, more that you can count," Madam Ama added. "Even if I'm afraid for you, I agree with Grannie. You won't know our kingdom until you see Kumasi. You'll see much that's new to you."

"When Nana's in Kumasi, he stays with my nephew, his cousin, Elder Kwadwo, the son of my younger sister," the Queen Mother explained. "You should meet your uncle in Kumasi. I'll talk to Nana soon."

Kwame and Kwaku smiled and felt encouraged, but then Kwame asked, "Can Baako come with us? We do everything together. He's our friend and he's thirteen. He should see Kumasi with us."

"You're right," the Queen Mother said. "Baako works hard and his father, Asare, will go with Nana. It would be good for Baako to be with you. I'll talk to Nana about all of you."

"*Medaase*, Grannie," Kwame said.

Madam Ama turned to Kwaku. "Tomorrow is *Adaepa*. We have to work to prepare for the *Adae* ceremony on Sunday. I hope that you'll come to the palace to help Kwame. Your father will be there. The elders will meet with Nana."

"Yes, I'll come and work," Kwaku replied. "I like to hear the drummers."

"My children," the Queen Mother said, "I'm happy to see you together. I have a surprise for you. An *odonko* gave me a honeycomb. The honey is rich and sweet. We'll share it."

"Ohhhhhh," everyone said together.

The Queen Mother picked up a bundle, unwrapped the leaves, and took out the honeycomb. She broke off pieces that dripped with honey and gave them out. Everyone sucked the honey with noisy slurping.

"So sweet!" Yaw Mensah exclaimed.

"Delicious," Akua agreed.

"Better than anything," Kwaku said.

"The true gold of the forest!" Kwame added.

"*Medaase*, Grannie!" Madam Ama said. "You've given us a perfect meal."

The Queen Mother smiled. "Wash your hands now," she said, handing a gourd of water to Akua.

"What a day!" Madam Ama exclaimed. "Kwame and Akua traded for peanuts and shea butter. I traded for corn paste, papayas, pineapples, and thick cloths from the savannah. We need them at night. I got a little gold dust but no cowries. I gave away carrots and people liked them. I'll try to sell some next week. It's time to go home now."

"I played in the river," Yaw reminded his family. Everyone smiled and started to pack.

WITHIN A FEW MINUTES THEY HEARD THE NOISE OF A CROWD COMING THEIR WAY. "I wonder what's happening," Madam Ama said as she and others stopped to look and listen.

The market manager led the crowd. With her were two strangers wearing elaborate cloths. One had a leather scabbard strapped to his waist and the other shook a large brass ring with many keys hanging from it. "Here come the tax collectors," Madam Ama explained.

When the manager arrived, she curtsied and said, "Greetings, Queen Mother. These men are from Kumasi. They want to see Nana but he's not here, so I brought them to you."

"*Medaase*," the Queen Mother responded to the manager and greeted the strangers, "*Akwaaba* – Welcome!"

"*Medaase*, Queen Mother. We are tax collectors for the Asantehene. Our sword and the brass ring with keys prove who we are," one of the men said in a serious manner. "We are here to see Tanosohene Nana Anyensu."

One tax collector took the sword from its scabbard to show the intricately carved wooden handle and curved metal blade, both covered with gold foil. The sword sparkled in the sunlight as he placed it flat across the palms of his hands to show the Queen Mother. The other tax collector shook the ring with keys vigorously, making the keys rattle loudly.

The crowd gasped. The sword and ring with keys were new to most people, but everyone understood their meaning. They and the elaborate cloths that the men wore showed the tax collectors' high rank. The crowd stood back, although some children pressed forward to see the sword and the keys better.

"You cannot travel alone. Where are your guards?" the Queen Mother asked.

A tax collector explained, "When we arrived, we bought food and our guards are eating here in the market. We will eat soon."

The Queen Mother rubbed the sword with her hands and lifted it and the brass ring with keys to judge their weight. "These objects are authentic," she said. "My son is expecting you. He'll return this afternoon. I'll tell him that you are here. When he is ready, the town crier will call you and the elders. Come to the palace at the top of the hill. Nana will lodge you in the palace."

"*Medaase*, Queen Mother," the tax collectors said together. They bowed slightly and left with the crowd following them.

"What a sight!" the Queen Mother exclaimed. "Kwaku, go now and tell your mama that the tax collectors are here. She'll let others know."

Kwaku agreed, saying, "I will. But first, what did you think of the sword? Fantastic, isn't it!" Everyone nodded.

"You can't cut anything with it. It's just a decoration," Kwame said. "Papa has two of them."

"Only important people have swords," the Queen Mother reminded everyone. "That makes the swords powerful."

"What about the keys?" Akua asked. "What are they for?"

"They tell us that tax collectors can unlock the chests where the Asantehene stores his gold," the Queen Mother explained. "The keys show us power, too."

"Papa has a chest for gold in his hut, but I've never seen keys," Akua said.

"That's right, Akua. All chiefs have to protect their gold," the Queen Mother explained. "Nana keeps the keys hidden in his hut." The children nodded with serious expressions on their faces.

Before leaving, Kwaku turned to Madam Ama and the Queen Mother to say, "*Medaase* – Thank you for lunch. I'll come to the palace tomorrow."

Madam Ama encouraged everyone. "We've had a good day and tomorrow is *Adaepa*. We'll be busy. Kwame, take the banana leaves that we used as plates and the lunch scraps to the dumping ground beyond the market. Then catch up with us. Let's go home now."

CHAPTER 7

Adaepa

THIS SATURDAY WAS CALLED *ADAEPA*, THE DAY TO PREPARE FOR THE SUNDAY *ADAE* CERemony. *Adaepa* was busy because no work could be done on the day of the *Adae,* which came every forty-two days. For the *Adae,* elders representing the Tanoso families gathered in the palace to bless the sacred stools of the grandfather chiefs and pledge loyalty to Nana.

On *Adaepa,* many men and women worked for a longer time than usual to weed and harvest on their farms. Families set aside water, food, and firewood for two days. Women and children also supplied water and firewood to the chief, who provided for those working at the palace. Elders met with Nana to take care of business and settle any disputes.

The early morning air was cool. Before breakfast Kwame, Akua, and Yaw Mensah swept the courtyards and collected water. They took breakfast to the main courtyard for the tax collectors and their guards.

With these chores done, Nana called everyone together at the hearth. Looking at the children, he said, "We'll be busy soon. I'll meet with the elders. *Nnonko* will repair the roof of the stool house. Your mother and other women will cook. My children, we'll need your help.

"Kwame, you will work with Kwaku, Baako, and other *nnonko* on the stool house roof. It's leaking and we can't let the sacred stools get wet. I want the roof repaired today.

"You boys will cut new palm fronds and vines and help the *nnonko* trim them and tie them into bundles to add to the roof. We won't take the old bundles off. The *nnonko* built the roof, and they know how to do this, but they'll need your help."

Kwame nodded in agreement but added, "Papa, we'll have to chop a lot of fronds and they're tough in the dry season. That'll be hard."

"Yes, it's hard work, Kwame, but I'm confident that you boys can do it. Start now by sharpening the machetes. The *nnonko* will be here soon. In the palm grove, look for fronds near the base of the tree trunks. Don't climb trees carrying a machete."

"Yes, Papa," Kwame replied. He felt honored to be trusted to work on the stool house even though he wasn't certain that he could do all that Papa expected.

Madam Ama spoke to her children. "I'll work with Aunties Abena and Adjowa to prepare peanut soup and fufu. Anyetata and other women will help, too. *Nnonko* will bring firewood and meat for our soup as well as plantains and cassava for fufu.

"I'll add vegetables from my farm and send *nnonko* to gather snails." Touching Yaw Mensah lightly on his head, she added, "They'll be the giant ones that you like, Yaw." Yaw Mensah smiled. "Children will shell peanuts.

"Akua, help with the peanuts. I'll depend on you to play with Yaw Mensah and the other children so they won't go near the hearth. We'll work hard together and then serve a fine meal."

Akua nodded. She loved helping when many people worked at the palace but wasn't sure that she could do so much. "Yes, Mama, I'll try," she replied.

"I'll be with you, Akua," the Queen Mother said, smiling.

"*Medaase*, Grannie," Akua whispered with gratitude.

Looking at Yaw Mensah, Nana said, "You should work, too, Yaw. I want you to help shell peanuts."

Yaw Mensah frowned, "Papa, that hurts my fingers."

"You'll get tougher, Yaw," Nana replied. "Use a rock to crush the shells if you need to." Yaw Mensah nodded to agree.

Madam Ama added wood to the fire. "We'll boil water to cook cassava and plantains first and then work on the soup," she explained to her children. "I'll need more wood and water soon. Kwame and Akua, greet people in the main courtyard. Yaw, stay here to help with the peanuts."

The first visitors were women carrying head loads of firewood. "Kwame, *bra aha* – come here," one of women called. "This wood's heavy."

"*Maakye*," Kwame and Akua greeted their neighbor as they lifted the bundle of branches off of her head.

"*Yaa*," she replied.

"Oh," Akua said, "this load is heavy. Are you all right?"

"Yes," the woman answered. "The wood is good so the fire will burn slowly. Thank you for helping. I'll greet your family and return home. I have my own cooking to do."

"Kwame, where are Kwaku and Baako?" Akua asked. "We need them. More people are coming."

"They'll be here soon. I'll take this wood to Mama. Help me put it on my head."

"I'm hungry just thinking about fufu," Akua said. "I should have eaten more this morning. I'll stay here for a little while, and then I'll help Yaw Mensah with the peanuts and eat some of them."

Several girls entered the main courtyard, balancing pots of water as head loads. Akua waved them to the family courtyard. The girls greeted Madam Ama and the Queen Mother, who thanked them. "Put the water here by the fire," Madam Ama instructed. "Please stay and shell peanuts with Akua and Yaw Mensah. You'll eat with us later."

"This will be fun," the girls agreed as they sat under a tree to work.

"I do this at home," one of the girls said. "I'm good at it. Yaw Mensah, use the fingers and thumbs of both of your hands to crack the shells. Don't try to crack shells with one hand." Yaw Mensah made slow progress. He wasn't enjoying the work even when the girls encouraged him.

"My fingers hurt," he complained. "I'll use a rock to crack the shells."

"Your fingers will get stronger," one of the girls encouraged him. "Eat peanuts while you're working. You'll feel better. Peanuts smell good and they taste great. You can look for a little rock, though, if you want to."

"I'll try more with my fingers first," Yaw Mensah replied with a slight smile. "Peanuts taste good."

Asare and Baako entered the family courtyard with four other *nnonko*, all carrying head loads. "*Maakye*, Queen Mother. *Maakye*, Madam Ama," each said.

"*Yaa*, Asare. *Yaa*, Baako," both the Queen Mother and Madam Ama answered.

"Madam Ama," Asare said. "I killed and dressed a duiker this morning. We have it with us now."

"*Medaase*, Asare, I'm pleased," Madam Ama replied. "I know that you helped kill a crocodile yesterday. *Medaase*. My family was safe. I hope that the *nnonko* will like eating the crocodile meat."

"It is my duty to protect the chief," Asare said. "We had a big meal last night with crocodile meat, and we're smoking the rest for later. I'll leave now to work at the new mine. Nana wants it dug deeper. My wife will be here soon."

"Work well, Asare," Madam Ama said. Looking at Baako, she directed, "Put everything in the storage hut near the big tree. Tell two *nnonko* to take an empty basket and look for snails on the far side of the stream. Then go with the others to the council room and ask what Nana wants you to do."

"Yes, Madam Ama," Baako replied. He spoke to the *nnonko,* who placed their loads in the storage hut. Two left to gather snails. Baako walked with the others to the council room, which was fully open to the main courtyard on one side. He saw several elders and Nana's spokesman, the Okyeame, seated on stools and talking. The men wore the full cloths and sandals appropriate for a council meeting. Nana wasn't there.

Baako and the *nnonko* stopped a short distance from the council room and waited until the Okyeame motioned for them to approach. Standing now, the spokesman addressed Baako. "Enter. What would you like?"

Baako entered the council room, which was one step above the courtyard. He felt shy facing the tall, well-dressed Okyeame, who carried an elaborate staff. The Okyeame smiled and welcomed Baako, who bowed his head slightly, saying, "Please sir, Madam Ama sent me. What does Nana want me and the other *nnonko* to do?"

"I'll ask him," the Okyeame replied. "Wait here." The spokesman went to Nana's hut, next to the council room, and returned quickly. "Nana wants the *nnonko* to add bundles of palm fronds to the first two tiers of the stool house roof. It's leaking. You, Kwame, and Kwaku will sharpen machetes and chop new fronds and vines. When enough fronds are ready, the *nnonko* will trim and bundle them and start tying them onto the roof. Don't remove the old bundles. The *nnonko* will know what to do. Help them after you cut new fronds."

"Yes, sir," Baako replied. "I'll go now." Stepping into the courtyard once more, Baako motioned for the *nnonko* to follow him and spoke to them in a low voice to explain the task. They said that they knew how to repair the roof. They found Kwame sharpening a machete.

Kwaku soon arrived. He saw his friends in the main courtyard, but first went to the small courtyard to greet the Queen Mother, Auntie Ama, Auntie Abena, and his own mother, Madam Adjowa, and to wave to the other children. Yaw Mensah ran to hug his cousin, saying, "I want to come with you."

"Let's find Kwame and Baako," Kwaku replied, taking Yaw Mensah's hand.

"What can I do?" Kwaku asked when he joined his friends.

"Papa wants us to help repair the stool house roof," Kwame answered. "We need to cut new fronds and vines. We've sharpened the machetes and the *nnonko* will help us get started in the forest. Yaw Mensah, go back to the family courtyard. You can't come with us."

"I'll help you," Yaw Mensah protested.

"We're going to use machetes, Yaw," Kwame said. "You're too little."

"Come with me, Yaw," Kwaku beckoned. "I'll tell Auntie Ama what Kwame, Baako, and I are going to do, and then I'll have to leave. I'll see you when I come back." Yaw Mensah agreed but walked slowly.

Accompanied by the two *nnonko*, Kwame, Kwaku, and Baako soon set off.

Joining Akua and her friends, Yaw Mensah explained, "I want to go to the forest with Kwame and the other boys. I'll help them chop fronds. I like the forest. It's getting hot now and the forest is cool."

"Yaw Mensah, you can't do that yet," Akua answered. "You need to help us."

"I want to go to the forest," Yaw Mensah insisted. "I don't want to stay here. I want to see spiders and monkeys. Come with me."

The Queen Mother had returned to her home and Madam Ama worked with other women to peel the cassava and plantains. Water in the cauldron was hot. "Can we take Yaw Mensah for a walk?" Akua asked her mother. "We'll go to the stream for a little while. He'll like that. We'll collect more water."

"All right," Madam Ama agreed, "but only for a short time. I need your help here."

Turning to her young son, she spoke softly, "Yaw Mensah, you are very fortunate that your sister and her friends will take you for a walk. Be strong and walk fast. Play in the stream, but then you'll have to work. Be sure to make noise on the path. Do you understand?"

"Yes, Mama, I'll be strong and I'll make noise," Yaw Mensah promised as he sprang to his feet. "I'm ready to go."

Kwame, Kwaku, Baako, and the *nnonko* welcomed the cool forest air as they followed the path. They walked past the log fence, the rocks, and the groves of oil palm trees and bamboo. At the far edge of the bamboo grove they left the path and continued toward the raffia palms, where they found several trees with low hanging fronds. The stems were tough. The work party chopped furiously to sever the fronds from the trunks.

Yaw Mensah, Akua, and her friends Atta and Tawia, soon left the palace on the same path, balancing water pots. They walked slowly. "Where's Kwaku?" Yaw Mensah asked. "I want to find him."

"The big boys walk fast and they've already left the path," Akua explained. "We can't do that. We don't have machetes and there might be snakes."

Yaw Mensah picked up pebbles and leaves from the path and threw them to the side. "I'll make the path clean for everyone," he said. He stopped to look at spider webs and tried to find the spiders. "Are they hiding from me?" he asked.

Rainforest tarantula

"You look big to the spiders," Akua replied. "You're scaring them. Come on, Yaw, walk faster. Aie! Look, a tarantula on the path! They don't spin webs. Watch out, Yaw. Don't step on it! Don't let it bite you."

"It's big," Yaw responded as he threw pebbles at the tarantula. "That's not the kind of spider that I was looking for. I didn't find it, it found me. I'll scare it."

"Where are the monkeys?" Yaw Mensah asked as he continued to look for animals. "I want to see them. We should have brought bananas for them."

"Oh, Yaw, if you feed monkeys, they'll always follow you to beg for food. That's a nuisance."

"I like monkeys and spiders. They're my friends," Yaw said, still walking slowly.

"Do you hear the parrots squawking, Yaw? They're really our friends. They talk to us."

"I like the parrots, too," Yaw Mensah replied. "I always talk to them."

When enough fronds and vines to begin repairing the roof were cut, two *nnonko* bound them into head loads and returned to the palace. The boys continued chopping.

Resting briefly, Kwaku said, "I'm strong, but this is hard work."

"The higher fronds aren't so dry," Baako observed. "They'll last longer on the roof and maybe they'll be easier to chop. I'll climb a tree to see."

Kwame and Kwaku watched as Baako found footholds on the rough trunk of an older tree and grasped the stubs of fronds that had been chopped off. Using the stubs as anchors, he climbed slowly and carefully, holding a machete in his right hand, until he was several feet off of the ground and close to the green fronds. He began chopping. "Watch out below. Here they come," he yelled, as fronds crashed to the ground. Kwaku and Kwame dodged them.

"These look good, Baako," Kwame called out as he and Kwaku stacked the fronds.

Baako was smiling as he tossed his machete to the ground and backed slowly down the tree. "I'm strong," he said, "but that was hard. I was careful so I didn't scrape my legs. I've watched my father do this, but he has a holster for his machete. That makes climbing easier. Nana didn't expect us to climb trees."

"I want to try," Kwaku said. "Green fronds are better. We can climb the younger trees where the green fronds aren't so high. Let's go."

"Papa told me not to climb trees with a machete," Kwame cautioned. "Maybe we can climb the trees and ask Baako to hand our machetes to us. Baako, can you do that?"

Baako agreed. He didn't want Kwame or Kwaku to be injured or Nana to be angry with him. "Be careful," he told his friends. "Anchor your feet and hold on while you're chopping."

Kwame and Kwaku climbed a short way up on separate trees. Baako climbed after them to hand each a machete. Kwame and Kwaku chopped off all of the fronds that they could reach from one position. Hearing fronds fall to the ground, Kwame bragged, "That sounds good. I like doing this. I feel stronger now."

"I could do this all day," Kwaku told the others, who shook their heads.

When Kwame and Kwaku finished chopping from one position, they tossed their machetes to the ground and moved or climbed down the tree. Baako retrieved the machetes and handed them back when the other boys were in position again. The boys stayed safe while they chopped enough fronds for the roof. When they stopped, they were tired but pleased with their success.

Kwame and Kwaku both thanked Baako. "We needed your help," they agreed.

"Let's work on vines now," Baako said, knowing to be careful since he was an *odonko*. He didn't want to embarrass his friends.

The boys found different kinds of trees nearby and cut vines off of their trunks. This was easy since many vines circled the trees near the ground. Twisting the vines, they made thick ropes and tied the fronds together to make three head loads. Baako and Kwame tied their machetes onto the loads. Kwaku kept his machete free to use if he needed it.

"Let's hurry," Kwaku said as they returned to the path bearing head loads of fronds. "I want to finish this job before we eat. It's getting hotter now. I'm sure that Nana and my papa will be happy with our work."

The boys delivered the fronds and vines to the stool house and then reported to the Okyeame, who thanked them and sent them back to the stool house to continue working. With the four *nnonko,* the boys trimmed the fronds, bound them into bundles, and delivered the bundles up the ladder to the roof. Everyone sweated in the full sun.

Head loads of palm fronds

— CHAPTER 8 —

Surprises

As Yaw Mensah and the girls followed the path through the bamboo grove, Akua's friend, Atta, proposed a race. "Who can go the fastest to the stream? I'll beat all of you even with a water pot on my head."

"You can't run," Tawia said. "Your pot will fall."

"Not if I hold it."

"If it's full of water?"

"Then I'd walk," Atta answered. "I don't want to spill water, but I can walk fast. We don't have water now, so let's run. Akua and Yaw Mensah, try to catch us."

The two girls ran, each holding on to her water pot. They soon rounded a curve and disappeared from Akua and Yaw Mensah's view.

Akua turned to walk backwards, looking at Yaw Mensah and encouraging him, "Come on, Yaw. Try to catch me!"

Yaw Mensah started running but stopped suddenly, pointed, and shouted, "Akua, look! Leopards! Look!"

Akua turned in time to see two leopard cubs, one chasing the other, running along the path away from her and Yaw Mensah. "Oh!" she shouted. "They're going to the stream. They'll catch my friends. We have to warn them."

Akua and Yaw Mensah ran as fast as they could, but the cubs ran faster. One cub stopped to look back before they both left the path. The children continued running and shouting, "Leopards! Leopards!" When they reached the stream, their friends stared at them in surprise.

"Why are you shouting about leopards?" Atta asked.

One cub stopped to look back.

"We saw two running on the path after you left," Akua explained.

"What? Are you sure? Do you know what leopards look like?" Atta questioned.

"Yes," Yaw Mensah affirmed. "Papa has a leopard skin. It's brown with black spots. It's very soft."

"Did you see big leopards?" Tawia asked.

"No, two cubs. One was chasing the other on the path," Akua explained.

"My papa says that there may be leopards in the forest, but we don't see them. Are you making this up?" Atta wanted to know.

"No, we really saw them," Yaw Mensah stated firmly. "You should believe us. I'm going to tell my papa. I know what leopards look like. He'll believe me. I want to go in the water now." Yaw Mensah took his cloth off, waded into the stream, and began splashing the girls.

Tawia turned to Akua saying, "If you really saw leopard cubs, we have to tell everyone when we go back. Where do you think their mother is?"

"I think that the mother and cubs went deeper into the forest," Akua answered. "They don't want to be near us. The cubs were cute, but it was scary to see them. Yes, we have to tell everyone when we go home."

"Okay, Yaw," the girls said. "We'll get some water first, and then we'll get wet, too." The girls walked upstream to fill their water pots. Returning, they set the pots aside, took off their cloths, and jumped into the stream. The four splashed each other, enjoying the warm water. After a good play, the girls got out, put on their cloths, and called Yaw Mensah. They heard voices from beyond the stream.

Looking up, they saw two *nnonko*, one with a large basket on his head. He called out, "*Maakye*," but said nothing more. Both extended their hands in front of their chests, each with his right hand in the palm of his left hand, to signal that they were friends. The children were not afraid. They greeted the *nnonko* politely.

Seeing that the children were alone, the *nnonko* motioned for them to follow. Akua turned to Yaw Mensah and said, "Come on. Let's go home now. We can race some other time."

"I'll carry some rocks," Yaw Mensah answered.

An *odonko* offered to carry Yaw on his shoulders, and Yaw Mensah accepted with relief. The little caravan made its way along the path with the *nnonko* in the lead, one carrying Yaw, the other balancing the basket of snails on his head, and the three girls balancing pots of water.

Akua was happy with the eventful walk and the surprising news that she and Yaw Mensah would share. "I wonder if the big boys are home yet," she said to her friends.

"Maybe they saw the leopards, too. Maybe the boys scared them. Maybe the leopards scared the boys."

AS THE MID-MORNING AIR GREW WARMER, WOMEN FROM TOWN CONTINUED TO BRING firewood, water, and now palm wine to the palace. More elders gathered in the council room.

Working at the hearth and under the trees in the family courtyard, women and girls prepared the afternoon meal. Tied to their mothers' backs, babies and young children peered over their mothers' shoulders to watch them work. Several girls played *Ampe*. Other children chased each other around the trees. The fragrance of peanuts sweetened the air.

Elders stood when Nana entered the council room and took his seat in the royal chair. The Okyeame opened the meeting. Each of the eight Akan clans was represented by an elder. Other respected men attended the meeting. Only the Okyeame spoke directly to Nana. He conveyed Nana's thoughts to the council and gave Nana a summary of the elders' remarks and recommendations.

An *okyeame* protected his chief from direct criticism or embarrassment while often embellishing a chief's words with proverbs or stories. Every chief had an *okyeame*. Some chiefs had several.

The Okyeame talked first about the tax collectors. "They met with several of us yesterday. Nana gave them permission to begin work today with an elder escorting them to the villages. Nana told them that he had new gold weights for the amount of a man's tax, the *domma,* a tenth of an ounce of gold dust. An elder will check that weight against the tax collectors' weight."

"Won't that annoy them?" an elder asked.

"They'll respect us more if we have our own weights," the Okyeame replied. "The circuit of our villages will take two days. On Tuesday they'll collect taxes from the men of Tanoso here in the palace. Nana sent the town crier out this morning to let people know. We'll meet on Thursday to divide a portion of the taxes among us.

"When all of the taxes are collected, we'll know the number of married men in our district, and this will tell us and the Asantehene how many soldiers we can send to his army. *Nnonko* won't be counted, but we can take them if we're called."

A younger council member commented, "Some men won't have the gold dust they need for the tax. Who will loan it to them?"

"Elders must take care of their families," the Okyeame replied. Council members murmured approval.

Returning to the palace, Akua's group entered the family courtyard at the back. From his position on the stool house roof, Baako saw the *nnonko* arrive and climbed down to meet them. He explained to Madam Ama, "The Okyeame said these *nnonko* should work on the roof with us. I'll tell them."

"*Medaase*, Baako. With two more *nnonko,* you should finish the roof before we eat. Thank the *nnonko* for the snails and for carrying Yaw Mensah." After Baako and the *nnonko* left, Yaw Mensah and the girls jumped up and down and clapped their hands.

"Mama, Mama," Yaw Mensah whispered. "I saw two leopard cubs running on the path. They were so cute. I want to go back into the forest and find them."

"Yaw Mensah, I know that you love the forest and see spiders and monkeys there, but leopards are rare. Are you sure you saw leopards?"

"Yes, I did. Ask Akua. She saw them, too."

"I did," Akua agreed. "They were running on the path in front of us just past the bamboo grove. I think they were running away from Kwame and the other boys. We didn't see their mother, and they didn't run all of the way to the stream. No one else saw them."

"That's right," the other girls confirmed. "We were at the stream and the cubs didn't come there."

"I'm sorry that you missed them," Madam Ama sympathized with the girls. "At least you played in the stream and collected water. Stay here now with Auntie Abena and Auntie Adjowa. Eat peanuts and bananas. I'll take Yaw Mensah and Akua to see their papa. Leopards are very valuable. He'll want to know if they're in his district. This is important news."

The Queen Mother agreed. "The ancestors are sending us a good sign. Leopards will bring us strength," she said.

"Akua and Yaw Mensah, come with me," Madam Ama instructed, motioning for the children to follow her.

"I want to show Papa my rocks, too," Yaw Mensah added.

The three hurried to the council room. Holding her children's hands, Madam Ama stood in the courtyard until the Okyeame invited her to enter. Nana and the elders waited.

Looking at the Okyeame, Madam Ama began. "I'm sorry to interrupt but Akua and Yaw Mensah just returned from the stream. They report seeing leopard cubs." Nana and the elders were surprised. Nana immediately told the Okyeame to invite the children to talk.

Akua began, "I was walking ahead of Yaw but backwards to look at him. He yelled at me about leopard cubs. When I turned around, I saw two leopard cubs running on the path. We chased them, but they went into the forest. We didn't follow them. I think that they were hiding in the bamboo grove, and Kwame and the other boys scared them."

Yaw Mensah burst out, "I saw two leopards cubs, Papa. They looked just like your leopard skin. I want to see them again. I found some good rocks in the stream. Here, look at them."

The elders chuckled. Nana smiled and turned to the Okyeame saying, "Thank the children. Tell them that the council will talk about leopards. Tell Yaw Mensah that I like the rocks."

After Madam Ama and the children left, Nana said to the Okyeame, "Long ago we killed or frightened away our leopards. Why have they returned? Has anyone else seen them?" The Okyeame turned to the elders to ask Nana's questions.

The elders talked among themselves. No one had seen leopards. Other thoughts were expressed.

"Maybe they are being hunted somewhere else and came here for safety."

"They'll find much game to kill here."

"As to what's going on now, I believe that there is a pair of leopards in the area and that the female delivered her cubs on our side of the river. The water is low now. She probably swam across looking for a safe place. She may leave her cubs in the forest while she hunts."

"The female must be hunting along the river bank. She'll find prey there, even a crocodile. Elder Kofi and Asare killed a crocodile yesterday. I've seen a crocodile near my farm where duikers and grasscutters drink in the river." Several elders nodded in agreement.

One of the village headmen had a story to tell. "Something strange is happening near my village. It's next to the river crossing and we hear hunters firing guns on the other side. At night they cross the river to our side. Akans know not to leave their own district to hunt. Maybe a prize like a leopard is tempting them."

Nana asked the Okyeame to question the man. "The river is the boundary of Nana's district. If hunters leave their own district to cross the river, they're breaking the law. What weapons do they bring?"

"They're not using guns on our side," the headman replied, "but we don't know what weapons they bring. In daylight we see their footprints and marks of their canoes on the bank. We've never seen the hunters, but we've heard them."

Nana conferred briefly with the Okyeame, who spoke to the elders, "Nana will talk about the hunters with the chief across the river. For all of you, look for signs of leopards on your land. We need to know if they've come back and if they're coming close to Tanoso or a village.

"If leopards are back, Nana wants us to protect them. They'll keep the forest in balance. Shelter your chickens and sheep at night, and you won't be bothered." The elders nodded in agreement.

An elder who hadn't spoken earlier raised his hand and was recognized. "Leopard skins are valuable. Every chief has one. They'll sell for a high price in Kumasi or even here. It will be hard for anyone to pass up the chance to kill a leopard."

Nana and the Okyeame conferred, and the Okyeame expressed Nana's thoughts to the group. "We have this land by the grace of *Nyame*. We must care for it even as we use it. If animals are in balance, people won't be threatened. We need leopards, not for their hides but alive in the forest. They'll eat snakes and crocodiles. They'll kill weak animals and keep the number of animals down. Nana hopes that none of you or members of your families will kill a leopard. A leopard skin should never be for sale in the Tanoso market."

"Yes, yes," elders showed their agreement.

The Okyeame signaled that it was time for other business.

Banana trees in the forest

— CHAPTER 9 —

Cooking, Roofing, and Ants

In the family courtyard Madam Ama, Auntie Abena, Auntie Adjowa, Anyetata, and other women surrounded the hearth to cut up the duiker meat and place it along with the snails into a cauldron of boiling water. They added peppers, okra, garden eggs, onions, and tomatoes. Children watched the work while fanning the women with the large leaves of banana trees.

"That feels good. What a relief! *Medaase*," the women said. The children smiled and laughed and fanned each other, too.

The Queen Mother joined girls, who were crushing shelled peanuts in small mortars. "Put the pestles on the peanuts and press hard," she told them. "If you pound the peanuts, they'll jump out of the mortars and you'll have to chase them."

The girls giggled. They already knew how to make the peanut paste that thickened the soup and gave it a delicious flavor. They loved their Queen Mother and wanted to please her.

"The paste tastes good," one of the girls exclaimed as she ate some. "I'm so hungry!" Other girls ate it, too.

"Peanut paste is my favorite food," one said. "I love the way it smells, and I could eat it all."

"Girls, leave a little for the soup," the Queen Mother suggested, smiling, as one of the girls delivered the paste to a storage shelter. "I love the way you're working. You're really helping."

Three women dragged heavy wooden mortars into the shade. Akua and other girls joined the women, bringing long wooden pestles for them to pound boiled plantains and cassava into fufu.

The girls sat on stools next to the mortars to turn the fufu dough while the women pounded it. A small bowl of water rested on the ground next to each girl, who dipped her hand into it to scoop up water and sprinkle the dough to keep it soft.

Using her right hand, each girl turned the dough. Left hands were used only for cleaning tasks. Movements were quick. The women and girls looked for the right consistency in the fufu, firm enough for two fingers to shape it into a small spoon to dish up the soup, and soft enough to swallow without chewing. Boom, boom, boom, the pounding sounds echoed. They were comforting, like music, because they meant that food would soon be ready.

Pounding fufu

Akua worked with Auntie Abena, who cautioned her. "I'll pound fast now."

"I'm ready," Akua replied.

"Here we go," Auntie Abena exclaimed in a cheerful voice as she began to pound the fufu faster and harder. Akua kept up, turning the dough quickly while keeping her hand wet without missing a beat. Beat, turn, beat, turn, beat, turn. Boom, boom, boom. Akua and Auntie Abena kept time together as did the others, perfecting the concert of drumbeats.

Akua admired the fufu when it was ready. "It looks perfect," she said. "I'm starved and it will be delicious. I'm ready to make more now."

"We're good partners," Auntie Abena assured Akua. "Deliver this batch while I get more plantains and cassava."

Receiving the fresh batch of fufu from Akua, Auntie Adjowa sprinkled it with more water to keep it soft and shiny, placed it in a bowl, and then in a storage shelter. The pounding and the aroma of spicy peanut soup assured everyone of a delicious meal to come.

THE STOOL HOUSE FORMED PART OF THE FENCE BETWEEN THE TWO COURTYARDS OF the palace and opened to the main courtyard near the tree. Working next to the fence, listening to the pounding of fufu and smelling the peanut soup, the boys and *nnonko* were encouraged to work faster to finish before eating.

Roofing the stool house was tough. Kwame, Kwaku, and Baako trimmed the fronds and bound them with vines to fit the lowest of the roof's three tiers. Four *nnonko* helped them and also climbed the ladder to tie the new bundles to the roof's framework. This addition would secure the roof against rain and wind once more.

The boys were impatient but respected the precise work of the *nnonko*. After a short time, an *odonko,* climbing the ladder on the far side of the stool house, called Baako. "Look at the driver ants," he said, pointing to the long column of black ants barely visible in the shadow of the fence. The ant column came from a neighbor's courtyard and entered the stool house from the back while some ants ventured out to explore both courtyards.

Baako was stunned and called Kwame and Kwaku. "Driver ants," Kwaku whispered when he saw them. "They eat everything including people! I know. They've tried to eat me."

"Let's see what's happening in the stool house," Kwame said. "Baako, tell the *odonko* to climb down the ladder so we can climb up." The boys knew that they were not supposed to look into the stool house, but this was an emergency and the door was locked. Each one climbed the ladder, separated fronds on the roof with

Driver ant

his hands, and looked inside.

"The stools are covered with ants," Kwame described them in a frightened voice. "We have to tell Papa and Mama. Baako, tell the *nnonko* what we're going to do." Kwame and Baako hurried to the council room and Kwaku to the family courtyard.

Kwame and Baako stood respectfully in the courtyard next to the council room and signaled to the Okyeame that they wanted to speak to him. The Okyeame soon beckoned to Kwame, who entered the council room and said, "Please sir, tell Nana that there are driver ants inside of the stool house. They're eating food that was left on the stools. They're going into the courtyards, too."

THE ELDERS HEARD KWAME, BUT THE OKYEAME REPEATED THE WORDS. THE ELDERS had encountered driver ants many times and knew what to do, yet Nana gave directions, replying to the Okyeame, "Tell the stool carriers to place embers from the cooking fire on the ant columns in the stool house and courtyards. They may open the stool house door to let smoke out. Tell the women what we're doing. They'll protect our food. Send out the town crier to tell everyone about the ants. The boys and the *nnonko* should help."

After repeating Nana's words, the Okyeame closed the council meeting. The elders dispersed to help control the ants at the palace and return to their homes to check for ants. One elder hurried to find the town crier. The stool carriers directed the action. Baako translated for the *nnonko*. Following directions, Kwame, Kwaku, and Baako chopped palm fronds into small shovels to carry embers.

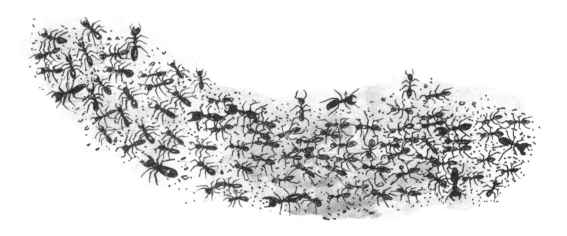

Column of driver ants

The *nnonko* sprinkled embers on the ant columns in the courtyards while the stool carriers entered the stool house to do the same. Large soldier ants acted as sentries along the sides of each column with their pincers pointed up to ward off attacks. Smaller worker ants plied each path. At times ants found human targets. "Aie, aie," people cried out when bitten, quickly backing away from the columns to brush ants off of their feet and legs.

Chickens fled. Women guarded the fufu and crops in the storage huts. Others gathered with children in small groups at a safe distance to watch. Elder Kofi, stood with several children in front of the stool house. "See how careful the stool carriers and *nnonko* are with the embers," he told them. "They'll set the ant columns on fire. That's the only way to kill the ants."

"Where did they come from?" Akua asked. "I've seen them on Mama's farm but never here. We always run away when we see them."

"The ants usually stay in the forest to eat bugs," Elder Kofi explained. "That's good for our crops, but when ants come into town, they threaten people. We must stay away from them."

"They march in long lines!" Yaw Mensah exclaimed. "Will they chase me if I meet them on the path? Will they chase us now?"

"They won't chase you," Elder Kofi replied. "They eat things that stay in one place or move slowly. They'll eat baby animals or animals that are tied up. People move fast so they won't eat us, but they'll bite hard."

"They're big, and there are so many of them. The columns are long and wide, like giant snakes!" Akua said. "Like pythons!"

Once the ants in the palace were destroyed or turned away, the boys, the *nnonko*, and several elders gathered more embers to cover columns outside of the palace. Other men joined the effort, and soon all of the ant columns in town were smoldering.

With their work complete, the elders returned to the council room and reported to the Okyeame, "We're safe from the ants now. Tomorrow morning we'll sweep the stool house and wash the stools. All will be ready for the *Adae*."

Madam Ama and the other women gathered again by the hearth. Children played once more. The boys and *nnonko* returned to their work at the stool house where the door had been left open. "We can't go inside, but I want to look at the stools again," Kwaku said to his friends. "Will you look with me?"

The boys peered into the doorway through the lingering smoke. The platform along the back wall held several stools, each lying on its side. The stool house had no windows and the light was low but the boys could see that some of the stools were decaying. The sight disappointed them.

"I never thought that I would see the sacred stools," Kwame said. "I'm a little bit afraid of them."

"Why does Nana keep them?" Baako asked. "They're too old to use and they're all black."

"When a stool is black, it means that the owner has died. His spirit comes back to the stool. I know that," Kwame explained. "The stools are on their sides so no evil spirits will sit on them."

Within a short time, repairs on the stool house roof were complete, and the boys stood before the Okyeame to inform him. Nana nodded to them, smiled, and thanked them through his spokesman. Kwame, Kwaku, Baako, and the *nnonko* retreated to the shade of the tree in the main courtyard to rest and wait for the meal.

"We did our work. What will the ancestors think tomorrow? Will they like it?" Kwaku asked his friends.

"I think they will," Kwame replied, "but they never tell us. We know that they're happy if our lives are good."

Nana soon called everyone together in the main courtyard. "We are blessed by your company and help as we prepare to honor our grandfather chiefs," he said. "Our meal is ready. Let us eat and afterwards bring out drums and horns to call the spirits of our ancestors."

Older children served peanut soup and fufu to elders in the council room. Women served others and themselves at the hearth and sat on stools to eat under the trees.

Most children sat on the ground to eat near Auntie Adjowa's stool in the family courtyard. She was a story teller and they hoped to hear a story after the meal. "This was a good morning and a busy one," she told them. "Thank you for your work. Our ancestors will be pleased."

Children replied, "You're welcome, Madam Adjowa."

"Thank you for helping us."

"The ants scared us."

"I want to eat now."

"I'm so hungry," Akua said. "We did a good job making fufu."

"It's smooth," one of girls agreed. "I love the soup, too. So peppery!"

"I shelled many, many peanuts," Yaw Mensah bragged. "My fingers are strong now!"

The girls laughed, and one said, "Yaw, you'll soon be as strong as a leopard!

Yaw Mensah grinned and ate eagerly.

— CHAPTER 10 —

Advice and Clans

EATING IN THE MAIN COURTYARD, THE OLDER BOYS TALKED WHILE THE *NNONKO* SAT nearby, silent. "I found good peanuts in the market yesterday," Kwame told his friends. "This peanut soup is great!"

"Tastes good," Baako agreed. "Too bad there's no crocodile meat in it." Kwaku and Kwame shook their heads.

"When will you bring us some crocodile meat to eat?" Kwame asked. "We want to try it."

"Soon, and you'll like it," Baako replied with a smile.

"Our *Adaepa* work is done," Kwaku said with pride. "We worked hard."

"Yes, but the ants were a surprise," Kwame declared. "It's good that we were all here and got rid of them fast."

Seeing the Okyeame approach, the boys stood up immediately and greeted him respectfully, their heads slightly bowed, "*Maaha* – Good afternoon, Okyeame."

The Okyeame returned their greeting and said quietly, "Come with me. Nana wants to talk to you." The boys stiffened, not knowing why the chief was calling them.

"Did we do something wrong?" Kwame asked.

"Is Nana angry because we looked at the black stools?" Kwaku wanted to know.

"Does Nana know that I climbed trees carrying a machete?" Baako was worried.

"Come with me," the Okyeame repeated softly.

They found Nana in the council room, sitting in his royal chair with Elder Kofi standing at his side. The chief smiled as the boys entered and greeted him. He returned their greeting and spoke in a quiet voice. "You worked well today to repair the roof of the stool house and drive the ants away. The elders and I are pleased."

The Okyeame and Elder Kofi clapped their hands quietly saying, "*Yoo* – Agreed."

The boys bowed their heads to show respect.

"You will soon be young men," Nana continued. "You are healthy. You work hard. You are learning the ways of the forest, how to farm, and how to hunt. The elders and I want you to be leaders of our people. Let us help you. Hear what I say.

"Listen to your history at the *Adae* ceremony tomorrow. Learn the blessings and the stories. Follow the *Sankofa* bird that walks forward while looking backward. You see one at the top of the Okyeame's staff. *Sankofa* birds let the past guide their future.

"Elders say that if a grasshopper's eyes extend beyond its eyebrows, it becomes ugly. When a grasshopper opens its eyes wide, it is looking down on people. This is a warning. Never look down on people. Respect your ancestors, your elders, and your friends. If you do, they will respect you and help you.

"Think carefully and speak well so that you may convince others of your ideas.

"Elders say that one head does not hold consultations. Make important decisions only after talking to others.

"In your friends, we see your character. Your actions and theirs will show us if you can be leaders. I hope that you three will remain friends and strengthen each other.

Sankofa bird

"Kwame," Nana continued, "you are my son, and you belong to your mother's clan. Honor her when you decide your future. Work hard to learn the skills that you'll need. Always consult with your Uncle Kwasi.

"Kwaku, you are the son of my senior sister. You belong to my clan, and you are the eldest son who might become the next chief. The Queen Mother selects the chief and asks the elders to approve. Show them that you are worthy. In the *Adae* ceremony listen to the reasons that we honor our grandfather chiefs. Learn what a chief must do.

"Baako, you are the son of *nnonko*. You have shown strength and skill in your work. You see your father's diplomacy as my foreman. Study him well. You are earning your freedom."

The boys remained quiet, struggling to understand the advice and why Nana was giving it to them at this time.

"I invite the three of you to join my delegation to Kumasi for the *Odwira* festival," Nana explained. "The walk is long, but you're strong enough, and you can help carry supplies. Leaders must make this trip. In Kumasi, you will see people from all parts of our kingdom. You'll see foreigners from outside of our kingdom. You will witness the chiefs pledging loyalty to the Asantehene and learn why our kingdom is powerful."

The boys looked at each other and showed their pleasure with smiles, slight jumps, and small hand claps. There was no need to talk. They all wanted to go to Kumasi.

Nana continued. "After a few more *Odwira* ceremonies, you will be young men. Kwame and Kwaku, you each owe allegiance to your mother's clan. As young men, you will move to the home of your mother's senior brother.

"Kwame, you will move to your Uncle Kwasi's home. Kwaku, you will move to my home. Baako, if I adopt you, you will owe allegiance to my clan and move with Kwaku to my home. In your new home, you will help build a sleeping hut. You will stay there until you marry and move to your own home. In this way we keep our families strong."

The chief folded his hands in silence, and the Okyeame spoke to the boys. "Nana talked to you directly and that is a compliment. You may go now." The boys returned to the courtyard, where they hugged each other and patted each others' backs.

"We're almost young men!" Kwaku cheered.

"We'll always be friends!" Kwame shouted.

"It's my dream! I want Nana to adopt me! I want to be free! I want to be Akan, but I'll never forget my mama and papa," Baako said with both happiness and apprehension.

IN THE COUNCIL ROOM, THE DRUMMERS AND HORN BLOWERS TOOK OUT THEIR INSTRU-ments and prepared to summon the ancestor chiefs. The soft drumming and the clear notes of the horns soon drifted through the courtyards and into town. Adults and children moved to the music. Nana and the Queen Mother were satisfied with preparations for the *Adae*. Early the next morning, after elders cleaned the stools and the stool house, all would be ready.

The Queen Mother was deeply pleased. *Adae* ceremonies were especially important for her because her brother's spirit would be summoned, and his blackened stool honored by the naming of his important deeds. She would feel close to him once more.

Most visitors left the palace with plans to return the next day to honor the ancestor chiefs. Some children stayed behind. The *nnonko* returned to their village. They, too, looked forward to the *Adae* because they could work on their own farms. Only Asare and Baako would come to the palace.

Clapping her hands over her head, Auntie Adjowa called children to the family court-yard to join her under a tree. Those already sitting near her snuggled in place. "Akua, ask Kwame and the other boys to come," she directed.

The boys came quickly. Kwame turned to Kwaku and Baako and said, "I think I know what Auntie Adjowa will tell us and Baako should hear it."

"Fine with me. I'm really tired," Kwaku said. Baako agreed, not knowing what to expect.

Auntie Adjowa talks about stools and families

Smiling at her audience, Auntie Adjowa spoke in a musical voice, "*Mema mo aha* – Good afternoon, my children. Rest now. I'll talk to you about our stools and our families. Do you see the stool that I'm sitting on?"

"Yes," children murmured, looking at the old wooden stool.

"Do you see other stools in the courtyard?" Auntie Adjowa asked.

"Oh, yes, many," children replied.

"Does every man and woman in this town have a stool?"

"Yes!" the children agreed.

"Do any of you have stools?" Auntie Adjowa asked once more.

"Yes," children replied again.

"Little stools," some added.

"Yes," Auntie Adjowa repeated. "Everyone has a stool, and we love our stools. Do you know how we make them?"

"Stools come from trees," one child said.

"You're right. We carve stools from tree trunks. Only in the forest are there enough trees to make so many stools. They show that we live among trees and that our people sit together to cook and eat and talk." The children listened with satisfaction and snuggled together.

"The outdoor stools are plain, but Nana and the Queen Mother have fancy stools that they keep indoors. We save the fancy stools of good chiefs so that we can remember them. When a good chief dies, the elders turn his stool black. Tomorrow I'll tell you how they do that. Only the elders who have the title of 'stool carrier' can handle Nana's stool or the black stools.

"We keep the black stools in the stool house here at the palace. Most of the time you don't see them, but, if you come to the palace early tomorrow morning, you'll see them. Elders will clean them in the courtyard and later honor them at the *Adae* ceremony. You're ready for that now." Children smiled to agree.

"LET'S TALK ABOUT OUR FAMILIES," AUNTIE ADJOWA CONTINUED. "EVERYONE BELONGS to a big family. You have a small family at home with your father and mother and brothers and sisters or even more people. Some of your aunts, uncles, cousins, or grandparents may live with you, too. You see that family every day." Children nodded.

"You have a bigger family, too, a clan, and in it are all of your grandparents, aunts, uncles, and cousins that you may not see often. You also have clan members from long ago who are your ancestors. All of the children in your family who will be born in the future are in your clan, too."

Children gasped, "Oh, so big. A clan is big," some murmured. "Where are all of these people?"

"You know some of them. You see them here in Tanoso or nearby," Auntie Adjowa continued. "Your ancestors and the children who have not been born live with *Nyame*. We don't know where they are, but they see us. They know what we're doing. They want us to live good lives, and if we do, they will help us."

"What should we do?" children asked.

"People in a clan should help each other in their homes and on their farms and when someone is sick. If members of your clan are traveling and come to your town, you must welcome them to stay with you and offer them food even if you don't know them. If they are in danger, you must protect them. If we help each other, our clans will survive."

Children nodded to show that they understood. Some said, "We do that already."

Auntie Adjowa smiled. "Yes," she said, "you have good families. Akans have eight clans and all of the clans are good. When you go home, ask your mother to tell you the name of her clan. That is your clan. We all belong to our mother's clan."

"*Oyoko* is the name of the first clan that came to the forest. Our Queen Mother is an *Oyoko*. She is my mother and Nana's mother, and so we belong to her clan. My son, Kwaku, is also an *Oyoko*." Auntie Adjowa smiled and rested for a moment while the children turned to look at Kwaku, who quickly sat up.

"*Oyoko, Oyoko, Oyoko*," children repeated the name because it sounded good to them.

"Some of you belong to the *Oyoko* clan. The rest of you belong to other clans."

"Auntie Adjowa, I want to belong to the Queen Mother's clan," a child said.

"Don't worry, my children. All of the clans are good. Soon you'll learn the name of your clan if you don't know it already."

"What about my father's clan?" a child asked. "Is he in the same clan as my mother?"

"I'm glad that you asked. Your father and mother belong to different clans, and you should know about your father's clan, too. Ask him the name of his clan. Your family will help his clan, but you don't belong to it."

Baako leaned toward Kwame, "Why did Nana say that I would belong to his clan if he adopts me? I thought that we would be brothers."

"Oh, you're different," Kwame answered. "I belong to my mother's clan, but if my father adopts you, you'll be in his clan, like Kwaku. I'm an *Agona*. The Queen Mother, Papa, Auntie Adjowa, and Kwaku are *Oyoko*. That's what you'll be."

Baako was confused. "Will we be in the same family, Kwaku?" Baako wanted to know.

"Yes," Kwaku replied. "I'm an *Oyoko* because my mother is a daughter of the Queen Mother. An *Oyoko* is always the chief in Tanoso. That's why I can be a chief, but Kwame can't."

"Can I belong to any clan that I want to?" a child asked.

"When you are born, everyone knows where you belong. You cannot choose your clan. You cannot change your clan. Tonight you have a job," Auntie Adjowa reminded everyone. "Ask your mother the name of your clan and tell me tomorrow. Are you ready to hear how Akans entered the forest?"

Snuggling closer together, children answered eagerly, "Yes, we are!"

— CHAPTER 11 —

The First Akans

"WHEN DID WE AKANS FIRST ENTER THE FOREST?" AUNTIE ADJOWA ASKED THE CHILDREN.

"We've always lived here," one child answered. "We're forest people."

"Where could we have lived before?" another child asked.

Auntie Adjowa smiled. "I have a story to tell you," she said. "Listen and then you will know.

"Long, long ago, the forest was ruled by animals. The forest was too dense and too dark for people to live here. Only hunters entered the forest. They knew how to talk to animals and follow their paths.

"One day, a hunter was walking in the forest with a honey badger, who said to him, 'Soon people will come to live in the forest. They will come from the sky or openings in the ground. You hunters must find good places for them to live.'

"The hunter was surprised and didn't know whether to believe the honey badger. 'Where will I find these people?' he asked.

"'At a sacred place in the forest, a woman will descend from the sky on a golden chain, and she will be the founder of the *Oyoko* clan,' the badger replied. 'The woman will carry a stool and take it to a different place where more people from other clans will appear. A stool means that people will sit together.'

An Akan stool

"'I will welcome these people,' the hunter replied, 'for we hunters are lonely and there is much land in the forest. Come with me now, badger, to greet the people.'

"These people were Akans," Auntie Adjowa explained. "They didn't know how to live in the forest then. There were so many trees that they could hardly see their way even in the daytime. They needed space and light to build villages and plant crops.

"Hunters brought the people meat and showed them good places to build villages and towns. Akans learned to build on hills to be high in the sky, near our ancestors, and safe from heavy rains and floods."

"Not safe from ants," one child added and others agreed. Auntie Adjowa smiled.

"Our people wanted to be near rivers and streams so that they would always have water to drink and cook and bathe. They needed flat areas to plant crops and enough land for hunting. Did our ancestors find a good place for our town here?" Auntie Adjowa asked.

The children were serious and nodded in agreement. "Yes," many said. "We have everything that you said. The hunters knew good places."

"From the beginning," Auntie Adjowa explained, "each village had a headman, and each town had a chief and a council of elders, just as we have now. The head of each clan belongs to our council. The chief's stool is the symbol of his land. When you walk through the big courtyard on your way home, look at Nana's stool in the council room. Nana will always protect it, just as he protects his people.

"Chiefs gave farms to people who wanted to join them and share their land. Some stool lands had more riches than others, especially in gold. As the chiefs of different stool lands became powerful, they sometimes fought each other for more land or gold or people."

"Do they fight with each other now?" a child asked.

"Not often, because we have a kingdom now," Auntie Adjowa assured the children. "We have many chiefs, but our king is more powerful than the chiefs, and he keeps the peace. Our king is called the Asantehene. He lives in Kumasi, the capital of our kingdom."

"Is the forest big?" one of the children asked.

"Oh, yes," Auntie Adjowa replied. "The forest is very big. Some of the traders who come to our market walk for many days from the ocean or from Kumasi. Nana and the elders will walk for eight days to Kumasi to see our king."

Children gasped. "Eight days," they repeated.

Baako gasped, too. "Eight days! That's a long walk, and then we have to come back." Kwame and Kwaku agreed.

"After all of the people in all of the clans arrived," Auntie Adjowa explained, "there still weren't enough people in the forest."

"Why did the chiefs need more people?" children wanted to know.

"To cut down trees, and build villages and towns, and clear land for farms and paths, and mine for gold. All of that is hard work. Families joined together to work, but they still needed more people."

"How did the chiefs find more people?" several children wondered out loud.

Auntie Adjowa looked very serious. "I'll tell you something important now," she said. "The chiefs brought people into the forest from outside of the forest. Our king still brings prisoners from the savannah who become *nnonko* for us. They are never free, but we adopt their children into our families. The children become Akan, and then they are free. That's how we get more people."

"I play with *nnonko* children," one child said. "They're like me."

"Akan families will probably adopt those children when they grow up," Auntie Adjowa explained. "Then they'll be free like you."

Baako turned to Kwame and Kwaku. "That's my story," he said. "My parents and grand-parents came from the savannah."

"The new people, where are they?" a child asked.

Auntie Adjowa smiled. "They belong to our clans. We never ask people where they came from. If you know, you must never say. All free people who live in the forest are Akan. They can't be anything else.

"Every clan has it own history. We all have to learn our clan's history and the stories about our forest and our people, just as I'm telling you now. You'll learn more from someone in your own clan."

"Auntie Adjowa, do animals still talk?" a child asked.

"No, long, long ago was a magical time when animals talked and welcomed our people into the forest.

"Oh, my children," Auntie Adjowa exclaimed. "Look at the sky. The sun is setting and it's time for you to go home. You'll have enough light to find your way. Tomorrow I'll tell you another story.

"Remember, you have a job. Tonight, ask your mother the name of your clan, and tell me tomorrow. If you come to the palace early in the morning, you'll see the sacred stools. We'll honor our grandfather chiefs at the *Adae* ceremony. You are ready for that now.

"When you return home, take your bath, eat something small, and go to bed. Close the door of your sleeping hut to keep the mosquitos out. *Dayie* – Goodnight."

The children got up slowly. "Thank you for the story, Auntie Adjowa," many said. "*Dayie* – Goodnight."

Holding onto each other and walking slowly past the council room, children saw an intricately carved stool set out for the *Adae* ceremony.

"Look, look," they said, as they pointed to Nana's stool

Nana's stool

and waved to the musicians. Children soon left the palace to find their way home.

"Baako and Kwaku, thanks for helping me today. I hope that you'll come back tomorrow," Kwame said. "I'd like some company."

"I'll come," Kwaku replied. "My mama and papa will be here, too."

"I'll be here in the morning with my papa," Baako answered. "He'll teach me more about throwing spears in the afternoon. Do you want to do that with us?"

"Yes!" Kwame and Kwaku responded eagerly.

"I'll tell Papa," Baako said, smiling. "I'm leaving now. I have a long way to go."

"Make noise!" Kwame said with concern for Baako.

"I will," Baako assured him.

The palace was quiet except for the soft beating of the drums. Nana, Madam Ama, and the Queen Mother sat on stools and talked. Akua and Yaw Mensah stretched out on the ground to build little huts with pebbles and leaves. Kwame lay nearby thinking about going to Kumasi with his friends.

"*Medaase. Dayie*," Nana said to his sister, Auntie Adjowa.

"*Medaase. Dayie*," the Queen Mother said to her daughter.

"*Dayie*. I'll see you tomorrow," Auntie Adjowa answered as she left the palace.

EARLY THE NEXT MORNING, ELDERS RETURNED TO THE PALACE TO PREPARE FOR THE

A black stool

Adae ceremony. The air was clear and cool, and everyone worked fast. The stool carriers opened the stool house door and removed the sacred black stools, placing them in the courtyard where they were seldom seen. Several elders swept the platform and the floor and made certain that there were no live ants inside the stool house.

Children throughout the town awoke at dawn and swept their courtyards but didn't go to the stream because they had collected extra water the day before. After eating breakfast, many hurried to the palace to join Kwame, Akua, and Yaw Mensah in front of the stool house. Elders motioned for children to stay back and not to talk. Most children obeyed, but the curious ones remained nearby.

Kwaku arrived with his father. Elder Kofi went to the council room, and Kwaku found Kwame. No one asked the boys to help. Only elders cared for the sacred stools. Seeing the stools again, Kwaku observed, "So many are old and falling apart. Only a few look solid."

"You're right," Kwame agreed. "The stool carriers have to be careful."

Asare and Baako entered the courtyard, sweating and breathing heavily. Asare went directly to the council room. He often attended meetings because Nana wanted him to be informed and available to help. Baako joined Kwame and Kwaku. He greeted them and they returned his greeting. "Why are you sweating?" Kwame asked.

"Papa and I were racing," Baako said, panting. "He won but I almost did."

"How can he run fast?" Kwame asked. "He's old."

Baako wasn't sure if Kwame was serious. "We like to race," Baako answered. "Papa's not old and he's strong. You saw him throw a spear. You'll see more when he teaches us how to throw spears. He can do that this afternoon if Nana agrees."

"I want to learn," Kwame replied.

"I want to learn, too," Kwaku agreed. "I'll ask my papa if I can come today. We have to know how to throw spears to be young men."

"What's going on here?" Baako asked, pointing to the stools.

"Elders are cleaning the black stools," Kwame answered.

To clean the stools and drive away evil spirits, elders made a paste of water, soot, and cut up sukubre leaves and rubbed it on the stools. They rinsed the stools, let them dry in the air, and returned them to the stool house, placing each on its side on the platform.

Nana's stool was placed just inside of the stool house, next to the door, upright on the floor. The only other contents of the stool house were two brass bells placed on the floor near the door.

An elder closed the door. The children were disappointed but waited, hoping to see more. Auntie Adjowa joined them. "*Mema mo akye* – Good morning, everyone," she said. "Kwaku, please find a stool for me."

"*Yaa*, Auntie Adjowa," the children replied.

"I'll stay with you and tell you what is happening inside," Auntie Adjowa promised. "I'll sit on an ordinary stool, but inside of the stool house are the sacred stools. You were fortunate to see them."

"We saw the sacred stools, and they're black," a child said.

"They're old. Some don't look strong," another child added.

"Yes, when a stool is black, it means that the owner has died. We save the stools of good chiefs so that we can remember them and honor them and ask for their blessing. Our grandfather chiefs live with *Nyame* and they see us."

"What makes stools black?" a child asked.

"When a good chief dies, the stool carriers rub egg yolks and soot on his stool and that turns it black. At the *Adae* ceremonies, the stool carriers rub sheep blood on the stools to keep them black. They'll do that again today. Did any of you count the stools?"

"There are a lot of them," some children said.

"There are ten stools, so we know that this district has had at least ten chiefs," Auntie Adjowa explained. "That tells us that the town has been here for ten generations or more."

"Oh," children gasped.

"Tanoso's old like the grandfather chiefs," one said.

Elders who were cooks for the *Adae* took over the hearth to boil eggs and plantains to offer to the spirits of the ancestor chiefs. Nana spoke briefly to the cooks and inspected the stool house. Satisfied with the arrangements, he returned to the council room where the elders, and now the musicians and historians, waited.

"We will begin," he said.

— CHAPTER 12 —

The Adae Ceremony

The Adae ceremony at the palace

AN ELDERLY WOMAN STANDING AT THE ENTRANCE TO THE PALACE WAVED A GOURD FULL of water over her head while saying a prayer. After pouring the water out, she placed the gourd on the ground and put a stone on it. This offering to local spirits prevented any disagreements among those attending the *Adae* ceremony.

The soft music of horns and drums filled the air. The head stool carrier opened the door of the stool house and waited outside while Nana, the historians, the musicians, and most of the elders walked slowly to join him. A few elders stayed behind to help with the ceremony later.

Sitting on a stool surrounded by children sitting or lying on the ground, Auntie Adjowa spoke, "Look, here come Nana and the elders, and they're wearing old cloths."

"Why are they doing that?" children asked.

"They don't look good," one child said.

"They're showing the grandfather chiefs that they are humble before their ancestors," Auntie Adjowa explained. "When the elders are inside of the stool house, they'll remove their cloths from their shoulders and tuck them inside their waists and take off their sandals to be even more humble. The grandfather chiefs protect those who are humble before them."

"Why?" a child asked.

"Humble people respect their ancestors. They care for their families and work together on their farms. They settle disagreements peacefully. They share the work of building towns and roads. They help each other. When we do these things, we are following our traditions.

"Soon you'll see a cook bring food for Nana to serve to the grandfather chiefs. To show his respect, Nana feeds his ancestors before he eats breakfast. You'll hear Nana ask the grandfather chiefs to bless us."

The head stool carrier poured water at the threshold of the stool house door, saying, "Grandfather chiefs, we celebrate the *Adae*. Receive this water and wash your hands. You will eat soon." The stool carrier stayed near the open door after Nana and the elders entered.

An *Adae* cook holding a gourd of boiled and mashed plantains mixed with palm nut oil, and boiled eggs chopped into small pieces approached the stool house and gave the food to the stool carrier, who passed it to Nana.

The elders stood facing the platform of black stools. Nana placed a small portion of the food on the side of each stool, repeating the same words at each but naming the different grandfather chiefs. He began, "Nana Akomea, at this *Adae* come and receive eggs and plantains to eat. Let this town prosper. Let us have many children, and let our families enjoy success."

The Okyeame intoned, "*Yoo!* – Agreed!" in a deep voice after each blessing.

Other elders chanted, "*Tie! Tie! Tie!* – Listen! Listen! Listen!"

"Do you hear the chants after the blessings?" Auntie Adjowa asked the children. They nodded.

"Soon a sheep will be presented to the ancestors. You need to know, my children, that Nana will sacrifice the sheep."

"Oh, no!" some of the children protested. "We don't want the sheep to die."

Consoling the children, Auntie Adjowa said, "It is sad for the sheep, but to honor the ancestors, the elders must spread blood on the stools and place fresh meat on them for the grandfather chiefs to eat."

When Nana completed the first blessing of the stools, an elder entered the stool house with a sheep slung across his shoulders. Nana addressed the spirits of the grandfather chiefs once more. "Come to see this sheep and prepare to receive its blood and meat. Let this town prosper. Let us have many children, and let our families enjoy success."

The Okyeame repeated, "*Yoo!*"

Elders chanted, "*Tie! Tie! Tie!*"

With a small knife, Nana sacrificed the sheep, which bleated in anguish. In the stool house and in the courtyard, the sheep's blood was collected in gourds. Elders laid the carcass on a plank in the courtyard to bleed, skin, and cut up. An elder returned to the stool house with a gourd of blood, which the head stool carrier spread with his hand on each stool to honor and preserve it.

Some children became frightened when the sheep bleated and found it difficult to watch the activity in the courtyard. They put their hands over their eyes or buried their faces in Auntie Adjowa's cloth. She soothed them, saying, "We feed our ancestors and give them palm wine to drink so they will watch over us.

"If this is difficult for you, keep your eyes closed. Soon you'll hear the historians chant the history of the grandfather chiefs. Listen, so you'll learn. Remember, our ancestors protect us, and Nana speaks to them." The older boys were fascinated, knowing that they would do this work someday.

Within a short time, portions of the muscle, fat, and internal organs of the sheep, cut into small pieces, were carried on a platter into the stool house. Elders also brought gourds of palm wine. Auntie Adjowa explained, "Nana will place the meat from the sheep on the side of each stool and fat at the base of each stool while he says more blessings. Listen carefully."

"Ancient ones who came from *Nyame*, receive our offerings and eat," Nana repeated the familiar words. "Permit me to have a long reign. Let our kingdom prosper. Do not let it act foolishly."

With each offering elders chanted, "*Tie! Tie! Tie!*"

The children heard the chants and then the ringing of the brass bells. "When the bells ring, you'll know that the grandfather chiefs are eating," Auntie Adjowa explained. "Next, Nana will pour palm wine on each stool for the grandfather chiefs to drink."

Soon a small group of elders took the sheep's head into the stool house on a plank.

"They'll put the head on the floor in front of the center stool to show the grandfather chiefs where the meat came from," Auntie Adjowa explained.

"Oh, I've never seen anyone carry a sheep head like that," one child said.

"It's so strange," another said.

"I can't watch," a third said.

The drummers and horn blowers accompanied the historians when they praised the grandfather chiefs and said their names and accomplishments. Chiefs do not act alone. They follow the advice of their councils to protect and serve their people. The historians praised chiefs who:

- treated their people with respect and listened carefully when they spoke their minds
- cleared land to provide more food for their people, who ate well and survived
- sent their hunters to save us from crocodiles
- rescued their people when floods covered the land
- dug mines to find gold and bring wealth to their people
- helped build the great-road that takes us to Kumasi
- fought with the Asantehene to defeat the Gonja in the savannah and bring more people into the forest
- handled disputes fairly and with care, and made sure that all of the gold weights used in the market were accurate
- always had time for their people.

"It's hard to be a chief," Kwaku said to his friends. "If I'm the chief someday, I'll have to learn so much and talk to my council and my *okyeame* and the Queen Mother, and then decide what to do."

"You have to work hard if you're a chief," Baako replied. "You see what Nana does."

"Do you really want to be the chief?" Kwame asked. "You could be a farmer. You would have an easier life."

"Yes, I want to be the chief. I want to help my people. I have to learn what to do," Kwaku answered emphatically. "You're my friends. You can help me."

"We'll help," Kwame and Baako agreed.

When the historians finished the chant, they, with Nana, the Okyeame, elders, drummers, and horn blowers, left the stool house. The head stool carrier closed and fastened the door.

Auntie Adjowa spoke quietly to the children. "You saw the sacred stools and you learned how the grandfather chiefs are honored. What can you tell me about our history?" Several children answered eagerly.

"The black stools help us remember the good chiefs."

"I know why ants like the stools. There's food on them."

"The grandfather chiefs like music."

"The sheep part is weird."

"I didn't know that grandfather chiefs could eat so much."

"The good chiefs took care of their people."

"What happens to the rest of the sheep's meat?"

"Hunters killed crocodiles."

Auntie Adjowa smiled and complimented the children. "You watched and listened carefully. Thank you for staying with me. The *Adae* is an important ceremony, and you'll understand more each time you hear the historians tell us about the grandfather chiefs. Oh, yes, the stool carriers will take the rest of the sheep meat home to eat.

"Nana and the elders will eat breakfast now, change into their finest cloths, and put on gold ornaments. The elders and village headmen will soon gather to pledge loyalty to Nana.

"Play in the courtyards and listen to the horns and drums. Join the dancing. Everyone likes to dance the *Adowa*. After we dance, come to the small courtyard. You can tell me your clan names, and I'll tell you a story."

"Yes, yes! *Medaase*, Auntie Adjowa," children replied as they stood and scampered away.

KWAME, KWAKU, AND BAAKO STAYED IN THE MAIN COURTYARD NEAR THE COUNCIL room, listening to the horns and talking drums create the rhythm and tones of histories and stories. They knew the story of the creation of the forest and said the words softly to the music:

> The stream crosses the path.
> The path crosses the stream.
> Which of them is the elder?
> Did we not cut a path to go and meet this stream?
> The stream had its origin long, long, ago.
> The stream had its origin in the Creator.

Talking drums and elephant tusk horns

"That's a good story, and the story of Nana's clan goes with it," Kwaku said. "That's my clan, too, the *Oyoko*. If Nana adopts Baako, it will be his clan."

"I want to hear the story," Baako said with interest.

"Tell the story," Kwame encouraged Kwaku. "I like it, too."

Kwaku began, "I've heard my mother tell this story many times. I think I remember it. The first Asantehene gave land to Nana Akomea, the oldest grandfather chief, to reward him for service in the army. We heard Nana bless Nana Akomea today. He brought his family here and invited people from all of the other clans to come.

"Hunters marked off enough land for farming and hunting and everyone worked together to build this town and the path to the stream. There was enough land for everyone."

"Nana and the elders have to make sure there's still enough land for all of the children, including *nnonko* children," Baako asserted. "Will they do that? I'll need a farm and so will my brothers and sisters."

"I think so," Kwaku answered. "If I'm the chief someday, I'll need land for all of my people, too. We'll always need a big forest for hunting. Nana and the elders know that. They keep Nana Akomea's black stool to remind them."

— CHAPTER 13 —

Wisdom

Nana followed by the Okyeame

We Are Akan

THE MAIN COURTYARD SOON FILLED WITH MEN, WOMEN AND CHILDREN FROM THE TOWN and nearby villages. The tax collectors joined the group. Everyone wore a fine cloth, and many wore gold rings and chains. Some men smoked pipes. Several elderly men and women used walking sticks and were shaded from the sun by colorful umbrellas borne by young family members.

The music of the drums and horns changed suddenly to a loud and strong beat announcing Nana's entry to the council room followed by the Okyeame. Nana wore a brightly colored *kente* cloth and gold accessories. A velvet band with gold decorations encircled his head. Gold chains hung around his neck. His hands and wrists were weighted down with gold rings and bracelets. Gold anklets chimed as he walked slowly and gracefully.

Once in his royal chair, Nana placed his feet on a leopard skin. Seated slightly behind Nana were family members and senior elders. The head of the *Oyoko* clan in Tanoso and the Okyeame sat to Nana's left. There, too, was a chair for the Queen Mother, whose arrival would close the ceremony. Other senior elders sat to Nana's right. The remaining elders, headmen, other respected men in the community, and the tax collectors stood in a wide circle in front of Nana.

Kwame, Kwaku, and Baako watched from the courtyard. "Nana looks so rich," Baako whispered.

"Chiefs have to look rich for celebrations. If the chief is rich, then everyone can be rich," Kwaku said. "The chief shares gold and food crops with his people. I'll do that someday. I want my people to be rich."

The Okyeame called the headmen and the clan heads by name. Each came forward, stepped out of his sandals, removed his cloth from his left shoulder, bowed from the waist, and pledged his loyalty to Nana, who responded with a slight bow of his head. This activity was slow and measured, giving Nana time to focus on each individual.

The Queen Mother in kente cloth

Later, with a welcoming smile, the Queen Mother entered the council room, wearing an elaborate *kente* cloth, an elegant headscarf, and a gold necklace. Her royal bearing revealed her authority. She curtsied in front of Nana before sitting down. With her arrival, the *Adae* ceremony officially concluded but the celebration continued.

The drummers and horn blowers joined by bell ringers played music for the *Adowa* dance. At first, men stayed in the council room to talk and drink palm wine. Women and children filled the main courtyard to sing and dance. Singers praised the grandfather chiefs. Men were drawn in. Nana and the royal party watched with pleasure.

Dancing the Adowa

People of all ages loved to dance the *Adowa* because it was open and free. Dancers made short walking movements that could be simple or intricate, fast or slow. Hands and fingers moved in waves, sometimes telling personal stories. Bodies twisted and turned. Many women waved a small white cloth. Some dancers displayed exceptional skill at interpreting the music with their whole bodies.

"Let's dance," Kwaku suggested. "It's fun."

"For a little while," Kwame replied.

"I'll try," Baako said, "but I really want to throw spears. I have to help Papa get ready to teach us."

Kwaku joined the dancers and moved his feet in intricate steps. Stretching out his arms, he turned around and around until he felt dizzy. He then lowered his arms and stopped turning but continued to move his feet keeping his hands on his waist.

Kwame moved forward and backward along the edge of the crowd, trying to copy some of the foot movements that he saw and listening closely to the women who were singing. Their voices encouraged him to move faster. He saw Akua and Yaw Mensah nearby and approached them. All three twisted and turned. Yaw grew tired and left the group to stretch out under a tree, where he continued to make the arm movements of a dancer. Akua and Kwame danced faster and faster.

Baako watched the dancers without quite standing still. He first moved his feet in small steps, imitating other dancers. Next he moved his arms and then his body and tried to connect all of the movements. "Come on," Kwaku encouraged him while Baako moved slowly at the edge of the crowd.

Once dancing, the crowd was lost to the music. Everyone moved feet, arms, and torsos freely. At times a drummer or horn blower would take over and play to the chief directly while the dancing continued. Nana nodded his head in reply. The Queen Mother, smiled with pride in the town and its people. She felt certain that the grandfather chiefs, especially her brother, were smiling too.

"They're ready for a story," Auntie Adjowa thought as she saw children sit and lie down in the courtyard. Walking to the entrance of the family courtyard, she clapped her hands above her head, and motioned for children to follow her to the tree, where she sat on a stool. Akua and Yaw Mensah were the first to come. Others soon joined them.

"Oh, my dears, you are good dancers," Auntie Adjowa complimented the children. "I love watching you. I'm glad that you're still here. Some of you were with me earlier. How many of you saw the stools of the grandfather chiefs?"

Hands went up and children cried out, "Me, me, me!"

"I saw so many stools."

"They're black."

"They're old."

Auntie Adjowa laughed, "You are right. Those stools are old just like the grandfather chiefs. It's good that you saw the black stools. You know they are special. We save the stools of chiefs who were wise. Only wise chiefs can have a black stool."

"I want you to know, though, that you don't have to be a chief to be wise. What is wisdom? What do wise people do?" Auntie Adjowa asked. The children had many ideas.

"They're good like the grandfather chiefs."

"They help people."

"They take care of people."

"They know how to do things."

"They're smart."

"All of you are right," Auntie Adjowa said. "Everyone should try to be wise. Every man and woman in our town will take care of you and teach you to be wise. If you are doing something that is wise, they will praise you. If you are doing something that you shouldn't do, they will stop you. You must obey."

"Even if they aren't in our clan?" a child asked.

"Yes, because the people in all of the clans take care of each other's children. We all live together. I'll tell you a story about why we can all be wise. First, I hope that you'll tell me the name of your clan. Did you ask your mother the name of her clan? That is your clan, too. Tell me the clan names."

"*Oyoko, Oyoko, Oyoko, Agona, Beretuo, Asona, Asokore, Ekuana, Asinie, Beretuo, Oyoko, Agona, Aduana, Ekuana, Asokore,*" children replied eagerly.

"Oh, so many families!!" Auntie Adjowa exclaimed. "Remember your clan's name because you must know where you belong."

The children began to tell each other their clan name.

"I'm a *Beretuo.* What are you?"

"I'm an *Oyoko.* What are you?"

"I'm an *Asona.* What are you?"

"You know the clans. I'm so proud of you," Auntie Adjowa proclaimed. "Now, for wisdom. I'll tell you a story about the spider, Kwaku Ananse. He's clever but not always wise. You will see what happened to him."

Kwaku Ananse,
the spider

"LONG, LONG, AGO, WHEN *NYAME* CREATED THE WORLD, HE PLANNED to share wisdom with people and animals. You could see and hold pieces of wisdom then. *Nyame* scattered the pieces in a forest clearing and invited animals and a person from each clan to come and take a share. *Nyame* spoke softly and the matter didn't seem urgent, so only one individual came right away. That was Kwaku Ananse, the spider, who walked very fast on the webs that he had spun in the forest.

"Ananse arrived in the clearing carrying a gourd. Quickly and quietly he scooped up all of the wisdom with his gourd and covered the gourd with a lid, which he tied on with vines. He smiled and said to himself, 'Now, only I will be wise. Everyone will have to come to me and ask me questions to learn what to do.'" Children gasped, knowing that that was bad behavior.

"With more vines, Ananse tied the gourd around his neck and let it hang in front of him. Slowly, he walked home across his webs. Even though he had eight legs, he couldn't walk fast because the gourd bumped his front legs. Ananse didn't care. He had his prize.

"When he arrived home, Ananse proudly showed his wife and children the gourd. 'What do you have in there?' his wife asked.

"'I've scooped up all of the pieces of wisdom in the forest and secured them in this gourd,' Ananse replied. 'Anyone who wants to be wise will have to talk to me. Many animals and people will come to see me. They'll pay me for wisdom. We'll have a lot of company. I'll earn a lot of gold.'

"'Oh, you're silly,' Ananse's wife said. 'You won't like having so much company. You will have no rest.'

"'Let me see,' Ananse replied.

"Ananse told the other animals that he had a gourd of wisdom, and they told the people, for animals and people still talked to each other then. Soon there were lines of people and animals who wanted advice. The visitors to Anansi's home asked many questions.

"'Where should I plant my corn when the rains begin? My harvest has been poor.'

"'There are too many monkeys on my land, stealing bananas. What should I do?'

"'I want to go to the river, but I'm scared of a python. What can I do?'

"'My children don't work hard enough on my farm. How can I encourage them?'

"'My neighbor has been harvesting my cassava. How can I stop him?'

"'I cannot get water from the river because of the crocodiles. Where is a safe place to collect water?'"

The children recognized the questions because they knew people who were trying to solve these problems. Auntie Adjowa asked them, "What would you say if someone asked you these questions?" Children offered answers.

"I'd tell people and animals to stay away from crocodiles."

"I'd tell farmers to plant corn in a clearing where the sun will find it after the rains begin. That's what my mama does."

"I'd tell people to give children bananas to eat so they would work harder on the farm."

"You have good answers," Auntie Adjowa said, "but Ananse didn't have good answers. He didn't like to think hard, and every question needed careful thought.

"'Are you wise enough to answer these questions?' Ananse's wife asked him. 'They'll take time to answer.'

"Ananse grew impatient. 'I don't want to spend my time answering these questions,' he declared. 'I'm going to hide the gourd high in a tree so that no wisdom is available. People will have to think for themselves.'

"Ananse found the tallest tree on his land. Once more he tied the gourd around his neck and let it hang in front of him as he started to climb the tree. After a few steps, he fell back. This happened many times because he couldn't hold tightly enough to the tree with the gourd hanging in front of him. He became more and more upset.

"One of Ananse's young sons who was watching his father had an idea. 'Try hanging the gourd down your back,' he suggested. 'If you do that, it won't get in your way when you climb.'

"At first Ananse dismissed the suggestion. 'Go away. Don't bother me,' he told his son. 'I'm busy.'

"When Ananse considered his son's idea more carefully, he realized that his son spoke with wisdom. Ananse hung the gourd on his back and was able to climb the tree swiftly. Watching from the ground, his son smiled with satisfaction.

"Once Ananse was high in the tree, he took the gourd off of his back and held it above his head. 'I thought that I had all of the wisdom,' he said to the spirit of the tree. 'I see now that my young son has wisdom that I must have left on the ground.

"'I know now that I cannot answer all of the questions that people ask. I would have time for nothing else. I will change my fate.' Ananse dropped the gourd to the ground, where it broke into hundreds of pieces, scattering wisdom widely.

"Animals who saw this told other animals, who told people. Many animals and people hurried to pick up pieces of wisdom and soon wisdom was shared by many.

"This is my story. If it be sweet or not, take some elsewhere and let some come back to me, just as wisdom does. You see, my children," Auntie Adjowa concluded, "we can all be wise. We can learn from each other. Tell me what you do that's wise." Children replied.

"I'm nice to my sisters."

"I take care of my baby brother."

"Every morning I collect water at the stream and sweep the courtyard. I'm getting wise."

"I crack open peanuts, and I'm getting wise, too."

"I help Mama trade in the market."

"I turn the fufu when Mama's pounding it. That's hard!"

"I look for pythons when I go to the river."

"I help my mama and papa weed their farms."

"You are good children," Auntie Adjowa said. "You're learning our history and how to be wise. Thank you for spending the morning with me! It's time for you to go home now. Find your family. We will see each other in town."

"*Medaase*, Auntie Adjowa," many replied as they stood to leave.

— CHAPTER 14 —

Spear Throwing

WHILE MOST PEOPLE DANCED THE *ADOWA*, ASARE AND BAAKO RETURNED TO THEIR VIL-
lage to prepare for a spear throwing lesson. Kwame and Kwaku met them on the path
next to the bamboo grove. They greeted each other. Each boy carried a machete. Asare's
machete was in a holster strapped to his waist.

"We'll go to a clearing in the raffia palms," Asare said. "Baako and I have already put
water, bananas, and spears there. The old trees with fat trunks are good targets. Are you
ready to learn how to throw a spear?"

"Yes, yes, yes," the boys answered eagerly.

Once in the clearing, Asare explained, "I'll get you started and watch you practice for
awhile. Then I'll return to my village. We're smoking crocodile meat. You can stay here
to practice.

"We brought old spears," Asare continued, picking one up. "Look at this one. It's as
tall as I am. Stand back and watch me balance it on one finger." The boys moved to give
Asare room. "When my spear is balanced, I can control it.

"Look, I've carved a notch in the shaft at my balance point," Asare said as he showed
the boys. "My hand knows where the notch is." Asare closed his hand around the shaft with
his pointer finger in the notch and lifted the spear to his ear. This is your starting point.

"Look at the spear tip," Asare continued, holding the spear out once more for the boys
to see. "It's strong and heavy. Our blacksmith makes them. The long base of the tip slips
over the shaft. It's hard to find the right branch for a shaft. You want one that's straight and
strong. You shape one end of it to fit into the base. You need a tight fit. Soon you'll make
your own spear. Check your spear every time you use it to make sure that the fit between
the shaft and the tip is tight." The boys nodded.

"Pick up a spear now. Find one that's about your height or a little longer. See if you
can balance it on your pointer finger. Stand away from each other and be careful with the
tip. It's sharp."

The boys looked through the spears and each picked one up and tried to balance it. "This tip's really heavy," Kwame said. "My finger has to be too close to it. I want a longer spear."

"Somebody short made this spear," Kwaku said. "My finger is almost all of the way to the tip. I want a longer spear, too."

"I found a spear that's long because I'm tall. This one's easy for me to balance." Baako showed the others.

"Keep looking until you find a spear that's the right length for you, and then find your balance point," Asare directed. "Put your hand where you'll hold the spear when you throw it, and then raise it to your ear. Stand apart from each other and face me." The boys followed directions. "Does your spear feel balanced in your hand?"

Asare gives a spear-throwing lesson.

"Mine feels balanced but heavy," Baako said. "Even if I'm strong."

"Same for us," Kwame and Kwaku agreed.

"Hold your spear tight. We'll talk about aiming and throwing. The hardest part is aiming. A hunter has to hit his target or he won't eat. You'll have to practice. That's where you'll put your time. Watch now. I'll demonstrate throwing a spear, but I won't throw yet.

"Imagine that you're hunting and carrying your spear next to the side of your body with your arm straight down." Asare demonstrated.

"You hear something and then see it. You lift your spear to your ear with your right pointer finger in the notch. You stretch out your left arm and point to the target. Keep your left foot pointing almost straight, step back with your right foot, and then lean back. Raise your spear and lean back more, and take your spear back as far as you can.

"Point your spear a little above the animal, shift your weight forward, and throw the spear with all of your strength. When the spear leaves your hand, your right pointer finger will point at your target. Hold still for a short time so you don't scare your target and then stand up straight."

Asare demonstrated in slow motion many times, and the boys copied him.

Asare told them to rest. "You're doing well," he said. "How do you feel?"

"Feel good."

"I pretended that I was throwing my spear at a duiker but it moved."

"I felt strong."

Asare smiled. "I want to see you do all of that on your own. I'll call out a target and you pretend to throw a spear at it. The fat trunk of that tree. The log to our right. The stump next to the log. Quick, behind us, the trunk of that tall tree." The boys pretended to throw at each target, and Asare made suggestions.

"Good practice. Do that again," Asare directed. The boys repeated their actions.

Asare critiqued their throws. "Good practice," he said with a smile. "Do it again and again."

When the boys had followed the routine several times, Asare asked, "Are you tired?"

The boys shook their heads to say, "No."

"That's good to hear," Asare replied. "We'll rest anyway. Drink water and eat bananas. I brought some crocodile meat for Kwame and Kwaku to try. Here you are, boys. Baako, there's some for you, too."

Baako bit into the meat heartily.

"It's good," Kwaku said after taking a small bite.

Kwame chewed a second bite and claimed that the meat tasted like chicken. "I can eat this," he said.

Kwaku disagreed. "It's more like fish," he said.

"It's like chicken and fish," Baako said with a smile. "I eat a lot of it."

"The women cook it in water with onions and tomatoes," Asare explained. "It's one of our favorite meals. It will give you energy."

AFTER A SHORT REST, ASARE INSTRUCTED, "LOOK THROUGH THE SPEARS AGAIN AND find two more that are as long as you are tall. Find your balance point on each one, and I'll carve a groove there. Try to hit the fat trunk of that raffia palm," Asare pointed to a target tree. "The thrower gets close. The rest of us will stay back. I'll throw first."

The boys watched closely as Asare's spear struck the tree trunk hard and stayed where it hit. Each boy threw three times. Spears sailed by the tree on both sides, and some fell short of the target. Two spears hit the target but not hard enough to pierce it. The boys both cheered and groaned.

"You're learning," Asare said to encourage them. "Let's do this once more." The boys repeated the exercise with similar results.

"I know that you're feeling disappointed," Asare said. "Don't give up. Sit down. Tell me what you think and what you've learned so far. Do you have any questions?" The boys shared their thoughts.

"I know how to hold a spear, but my arm's too weak to throw one."

"The spear gets heavier every time I throw it."

"It's hard to make the spear go straight, and animals move anyway."

"If I can't hit a fat tree, how can I hit a skinny animal?"

"I could do better hunting with a machete than with a spear."

"How fast does a spear have to go to kill an animal?"

"How can I get close to an animal in the forest where there are so many trees?"

"You have good questions," Asare said. "I'll answer them as we go. Throwing a spear looks easy but it's hard. You're just starting. With practice, you'll learn. Before you think about hunting, you have to work on aiming."

"I've been doing that already," Baako said. "It's still hard."

"Stand close enough to your target to hit it hard when you throw. You get only one chance. Practice leaning back and throwing with your weight behind the spear. When you work on your aim, look at your target at all times and keep your left arm and hand pointed at it."

"How long will take us to be good at spear throwing?" Kwaku asked.

"Keep practicing. Nana wants you to go hunting with us in the next dry season. Before then, we'll work on throwing a spear at an animal."

"Duikers and grasscutters and snakes and crocodiles?" Kwaku asked.

"Yes, but no crocodiles for a long time," Asare affirmed. "Work today until you can hit the trunk of the fat tree. Try to throw hard enough for your spear to stay in the trunk. Get close to the trunk if you need to. When you're practicing, only one person at a time should throw. The others stay behind him. Do you understand?"

The boys said an enthusiastic, "Yes! Yes! Yes!"

"I'll stay for one more round of throwing," Asare said. "I'll go first."

Asare picked up his spear. His expression changed suddenly as he motioned for the boys to back away from the tree. Everyone heard hissing and followed the sound to see a fat puff adder, hiding in a few leaves, and watching them from under their target tree. The snake raised its head to a striking position.

"There's a real target," Asare observed. "Everyone stay quiet and watch how I do this."

Asare took several steps to the side and toward the puff adder but stayed out of its striking range. The snake didn't move. Asare raised his spear to touch his ear. He stretched out his left arm and pointed to the puff adder with a finger of his left hand. He leaned back and threw his spear to pin the snake to the ground. The boys gasped and watched the snake writhe. No one talked. After several minutes, when the puff adder's body quieted, Asare chopped its head off with his machete.

Smiling to ease the tension, Asare said, "That's better target practice than I planned."

"Your throw was so good," Kwaku complimented Asare. "That snake was dangerous."

Asare dug a hole with his machete to bury the snake's head and tossed its body away from the clearing. "Vultures will eat it," he said. "A snake's head will be poisonous for a long time. Never leave one out."

"Papa, your aim was perfect," Baako said.

"If all of you practice, you'll be able to do that," Asare replied, smiling. "Not all animals move fast. A puff adder moves slowly and is an easy target but you can't get close to it. Let's pretend that our fat tree is a puff adder. It won't move. I'll watch you throw your spears once more, then I'll leave. Keep practicing. You're learning fast. Eat all of the bananas and drink the water. When you're done, bring the spears to the *nnonko* village."

"*Medaase*," the boys said to Asare as they picked up their spears once more.

CHAPTER 15

A Baby's Birth and the Work Week Begins

A MESSENGER WOKE THE QUEEN MOTHER LATE IN THE NIGHT. "QUEEN MOTHER, QUEEN Mother, come quickly," she said. "My sister may deliver at any time. She needs you."

"I'm coming. Wait in the courtyard," the Queen Mother replied, getting up immediately. She dressed, splashed water on her face, and smoothed her hair. "I'm ready," she said, stepping outside. The two walked quickly with moonlight to show the way.

Whenever possible, a woman returned to her mother's home to give birth, as had the young woman in labor. She wanted to be with her own clan, whose women would care for her.

Entering the young woman's hut, the Queen Mother greeted her.

"*Akwaaba*, Queen Mother," the young woman replied. "Thank you for coming." She sat on dried plantain fiber that had been spread for cushioning on the floor. Surrounded by clanswomen and midwives, she leaned against one of them, who held her shoulders while her face twisted in pain.

"I want to be here," the Queen Mother said. "I've known you all of your life."

Turning to the midwives, the Queen Mother asked, "How long has she been like this?"

"For most of the night. This is her first baby, and it's coming slowly," a midwife answered.

"She's always been healthy. Her fevers were mild," the Queen Mother recalled. "We have to be patient."

Family members cared for the young woman tenderly by giving her sips of water, wiping the sweat from her body, and encouraging her. She wanted to lie down, but the older women said, "No, sitting is better." They rubbed her back and her legs to help her relax. The Queen Mother held the young woman's hand.

When the sun had risen, and after the Queen Mother and the others had taken turns eating breakfast, the baby was ready to come. The young woman pushed a final time, and a baby girl was born. The baby gasped for breath and cried. The midwives welcomed her crying, cleaned her, wrapped her in a cloth, and held her tightly.

The Queen Mother, the clanswomen, and the midwives were pleased that the birth was accomplished, and that the mother and baby were well. Family members bathed the mother, gave her a fresh cloth, and let her lie down. She rested and cradled her newborn daughter with great happiness.

"The ancestors have sent a healthy child. We are blessed," the Queen Mother said, and all agreed.

The messenger informed the baby's father of the birth, and he came to welcome his child. He greeted his wife and picked up his daughter.

"She's beautiful," he said. "Today is Monday. Her day name will be Adjowa. I'll pray to *Nyame* and my ancestors to let her stay so that I may give her a second name at her outdooring."

While Nana's family ate breakfast, the messenger came to say that her sister had successfully delivered a baby girl, and that the Queen Mother would return soon.

"Wonderful! She's Adjowa, a Monday girl!" Akua said, jumping up and down with excitement. "I want to see her. Too bad it's not Wednesday, then she would have my name. I'm Akua, a Wednesday girl."

"I'm Yaw, a Thursday boy," Yaw Mensah added.

"You are our third child," Nana added. "I gave you the second name, Mensah, after one of my uncles who was a courageous man and the third son in his family. Your mother and I hope that you'll grow up to be courageous, too."

"Yes, I'm Yaw Mensah, a courageous Thursday boy," Yaw Mensah stated with pride.

"I'm a Saturday boy," Kwame said.

"You are Kwame Okoto. I gave you a second name from my father," Nana reminded everyone. "Okoto means calm and humble. You are following his good example."

"Kwame Okoto, that's a good name," Kwame agreed.

Nana continued, "Akua, I gave you the second name, Anane, that comes from the Queen Mother, who was the fourth born in her family. Akua Anane is a beautiful name."

"Akua Anane. I like my name," Akua responded. Turning to her mother, Akua said, "Mama, you are Madam Ama, a lady born on Saturday." Mama smiled and nodded.

The children looked at Nana. "Papa, what day were you born?" Yaw Mensah asked.

"You children call me 'Papa' and everyone else calls me 'Nana.' No one uses my day name but I have one. I was born on Sunday," Nana explained, "and so I'm Kwasi."

The children laughed. "Oh, it's funny to think that your name is Kwasi, just like our Uncle Kwasi," Akua said. "For you, I like Papa, better." Kwame and Yaw Mensah agreed.

"I like that name, too," Nana replied. "The new baby won't have her full name until she's eight days old. If *Nyame* allows her to stay, she'll have an outdooring."

"We'll give her waist beads with little gold nuggets," Madam Ama said. "Her father will give her gold earrings. We'll all welcome Adjowa to Tanoso."

"Now to our work," Nana said. "This will be a busy week. We'll begin the yam harvest and have a good supply of yams before I leave for Kumasi. We can't eat yams until the Asantehene does, but when I return from the *Odwira*, we'll be ready."

"I love yams. They taste so good in fufu," Akua said with interest.

"Kwame, you, Kwaku, and Baako will work with us today," Nana continued. "This morning we'll meet Elder Kofi, the Okyeame, and the other boys, along with Asare and several *nnonko*, at the marketplace and work between the river and the Tano Road. We have easy access to those fields, and I want to be near the river. There may be a leopard hunting along the banks. I'll bring a gun to scare it. I want leopards to return, but I'll protect my people."

"Take me with you," Yaw Mensah said. "I want to see a leopard again."

"I know you would like to come, Yaw Mensah, but not yet. When you're a little older," Nana said softly. "For now, you'll work with your mother."

"Akua and Yaw Mensah, I'll need your help, today," Madam Ama said. "Anyetata will bring water to wash our cloths. She and one of her daughters will work with us this morning. The Queen Mother may need us when she visits sick people in the afternoon."

Akua was pleased, but Yaw Mensah looked sad. Akua encouraged him. "We can play with the children of the sick people after we wash our cloths," she said. "That'll be fun."

Yaw Mensah didn't smile. "I want to see a leopard," he repeated.

Early morning was the best time for a dry season harvest because the air was crisp, while dew dripped from the leaves of tall trees left standing on the farms, cooling those who worked below.

Asare, Baako, and other *nnonko* arrived first at the marketplace carrying machetes, hoes, grinding stones, and large baskets. Some baskets were empty and others contained food for the afternoon meal. The market was closed yet filled with forest sounds and the music of the nearby Tano River. Grinding noises soon overwhelmed the natural forest sounds as the *nnonko* sharpened their tools.

The *nnonko* resembled brothers, of medium to tall height, thin, and muscular. Their hair was cut short, and their faces were clean shaven, revealing the long scars on their cheeks. As Gurunsi people of the savannah, they were farmers and fishermen before they were captured and brought to the forest as prisoners. Akans welcomed their knowledge and skill in farming. The *nnonko* looked healthy but poor since they wore old cloths tied around their waists and walked barefoot.

Asare was tall and stood out as well groomed and better dressed, wearing sandals. His facial scars, too, were prominent. Baako resembled his father but bore only a single, short scar on his left cheek.

When the *nnonko* had accomplished their task, Asare spoke to them, "We'll move from one field to the next along the river. Nana will tell us which crops to harvest. He'll work with the boys first to make sure that they'll harvest yams without damaging them. The boys may work with you later. You'll have to tell them what to do."

Nana and Kwame arrived at the marketplace along with Elder Kofi, the Okyeame, Kwaku, and four more *nnonko*. Nana carried a gun and the others carried large baskets and tools. "*Mema mo akye* – Good morning, everyone. I hope you are well," Nana said to the group in his friendly manner as everyone gathered around him. "We have a long morning ahead, but we'll finish by mid-afternoon and eat in the village near the river crossing." Asare translated for the *nnonko*.

"We'll harvest yams first, and then corn, cassava, bananas, and plantains. Pick up any kola nuts that you find on the ground. We'll follow the Tano Road to the fields and leave the crops that we harvest on the side of the road to pick up when we return. Asare and I will come to each plot to see if you need us. The boys will work together. I'll get them started. Elder Kofi and the Okyeame will work with their *nnonko* in my fields. I'm grateful for their help.

"We know that leopards have returned. This is a welcome surprise and we need to learn more. I'll protect any leopards that are here but I'll also keep my people safe. I've brought a gun today. If you see any signs of leopards, let me know. If there's one nearby, I'll fire my gun to scare it." Asare translated for the *nnonko* who recoiled. He reassured them.

Nana turned to the Okyeame and asked for the small gourd of *akpeteshie* that he carried. "Before we start," Nana said, "I'll say a prayer and pour a libation." He held the gourd above his head. Leaning forward, he poured some of the *akpeteshie* on the ground after saying each phrase of the prayer:

> *Nyame*, almighty God, you, who created heaven and earth,
> with this *akpeteshie* we glorify your name.

Mother Earth, *Asase Yaa*, I return the *akpeteshie* to the earth to honor you. Come and drink. You'll see us care for the earth. Bless us with a plentiful harvest.

Nana then called upon the spirits of the trees and rocks and especially the spirit of the Tano River.

Come spirits, come, and see us work. Bless our work and take care of us.
Give us a generous harvest.

With the libation concluded, the Okyeame responded, "Thank you, Nana, for the prayers well said." The group picked up tools and baskets and walked to the road with the sounds of birds and insects following them. Dry leaves rustled. The air remained cool and still. Nana, Elder Kofi, and the Okyeame gave instructions to their *nnonko,* and Asare translated as the group walked along the great-road toward the fields.

NANA, WITH HIS GUN, AND THE BOYS, CARRYING BASKETS FILLED WITH BANANAS, gourds, machetes, hoes, and a grindstone as head loads and in their hands, turned off of the road, taking a path to the first field next to the river. Here, most of the tall trees had been felled, but stumps and large branches, left to rot and replenish the soil, dotted the area. The plot had been carefully weeded during the rainy season so at least fifty yam plants had grown thick and tall, each from a small mound.

Standing at the edge of the plot, Nana put his gun on a rock and said, "Let's look this area over. We cleared it four dry seasons ago. It gets enough sun for the vines to grow well, so one or two good-sized yams should be in each mound. After this harvest, I'll let the field lie fallow."

The yam vines curled up bamboo stakes and were covered with leaves that had turned yellow. "The vines are so tall," Kwame observed. "When I weeded here in the rainy season, they were shorter than I am. Now I can't see the top of them, and I can't see the mounds either. The big leaves look like pointy crocodile faces. I see hundreds of yellow crocodiles staring at us. They're scary!"

Baako and Kwaku agreed. They put down their head loads and hid behind tall vines to hiss like crocodiles. "I'm a crocodile. You're the hunter, Kwame!" Kwaku called. "Ssssssssss. Find me. Ssssssssss."

"I'm over here," mimicked Baako, hissing, too, like a crocodile about to attack. "Find me first."

Field of yam vines

Baako and Kwaku ran from vine to vine hiding from Kwame, hissing and then jumping out in the open. "I'll find you," Kwame answered as he looked behind the vines.

"Here I am," yelled Kwaku, leaping from behind a tall vine. "I'll eat you!" Kwaku cried out and chased Kwame.

Baako ran out into the open. "I'm the crocodile king!" he yelled as he jumped over a stump and disappeared again.

Running fast, Kwaku jumped over the same stump and then cried out, "Ahhhhhh! Ahhhhhh!" as he bent down and swatted a tsetse fly on his foot, splattering blood everywhere.

"What's wrong, Kwaku?" Baako asked.

"I'm hurting," Kwaku yelled. "A tsetse fly bit my foot! It was hiding in the stump. It meant to bite you, not me." Kwaku held his foot where the tsetse fly had left a puncture wound. "My foot hurts."

Nana and Baako quickly joined Kwaku. Kwame picked up a gourd and ran to get water from the river. Looking at the bite, Nana shook his head and said, "The tsetse fly had eaten well, Kwaku. It was full of blood. The bite will hurt for awhile, but you should be okay."

"That tsetse fly was as big as a bee," Kwaku proclaimed. "It bit me hard. I hit it hard. It won't bite anyone else."

"We have to be careful here because tsetse flies and ants like the cool holes in the stumps and logs and the shaded areas around the vines," Nana reminded the boys. "Rats like the vines, too."

Kwaku and Baako shuddered.

"I hate all of those things," Baako groaned. "The forest is full of bugs. Crocodiles don't bother us in the fields, but bugs do."

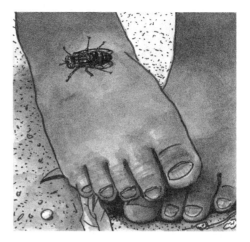

A tsetse fly bites.

Nana smiled. "We have to be careful, but plants and animals give us food. We live with them. Use your machete or your hoe to shake the vines when you get close. That will scare any tsetse flies or snakes or rats hiding there."

Kwame arrived with water to splash over the bite and wash the blood off of Kwaku's leg. "Feels good," Kwaku said. "*Medaase*, Kwame."

"Sorry about the bite," Kwame answered,

"Can you work, Kwaku?" Nana asked.

"Yes, Nana, I'm ready to work," Kwaku replied.

"Let's start," Nana said.

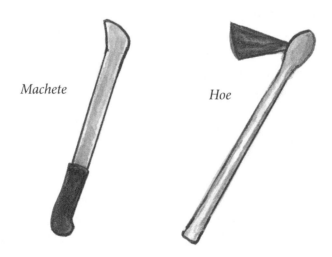

Machete   *Hoe*

Farming tools

— CHAPTER 16 —

Harvesting

Looking at the boys, Nana began, "You've been planting and weeding on farms for a long time. Now you're strong enough to harvest yams. They're important. You have to raise yams to be a real farmer."

"Why, Papa?" Kwame asked.

"Yams were our first crop in the forest, and they're still the most important one. If nothing else will grow, yams will. We can't live without them. Let's work together for a while, and then you'll be on your own."

The boys murmured, "Yes."

"Our machetes are sharp," Nana continued. "Don't cut yourselves or each other or the yams. Machete cuts are a lot worse than tsetse fly bites, and yams won't keep long if you damage them. Are you ready?"

The boys murmured, "Yes," once more.

Nana tucked his cloth in at his waist, picked up his tools, and approached the nearest mound. He extended his machete, and shook the yam vine. "Let's see if we find snakes or tsetse flies or lizards or grasshoppers or a little mongoose," Nana said, smiling. "Stand back until we know."

Nana shook the vine again, top to bottom. "That's good, no animals." The boys advanced to the mound and stood around it as Nana put one foot on it. "First, cut the leaves off of the vine and toss them to the side. Watch me make short chops. With sharp machetes you can do this easily." Nana demonstrated, and leaves fell from half of the vine. He stepped to the other side of the mound and repeated the action.

"Put the leaves in a pile off of the mound," Nana instructed. The boys did the job quickly and stepped back to view a leafless vine curling up a bamboo stake. "Looks like a snake, doesn't it?" Nana said. The boys groaned.

"Chop through the vine and the stake near the ground and toss them on top of the leaves. You'll come back later to chop and spread all of this on the field so it will decay quickly.

"See the stem that's still in the ground," Nana said, "that's the handle to hold while you dig with your hoe. Wiggle it while you're digging around the base of mound. I hope to find one or two yams in each mound. If there are more, they'll be small. Watch me."

Wiggling the stem slightly at first, Nana used his hoe to make a trench in the soil around the mound. He wiggled the stem harder and dug deeper. Soon he was able to pull the stem and the attached yams out of the mound.

"Look at this," Nana said with a smile. "Two beautiful yams. They're almost as long as my arms and twice as thick, and I didn't nick them with my hoe. Kwame, start a pile of yams on the side of the field," Nana directed as he cut the yams off of the stem and gave them to his son. "Now, I want to see each of you give this a try. Baako, you're first."

Baako could reach the top of a vine with his machete. He stepped up to the nearest vine, shook it, and waited to see if any animals ran out. None did, so he quickly chopped all of the leaves off and tossed them aside. "Those crocodile faces are gone now," he said to his friends, who grinned. Baako finished by cutting the vine and the stake.

"Good job," Nana said. "Let's see the yams." Baako grasped the stem, wiggled it while digging, and came up with a single yam. "Only one but it's big and you didn't cut it. Perfect." Both Nana and Baako were pleased. "Add the yam to the pile and start working on another mound, Baako. I'll see how Kwame does now."

NANA AND KWAME STEPPED TO A NEARBY MOUND. KWAKU FOLLOWED. KWAME checked for animals and chopped off leaves with short, quick strokes of his machete. "That's good," Nana said. "Quick chops holding your arm close to your chest are the best."

The vine was tall. Kwame couldn't reach high enough with his machete to chop off the leaves at the top. He held onto the stake and stood on his tip toes, but sank in the soft dirt of the mound. "Papa, I'm too short for this vine," he said.

"You don't need to reach the highest leaves because you can get them after you chop the vine down. Do that now," Nana instructed. Kwame followed Nana's instructions, cutting the vine and stake and digging up a large yam. "Beautiful yam. Add it to the pile. You're ready to work on your own now, but see how Baako's doing first." Kwame agreed and set off.

"Kwaku, how is the bite?" Nana asked.

"It's itching."

Looking at the bite, Nana said, "It's not bad, but it will itch for awhile. Keep it wet and rub it a little. That might help. Watch for more tsetse flies. They're worse than mosquitoes. Are you ready?"

"I'm ready," Kwaku said as he approached a mound.

Kwaku checked for animals and worked carefully, chopping off all of the vine's leaves except those at the top. "The vine looks like a skinny dancer now with lots of hair," he observed. "I'll pull up his feet and let him dance." Kwaku cut the vine and the stake, and tugged on the stem while digging with his hoe. He found two medium sized yams, each as long as a man's foot. "Look at these feet," he cried out. "They're big for such a skinny guy!"

Nana smiled and laughed. "Kwaku, you've done well," he said. "I'm happy with this crew."

Kwaku smiled, too. He wanted to please Nana. "I'm ready to go on by myself," he said quietly. "But first I want to show Kwame and Baako the big feet."

Nana circulated among the boys to watch them work, make suggestions, praise them, and harvest yams from a few more mounds. He was skilled and worked fast, giving the boys a model to follow. Nana was an expert farmer, although he didn't often do routine work. He took pride in his carefully tended and highly productive farms, knowing that successful farming was essential to his people's survival.

As the sun rose higher and the air grew warmer, Nana called the boys together. "You're working well. It's time to rest and sharpen our machetes." The four gathered at the riverside, scanning the banks for crocodiles and snakes before wading into the shallow water and splashing each other.

"Feels good, feels good," Kwame cheered. "I'm definitely not going to be a farmer when I grow up! This work is too hard."

"What will you do?" Nana asked with curiosity.

"I'll be a trader and travel to different places. I'll buy all of my food."

Nana smiled and replied, "You'll need good farmers to supply your food. Maybe Kwaku and Baako will help you." Kwame smiled, too.

Kwame brought the grinding stone to the river bank and filled a gourd with water. Nana carefully ground the machete blades against the stone while Kwame poured water on the blades to keep them cool. Once finished, Nana dried the blades with leaves and tested them on nearby vines.

"They're sharp again," he said, turning toward the boys. "Drink water and eat bananas. When you've finished harvesting yams, stack them along the road. Then come back to the field. Chop the leaves, vines, and stakes and scatter them around the field. There's a lot to do.

"We'll eat near the village by the river in the mid-afternoon. When you finish here, look for Asare. He'll give you another job. Work well." Nana set off with a hurried walk, picking up his gun as he left the field.

The boys continued harvesting, working further and further apart without talking. The chattering of birds kept them company. By midmorning, they had dug up all of the yams and stacked them along the Tano Road. They finished the rest of the work quickly and left their tools next to the road as well.

"We're finished! We did it!" Kwaku shouted with his arms raised up in the air as they returned to the field.

"Did it! Did it!" Kwame and Baako echoed.

Tired but happy, the three stood in the middle of the field, put their heads together, their arms on each other's shoulders, and danced in a circle, chanting, "Did it! Did it! Did it!"

"There's time to go into the river before we look for another job," Kwaku exclaimed. "We're ahead of time. Race you to the river."

KWAME, KWAKU, AND BAAKO RAN TO THE RIVER, CHECKED QUICKLY FOR CROCODILES, threw their cloths on the bank, and jumped in. They immersed themselves in the warm water, rinsing off sweat, and splashed each other to celebrate a job well done. Staying close to the bank, the boys floated with the current, sometimes rolling over in the water and touching the river's bottom, pretending to be fish, while watching for rocks. They waded back upstream to get out and eat bananas, certain that Nana would be pleased with their work.

"Have you ever crossed the river?" Baako asked the others. "I've never tried. I don't like to go far from the bank. I don't know how deep the water is in the middle."

"I like to splash in the river and the stream," Kwame replied. "We can all float, but I can't really swim like the people who live next to the ocean. I want to stay away from rocks, and I don't like deep water either. Anyway, the Tano is the border of Papa's district. We're not supposed to cross it."

"I love the water but I'm careful," Kwaku added. "I've seen men riding logs down the river and the logs twist in the current. The riders have trouble staying on them. That's dangerous work. A log could dump a rider and escape."

"Those men can swim," Kwame said. "You have to swim if you take logs to the ocean. I don't want to be in the river with logs either. I can't move fast enough to get out of the way of a wild log."

"Kwaku, you know about farming," Baako said, changing the subject. "Are you going to be a farmer if you're the chief?"

"I'll have farms if I'm the chief," Kwaku replied, "just like Nana does. My *nnonko* will do the hardest work and also mine for gold. Even when our family helps, we can't do everything."

"Baako, do the *nnonko* like working here?" Kwame asked. "They're good farmers."

"Our lives aren't bad, but we have to do the hardest work like farming, chopping trees down, and working in the pit mines," Baako commented carefully. "I don't have to work in the mines often. I hate to do it.

"We have enough to eat and we're safe and Nana is kind to us, but the *nnonko* are always strangers in the forest. Most don't speak Twi. They can't do anything except work. They might want to escape, but they don't know how to find the savannah, and they can't ask anyone. If they escaped, they would probably be captured again and might get a bad owner.

"The *nnonko* who have families here don't want to leave. They know that their children will probably be free. That's what my papa says. I hope that Nana will adopt me and my brothers and sisters. Do you think he will?"

"I think he'll adopt you," Kwame said. "You work hard and he likes you. I don't know about your brothers and sisters. Asare is Papa's foreman, and that's important. He wants both of you to be happy. If you're free like us, Baako, you'll have a farm, and you'll be able to go places. You won't have to work in the mines anymore. Akans don't do that."

"If Nana adopts me, I'll be Akan like you. I'll stay here with my mama and papa and sisters and brothers. I speak Twi. I know the forest. I don't know the savannah. I don't even know where it is."

Kwaku interrupted, pointing across the river, and whispered, "Look!"

Stalking a crocodile

The boys fell silent, focusing on a frightful sight. A crocodile lay on the opposite bank, its snout touching the water. Its face looked far more menacing than yam leaves. "Let's run," Baako said. "Crocodiles swim fast."

"Wait! Look behind the crocodile," Kwaku cautioned, still pointing. "There's a leopard on the rock. It's going to attack the crocodile."

"You're right," Kwame said. "Should we stay or run?"

"Let's watch and then run," Baako said.

The leopard approached the crocodile slowly from behind, seeming to tiptoe, and suddenly pounced on it. Grasping the back of the crocodile's neck in its powerful jaws, the leopard lifted it into the air and bit hard. The crocodile fell limp. The leopard released it, letting it fall to the ground, and quickly dragged it away from the river by its tail.

Without a word the boys stood up, grabbed their cloths, and ran. They stopped only when they reached the Tano Road, where they picked up their supplies. From there, they walked fast toward the next field, stunned by the hunting scene that they had witnessed. They looked at each other in disbelief.

"We saw a leopard kill a crocodile!" Kwame exclaimed. "Can you believe it?"

"Yes!" Kwaku and Baako replied together.

"I didn't know that leopards could do that," Kwaku said.

"I didn't either," Baako added. "My papa told me that leopards can swim so they have to fight crocodiles."

"Do you think the leopard will swim across the river?" Kwaku asked.

"It has a lot of food now, and Papa says leopards don't like to be near people," Kwame answered. "I hope he's right and that it won't cross the river. We have to tell him what we saw. Tsetse flies and mosquitoes bite us, but crocodiles and leopards can eat us."

— CHAPTER 17 —

Farm Work and Town Work

THE BOYS STOPPED AT SEVERAL FIELDS BEFORE FINDING ASARE, WHO WAS WORKING WITH other *nnonko* in a plot of corn and cassava. When they told him what had happened, Asare was alarmed. "I have to warn Nana," he said. "He and the elders are on the river path looking for signs of a leopard. I'll find them. You boys stay here and work. The *nnonko* will show you what to do. Baako, you translate."

Asare spoke briefly to the *nnonko* and left. Despite the heat, he ran. The news was important, even shocking. Nana didn't want the leopard to be killed, Asare knew, but he didn't want the leopard to threaten people either.

While the boys were talking to Asare, the *nnonko* drank water and wiped sweat from their bodies. They poured water over their heads to cool themselves. After Asare left, Baako told the *nnonko* what had happened. They were intrigued and remarked that they wanted to see such a sight, too. They knew crocodiles and lions from the savannah, but they had never seen a leopard.

"What do you want us to do?" Baako asked.

"Start by harvesting corn, and then cut down the stalks and pile them at the end of the rows. We'll chop them up later. We'll give you five rows." Baako translated for Kwaku and Kwame.

The field included many rows of tall corn stalks and leggy, big leaved cassava bushes. The long rows curved around numerous tree stumps. Fresh ears of corn had been harvested months ago, but some ears were left on the corn stalks to dry. Akans scraped the dried kernels off to sell to traders, who sold them again to coastal people to grind into flour for the sour dumplings called kenkey.

"Let's begin," Baako said.

Before picking up his machete, Kwame turned to walk to the river. "I'm thirsty and I want to pour water over my head to feel cooler," he explained. "While I'm at the river, I'll check for crocs and look for the leopard." Kwaku and Baako followed him.

Once back, the boys started working on the corn, chopping the dried ears off of the stalks and piling them in baskets. This was easier work than harvesting yams, and they made quick progress.

Baako had an idea. "My friends," he said, "I'll stand away from the rows of corn. Chop off the ears and throw them to me. I'll catch them and put them in baskets. We'll work faster that way."

Dust flew. Kwame and Kwaku chopped faster and faster and tossed the ears to Baako, who caught them first with his right hand and then his left, back and forth, and dropped them into a basket. The dry season dust that had gathered on the corn stalks filled the air and soon covered the boys' heads and shoulders, making them cough. They didn't stop. This was too much fun.

"One, two, catch this!" Kwaku shouted.

"Got it," Baako yelled.

"Three, four, here's more!" Kwame howled.

"Five, six, these aren't sticks," Kwaku called out.

"Got them, too," Baako yelled again.

"Seven, eight, nine, these are fine," Kwame shouted as he launched three.

"More, more, more," Baako shouted.

"Nine, ten, let's begin again!" Kwaku cried out.

When one basket was full, Baako ran with it to the end of a row, and hurried back with an empty basket, daring Kwame and Kwaku to work faster. "Hurry, but don't cut yourself," he warned. When they had filled many baskets and finished harvesting five rows of corn, they sank to the ground to rest.

Baako laughed. "With all of this dust on us, we look like spirits!" he said to his friends.

The three ran to the river, checked again for crocodiles and the leopard, and washed off the dust. "Let's dunk our heads in the river," Kwaku said. "I can barely breathe. We found a new way to work. What do the *nnonko* think, Baako?"

"I'll ask them. Let's go back now or they'll be mad," Baako answered.

Returning to the field, Baako spoke to the *nnonko* and reported to Kwaku and Kwame. "They were surprised by the way we worked and that we were having fun. They said that they couldn't do that because Asare wouldn't like it. They aren't sure if we're serious. We have to show them that we are.

"They want us to chop leaves off of cassava bushes now and leave the stalks. Asare wants the *nnonko* to dig up only a few cassavas since they don't stay good for long. The stalks look like elephant tusks with no elephants."

"We're surrounded by big animals today," Kwame commented. "I hope these elephants will stay in the ground."

"They won't chase us," Baako said.

"The cassava in the ground is a buried treasure, something like gold," Kwaku observed. "This will be easy."

Carrying water pots as head loads, Baako's mother, Anyetata, and his sister, Atoyene, who was Akua's age, arrived at the palace early to help Madam Ama and Akua wash cloths in the family courtyard. The women greeted each other warmly. Anyetata poured the water into two cauldrons. The women and girls worked intently.

"Yaw Mensah, bring your cloths here and help us," Madam Ama instructed.

"Yes, Mama. I like to get wet."

The women washed and rinsed the cloths, and the girls hung them to dry on vines strung between the trees and the fence. Dancing around the cauldrons and dipping his hands in them at times, Yaw Mensah washed himself as clean as the cloths. "This is my bath for today," he laughed.

As they worked, Akua taught Twi words to Atoyene. Akua pointed to one of the huts. "*Fie*," she said, and Atoyene repeated the word. Akua pointed to the water and said, "*Nsuo*." She pointed to the tree and said, "*Dua*," and to a water pot and said, "*Ahena*."

When Atoyene repeated, "*Fie, nsuo, dua, ahena*," with a perfect accent, Akua clapped her hands and cheered. The girls communicated well.

The Queen Mother joined the group in the late morning.

"*Maakye*," each greeted her. Akua was pleased that Atoyene knew the greeting.

"*Yaa*," the Queen Mother replied, smiling.

"How do you feel?" Madam Ama asked. "Were you up all night?"

"I slept a little last night and more this morning. I feel well," the Queen Mother replied. "The birth was smooth, and a beautiful baby girl has joined us. We thank our ancestors. We'll see her at her outdooring. I'll leave soon to visit sick people."

"We'll go with you. We're almost ready," Madam Ama said. "I'm boiling eggs and plantains to take with us."

"Good," the Queen Mother replied. "Most people will be working on their farms today, but a few will be home if someone is sick. We'll take the food and water to give out. I'll gather my supplies while you have lunch and then we'll leave."

WHEN ASARE CAUGHT UP WITH NANA, ELDER KOFI, AND THE OKYEAME, HE WAS OUT of breath and struggled to tell them about the crocodile and leopard. Nana stiffened with surprise when he heard the account and spoke slowly as he thought about it. "I believe we have two leopards here. The female is staying with her cubs on our side of the river while the male is across the river. I want to protect them all."

"The harvest is coming well," Asare added. "We'll be almost finished for the day before we eat."

"*Medaase,* Asare. Return to the harvest now, but walk. Send two *nnonko* ahead to prepare our meal." Asare agreed and left.

Nana turned to his companions, "My neighbor's people may be hunting for a leopard with guns. Some may cross the river at night to look for it on our side. We need to persuade him to stop them. They should never cross the river to hunt in my district. Akans know to respect district boundaries. Maybe his *nnonko* are doing this."

"The chief is young and new on the stool. He may want a leopard skin for his court or to sell," Elder Kofi said. "The skin would bring a high price in Kumasi. Can you match the price?"

"I want to meet with him privately," Nana explained. "I'll ask him directly if anyone has seen a leopard in his district. If anyone has, I'll offer him gold to protect it. I'll match the price of a leopard skin in Kumasi."

"I like the idea if he'll meet with us today," the Okyeame said. "You're humble and he may accept. If he wants to wait, I'll be suspicious. His elders may be too strong for him."

The three continued to the village, where the headman greeted them. The Okyeame reported on the progress of the harvest.

"Another matter," the Okyeame said. "You know that two days ago Nana's younger son saw two leopard cubs on the path between Tanoso and the stream. Today the boys with us saw a leopard kill a crocodile on the other side of the river." His audience reacted with surprise and caution.

"I've never heard of such an attack," the headman said. "The leopard is powerful. It's confirmed now that there's a leopard with cubs nearby and maybe a second one across the river. We'll be safer from crocodiles and pythons, but we'll need to shelter our animals at night."

The Okyeame continued, "You told us at the council meeting that hunters were crossing the river at night near your village. Nana, Elder Kofi, and I want to speak to the chief across the river. He's new and we should meet him."

The headman was encouraged. "I welcome your help. I don't want hunters crossing the river. I don't know what they'll do on our side. I'll send messengers to tell the chief that you want to see him. He lives nearby. He has to receive you and send people to escort you."

"*Medaase*," the Okyeame replied.

"I invite Nana, his elders, and the boys to eat with me and my elders. We have much to talk about," the headman said.

Nana responded directly. "We accept and thank you."

In the early afternoon Anyetata and Atoyene left the palace. "*Meh ko fie*– I'll go home," Atoyene told Akua proudly.

Akua clapped, smiled, and waved goodbye.

"*Medaase*," Atoyene replied.

The Queen Mother, Madam Ama, Akua, and Yaw Mensah left the palace and descended the hill toward the marketplace. Stopping at each home, they called out, "*Agoo* – May we come in?" and waited for a reply. Most people were working on their farms, but in some homes they found a sick or injured person who needed comfort.

When they heard the welcoming reply, "*Amee*," and saw someone approaching, the Queen Mother and Madam Ama entered to inquire about the family's health.

Akua and Yaw Mensah joined other children in the main road. Akua found girls playing *Ampe*. Yaw Mensah followed children running down the hill and walking up, sometimes chasing each other. They seemed to float in the air, often with their arms extended for balance. Down with cries of happiness, up with groans.

Along the road elderly men sat on stools in small groups and talked while smoking pipes and encouraging the children. Some men played *Oware*. Sheep and chickens crossed the road looking for plants, insects, and seeds to eat before continuing to the river. Running children circled the bleating and squawking animals and hurried them along.

In the first home the Queen Mother and Madam Ama were greeted warmly, "*Maaha* – Good afternoon, Queen Mother. *Maaha*, Madam Ama. You see my grandson who fell and injured his eye."

The Queen Mother found a boy with a swollen eye, whom she greeted and asked, "What happened to you?"

"*Maaha*, Queen Mother. I was running and fell down. My eye landed on a rock. That hurt." The Queen Mother untied the cloth around the boy's head and looked at his eye. The boy whimpered.

"You hit your head hard," she said. "There's a big bump. I'll wash your eye and make a poultice with wet leaves to tie over it. That should make the swelling go down. Are you a good runner? Were you running fast? "

"Yes. I'm very fast."

"Your eye will heal soon. Don't run until the swelling goes away. I'm leaving you some boiled eggs. Eat them so you'll get better." The patient agreed, and his grandmother approved.

In a second home the Queen Mother and Madam Ama found a man with a high fever. To cool his forehead the Queen Mother again made a poultice of wet leaves. "Keep his forehead damp and cool," the Queen Mother told the man's wife. "The poultice will hold water for a long time. I'll leave you some leaves to use later. If the fever doesn't break, call the herbalist tonight. Do you have more water?"

"We're almost out, but my sister will go to the stream with her children to collect more. When she returns, I'll go to my farm to harvest cassava and plantains for dinner. One of us will be here to watch my husband all day."

"I'll call my children to help collect water," Madam Ama said. Arriving a short time later, Akua and Yaw Mensah greeted Madam Afua, who would lead the group to the stream. Speaking to Akua, Yaw Mensah, and her own children, Kwabena and Yaa, Madam Afua said, "We'll walk fast and rest at the stream. Let's go!"

— CHAPTER 18 —

Negotiating

THE AFTERNOON GREW INTENSELY HOT. AFTER THEIR MEAL, NANA AND THE ELDERS sought refuge in the shade of a tree in the headman's courtyard. *Nnonko* stretched out on the river bank and chewed kola nuts. Nearby, Kwaku, Baako, and Kwame dangled their feet in the water.

"We saw a leopard kill a crocodile today. I almost can't believe it," Kwame said. "I remember the crocodile that Elder Kofi and Asare killed. Do you remember it, Baako? It was huge. The leopard we saw today is smaller but it's strong."

"I don't want to be close to crocodiles or leopards," Baako answered. "I want them to stay on the other side of the river. We'll have to learn to shoot guns to be safe from leopards."

"Papa doesn't want us to shoot leopards, just scare them. When we're farming now we'll have to watch out for them. If I'm a trader, I won't be near leopards."

"Kwame, if you have a big trading business, you won't be near leopards but you'll be gone a lot," Kwaku said.

"I might have a big business. *Nnonko* would work on my farm here and carry my crops and merchandise to sell in the forest markets. I'd go to Kumasi sometimes. I'd travel in the dry season when the roads are good. Baako and Kwaku, you could come with me. Don't you want to see new places?"

"Yes!" Kwaku and Baako answered together.

"Where do you want to go?"

"I want to go to the savannah," Baako answered. "Papa told me that the grass is tall and makes waves in the wind. You can see for a long way because there aren't many trees. If we find Gurunsi people, I'll talk to them and translate for you."

"That would help me in the savannah, but what about the coast?" Kwame wondered. "We could go out in the ocean in a canoe. Maybe go fishing."

"I want to get wet in salt water," Kwaku said. "I don't know if salt water is warm or cold. What language do the people there speak? Can we talk to them?"

"Papa said coastal people near us speak Fante and that's like Twi.," Kwame replied. "We could understand them. Other coastal people speak Ga and Ewe. We'd need a translator to talk to them."

"We'd have to be careful," Baako cautioned, "because the Asantehene sends prisoners to the coast to sell to the whites. My papa told me. He said a lot of prisoners are Gurunsi, like me. No one knows what happens to them when the whites take them away. I don't want anyone to sell me."

"You have an Akan scar and you speak Twi," Kwaku reassured Baako. "You would be safe with us."

"Kwaku, you're Akan and you speak Twi, but you don't have a scar. Why not?" Baako asked.

"I'm in a royal family and chiefs can't have any scars on their body. The Fante know that. Nana doesn't have a scar either."

"Do the whites know?" Baako asked again.

"Maybe not, but we'll be safe in Kumasi. I want to see the prisoners' market there," Kwaku said. "I want to see what the prisoners are like and find out what happens to them."

"I want to see them, too. If they're Gurunsi, I can talk to them," Baako said. "Kwame, do you think Nana or any of the elders will buy prisoners when we go to Kumasi?"

Kwame was uncertain. "Papa said that he's never bought any *nnonko*, but I'll ask him to be sure. I hope he doesn't."

"Baako, if I'm the chief someday," Kwaku said, "I'll want you to be my *okyeame*. You speak well, and you could translate for me when I need to talk to *nnonko*."

"Maybe. I'm already translating," Baako replied with caution.

SEEING NANA, THE BOYS STOOD UP TO GREET HIM. "*MAAHA*, NANA."

Nana returned their greeting and said, "The *nnonko* told Asare that you worked hard. I'm pleased to know."

"Papa, we figured out how to harvest corn faster."

"What did you do?" The boys explained and Nana chuckled. "It's good to find a way to make your work go fast as long as you can do everything. You worked faster?"

"Oh, yes," Kwaku answered. "Much faster!"

"Did you get tired?"

"Not so tired," Kwame answered. "When we tossed the ears of corn we didn't have to bend down. That was easier and faster but we got dusty. We poured water over our heads to stay cool and wash off the dust."

"The rest of us might try your idea," Nana said. "I'll tell the *nnonko* that they can do that if they want to. They'll keep harvesting today until the sun is half way down in the sky. I have another job for you now. It concerns leopards." The boys were alert.

"I think that hunters from across the river are looking for a leopard and might shoot it. The headman here says that his people hear guns firing at night. Some hunters have been crossing the river but without guns. They have to be looking for something special. Both sides of the river are Akan territory but different districts. When hunters cross the river, they're coming to my district, and I want to stop this."

"What will you do, Papa?"

"The Okyeame, Elder Kofi, and I plan to meet with the other chief later this afternoon. I'll tell him what we know about leopards and ask his help to protect them. I'll ask him to stop his people from coming to my district. Do you want to come with us?"

"Yes, Nana."

"Yes, Nana."

"Yes, Papa."

"Good. You'll see how we handle this. Wash in the river but check for snakes first. I'll find you in the village."

Python on a bank of the Tano River

THE CHIEF ACROSS THE RIVER SENT AN ELDER AND TWO OARSMEN TO ACCOMPANY Nana and his party. The crossing was swift and smooth. Elder Kofi pointed to a python on the river bank, waiting to strike a passing animal. Nana readied his gun, but the snake stayed its distance.

Nana and his group followed their escorts to a town where they were welcomed by the chief, his *okyeame*, and two more elders in the palace courtyard. Nana placed his gun on the ground, just inside the courtyard. Those carrying machetes placed them nearby. Standing face to face, the two chiefs bowed to each other slightly, the cordial and respectful greeting of chiefs of equal rank.

"*Akwaaba* – Welcome. I am Nana Somfo of the *Agona* clan," the host said.

"*Medaase*. I am Nana Anyensu of the Tanoso district. *Oyoko* is my clan. I regret that we haven't met before. Thank you for agreeing to meet with me with no notice."

"I'm new on the stool. I've been chief only since the rainy season."

"My wife belongs to the *Agona* clan," Nana said with a smile. "Its symbol is the parrot, the wisest and noisiest bird in the forest. *Agonas* are always talkative and smart!"

The younger chief smiled also. "The falcon, the most feared bird in the forest, is the symbol of the *Oyokos*. A parrot knows to be careful when talking to a falcon."

Nana bowed his head again slightly. "I want to talk about hunters from your district who may be crossing the river to hunt in my district, and about leopards who may be returning to this area. I seek a conversation with my *okyeame* present and I would like to include these boys. They would say nothing but would learn how we handle the matter. They may live to see leopards roaming our forest again."

"My *okyeame* and I will be pleased to talk to you and your *okyeame,* but this is a private matter. Let the boys stay in the courtyard with the elders. We will give them refreshments."

Nana was disappointed but agreed. The negotiating group of four walked to the council room and sat on stools. In this private setting, the chiefs spoke to each other directly. The other elders, the boys, and the oarsmen remained in the courtyard.

"Thank you again for meeting with us today," Nana began. "The headman of the village near the river on my side told me that his people hear gunfire at night on your side, and then hunters cross the river to continue their hunt in my district but without guns. Do you know about this?"

With a careful choice of words and a restrained tone, the second chief replied. "Hunters in my district use the light of a full moon to go out at night. They hunt along the river where we've chopped back the brush. They're looking for duikers, grasscutters, and porcupines. They sometimes see crocodiles and have killed one.

"The hunters are both free men and *nnonko*. They use guns, spears, and bows and arrows. If they've crossed the river, they've acted without my permission. I'll tell them never to do that. I hope that they did no harm on your side."

"They did no harm," Nana replied, "but they worried my people, who didn't know what was intended. I will expect the hunters to follow your orders. I appreciate your help.

"Another matter," Nana continued. "Have you or any of your hunters seen a leopard?"

"I'm intrigued with the question," Nana Somfo replied. "One of my *nnonko* reported seeing a leopard on the river bank recently. I didn't know whether to believe him. Has anyone seen a leopard on your side?"

"A few days ago my younger son saw two cubs on a path near Tanoso."

"The female must have been nearby. Perhaps the male, too."

"Today my older son and the other two boys saw a leopard on your side. They watched it kill a crocodile."

Nana Somfo and his *okyeame* gasped. "That's remarkable," the chief said. "I didn't know that could happen. The spirit of the Tano River must be very strong. The leopard felt it. Are we in danger?"

"Everyone should shelter sheep and chickens at night. Leopards won't bother people unless we threaten them. I want to protect any leopards that return to our area," Nana Anyensu emphasized. "The forest is out of balance. There are too many crocodiles and pythons that threaten our people. There are too many duikers and monkeys that eat our crops."

"Leopards won't survive here," Nana Somfo predicted. "The price of a leopard skin in Kumasi is very high. Someone will kill any leopard that returns and sell the skin."

"Not if the chiefs and elders decide otherwise. We can place a severe punishment on anyone who traps or shoots a leopard. We can forbid leopard skins from being sold in our markets. No hunter can kill a leopard in secret. For your help I offer you the price of a leopard skin in Kumasi."

"It will take many years, maybe even a lifetime, for leopards to return."

"That's why I wanted the boys to hear our deliberations. They will be leaders one day. It will be a difficult task, but we can do this. We can have leopards once more."

"You bring me a serious question," Nana Somfo replied. "I'll talk to my elders, then I'll send a messenger to tell you of our decision. Will you go to Kumasi for the *Odwira* celebration?"

"Yes. Are you going?"

"Yes. This will be my first trip to Kumasi. I want very much to see the city and the Asantehene. I hope that we will see each other there."

"I hope so, too. Thank you for receiving me and listening to my ideas. Please send me your reply soon. I want to know your decision before traveling to Kumasi. A falcon and a parrot must work together," Nana concluded.

"I agree, and I will try," Nana Somfo replied. "I'm glad you came. The oarsmen will take your group back."

"*Medaase.*"

Once returned to his district, Nana told Elder Kofi and the boys about his discussion with Nana Somfo and added that he was encouraged.

"Nana, I want to tell you something," Baako said.

"What is it?"

"In the courtyard the oarsmen were talking in Nankane. They didn't know I understood them. They said that they had seen a leopard on their side of the river a few times and always at night. It ran when hunters fired their guns. Hunters crossed the river to look for it but didn't find it. I don't know if they've told their chief."

"This is serious, Baako. Thank you for telling me."

Turning to his group, Nana said, "I want all of you to come with me tomorrow night to sit by the river and learn what the hunters are doing on the other side. I'll tell the headman. We'll eat in his village and spend the night there."

The elders and boys agreed. "We need to save the leopards," Kwaku said. "If I'm the chief someday, I'll protect them."

"We will, too," Kwame and Baako confirmed.

"The leopards need us," the Okyeame agreed.

"Our harvest is going well," Nana said to the Okyeame and Elder Kofi. "Your help means that we'll all have yams to eat after we celebrate our own *Odwira*. Asare, bring the *nnonko* back here tomorrow to keep harvesting along the river. Dig up all of the yams. Watch for a leopard.

"We'll walk to the road now and carry home what we've harvested."

— CHAPTER 19 —

Yaw Mensah Is Missing

CARRYING A MACHETE AND A HEAD LOAD OF BANANAS, MADAM AFUA SET OFF ON THE path to the stream at a brisk pace with Akua, Yaw Mensah, Kwabena, and Yaa following her. "Is this too fast?" she asked. There were several responses.

"No, we're strong."

"We can do this."

"We know the path."

"We just passed the log fence," one child observed.

Colobus monkey

"Let's play a game," Madam Afua proposed. "I'll tell you what I see or hear, and you tell me if you see or hear the same thing and where. I hear monkeys."

"I hear chattering, but I don't see any monkeys."

"Where are they?"

"There's one on the boulder. It looks sad. Its tail is so long."

"They're high in the trees, too. Watch for leaves that move," Madam Afua suggested. "They show you where monkeys are."

"I see them now."

"So many monkeys!"

"Are they following us?"

"Yes, I think so. I see spiderwebs, but spiders don't make noise," Madam Afua said. The children laughed at the idea of noisy spiders.

"So many webs."

"I see a spider on its web. Maybe it's Ananse."

"I'm glad we don't see tarantulas. I don't want to step on one."

"Do you hear insects?" Madam Afua asked. "Are they buzzing in your ears?"

"I hear them, but I can't see them."

"I know where they are when they bite me!"

"Do you mean mosquitoes?"

"Yes!"

"Do you still hear the monkeys?" Madam Afua asked once more.

"I see leaves moving in the trees."

"Leaves can move and make noise when wind is blowing."

"Look behind the leaves. Do you see any monkeys?" Madam Afua prompted the group.

"Yes, many monkeys hiding there. They're watching us."

"I hear squawking parrots," Madam Afua proclaimed, raising her voice over the loud noise.

Grey parrots

"I see them, too."

"They're over our heads. So many of them."

"They're hard to see."

"They're following us like monkeys do."

"Walk faster," Akua urged Yaw Mensah. "We have to keep up. Madam Afua wants us to hurry."

"I'm walking as fast as I can. I'm hungry. I want to eat," Yaw Mensah answered.

"You can eat at the stream. Madam Afua is bringing bananas. Come on!"

As Madam Afua had warned, the pace was fast, and they reached the stream quickly. Once there, she directed, "Fill your pots with water and then sit down to eat."

Everyone soon sat on or near the path, happy to rest and eat bananas, when a noise disturbed them.

"Oh no, monkeys are coming," Madam Afua warned. "They'll want our bananas. Throw your bananas away from the path. I don't want the monkeys to get near us.

"I'll move the stalk. We'll get more bananas later. If the monkeys come close to us, don't touch them, don't fight them. The adults are strong. Just let them walk by. If we don't hurt them, they won't hurt us."

A troop of Colobus monkeys, including adults, young ones, and babies carried by their mothers, approached from the far side the stream. At first they walked slowly but sped up as they neared the stream.

"Stay calm," Madam Afua told the children. "Come, stand next to me." She wrapped her arms around them. "Don't say anything."

Making whooping noises, the monkeys crossed the stream and walked slowly on both sides of Madam Afua's group. Some monkeys ate the bananas that the children had thrown away. Others investigated the stalk lying nearby. They broke bananas off, stopped to peel and eat them, and then walked on.

"Don't move. Don't talk," Madam Afua whispered to the children. "The monkeys won't hurt us. They'll go away."

A young monkey approached Yaw Mensah, who was hiding a banana under his arm. "Don't take my banana," Yaw Mensah shouted when the monkey grabbed the banana and hurried away.

"Yaw, don't shout. Don't move!" Akua whispered, gripping her brother's shoulder.

Yaw Mensah broke free of Akua's grasp to chase the thief. "Yaw, stop, don't chase the monkey. Come back," Akua shouted.

Yaw did not stop. "I want my banana! Give it back to me!" he demanded of the monkey, now traveling fast with its troop. Yaw ran after them.

Madam Afua was alarmed. "Everyone stay here," she said as she watched Yaw Mensah closely. She called in a stern voice, "Yaw Mensah, stop. Come back. Don't chase the monkeys."

"I want my banana. I want my banana. Give me my banana," Yaw Mensah yelled as he ran. "I don't care if you go into the forest. I'm coming after you."

Yaw Mensah chased the monkeys as they passed the termite mound and left the path to run across the open area. They entered the forest on a narrower path used by hunters and Yaw Mensah followed them.

Madam Afua was distraught. Yaw Mensah should have obeyed her. "My dears," she said to her group. "Pick up your water pots. I'll carry Yaw's. We'll start walking and try to find Yaw Mensah." The children were confused by Yaw Mensah's behavior and followed Madam Afua willingly.

The group stopped where Yaw Mensah had left the path. The grass was bent over and the bushes were broken. Banana peels littered the ground. "The monkeys left the path here," Akua said with certainty. Madam Afua agreed.

"Yaw, Yaw, Yaw," everyone called. There was no reply, but nearby parrots screeched.

"The parrots may be telling us that something unusual is happening," Madam Afua told the group. "Maybe they're watching Yaw."

"Akua and Kwabena, leave your water pots here and run to town. Akua, tell your mother and the Queen Mother what happened and ask them to tell the town crier to let everyone know. We need people to come and look for Yaw Mensah. Kwabena, tell your auntie about Yaw and help her in any way you can. Yaa and I will wait here for a search party."

Akua was truly frightened. She grabbed Kwabena's hand and the two ran as fast as they could along the path that was covered with leaves, dry now but still slippery. The children were careful but raced even as they climbed the hill to town. They were relieved to see the log fence.

"We're here!" Akua said in triumph, although she and Kwabena were breathing hard. "Kwabena, go home and tell your family what happened. I'll ask the old men where Mama and Grannie are." Akua soon found the right home and called, "*Agoo*," at the entrance.

"*Amee*," came the reply and Akua entered. She greeted everyone and in a breathless voice described what Yaw Mensah had done. Madam Ama and the Queen Mother were alarmed. Madam Ama responded immediately.

"I'll tell the men sitting along the road. One of them will let the town crier know and send someone to call Nana. We need a search party. I'll go to my sister's home for help. Akua, tell Madam Afua's family what we're doing and then stay with the Queen Mother at the palace. Nana will look for you there."

Within minutes, Madam Ama and one of her nephews, both carrying machetes, left on the path to the stream.

BY LATE-AFTERNOON BASKETS OF YAMS, CASSAVA, CORN, BANANAS, PLANTAINS, AND kola nuts lined the great-road near Nana's fields. The *nnonko* ferried most of the harvest to the palace, but Asare set aside some baskets for his village. *Nnonko* took them to the marketplace, where they planned to stop and bathe in the river before returning home.

As the group approached the river, two *nnonko* spoke loudly to one another while pointing at the ground. Baako translated for Kwaku and Kwame. "They see leopard tracks. Big ones and little ones. The female and her cubs were here this afternoon."

"The spirit of the Tano River blesses us," Kwame said. "Papa will be happy."

"What will we do if we see leopards now?" Kwaku asked.

"Run," Baako answered quickly.

The clanging of the town crier's bell soon reached the marketplace. Alarm spread through the group with the news about Yaw Mensah. Asare directed all but one of the *nnonko* to take the baskets of crops to their village immediately using the path along the river. "Look for Yaw Mensah on the way, and then from our village, walk toward town on the main path and bring spears. Tell everyone that Yaw's missing. We'll look for him."

Asare sent the remaining *odonko* to tell Nana what had happened and stay with him to help. To the boys, Asare said, "Let's go to town. Bring machetes." The marketplace emptied quickly.

Baako and Kwaku each told Kwame that he was sorry that Yaw was lost and pledged to help find him.

"He's probably looking for leopards," Kwame said. "He's always curious. Maybe he went into the forest at the place where he saw the cubs."

"I hope that we find him before dark," Kwaku said. "He'll be scared and cold if he has to spend the night in the forest."

At the palace Asare and the boys learned from the Queen Mother and Akua more about Yaw Mensah. Men and women returning from their farms heard the news. Four men, including two drummers, organized a search party that Asare and the boys joined. They informed the Queen Mother of their departure. Drums would keep members of the search party in touch as they tried to communicate with Yaw Mensah.

FOLLOWING THE HUNTERS' PATH, YAW MENSAH STUMBLED OVER ROOTS AND SCRAM-bled around low bushes, sometimes tripping over rocks or fallen branches. He picked up a stick to push away spider webs and hold back foliage. He winced when twigs scratched his bare arms, legs, and chest.

"Wait, wait for me!" Yaw Mensah yelled as he ran after the monkeys. When he saw them climb a tall tree, he stopped, looked up, and shouted, "You stole my banana. You stole everyone's bananas. That's not fair."

When Yaw Mensah reached the tree, he started to walk around it, still yelling at the monkeys. The path disappeared under vines. Yaw Mensah climbed over the vines but then fell through them into a dark hole. "Aie," he yelled. "What's happening to me? Where am I?" Yaw Mensah asked himself as he landed on a pile of even more vines.

"This is a pit trap," Yaw Mensah realized, squinting in the low light to see if there were any animals in the pit. He didn't see or hear any. When he tried to stand, he knew that he had hurt his right ankle, so he found a comfortable way to sit.

Yaw Mensah loved the forest and he wasn't afraid, but he had never been in a pit trap. "Someone will have to get me out," he thought. "How can I tell anyone where I am? The monkeys won't do that." Yaw Mensah heard the parrots screeching in nearby trees. "I hope they know I'm an *Agona* and parrots are my symbol. I'll talk to them.

Flock of grey parrots

"Parrots, you're smart. You can help me. I'm an *Agona*. I'll always protect you, and I need your help now. Show someone where I am. Find someone to come look for me. Madam Afua will come. Mama and Akua will come. Papa and Kwame will come. Uncle Kwasi will come. I want to get out of here. A porcupine might fall in, or a snake or something. Fly away now and look for someone."

The pit was quiet except for the buzzing insects. Yaw Mensah relaxed, hoping that the parrots had understood his message. As his eyes grew accustomed to the low light, he saw that the vines were fresh, meaning that hunters were watching the pit. "Maybe they'll come by soon," he said to himself. "They would find me."

Seeing a pile of leaves in a corner, Yaw Mensah scooted in that direction and probed with his stick. Beneath the leaves was something brown and soft. "It's a big snake that's asleep," he thought. "It's all coiled up. Probably a python. Papa says that they sleep when they're full. I don't want to wake it up. I don't want it to eat me. I want out of here."

Yaw Mensah was terrified now. He crawled as far away from the snake as he could and held on to the stick. He yelled, "Help! Help!" and tried to pull himself out of the pit using hanging vines, but he wasn't strong enough. He sat on the pile of vines once more, held the stick in his hand, and stared at the leaves where the snake slept, while yelling for help as often as his strength allowed.

Madam Ama and her nephew soon joined Madam Afua and Yaa on the path and greeted them. "I'm very sorry that Yaw Mensah disobeyed you," Madam Ama apologized. "He knows better. Everyone in town will soon know that he's lost in the forest. More people will come to look for him."

"I'm sorry, too, that he didn't obey," Madam Afua agreed. "He left the path here to chase the monkeys. I hope that he stayed nearby. We've been listening to the parrots screech. They may have found him. Tell the search party to listen, too. Yaa and I will return to town now and make sure that people are on the way to help you. We need a search party with drummers. We won't stop until we find Yaw. We'll take the extra water pots with us."

"*Medaase*," Madam Ama said with genuine gratitude. "We'll wait here. Animals will chatter because we're here and that might help Yaw find us. We will hope."

---- CHAPTER 20 ----

Searching and Taxes

THE SEARCH PARTY FOUND MADAM AMA AND HER NEPHEW ON THE PATH. ARMED WITH spears, machetes, and knives, three men, including Asare, soon stood across the open area and walked slowly forward in the direction that Yaw Mensah had taken. One drummer walked a few paces behind them beating a slow rhythm that was repeated by the drummer who stayed on the path. The drummers kept the two groups in touch.

Mama asked Kwame, Kwaku, Baako, and her nephew to stand along the path on both sides of her in case Yaw Mensah walked out of the forest on his own. "Look for animals running out of the forest. Yaw might frighten some," she told them. The boys understood. Each holding a machete, they stationed themselves along the path with Baako nearest the stream.

Asare explained to the men crossing the open area with him, "There's a hunters' trail ahead. I'll walk along it. Beware of pit traps." The men walked slowly and cautiously, chopping brush with machetes and probing piles of vines with spears. They looked carefully for snakes, spiders, and ants. Larger animals fled. Beyond the open area, the vegetation grew thick and tall trees blocked the sunlight. Progress was slow.

When the men lost sight of each other, they called out, "*Agoo*," and listened for a reply over the forest noise of screeching parrots, cawing crows, and buzzing insects. Suddenly Asare shouted, "Leopards, leopard cubs, leopard cubs!!"

Everyone stopped. "Let's get together," one said. They searched for each other through the foliage.

"I saw two cubs playing in the underbrush," Asare explained. "The parrots were telling us about them. I didn't see their mother, but she's certainly in the area."

"This is good news for us, but not for Yaw Mensah. I wonder if he saw them, maybe chased them," the drummer said. "We need to find him before dark. Let's continue and I'll keep drumming. Yaw Mensah might hear us."

"Listen to the parrots. Maybe they'll help us find Yaw," Asare suggested. "There's a pit trap ahead. I'll check it."

The men spread out once more. Drumming began again, and the second drummer responded.

At the bottom of the trap Yaw Mensah heard only faint sounds but a new sound encouraged him—drumming. "Someone's drumming for me," he thought. "They're drumming for me. Someone's looking for me." Yaw Mensah pulled himself up holding on to the vines and yelled, "I'm here. I'm here." There was no response.

Approaching the pit trap, Asare saw a hole in the vine covering. He walked to the edge and called, "Yaw Mensah, are you down there?"

"Yes, yes, I'm here!" Yaw Mensah yelled. "Asare, I'm here at the bottom of the pit. I want to get out! There's a python in here."

"Are you hurt?"

"I hurt my ankle, so I can't walk, but I'm almost all right," Yaw Mensah said with great relief. "I'm so happy that you're here. Did the parrots tell you where I was?"

"They helped me find you, Yaw. Other men are coming. We'll get you out. What's the python doing?"

"It's sleeping."

"That's good. Stay away from it."

Asare called to the other men and then picked up a long tree branch to lower into the pit. "I'll come down for you on the branch, Yaw. Be patient."

Asare told the others about the snake. "When I'm in the pit, be ready to hand me my spear. We'll get Yaw Mensah out, and then I'll kill the snake. Yaw thinks it's a python and that it's sleeping."

"Pythons sleep for a long time after they've eaten," the drummer commented. "Yaw's lucky. He could have been its dinner. I'll drum with a fast beat now to say that we're returning."

"Stay where you are," Asare told Yaw Mensah. "I'm coming now." At the bottom of the pit, which was slightly deeper than his height, Asare used Yaw's stick to uncover the python and confirmed that it was in a deep sleep.

Turning back to Yaw Mensah, Asare said, "You're right, Yaw. That's a python and it's sleeping. That's good. I'm glad we found you. Were you scared?"

"I'm not scared," Yaw Mensah replied. "I just don't want to be in a pit trap with a python. I want to go home."

"We'll get you out," Asare said as he boosted Yaw Mensah along the branch. "Climb with your hands. I'll hold your legs. Someone at the top will pull you up. I'll stay here and kill the python." Hand over hand, Yaw Mensah climbed up the branch until the men above pulled him out of the pit.

"It's good that we found you, Yaw," one of the men said. "Are you hurt?"

"I hurt my ankle, but I'm all right," Yaw Mensah replied. "I don't like the pit."

"Hunters make traps to catch animals. You got caught."

Asare held his spear in a throwing position as he uncovered the python. The long snake was tightly coiled. Asare stabbed it throughout its body until it became limp.

Asare pulled himself up out of the pit. He left the branch in the pit and the hole on the top exposed so that he and other *nnonko* could find the trap easily and retrieve the python. Putting Yaw Mensah on his shoulders, he said, "Let's hurry. The sun is going down."

WHILE WAITING ON THE PATH, BAAKO GREETED TWO *NNONKO* WHO APPROACHED from the far side of the stream.

"Madam Ama," Baako said. "These *nnonko* worked with Asare this morning and took baskets of crops to the palace and to their village. On the river trail they saw the two leopard cubs! Not long ago! Maybe we'll see them, too. Maybe Yaw's seen them!"

Madam Ama greeted the *nnonko*. "I don't know what to think," she said, feeling increasingly worried. "Let's see what the search party found. They're coming back now. The cubs are little. I wonder where their mother is?"

When the search party returned each group reported its news. Madam Ama hugged Yaw. "You're safe, my son. We want to see you home again. Let me look at your ankle."

"Yes, Mama," Yaw Mensah replied. "I'm glad to be out of the pit. It was dark down there. A python was in the pit with me."

"Yaw, Yaw, you're back. That's good, but why did you chase the monkeys?" Kwame asked.

"They stole our bananas. I want to go home," Yaw Mensah said. He smiled but said no more because he knew that he should not have left the path. He squealed in pain when Madam Ama turned his ankle.

"Yaw Mensah is safe, and the leopards are nearby," Madam Ama said to everyone. "We thank our ancestors who care for us. I thank all of you, and I apologize for Yaw's failure to obey. We will talk to him." The others sympathized but planned to scold Yaw Mensah when they saw him later. Madam Ama understood why. His behavior had endangered them all.

Madam Ama thanked Asare, especially, for Yaw Mensah's rescue and he replied, "It's our duty, Madam Ama. Yaw doesn't understand the forest yet."

"Yes, the ancestors protected him, even from a python," Madam Ama replied.

Talking to the newly arrived *nnonko*, Asare explained, "I killed a python in the pit on the hunters' trail. We'll take it home to eat." The two groups said good-bye and departed.

TALL TREES ALONG THE PATH BLOCKED MUCH OF THE LIGHT AS THE SUN SET, BUT THE path to town was familiar to everyone. One of the men carried Yaw Mensah on his shoulders. The older boys named the animals that they had seen run out of the forest: a honey badger, three duikers, two grasscutters, a mongoose, a porcupine, and six rats.

"The animals might have been running from leopards, not from people," Kwame said. "I wish we had seen the leopards."

"I saw monkeys and a python, and I heard parrots!" Yaw Mensah boasted, smiling now about his adventure.

Nana was waiting at the palace when Madam Ama and the search party returned. He picked Yaw Mensah up and hugged him. "We're glad that you're safe at home again, Yaw, but you must learn that leaving a forest path is dangerous. Never do that again. Do what adults tell you."

"Yes, Papa," Yaw Mensah responded. "I'm sorry."

To the others Nana said, "Thank you for your work to find Yaw Mensah. You saved his life. I regret that he placed your lives at risk."

When Nana heard about the leopards, he was pleased, saying, "Leopards are definitely here."

Weighing gold dust

EARLY THE NEXT MORNING THE TAX COLLECTORS walked through Tanoso jangling the keys on their brass ring and repeating "*Mema mo akye* – Good morning to everyone." This signaled that they were ready to collect taxes at the palace. When they returned, the Okyeame welcomed them and showed them to the council room where Nana waited. They greeted Nana and he replied.

"I hope that you were successful collecting taxes in my villages. How many men have paid?"

"In twelve villages we collected taxes from one hundred fifteen men who are married, can carry a gun, and work a farm," a tax collector replied. "How many will we see today?"

"This morning you should see fifty-five men who live in town. You'll work in the courtyard. Clan heads will verify that all of the men in each clan have come."

"We're ready to work fast and then divide the total with you. We'll leave for Kumasi this afternoon," one of the tax collectors replied.

The tax collectors opened their shoulder bags and took out leather pouches containing a balance scales for weighing gold dust, a gold weight, a brass spoon to handle the gold, a feather to brush the gold from the scales to a pouch, and cowrie shells for record keeping.

"I'll put out my gold weight for the tax," Nana said. "We'll make sure that our weights agree." The tax collectors were not surprised since the village headmen had done the same.

Nana put his *domma* weight, one tenth of an ounce, on one pan of the balance scales. A tax collector placed his on the second pan. The two pans moved up and down briefly and were level when they stopped.

"The weights are equal," Nana observed with satisfaction and the tax collectors agreed, leaving their weight on the scales while Nana removed his. "Men are arriving now. Let's start," Nana said to the Okyeame.

Gold weight, the domma

Elder Kwasi stepped up first, greeted the tax collectors, and untied a leather pouch. Using the tax collectors' brass spoon, he placed a small amount of gold dust on the scales' empty pan. He kept the gold dust away from his face knowing that his breath might scatter it.

Seeing that there was too much gold dust, he removed some by brushing it with the feather back into his pouch. Having verified that the weight of the gold dust equaled a *domma*, the tax collector brushed it into his pouch. No one touched the gold dust because it would stick to skin.

The second tax collector handed Elder Kwasi a cowrie shell to verify his payment and placed a second shell into a box to keep count of the number of men who paid. Elder Kwasi bowed slightly as he stepped aside for the Okyeame and others to pay their taxes.

Elder Kwasi found Madam Ama, Kwame, Akua, and Yaw Mensah in the family courtyard. He planned to accompany his sister, Kwame, and Akua to work on their family's farm. He would be responsible for the children when they were grown and took time to get acquainted with them. To the children he was "Uncle Kwasi."

Uncle Kwasi lifted Yaw Mensah in his arms and spoke to him quietly. "Yaw Mensah, as your senior uncle, I'm worried when you disobey adults. We protect you. You're not safe in the forest alone. You know about the leopards. What about snakes and ants and crocodiles and tsetse flies?"

"I'll obey now," Yaw Mensah replied. "I like animals, just not the scary ones like the python or the monkeys that steal bananas. I'll obey. I'll stay safe."

"We depend on you, Yaw Mensah. Stay here today and help your grandmother."

"I will, Uncle Kwasi," Yaw Mensah replied, "I promise."

CHAPTER 21

Madam Ama's Farm and Leopards

READY TO LEAVE FOR HER FARM, MADAM AMA HUGGED YAW MENSAH SAYING, "HELP your grandmother today. I depend on you. Your ankle will heal soon."

"I'll help Grannie," Yaw Mensah replied. "I want to go to your farm when I can walk, Mama. I like to work there."

Madam Ama picked up a basket containing hoes and machetes. Akua placed a basket holding lunch and extra cloths on her head. Kwame balanced a basket with an empty pot to fill with drinking water, carried a machete in one hand and, in the other, peelings from cassava and plantains wrapped in a banana leaf to place in the town's dumping ground.

Madam Ama's senior brother, Elder Kwasi, accompanied the group carrying a spear and a gun. They descended the hill walking away from the marketplace, passed the log fence, and waited as Kwame hurried to the dump. After a short distance, they left the road on a path toward the river.

"My vegetables have grown well, especially the carrots," Madam Ama told her brother. "I've fed my family and sold much of the crop in the market and earned a good income. I want our family to clear more land for vegetables. Our sisters are interested, too."

"Sister Ama, let's see how close to the river we can farm before asking Nana for more land," Elder Kwasi replied. "There's timber to harvest near the river. When that's gone, more land will be open, and we can farm some of it. Since Nana's gold mines near the river have been rich, I want our *nnonko* to dig a mine near the bank to see what we find."

"We don't have enough *nnonko* to dig and work a new mine," Madam Ama replied.

"I'd like to buy a family in Kumasi," Elder Kwasi explained. "That would be another man to dig the soil and another woman to wash it."

"That's hard work. It would be good to have more help. Do we have enough kola nuts to buy a family?"

"I'm not sure. I don't know the price of prisoners now. We may be able to buy just one man. I'll do that if I can't afford a family."

Madam Ama turned to Akua and Kwame. "Uncle Kwasi told me that an *odonko* will join us today and bring a child. Let's teach the child some Twi words while we work."

"Yes," Akua agreed with enthusiasm. "I can do that."

REACHING THE FARM, THEY GREETED THE *ODONKO* AND HIS CHILD. "OH, HE BROUGHT a girl," Akua said. "She's my age." Neither Madam Ama nor Elder Kwasi spoke Nankane, and the *odonko* didn't speak Twi, but weeding and harvesting were familiar activities that they could do together.

Madam Ama took hoes from her basket. She motioned for the *odonko* child to come to her, saying, "*Bra aha* – Come here." The child's father knew the words and translated for his daughter. The child responded, although she was shy with the new people. Her father smiled and patted his daughter on her head, saying her name, "Asa."

Madam Ama demonstrated to Asa how to hold a tall weed by its stem and use a hoe to dig up the roots. Madam Ama placed Asa's hands on top of her own and the two worked together, repeating the Twi words for hoe – *aso*, and weeds- *nnwira*.

"Weeding's never interesting, but it's important," Uncle Kwasi said to Kwame and Akua with a smile. "I'll show you how I do it, and then you can show me how you do it." Kwame and Akua smiled, too, as each picked up a hoe and started this familiar work.

Uncle Kwasi was efficient and thorough, a good model for Kwame and Akua with his hard work and good cheer. As he watched his niece and nephew work, he complimented them while making an occasional suggestion. "Dig deeper to get all of the roots. Dig all around a weed before you pull on the stem. Pull the stem harder. Put all of the weeds that you chop at the end of the row. This field may be yours to farm some day," he said. "Let's take good care of it."

"Uncle Kwasi, I want to be a trader and travel to the savannah and the coast," Kwame explained. "I want to see our kingdom. I don't want to farm. I don't like farming."

"Where will you live?" Uncle Kwasi asked. "What if you have a wife and children? How will all of you eat?"

"I'll earn gold to buy things in the market," Kwame replied. "My wife can farm on her clan's land. We'll live in Tanoso, and I'll travel in the dry season. Kwaku and Baako might come with me on trips. We've talked about that."

"Kwame, it's good to travel. You, Kwaku, and Baako will soon visit Kumasi and see new things. I hope that you'll like the city. You'll see what traders there do.

"As for farming," Uncle Kwasi continued, "everyone has to know how to farm. We'll always need food and there might be times when you'll need to farm and hunt, too."

"Asare is teaching Kwaku, Baako, and me how to throw a spear," Kwame replied. "He said we might be able to go hunting in the next dry season. I hope that we can, but we'll have to practice a lot."

"Asare's a good teacher. Learn from him. Your mother, Nana, and I will work with you, Akua, and Yaw Mensah on farming. Keep thinking about being a trader and we'll keep talking about it."

"I know that farming is hard," Akua said, "but I like to be in the fields with Mama. I like to help her in the market and see all of the people there. I like her vegetables, too, even the carrots."

"You're doing well," Uncle Kwasi complimented Akua. "Your mother is a good teacher."

"We even teach Twi to the *nnonko* children," Akua said. "I'm a good teacher, too."

"Both of you are working well," Uncle Kwasi said. "I'll go to the next fields now to find my other sisters and their children. We'll have lunch with you."

As Akua and Kwame worked closer to their mother and Asa, they heard Asa use Twi words and they praised her. Asa seemed comfortable with her father working in sight. Soon the group was weeding and talking together. After weeding several rows, Madam Ama encouraged the children, "I know this is hard work," she said. "You're doing well. We'll stop for a rest soon."

Only Akua responded. "Mama, weeding is the worst. I don't understand how weeds can grow so fast."

WHEN THE *ODONKO* FINISHED WEEDING HIS SECTION, HE WALKED TO THE RIVER TO collect water. Everyone stopped to rest, drink water, and eat bananas. Akua and Kwame looked forward to harvesting the okra and garden eggs next. They were planted in the same rows because their growing habits were different but compatible, and they were easy to harvest.

The tall okra plants grew upright, tied to bamboo stakes, at the back of each row. The okra pods stuck their pointy noses into the air. The garden egg bushes were short. The garden eggs were white, like chicken eggs, only bigger and easier to see.

After the rest Madam Ama gave Akua a small machete and reviewed how to chop vegetables off of their stems. Kwame had already started with a larger machete. "Akua, hold vegetables firmly and chop the stem once with the machete. No big swings. Just a quick, short chop. If the first chop doesn't work, try again."

Akua wanted to be the teacher now. She harvested an okra pod and handed it to Asa saying, "*Nkruma* – Okra."

Asa repeated, "*Nkruma, nkruma.*" Akua clapped her hands.

Akua harvested a garden egg and showed it to Asa saying, "*Nyadoa, nyadoa.*"

Asa smiled. She touched the garden egg and repeated, "*Nyadoa, nyadoa,*" and then held up the okra pod up saying, "*Nkruma, nkruma.*" Akua clapped.

Asa carried the baskets for the harvested vegetables. Madam Ama, Akua, and Kwame worked fast and made a game of handing or rolling the okra pods and garden eggs to Asa while naming them.

The musical sounds of "*Nyadoa, nyadoa, nkruma, nkruma, nyadoa, nkruma,*" rang out as Asa skipped along picking the vegetables up. Madam Ama was pleased with their progress.

After a full morning of weeding and harvesting, Madam Ama's group stopped for lunch. Elder Kwasi returned with his other sisters and their children. Everyone spread cloths on the ground and sat down to eat.

The *odonko* went to the river for water again. He was agitated when he returned and spoke to Elder Kwasi. With hand motions and by drawing on the ground, he explained that he had seen a leopard across the river.

Uncle Kwasi looked alarmed when he told the others. "I don't know if the leopard is the male or female. The *odonko* didn't see the cubs. I'll fire my gun to scare it."

"Oh, I want to see it before your scare it!" Kwame said.

"Me, too!" Akua added. The others agreed.

"I'd like to see it, myself, " Elder Kwasi said. "Let's go to the bank. Look for crocodiles and pythons first."

The group approached the bank slowly and carefully. Seeing no crocodiles or pythons, they lined up next to the water to watch and wait. Elder Kwasi stood nearby, holding his gun. Within a short time a leopard emerged from behind a large rock and approached the water.

"Oh, it's beautiful," Akua said.

"We have to save leopards," Madam Ama affirmed, and all agreed.

"I'll scare it now," Uncle Kwasi said as he turned to walk a short distance into the forest to load his gun and fire. The group soon heard the shot and saw white smoke. The leopard sped away.

Elder Kwasi was satisfied that everyone would be safe but wanted to finish eating, complete the harvest quickly, and return home. "It's not good to be here if a leopard is nearby, even across the river," he explained.

Elder Kwasi holding a long Dane musket

"Did we see the male or the female?" Kwame asked.

"I don't know," Elder Kwasi answered. "We didn't see the cubs, but we know that they were on our side of the river yesterday. Their mother can swim and carry them in her teeth, so we may have seen the female."

Madam Ama interrupted, "I want us to pull the carrots in my field before we leave. We'll return tomorrow to harvest more for the market."

Work concluded quickly. Akua, Kwame, and Madam Ama waved to Asa and her father when they left on the river trail.

"*Medaase*," Asa answered, smiling and waving.

LATE IN THE AFTERNOON NANA, THE OKYEAME, ELDER KOFI, ELDER KWASI, KWAME, and Kwaku walked along the main road toward the marketplace. The men wore full cloths with a white background to be visible at night. This was an unusual sight because such cloths were normally reserved for holidays.

People walking or sitting along the road were curious as they called out greetings to the group and waved. Nana and the others replied.

The group walked fast. "We're four days past the full moon, but there's still enough light to hunt at night," the Okyeame observed. "Any hunters across the river should see us."

The group continued on the great-road beyond the marketplace. A man holding a burning torch waited for them at the path to the village. He escorted them to the village where the headman greeted them warmly, "*Akwaaba*."

"*Maadwo* – Good evening," Nana replied.

The villagers shared a generous meal with their guests. The men sat together after dinner to drink palm wine, smoke pipes, and talk. The boys played *Oware*.

After a long evening, Nana stood and said to the group, "We've had a good meal and a good visit. I thank the headman and his council. Let's go to the river now to watch for hunters. The Okyeame will carry a loaded gun. If we see a leopard, he'll fire into the air to scare it. I want leopards to live in the forest but not near villages."

With the headman and several of his people, Nana's group approached the favored crossing point on the river bank and sat on chairs, stools, and mats. The river flowed slowly, partially covered with leaves. The water level was low and rocks were visible. Enough moonlight reflected off of the water for the group to see the opposite bank where brush and trees had been cut back.

Sounds of the flowing water and the noise of insects filled the air. A slight breeze blew toward the group, carrying its scent away from the river. The scene was peaceful. Nana felt certain that his group was visible to the opposite bank. He wanted hunters there to know of the group's presence.

"It's calm here, but it feels scary," Kwame whispered to Kwaku, knowing that he was supposed to be quiet. "Do you think hunters are across the river? It's light enough for them to hunt without torches tonight. We saw a leopard on their side at Mama's farm this morning. It could be nearby."

"Maybe hunters are hiding and waiting for it," Kwaku replied. "We saw a python on the other bank when we crossed the river. Are there enough people here to scare snakes? I hope so."

Nana, pointed across the river saying, "I see a reflection close to the bank. It may be coming from a knife blade. Watch." Two duikers walked out of the forest to the river. Arrows felled them. Gunshots rang out. A leopard ran out of the forest downstream from the observers and leaped into the water.

Nana's group stood to watch the powerful beast swim as none of them could. It emerged from the river on their side and climbed onto a massive boulder. With its lean muscular body silhouetted against the sky, the leopard twitched its tail with patience seeming to wait for recognition. When the Okyeame fired his gun, the leopard jumped to the ground and disappeared into the forest without making a sound.

The leopard's silhouette

The group was stunned. "Nana, you called the leopard!" the headman proclaimed.

"I've never seen a leopard before," an elder exclaimed in wonder.

"It's a powerful animal, worthy of our respect, a symbol of royalty," the Okyeame said.

"A magnificent animal! A magnificent animal!" Nana pronounced. "We're fortunate to have seen it! It's very rare, very rare, but I hope that we'll see it again. Our ancestors want us to protect leopards, and we will. Our presence makes that clear. The hunters across the river know that now. They'll tell their chief."

"Papa, why did the hunters on the other side fire their guns? Did they want to scare the leopard or kill it?" Kwame asked.

"We'll never know, Kwame, but they know that we're watching."

— CHAPTER 22 —

Honoring Asase Yaa

No farming took place on Thursdays. Everyone worked at home or in town or in a village. This Thursday Nana met with his council while the Queen Mother and Madam Ama visited sick people. Kwame carried Yaw Mensah to the home of one of his aunts, where Akua stayed to play with him. Kwame then joined Kwaku and Baako to throw spears.

At the edge of the council room, with the elders present, the Okyeame poured *akpeteshie* on the ground saying, "*Asase Yaa*, Mother Earth, we honor you with this libation. We do not farm on Thursdays so you may rest. Be aware of our efforts and bless us with a plentiful harvest."

Opening the council meeting where ten elders had assembled and were sitting on stools, the Okyeame announced, "We'll talk first about the return of leopards. Five sightings and on both sides of the river. Two adults and two cubs are here. What are your thoughts?"

"When children go into the forest to collect water, they're in danger."

"Leopards usually hunt at night. They won't attack children during the day."

"Some hunt during the day, certainly a female with cubs."

"Leopards will kill our sheep."

"Not if we corral sheep at night. Put a roof on your corral and keep sheep near the town or a village or in your courtyard. Sheep will be safe."

"A gunshot will scare a leopard."

"Will the chief across the river protect them?"

"Hunters were crossing the river at night to our side, certainly to hunt for a leopard."

"Nana talked to their chief, but we don't know yet if he'll agree to protect leopards."

"How can leopards help us?"

"The forest will be balanced again. Too many small animals spoil our crops now."

"Leopards will kill crocodiles and snakes. We'll be safer in the forest."

"Leopards won't bother people unless we threaten them."

Nana motioned for the Okyeame to talk to him. The Okyeame then repeated Nana's words. "More of our communal labor will be guarding the river near the marketplace. There is a guard on market days now. Soon there will be a guard each morning to look for leopards and crocodiles. It will be safe for everyone to collect water and do washing there.

"Nana will call for men to cut down more trees near the town and villages and along the great-road. Leopards spend most of their time in trees and this will keep them away from people. We can learn to live with leopards again."

"Someone will kill the leopards for their skins."

"Not if councils protect them."

"We can protect them. We will."

The Okyeame voiced Nana's thoughts once more. "The leopards kept strangers out of our forest in the past, and we were never invaded. We should welcome leopards again for our protection."

The elders talked briefly among themselves and one rose to speak. "Thank you, Nana, for protecting the leopards. My grandfather remembered them. I want to see them. Others in the council expressed approval. The Okyeame reported to Nana, who accepted the consensus.

THE OKYEAME MOVED THE DISCUSSION TO TAXES. "FIFTY-FIVE MEN IN TANOSO AND a hundred and fifteen men in twelve villages paid a total of seventeen ounces of gold dust. Remember the division, 3/7 is for the Asantehene, 1/7 is for the tax collectors, and 3/7 remains here for Nana to divide among us. Nana will give each clan head gold dust equal to the taxes of five men. To each village headman, he will give gold dust equal to the taxes of two men. Use this for the welfare of your people. Nana is generous because he's giving you most of the amount that he received." Council members murmured approval.

"Our district has more than 1,000 people," the Okyeame continued. "There are 170 married men and 200 married women because some men have two wives. There are 650 children, and the *nnonko* village has about 100 adults and children. With this number of people in his district, Nana can carry a horse tail switch in the *Odwira* parade in Kumasi.

"Nana's district is large and rich. Nana believes that we have room for more free people who would make us stronger and safer. Other chiefs won't move onto our land. When we send soldiers to the army, there will be enough people at home to farm. We'll never be hungry. More people will attract more traders. A bigger market will attract more buyers for our crops and other goods. Our district will prosper."

The elders received the information cautiously. One raised his hand, and the Okyeame recognized him. "We have to balance more people with the return of leopards," he said. "Tanoso and our villages can grow, but we need dense forest to attract leopards and for our own hunting." Others agreed.

"Nana's land is vast," the Okyeame replied. "He wants the Asantehene to reward soldiers by sending them here with their families where he can give them land. They'll find clan members in Tanoso. We can welcome more people, but we'll have to use our farm land better. We'll clear more land, but our fields will be closer together."

"There are *nnonko* children that we will adopt," an elder commented. "Nana will give them land, and they'll become farmers like the rest of us. This will increase our number."

"We have to make room for them and our own children, too," another elder added.

"We'll always need *nnonko* to mine and wash the ore because Akans don't do that work. When we adopt the *nnonko* children, we'll have to buy more adults."

Nana spoke to the Okyeame, who repeated his words. "We'll provide our children with farms when they are old enough, but the Asantehene can send us families who will farm right away. Nana will offer this plan at the council of chiefs in Kumasi. Yes, we will always have *nnonko*. Anyone who needs to buy *nnonko* now should join Nana's delegation to Kumasi."

"We need to plan our trip to Kumasi before we distribute the taxes," an elder said.

"Let's take a short rest and then talk about Kumasi," the Okyeame proposed. "Nana will give us news of the Asantehene's defeat of the Fante."

CHILDREN DID THEIR CHORES EARLY WHILE THE MORNING AIR WAS COOL. THEY SWEPT courtyards, collected water, took food waste to the dumping ground, washed cloths, cleaned chicken coops, collected eggs, and let chickens out, untied and fed sheep, and cared for their brothers, sisters, and cousins. Some stayed home afterwards to do other work, but many played in courtyards and on roads in town where the elderly sat on stools to watch over them. Tanoso rang with children's shouts and laughter when the council resumed its meeting.

Nana spoke to the Okyeame, who conveyed his words to the council. "In the rainy season, the Asantehene led the army himself to defeat the Fante. The Fante have defied the kingdom for a long time by blocking our trade with whites on the coast. Recently, they hid fugitives and killed ambassadors from the kingdom. The Asantehene had to act.

"Our army met strong resistance. Our soldiers burned many towns and villages. There was a tragic battle at the fort in Anomabo, where hundreds of women and children had taken refuge. On the beach the Asantehene fought both the Fante army and the whites who fired from their fort. In the end, Fante soldiers fled and the whites sued for peace. The Asantehene lost 2,000 men, and the Fante lost more. People say that the beach was red with blood and strewn with bodies." The elders reacted strongly, uttering words of regret and alarm.

"Osei Tutu Kwame is the first Asantehene to see the ocean," the Okyeame recounted. "At Anomabo he struck the ocean with his sword, and the splash of water looked like a whale's spout. Now people are calling him Osei Bonsu—Osei the Whale. Perhaps some of us will see the ocean, too." Elders smiled even through their tears.

"The Asantehene remains with some of his soldiers in Fante territory," the Okyeame continued. "He may not be in Kumasi for the *Odwira*." The elders gasped. This was unknown.

"Will there be a festival?" an elder asked.

"The tax collectors assured Nana that the Kumasi council of chiefs will celebrate the *Odwira* even if the Asantehene cannot be there. We will travel to Kumasi."

"Has the Asantehene been defeated? Is he hiding that from us?" elders wanted to know.

The Okyeame was adamant, "The Asantehene was victorious, but there are Fante rebels who have not surrendered. He's determined to defeat them."

"What will happen to them?" an elder asked.

"He'll kill them or sell them to the whites. The rebels will not succeed. They don't know the strength of his army," the Okyeame concluded.

"The Asantehene didn't call us for this war," Nana spoke once more to the Okyeame, who repeated his message. "We know that the Fante remain strong. They trade for guns directly with the whites. If they continue to rebel, the Asantehene may call us to fight. We would bring our own guns. He would supply the ammunition. Nana is a man of peace, but he will prepare us for war in case we have to fight."

The elders said, "*Yoo*," in unison to show agreement.

The Okyeame affirmed the sentiment. "We are all men of peace," he said, "but we will be ready for war."

"On this trip Nana will buy guns, gunpowder, and musket balls to help us prepare. Each of you should have your own gun. Nana will divide ammunition among us."

The elders talked among themselves to support Nana and praise the Asantehene. "The Fante have so many guns," an elder said. "We definitely need more." Others agreed.

Another elder added, "I want more ammunition so I can practice shooting. It's too expensive for me to practice now."

Several elders shared this view, and one added, "I praise Nana. I don't want to go to war, but if I have to, I want to be well armed."

A senior elder raised his hand, and the Okyeame recognized him. The elder rose and stepped forward. "What does Nana expect of the council?" he asked. "Some of us have been to Kumasi, but not everyone. We're prepared to help, but it's a difficult trip. We have to walk eight days from Tanoso to Kumasi and then return. We'll have to prepare our families for our absence."

THE OKYEAME CONTINUED. 'NANA WILL LEAD OUR DELEGATION TO KUMASI FOR THE *Odwira* festival. We'll leave on the day after the next *Adae*. When we return, we'll celebrate our own *Odwira*. We'll eat yams for the first time this dry season to welcome the new year. If we harvest yams now, we'll be ready. Nana believes that *Asase Yaa* will honor us with a bountiful crop."

The elders clapped with approval.

"To celebrate the *Odwira* in Kumasi, we need a group big enough to honor the Asantehene and show our strength. Nana will bring five *nnonko* to carry food, supplies, and his regalia, along with kola nuts and corn to trade. Asare will come as the foreman. Kwame, Kwaku, and Baako will join us for the first time to help carry supplies." The elders murmured approval.

"Nana wants five of our council to come, each bringing two *nnonko,* at least two village headmen to carry Nana's swords, plus two drummers and two horn blowers. Our delegation will have over twenty-five people. Nana's clan will welcome us to Kumasi and give us shelter. If you want to stay with your own clan, you may." The Okyeame paused now to hear what the elders thought.

One elder commented, "We will thank Nana's clan for receiving us. But such a number! That will cost a lot."

"We must show strength," the Okyeame reminded the council.

Another elder with permission to speak said, "You're right. We must show strength to be respected. Will Nana help us pay for the trip?"

"Yes, Nana will contribute from his treasury," the Okyeame replied. "He'll pay for some of the food on the way, but those who come should bring gold dust to buy more. Take care of your own business when you're in Kumasi. That will help you pay for the trip, but don't overload your *nnonko*. Remember that on the return trip, they'll have to help carry the guns and ammunition that Nana buys."

The elders talked among themselves. "My *nnonko* will carry cassava to eat on the way and kola nuts to trade in Kumasi. I'll buy tools and cloth in Kumasi to sell in our market," one said. "I'll keep an *odonko* free to carry guns and ammunition on the way back. I'll still make a profit."

"I'll buy glass beads to sell here," another elder said. "Women and girls like them and will pay a good price. They're small and easy to carry."

The elders identified five of their number for the trip and two headmen volunteered to come. When the council agreed on plans that the Okyeame judged favorable, he closed the discussion and reported the outcome to Nana. With Nana's approval, the meeting concluded.

Before the elders left, Elder Kwasi rose to speak, "Tonight I'll honor the yam harvest and the *Odwira* celebrations by telling the story of Osei Tutu, our first Asantehene. I've done this for many years. I invite you, your children, and your grandchildren to come."

The elders applauded.

CHAPTER 23

The First Asantehene

CHILDREN AND ELDERS MADE THEIR WAY TO THE PALACE IN THE MOONLIGHT. REGAL in his full cloth, Elder Kwasi welcomed them in his sonorous and musical voice. "*Mema mo adwo* – Good evening everyone," he said. Children sat or lay down on the ground of the main courtyard. Elders sat on stools. Kwame, Kwaku, and Baako huddled nearby even though they knew the story. They always liked hearing Elder Kwasi tell it.

"I honor our yam harvest and the beginning of each new year by telling the story of Osei Tutu, our first king, and how he created our kingdom," Elder Kwasi began. "Are you ready?"

"Yes, yes, yes!" came replies as children squirmed to be comfortable.

"Long, long ago Akans had strong clans, but we were not united. There was no kingdom. Akan groups living in different parts of the forest took separate names and sometimes fought each other over land and gold."

"Oh, that's scary," one child said. "I don't want to go into the forest now."

"Wars once made our lives dangerous," Elder Kwasi explained. "Most of the time now, we have peace in our kingdom."

"My story starts with an Akan group called the Denkyira. They had a kingdom and with their strong army they conquered other Akan groups including a group called the Asante. The Denkyira made the Asante give them gold and palm oil. The Asante were always poor.

"The Denkyira king wanted more power, and he said to an Asante chief, 'Give me one of your nephews, one who may become a chief. I'll treat him well in my court, but I'll keep him so you won't attack me. He'll be safe as long as your people give me gold and palm oil.'

"The Asante chief was very sad because he loved his nieces and nephews, but he could not refuse. He sent the Denkyira king his nephew, Osei Tutu, who was about sixteen years old, along with servants to take care of the boy."

"That could be me," Kwaku said to his friends as he sat up to listen carefully. "I wouldn't want to go to the Denkyira. They could hurt me. I would miss my family." The story worried him even though he had heard it before.

"Osei Tutu was afraid," Elder Kwasi continued. "He loved his large family, his grandparents and parents, uncles and aunts, brothers and sisters and cousins, and he didn't want to leave them. He didn't want to go to the Denkyira court, but he had to. The Denkyira king, however, was kind to him. Osei Tutu spent at least ten dry seasons with the Denkyira. He didn't see his family at all."

"Oh," the children groaned. "That's sad."

"You're right," Elder Kwasi said. "It was sad. The Asante did not fight the Denkyira then because they wanted to protect Osei Tutu.

"The Denkyira king saw that Osei Tutu was smart and strong. Osei Tutu could run fast, throw spears well, and shoot arrows accurately. He also spoke well. The king wanted Osei Tutu to join the Denkyira and trained him and his servants to be soldiers."

"Osei Tutu wouldn't leave his family. That would be terrible. Why would he do that?" Kwaku asked his friends. "He didn't have to."

"We need to learn to throw spears like Osei Tutu did. That made him strong, and you have to be strong to be a king," Baako replied.

"The Denkyira army fought with guns, and in those days very few Akans had guns," Elder Kwasi explained. "Osei Tutu wanted to learn how to use guns."

"We have guns now," one of the children said.

"Yes," Elder Kwasi replied. "Later, all Akans got guns."

"The Denkyira king wanted a bigger kingdom. He asked Osei Tutu and his servants to fight with the Denkyira army against nearby Akan people. Osei Tutu agreed, and in a fierce battle, he and his servants swam across a river and helped defeat an enemy of the Denkyira. They took gold from the enemy's chief. The Denkyira king demanded that Osei Tutu give him the gold, but Osei Tutu refused."

"Aie!" exclaimed the children all together. "What happened?"

"The Denkyira king was angry because Osei Tutu wasn't loyal to him. The king tried to arrest the Asantes, but they escaped and returned home. Osei Tutu's family welcomed them and hid them when Denkyira soldiers came to look for them. The soldiers never found Osei Tutu or his servants."

"Osei Tutu didn't really leave his family. He was only fooling the Denkyira king," Baako said.

"That was dangerous," Kwame added.

"Osei Tutu realized that he wouldn't be safe at home," Elder Kwasi explained. "He left to stay with another Akan people, the Akwamu, who were friends of the Asante. The Akwamu chief also trained Osei Tutu and his servants in warfare because there was much fighting then among Akans. While Osei Tutu was with the Akwamu, his uncle died. Osei Tutu and his servants were sad."

"Oh, oh, oh," the children cried out. "What happened then?"

"The Queen Mother and elders selected Osei Tutu's younger uncle to be their new chief. He sent a message to Osei Tutu asking him to come home and fight with him and his army.

"While Osei Tutu was deciding what to do, a priest, Okomfo Anokey, stepped forward to advise him," Elder Kwasi continued. "The priest knew how to speak with the spirits of trees and rivers. He told Osei Tutu that it would be dangerous for him to join his family's army because certain spirits did not favor his uncle. Osei Tutu followed this advice and did not return home."

The children shuddered and snuggled together. Baako followed the story closely. He had never heard it. Kwame and Kwaku smiled broadly because they loved the story even though it scared them.

"Okomfo Anokey was right," Elder Kwasi explained. "Spirits were against Osei Tutu's uncle. He died in battle. His army was defeated."

Children sighed. They didn't like the bad news.

"This was unfortunate, but what happened next was good. The Queen Mother and the elders believed that Osei Tutu was smart and courageous. They selected him as their new chief and sent a messenger to ask him to come home.

"The priest told Osei Tutu to accept the honor. He agreed, and the messenger returned to tell the Queen Mother. Before he could leave, Osei Tutu became very sick with small pox. His servants and the priest took care of him and he recovered. Osei Tutu always believed that the priest had summoned spirits to heal him."

"Oh," the children sighed with relief.

"When he was well again, Osei Tutu returned home with his priest and servants to become the chief of his district."

"He was a good chief, like Nana, but he had to fight," Kwame said. "I don't want Papa to fight."

"THE AKWAMU CHIEF GAVE OSEI TUTU GUNS AND AMMUNITION TO TAKE HOME AND invited him to trade for more. Osei Tutu trained his district's army to fight as he had learned to do from the Denkyira and the Akwamu. He knew that guns were important, but that good commanders with brave soldiers were more important. He wanted other Asante chiefs and their soldiers to join him to form a powerful army. He wanted to teach them how to use guns.

"The other Asante chiefs resisted. Osei Tutu bargained with them. He offered them guns and ammunition if they elected him their king. He told them that a large Asante army with good commanders and armed with guns could defeat the Denkyira. The chiefs wanted to know more.

"'Guns make a loud noise and white smoke that frighten enemy soldiers because they don't know where the danger is coming from,' Osei Tutu explained. 'Musket balls will kill some and others will run.

"'Soldiers have to learn to load guns carefully and shoot them quickly. Reloading takes time. Soldiers have to keep their gun powder dry when it's raining. In a united army, some soldiers will fight with guns and others with spears and bows and arrows, as we always have. Together all of these weapons will make us powerful.'

"'How can we protect ourselves?' chiefs asked.

"'Thick war smocks will block musket fire,' Osei Tutu answered.

"'How can we get guns, powder, and musket balls?'

"'We'll trade gold to get them from other Akans or the whites. It will be hard, but I know we can do it even if some Akan groups try to stop us.'

"The chiefs wanted guns and needed a leader who could teach them how to fight with guns, but they had never had a king. They thought carefully about Osei Tutu's offer.

"Osei Tutu promised to share power with the other Asante chiefs. 'You'll be my council,' he said. 'You'll be commanders in a united Asante army.' After much deliberation the chiefs accepted Osei Tutu's offer. They elected him as the Asantehene, the king. Osei Tutu brought their soldiers together to form an army, and taught them how to fight with guns.

"The Asante Kingdom grew as its army defeated other Akans. The Asantes were finally strong enough to defeat the Denkyira, kill its king, and make the people join the Asante Kingdom. Over many years, almost all of the Akan groups were united in the kingdom that was ruled from Kumasi with the help of district chiefs like Nana. We are in the Wassa group of Akans, and we are part of the Asante Kingdom."

The children clapped. "The kingdom is all of us," one said.

"You've listened well, my children, and there is more," Elder Kwasi said. "Before I continue, stand up and run around and jump up and down. You need to move. Drink water if you're thirsty, and eat a banana if you're hungry." The children were happy to follow the instructions.

"I didn't know that guns were so important," Kwame said to Kwaku and Baako. "We'll have to learn to shoot guns when we're young men. All Akans have guns now. There are still wars. Papa talks about them."

"We might have to be soldiers someday," Kwaku added.

"Spears and bows and arrows are better. We can see where they go," Baako said. "I don't know about guns. *Nnonko* don't have guns. Has Nana fought in a war?"

"I don't think so," Kwame answered.

"I don't want to fight in a war," Baako said. "I don't want to kill people. We could get killed or captured like my parents. We could be sold to the whites. They would take us away from the forest."

"I want peace in the forest," Kwaku said. "Guns are dangerous. They killed the leopards."

"I want to hear what Osei Tutu did next," Baako said. "I have to know."

ELDER KWASI MOTIONED FOR CHILDREN TO GATHER ONCE MORE AROUND HIS STOOL as he sat down. Children squeezed together, welcoming the mystery of the story. When they were comfortable and quiet once more, Elder Kwasi began. "Osei Tutu was strong and brave. He trained his soldiers well. He won many battles and lived for a long time. Even as an old man, he fought with his army, but he made a mistake."

"Oh, no," children said, paying close attention.

"An Akan group called the Akyem rebelled against the kingdom. Osei Tutu thought that the Akyem were weak because their army was small. He left his war smock at home when he led his army against the Akyem. When Osei Tutu was crossing the Pra River in a canoe, Akyem soldiers hiding along the bank shot him. He died quickly and fell into the river. His body was never found. His people were distraught. They had lost their king."

The children cried out, "Oh, no. We thought he was smart. He made a bad mistake."

"Why didn't the priest warn him?" Baako asked.

"Maybe the priest had died by then," Kwame suggested.

"Osei Tutu was smart but proud. He looked down on the Akyem. Let this be a lesson for you," Uncle Kwasi warned. "Never look down on anyone or anything. Don't be proud. Be humble. Osei Tutu did not learn."

Elder Kwasi waited for a few moments and then said, "My children, all of this happened long ago. We must always remember Osei Tutu as our first Asantehene and how he created our kingdom. We must ask for his blessing.

"Osei Tutu belonged to the *Oyoko* clan, like Nana and the Queen Mother and many of you. Nana's ancestors served Asantehene Osei Tutu and received this land from him. You have learned that we have had ten chiefs since that time."

"Yeah, yeah, yeah!" a chorus of children chanted.

"I'm an *Oyoko*," one of the small boys said. "Can I be the Asantehene someday?"

"You would be a good Asantehene," Elder Kwasi assured him, "but you would have to live in Kumasi."

"I'll tell my mama," the boy replied, smiling.

"There is more to know about why our kingdom remains strong," Elder Kwasi said. "Rest for a few minutes, my children, and then I'll tell you what happened next."

CHAPTER 24

The Golden Stool and the Outdooring

"WE REMEMBER OSEI TUTU BECAUSE HE WAS OUR FIRST ASANTEHENE," ELDER KWASI reminded his audience. "The Asante Kingdom has remained powerful. The Asantehenes have kept peace in the forest. They've defeated the kingdoms of the savannah. Asantehene Osei Bonsu, our sixth Asantehene, holds the royal stool now. He's a strong general for our army and a powerful leader for our people.

"Long ago, when our kingdom was new, it needed a powerful symbol to hold people together. A king and an army were not enough. Do you remember the priest, Okomfo Anokey?"

"Yes," most children replied.

"The priest was clever. He thought of a stool."

"Why?" a few children asked. "What can a stool do?"

"Then, like now, stools were everywhere. We used stools to sit together to work and talk and eat. I'm sitting on a stool to tell you this story. When a new chief is selected, we say that he is enstooled."

"What else would we say?" a child asked.

"Every chief has a royal stool, and we say that the land he cares for belongs to his stool. If a chief does well, after he dies his stool will become a black stool kept in a sacred stool house and honored at the *Adae*. Do you remember?"

"Yes," children responded.

"Auntie Adjowa told you about the first Akan person who came into the forest. She carried a stool. Do you remember?"

"Yes," children responded once more.

"Since stools have always been important for Akans, Okomfo Anokey thought that a special stool would be a good symbol for the new kingdom. He wanted everyone to be loyal to a special stool, a golden stool, that would always exist no matter who was the king."

"Oh," children gasped.

"Akans know about gold because it comes from our rivers and hills," Elder Kwasi reminded the children. "We have gold jewelry and gold decorations. We shop in the marketplace with gold dust. Our gold is beautiful. Imagine a golden stool.

"One day the priest asked everyone in Kumasi to come to a large open area in the city where he had built a fire. Many people gathered. Drummers came with drums; horn blowers brought their horns; soldiers carried bows and arrows, spears, and guns. Osei Tutu and his *okyeame* came. The Queen Mother came. Most people stood, but Osei Tutu and the Queen Mother sat on chairs and were protected by umbrellas. Everyone waited patiently wondering why the priest had called them together. What do you think happened?"

"We don't know. Tell us," several children answered while wiggling to make themselves more comfortable.

"Listen closely," Elder Kwasi whispered as he smiled, stood, and extended his arms to his sides.

"Okomfo Anokey stood near the fire, in front of the crowd. 'Thank you for coming,' the priest said. 'Look up in the sky.'" Elder Kwasi raised his arms to the sky and the children followed them with their gaze. "Black clouds and smoke from the fire blocked the sun. The drummers beat their drums. The horn blowers blew their horns. The soldiers fired guns into the air, making a loud noise and creating white smoke."

Elder Kwasi looked up to the moon and shaded his eyes with his hands. "A shiny, golden object descended slowly through the smoke. People gasped and squinted as they watched it come closer and closer. Finally everyone saw that it was an elaborately carved wooden stool covered with gold. The stool came to rest very lightly on Osei Tutu's knees.

"The crowd gathered around the Asantehene and many exclaimed, 'Look at this stool. It's golden. This is a miracle!' Osei Tutu stared at the stool in wonder."

"A golden stool," several children gasped.

Elder Kwasi looked at the children once more. "The priest spoke. 'This stool contains the soul of our kingdom. As long as the stool is safe, we will have good health and remain powerful. If the stool is destroyed, our kingdom will be lost.' The people of Kumasi stood silent as they heard the message."

"Oh," Baako whispered. "I can't imagine a golden stool." Kwame and Kwaku smiled.

"People throughout the Asante Kingdom wanted to honor the Golden Stool," Elder Kwasi explained. "They buried their old stools and carved new ones to use in their homes and as royal stools. They thought of the Golden Stool as the kingdom's first stool."

"Many traditions have grown up around the Golden Stool," Elder Kwasi continued as he sat on his stool once more. "Some Asantehenes have carried it into battle to inspire their soldiers. Now it's kept in the Asantehene's palace in Kumasi. No one sits on it. It never touches the ground. When an Asantehene brings it to a ceremony, it rests on its side on a chair next to him so that no evil spirits will sit on it. For a celebration, it's sometimes paraded under its own umbrella. People can look at it but never touch it."

"We've seen black stools," a child said. "I want to see the Golden Stool."

Descent of the Golden Stool

"You will see it if you go to a celebration in Kumasi," Elder Kwasi explained. "That tradition started when Osei Tutu asked all of the chiefs to come to Kumasi every dry season for the *Odwira* festival. He showed them the Golden Stool to let them know that it was safe and that he would always protect it and protect them. In return, they pledged their loyalty to him.

"When Nana and the elders go to the *Odwira* festival in Kumasi, they will see the Golden Stool. Do any of you want to go to Kumasi?" Elder Kwasi asked.

"Me, me, me, me!" children said, and many raised both hands and clapped to show their enthusiasm.

"Someday many of you will visit Kumasi and see the Golden Stool," Elder Kwasi assured them. "Even if you don't see it, the stool protects you because it contains the soul of our kingdom."

"Uncle Kwasi is a good story teller. I can remember his words," Kwame said with pride to his friends. "We'll see the Golden Stool soon. I want to know what it's like."

"We have to walk a long way to Kumasi," Baako added. "I hope we'll see it."

"I'm not sure that I believe this story," Kwaku said shaking his head. "Did *Nyame* send the stool?"

"Be careful, Kwaku," Kwame cautioned. "Papa says that the Golden Stool is powerful just like the black stools. We have to honor our ancestors and our king. We have to be humble."

"What about me?" Baako asked. "My mother and father are from the savannah. I don't have ancestors in the forest."

"I'm sure that Nana will adopt you and give you ancestors," Kwaku explained. "You'll be in his clan, and that's my clan, too. You have to have a clan. You'll be an *Oyoko* like me and you'll have *Oyoko* ancestors like Osei Tutu."

"But what about my real mama and papa?" Baako questioned.

"Nana will protect them, but he won't adopt them," Kwame said. "They'll keep their ancestors from the savannah."

Baako did not respond. He wanted to think about his ancestors in the savannah and talk to his mother and father about them.

"My children, you've listened well to a long story," Elder Kwasi concluded. "Can you tell me now what a king is and what a kingdom is?" Many children answered.

"Osei Tutu was our first Asantehene. That means he was our first king."

"Osei Tutu was like a chief but he had more land."

"Osei Tutu had a big army."

"His soldiers had guns."

"He was brave."

"He made us safe, but he had to fight in wars."

"The Asantehenes like to eat yams. That's why there's an *Odwira* festival."

"The whole forest is the kingdom, and it has a Golden Stool."

"You are all right. You've listened and learned well. Remember the name of your first king, Asantehene Osei Tutu. We have a different king now, Asantehene Osei Bonsu. Nana will see him in Kumasi. I hope that someday all of you will see our king and the Golden Stool.

"This is my story. Share it with others. Thank you for coming," Elder Kwasi concluded.

The children rose stretching and yawning, holding on to each other, and ready to return to their homes. "*Dayie* – Good night, Elder Kwasi. Thank you for the story," many said as they left.

EARLY MONDAY MORNING NANA AND HIS FAMILY ARRIVED AT THE HOME OF THE grandparents of the new baby girl to celebrate her outdooring. They and the other visitors greeted each other and the grandparents while waiting in the courtyard. Madam Ama handed the grandmother a package of beads.

The baby's father arrived with gifts: two metal bowls, a metal spoon, a new mat, a cloth, a pillow, and a pair of gold earrings, which he took inside of a hut to his wife and daughter.

The mother dressed in her best cloth and spread white clay on her chest, shoulders, and arms. She rubbed the baby's body with shea butter, and darkened her eyebrows with charcoal. She placed beads around the baby's arms, legs, and waist, attached the earrings, and wrapped her daughter in the new cloth. Mother and baby were resplendent and ready to meet their guests.

The morning sun shone brightly. The new parents brought their daughter into the courtyard and laid her on a mat. The father picked his daughter up in both hands, held her above his head, and chanted, "Adjowa, we place you here in the sun to take away the cold air of the spirit world. Feel the warmth of the sun. You have come to stay, and we welcome you."

The guests responded, "*Yoo, yoo, yoo!*"

The father placed his daughter on the knees of her grandfather, who sat on a stool. The grandfather proclaimed, "I call my ancestors. My son now has a child, and he has brought her to me. I will name her Adjowa Kraa after my mother, her great-grandmother, who was a wise and patient woman. May she grow up to have these qualities and continue to meet me here so that I may give her food with this metal spoon."

The grandfather gave Adjowa Kraa a few drops of water and handed the infant to her mother, who kissed the baby's head and smiled through her tears.

Nana offered a blessing, "We welcome Adjowa Kraa to Tanoso. We will help her and guide her as she grows. She is part of our future."

The Queen Mother offered another blessing, "This is a glorious time. We welcome new life to our community. Adjowa Kraa, we need you in our lives."

Adjowa Kraa's grandmother added with affection, "When I take her to the marketplace, I will feel her at my back and know that she is with me."

"She's so cute," Akua whispered to her family. "I'll play with her and I'll teach her how to play *Ampe*. She has to learn!"

"I'll teach her how to play *Oware* as soon as I learn," Yaw promised. "I think she's smart."

"It is good to have a new baby in town. We'll see her in the marketplace," Madam Ama affirmed.

"Congratulations to all," Nana added and then turned to walk to the doorway. To his family, Nana said, "We've celebrated new life. Now we'll go to our fields."

Part Two:

THE ASANTE KINGDOM

Main street in the capital city, Kumasi

— CHAPTER 25 —

To Kumasi

At dawn those traveling to Kumasi gathered in the palace courtyard. Madam Ama and Akua served warm porridge, which was accepted with gratitude.

Kwame, Kwaku, and Baako ate eagerly as they checked through the personal items that each would bring: two extra cloths, a hooded cloak and a scarf that were presents from the Queen Mother, a sleeping mat, and small gourds for eating and drinking.

Kwaku and Baako would carry their personal supplies as well as Kwame's, fitted into large baskets with cloths, scarves, corn, and cassava belonging to others. Kwame would carry a pot full of water. Wearing cloths tied around their waists and walking barefoot, each would balance a heavy head load.

"I'm ready for the trip, Mama. I'm so happy," Kwame declared. "I'll tell you all about it when I come home. Kwaku, Baako, and I will go ahead of the delegation now so we can see everyone walk down the hill before we join in. Please tell Papa."

"I will," Madam Ama replied, smiling. "Take Akua and Yaw Mensah with you so they can see the delegation, too. Say 'Good-bye,' to your grandmother before you leave. Kwame, I'm glad that you're going to Kumasi. You'll see what a big city is like. Travel safely." She hugged her son tightly, pleased that he would make this long trip but fearful of the risks.

Kwame joined his friends, explaining, "I have to take Akua and Yaw Mensah with me." Within minutes the five children reached the bottom of the hill. Others from town joined them.

"Here they come!" Kwame shouted as the drummers followed by the horn blowers came into view. The drummers carried small drums hanging by straps from their shoulders. Their steady beat paced the expedition. The horn blowers followed, pointing their horns to the sky as if to prod the sun with piercing sounds.

"They are so loud. Everyone in the villages will hear them!" Kwaku said as he jumped up and down. Nana and the elders followed.

The headmen came next. Asare led the *nnonko* at the back of the delegation. The headmen and *nnonko* balanced large baskets of supplies and food, bundles of Nana's regalia including two umbrellas, gold accessories, two swords, and his stool, three guns, and machetes. Several, including some *nnonko,* carried a machete or a spear, or wore a holster with a knife.

Spectators waved enthusiastically and shouted greetings. The delegation looked rich with Nana and the elders wearing fine cloths and boots. Others wore waist cloths and sandals. The *nnonko*, except for Asare, walked barefoot.

"Papa, Papa," Akua and Yaw Mensah called out.

Nana, the elders, and the headmen smiled and waved. The *nnonko* looked straight ahead but smiled and seemed to share the excitement. Baako waved and called greetings to the *nnonko* in Nankane. He had never seen so many of his people in town, and he wanted to show his support. They didn't respond, but Baako didn't mind. He knew that they were working hard.

The sounds of drumming and horn blowing still filled the air when the last of the delegation walked by. Turning to Akua and Yaw Mensah, Kwame said, "Go home now. I'm leaving with Papa."

Akua cautioned her brother, "Kwame, be careful. Kumasi is far away."

"I'll be careful," Kwame replied. "Help Mama and Grannie while I'm gone."

"*Nanteyie* – Walk well, Kwame, Kwaku, and Baako," Akua and Yaw Mensah said as they turned to climb the hill.

"Let's catch up," Kwaku urged the other boys as they began to walk fast.

"Where do we fit in this parade?" Baako asked. "Can I stay with you?"

"We'll all stay together," Kwame answered. "Let's walk behind Nana and the elders for awhile. It's too noisy in the front. The road is wide, so we can get to the front later and see what's coming."

A short distance out of town, the delegation stopped. The musicians put away their instruments but remained in front to play again when the group approached a village. Travel quickly resumed so the delegation could reach the next town with a shelter and provisions for travelers by late afternoon. No one traveled at night.

THE EXCITEMENT OF THE DEPARTURE PROPELLED THE DELEGATION THROUGH THE morning even as the air grew hot. The group had the road to itself for much of the time, and the setting was quiet, filled only with their talk. They occasionally met or passed men and women carrying head loads bound for or returning from farms. When approaching a village, the musicians took out their instruments and played to announce the group's arrival. Members of the delegation waved to villagers who greeted them.

When the walk was well underway, Kwame turned to his friends and said, "This pot is too heavy. Do you want to drink some water?"

"Good idea," Kwaku answered. "Baako, do you want water, too?"

"Yes, but we have to be careful," Baako cautioned. "We don't want to run out while we're walking. We don't know where the streams are."

The boys stopped. Kwaku and Baako set their own baskets on the road, and together took the pot off of Kwame's head.

"I'll get the drinking gourds," Baako said. Kwame poured water, and the boys drank slowly.

"This feels good," Kwame said. Kwaku and Baako agreed. "I've never been far away from Tanoso. The forest looks the same, but walking on a big road is different. There's so much sun. It's so hot."

"We have scarves. Let's wrap them around our heads to keep cool," Kwame proposed. The boys did this and felt relief.

They soon rejoined the delegation and worked their way to the head of the group. "Now we can see where we're going," Kwaku said.

Throughout the morning the delegation maintained its pace. Everyone sweated in the sun, and some elders wrapped scarves around their heads. Several *nnonko* wore scarves. Their head loads also protected them. The group paused to drink water from time to time.

When the sun was high, the delegation stopped to eat a quick meal and drink water. Some *nnonko* chopped kola nuts open and chewed them with relish. The juice from the nuts gave them energy and quenched their thirst.

"Take a kola nut to chew even if you don't usually do that," Nana encouraged the others. "There are plenty in this basket," he said, as he picked up a handful to pass out, keeping one for himself. "They'll help on this long walk when we're in so much sun."

"*Medaase*, Nana," many in the group responded as they took kola nuts.

Asare approached Nana to let him know that the *nnonko* were doing well. "We'll repack some of the head loads tonight. My people grew up in the savannah, and they're used to the sun. The kola nuts help. We won't get thirsty."

"Are any of the *nnonko* worried about returning to Kumasi where they were once prisoners?" Nana asked.

"Remember, I was once a prisoner there with my parents and grandparents," Asare answered. "I was a child then, but I remember, and I used to be fearful. I'm settled in the forest with my family now, and I'm not worried. Some of the others could find it hard."

"They'll stay outside of Kumasi on my cousin's farm, but they'll have to be in the city some of the time. Do you think that any will try to escape?" Nana asked.

"I don't think so. It would be difficult for them to find their way back to the savannah, and they have families on your land now," Asare replied. "They're safer there."

"They won't succeed if they try to escape," Nana said, "but it might be hard for them if my people buy *nnonko*. Let them know that this could happen. If it does, we'll need their help to take new *nnonko* back to Tanoso."

"I'll talk to them," Asare replied.

Nana circulated among the elders to talk, and later he asked the boys to join him. "What do you think of our travels, so far?" he asked.

"It's good to walk with a group," Kwaku replied. "Will we see more people on the road?"

"Maybe, but my district is at the edge of the kingdom. There won't be many chiefs behind us," Nana replied. "How are your feet?"

"My feet are getting sore, but it's not too bad. The road is smooth," Kwame said.

"My feet are okay," Baako said. "I never wear sandals."

"You boys are growing too fast to wear sandals," Nana replied. "Your feet are tough. When you stop growing, you can have sandals, even boots for long walks."

"We'll soon leave my stool land," Nana observed. "I want to talk to the chief of the next district tonight. I hope he hasn't already left for Kumasi."

"Papa, did you bring your gun? How many machetes and spears do we have? Are we safe?"

"Kwame, we're forest people," Nana answered. "We always have our machetes, knives, and spears with us. The great-roads are safe, but we're prepared to handle animals, cut back bushes, dig holes, peel cassavas – so many things.

"The Okyeame and two other elders brought guns. We have them for our safety, but at the *Odwira* festival people like to fire into the air to make noise and smoke and honor the Golden Stool. People who shoot use only gun powder, no musket balls."

"I feel better now, Papa," Kwame said. "I'm glad that we're safe from crocodiles." Nana patted Kwame's shoulder.

"Look ahead," Nana said. "Do you see *nnonko* repairing the road? They're filling cracks and weeding."

"Yes, I see many *nnonko*," Kwaku replied.

"It was a big job to build the road, and it has to be maintained well," Nana continued. "If the road isn't good, travelers will tell the Asantehene."

The group waved to the *nnonko* who stood and waved back.

"Are your head loads too heavy?" Nana asked.

The boys looked at each other, not certain what to say. "Water is heavy," Kwame answered, "but I can carry it. I want everyone to keep drinking water so my load will get lighter."

"My basket's okay," Baako said. "I carry this much most days."

"Mine's all right," Kwaku replied.

"I'm happy with your work," Nana reassured them. "You can trade head loads if you want. We'll reach our destination before dark. The *nnonko* will bring water from a stream to the camp. We'll have time to bathe before we eat.

"I'll hire women to cook for us. We'll buy meat and vegetables for a soup, and use our own plantains and cassava for fufu. Kwame, find out where the best water is and refill your pot after we eat."

"I will. I'll be tired tonight, Papa, but I'm really happy to be on this trip."

"I'm glad you boys are here," Nana said. "You're already strong from working on our farms. You'll get stronger as we travel."

The delegation continued at a good pace even as the group tired. In the mid-afternoon, Nana recognized the terrain and knew that the group was approaching the town where they would spend the night. He told the Okyeame to signal the group to stop for a brief rest. The Okyeame explained Nana's plans for the evening and asked the musicians to play to announce the group's arrival.

WHEN THE DELEGATION ENTERED THE TOWN, NANA AND THE LOCAL CHIEF GREETED each other with pleasure. Each bowed his head slightly and removed his cloth briefly from his left shoulder. They were friends from Nana's earlier trips. The local chief invited Nana and the elders to his council room to rest and talk.

The Okyeame asked the boys, one other elder, and Asare to join him while he talked to the camp manager and paid for the shelter, the evening meal, and breakfast for the group. The supervisor showed them the shelter, which included several huts, hearths with firewood, a path to a stream, and a latrine.

The headmen and *nnonko* put down their loads, stretched, and walked around to relax and fetch water for drinking and bathing. Women from the town prepared their meal.

When soup and fufu were ready, women served the chiefs and elders in the council room and others at the hearth. After the meal several men took out chewing sticks to clean their teeth. Some smoked pipes. Small groups played *Oware* by digging holes in the ground and gathering stones to play with. Others took out boards and playing pieces for checker games. Children from the town, curious to see the travelers, crowded around the camp. Nana talked to the local chief.

"The tax collectors visited us and hurried back to Kumasi," the chief told Nana. "They were satisfied with the condition of the Tano Road."

"Did they talk about war with the Fante?" Nana asked.

"Yes, the Asantehene defeated the Fante army, but he remains on the coast to capture rebels. Both sides lost many soldiers in battle and also because of smallpox. The disease is deadly."

"That's what we heard, too. Did you send soldiers for the war?" Nana was curious.

"No, the Asantehene didn't call us. He's saving us for another time. I'm glad because some of the soldiers may have taken smallpox to their towns. That's a disaster." Nana agreed.

"Do you think that the Asantehene will return to Kumasi for the *Odwira*," the local chief asked.

"I don't know," Nana replied. "His presence in Fante territory will secure peace, but the *Odwira* is important for the chiefs. If he's not in Kumasi, we'll need to know why."

"We have to go to Kumasi to learn what's happening," the local chief agreed. "I'll leave in two days. Rest now. I'll see you in the morning. *Dayie – Good night.*"

"*Dayie*," Nana replied.

As the sun set, an elder called children together at a travelers' hearth.

Garden eggs

"A story, a story, let me tell you a story," he began in a friendly voice as he sat on a stool with children surrounding him.

"Good," Kwaku said. "I'm too tired for a game."

"Do you like garden eggs and okra?" the story-teller asked the group.

"Of course," Kwame answered. "We always eat them in soup."

The younger children nodded and answered loudly, "Yes! Yes! They grow on our farms."

"Then listen to my story and learn why garden eggs grow near the ground and okra stands up tall," the storyteller said.

"There was a time when okra and garden eggs lived next to each other and used the same courtyard.

As you know, they have different shapes. Garden eggs are small and round and grow on short bushes. Okra bushes are tall, and okra pods are long and lean and pointy. Because of their different shapes, the two could help each other. The garden eggs hoed the ground and dug out yams and cassava. Standing tall, the okra harvested corn and palm nuts.

"The okra and garden eggs were peaceful neighbors for a long time, but they couldn't agree on one thing – where to put their trash.

"Finally, the garden eggs told the okra, 'We're ashamed of the way the courtyard looks. There is too much trash here. Help us dig a hole for the trash.'

"The okra refused to help. 'We don't like digging,' they said. 'We're tall, and digging is hard for us.'

"'Then we will do it ourselves,' the garden eggs replied, and they did.

"Seeing this, the okra said, 'Bring us the hole so that we may see it.'

"'Since *Nyame* created us, have you ever seen anyone lift a hole?' the garden eggs asked. 'As for you, fill a strainer with water for us to drink. When you do that, we will bring the hole for you to see.'

"'Do not take us for fools,' the okra said, 'or we will beat you.'

"'Do not take us for fools,' the garden eggs retorted, 'or we will beat you.'

"The garden eggs and okra argued so loudly that *Nyame* heard them and sent a

Okra

vulture to bring a garden egg and an okra pod to talk to him. The two spoke the words that were in their mouths, and *Nyame* listened carefully. He consulted his councilors and made a decision. His spokesman pronounced a judgment against the okra.

"This is why we still see garden egg bushes growing close to the ground, for they are thanking *Nyame* for his judgment. Okra bushes stand up tall, and the okra pods point their noses to the sky to say they will fight because *Nyame* gave the wrong judgment.

"As for us people, we accept *Nyame's* decision, and eat both garden eggs and okra in our soup.

"This is my story. If it be sweet or it if be not sweet, take some elsewhere and let some come back to me."

The local children clapped to thank the storyteller. Kwame, Kwaku, and Baako smiled broadly and thanked the story teller, too. "We'll sleep better now," they assured him.

"Mama grows garden eggs and okra on her farm," Kwame said. "I hope she knows this story. I'll ask her when I'm home."

The boys returned to their hut to unroll their sleeping mats. Each put on his cloak, and covered his head with the hood. "Mosquitoes won't bite us now, and we'll be warm," Kwaku said. The boys stretched out and quickly fell asleep.

CHAPTER 26

The Long Trip

THE TRAVELERS ROSE AT DAWN AND GREETED THE COOL MORNING AIR WITH YAWNING and stretching, and they washed with the water collected the night before. Women from the town prepared a breakfast of bananas and rice porridge sweetened with honey.

"I slept great," Kwaku said. "All of that walking yesterday made me tired. I wasn't cold last night with the cloak. I love the hood. Mosquitoes didn't bite my ears."

"Same for me," Kwame agreed. "I'm going to wear my cloak for a little while to stay warm. We won't have to sweep courtyards this morning, but we'll probably have to sweep the shelter."

"I'll see children on my way to the latrine," Baako said. "I'll tell them to come help us sweep and then eat with us. That's only fair. They listened to the story last night. I'll hurry. I'm starved."

The boys rolled up their sleeping mats and repacked them, and soon joined the others around the hearth to eat breakfast. "Papa says we should drink a lot of water since we're in the sun so much," Kwame said. "I'm already thirsty."

Nana thanked the local chief for his hospitality. "I hope that we see each other in Kumasi," he said.

"I hope so, too," the local chief replied. "My group will depart tomorrow. All of the delegations to Kumasi that use this road have passed by now. Have a safe journey."

Within a short time the Tanoso group set off with drums echoing and horns blaring. Everyone walked with renewed energy in the cool morning air. Local children waved and shouted, "*Nanteyie* – Safe journey." Kwame, Kwaku, and Baako waved as they walked just behind the musicians. They liked seeing the road ahead.

Nana soon confided to the Okyeame, "The local chief told me an interesting story. The delegation of the young chief, the one who's our neighbor, stayed with him two days ago. The chief was bringing an unusual gift for the Asantehene, a leopard cub."

"Oh, no!" the Okyeame reacted to the news. "Where did the cub come from?"

"Our neighbor said that his *nnonko* had found it in a pit trap. He's feeding it sheep's milk when he can find it, and otherwise soup. I thought that he would agree to protect leopards, but he didn't let me know. He must believe that he's protecting this one while gaining the favor of the Asantehene."

"Will the Asantehene accept the gift?"

"Perhaps," Nana replied, "but we all know that it's difficult to raise a wild animal. It's likely to die in captivity, so the Asantehene might release it while it's alive. He'll understand that the young chief wants to honor him, but I think the king will want to protect the cub, as we do," Nana replied. "It's a valuable animal. Let's think about what we can do."

THE TANOSO GROUP WALKED STEADILY EVEN AS THE AIR GREW WARMER. INDIVIDUALS stopped at different times to drink water, and several wore a scarf. The *nnonko* chewed kola nuts, and Nana offered kolas to others. Only a few took a kola to chew, but the number was greater than on the day before.

The boys identified the few monkeys and birds that came into view. "Animals like the forest better than a great-road," Baako commented. "The cover is better for them in the forest."

"No webs or spiders on the road," Kwame added.

"No snakes or tsetse flies or ants," Kwaku observed. "That's good. Rats run across the road. They're not afraid of anything. We won't see duikers or porcupines. They like trees and shade and water."

"Look ahead," Baako said.

"Baboons!" Kwame replied. "Why are they here?"

The Okyeame and Asare called for the group to stop. They counted almost twenty baboons on the road. Five guards stood in the middle of the road on the near side with spears and machetes. The guards worked for the local chief and were paid by the Asantehene to keep the road safe.

"Asare and I will find out what's happening," the Okyeame said, and the two walked forward carrying spears.

The Okyeame greeted the guards and explained, "We're on our way to Kumasi from Tanoso. What's happening with the baboons?"

"Greetings," the spokesman for the guards replied. "We're trying to drive this troop away. They want our food. Be careful. They've backed off, but they may charge. Are you carrying food?"

"Yes, in the head loads," the Okyeame answered.

"Wait here until the baboons leave," the guard cautioned. "They're bold."

The Okyeame and Asare returned to the group with the message. Nana told everyone to set head loads down, rest, and drink water. The guards' spokesman joined them and greeted Nana.

"We don't usually see baboons," he explained. "We think that the war with the Fante drove them from the coast into the forest, and that the large monkeys chased them here."

"Asare, tell the *nnonko* to take their machetes out," Nana instructed. "I'll tell the headmen. We're a big group. We'll help drive the baboons off."

"Thank you. We welcome your help," the guard said.

Nana gave directions. "We'll leave the head loads here with the boys and elders. I'll stay here, too, while the headmen and *nnonko* spread out across the road with the guards and walk toward the baboons waving machetes and spears and making noise. Don't let the baboons circle around you, and don't kill any. Asare, let the *nnonko* know. The Okyeame will lead the way."

Baboons on the great-road

Holding machetes, Kwame, Kwaku, and Baako stood with the elders near the head loads. The guards, headmen, and *nnonko* approached the baboons, making hissing sounds and waving their arms and weapons and scarves. The baboons stood their ground and stared at the advancing phalanx. The men reached the baboons and nudged the larger animals. Most of the baboons turned and walked away slowly.

Suddenly one large male baboon stopped, turned, and charged Asare, grabbing his spear. Asare held on to his spear, pushed back, and the two struggled. Other *nnonko* tried to help Asare, but he shouted to them, "Let me do this." Some of the larger baboons turned now to face the men and spit at them. Baboons on each side of the road evaded the men and rushed toward the head loads.

"Here they come," Baako shouted.

"Swing machetes in front of you," an elder instructed.

Waving machetes and yelling, Kwame and Baako worked side by side to drive two baboons away. "They think that we're one big person," Baako said with relief.

"We're big enough to scare them," Kwame replied.

Kwaku stayed near the head loads and swung his machete. A baboon approached and spit at him. Kwaku backed away and stopped swinging. The baboon brushed past him, leaped onto a basket, and began taking everything out.

"Stop," Kwaku yelled while trying to push the baboon off of the basket. "Don't take our fish. Don't take our bananas. We need to eat."

The baboon resisted. Kwame and Baako quickly approached the baboon from behind, yelling at it. Each grabbed one of the baboon's shoulders and pulled. The baboon resisted. Kwaku began swinging his machete in front of the baboon once more. The baboon finally gave up and left.

The baboon holding Asare's spear did not let go, nor did Asare. Asare and the baboon stood face to face. Each tugged, and together they rotated the spear from side to side. The baboon made grunting noises, and Asare uttered a high pitched screaming sound to frighten the baboon. Other baboons had retreated, freeing more *nnonko*, who came to Asare's assistance. This time he welcomed them.

Two *nnonko* approached the large baboon from behind and grasped and pulled on his shoulders. He growled but seemed to sense that he was outnumbered and moved away, returning slowly to his troop, looking behind from time to time.

Nana called everyone together. "Asare, you did well," he said. "You're strong. Thank the *nnonko* for their help, and tell them that we'll rest now for a short time, drink some water, and then start out again." The elders patted each other on their shoulders to show relief that this encounter was over.

"Thank you for your help. The road ahead is good. Travel well," the spokesman for the guards said to Nana.

The Okyeame complimented the boys. "You were brave. Baboons are tricky. They usually don't attack, but they're experienced robbers. They'll push you out of the way to steal from you."

"We never see baboons around Tanoso," Kwaku said. "I wasn't sure what to do."

"Crocodiles keep baboons away from the river near Tanoso," the Okyeame explained. "We might see them again here. I think that the guard is right. The war with the Fante probably drove them here."

THE MORNING OF THE TRIP'S SECOND DAY WAS THE MOST EXCITING. AFTERWARDS, the days were long with little variety. Everyone knew that they would arrive at their destination on the eighth day. They balanced walking, talking, drinking water, resting, and eating to keep a steady pace.

The travelers' shelters were always ready for them.

Fallen trees and other roadblocks had all been cleared from the great-road, and the Asantehene's guards patrolled to promote quick and safe travel. The Tanoso group greeted the guards and looked forward to learning news of the road from them. Excitement built as the delegation approached Kumasi.

Kwame, Kwaku, and Baako woke before dawn on the eighth day. "We're almost there!" Kwaku whispered to the others.

"Yes! Yes!" Kwame agreed. "I knew we could do it. This trip is hard, but now we'll see Kumasi."

"We have to walk back," Baako reminded them, "but not right away. Let's get up."

The boys quickly joined the others to eat breakfast, repack the head loads, and sweep the shelter. The routine was familiar and quickly accomplished. Nana thanked the local headman for his hospitality. Several people came to say, "*Nanteyie.*" With the musicians playing and leading the way, the Tanoso delegation departed.

Knowing that they were close to Kumasi helped the musicians and the boys begin with a fast pace. The headmen and *nnonko* kept up easily because their head loads were lighter now that the delegation had eaten the food that it started with. The cool morning air helped, too. Closer to Kumasi, the terrain slowed the group. They climbed hills with care and descended slowly, rebalancing the head loads.

While walking, Nana and the Okyeame talked quietly. "Our trip has been long and our group has done well," Nana said. "The boys are strong from their farm work, but the trip has tested them. They've become even stronger. I'm pleased with them.

"We'll have three days to take care of business before the *Odwira*," Nana continued. "We need to learn if the Asantehene is in Kumasi. We need to know if we're at peace with the Fante. I want to find Nana Somfo and talk about the leopard cub."

"There is much to learn right away," the Okyeame agreed.

"When we arrive at Elder Kwadwo's, home, we'll unload provisions and store them there. Our *nnonko* will stay on his farm with his *nnonko*. Tomorrow will be a day of rest for them. They'll have work after that, and Asare will bring them into Kumasi on the fourth day.

"I'll show the boys around Kumasi tomorrow," Nana continued. "I want to introduce them to the city. I'm looking forward to that."

"Maybe they'll want a day of rest, too," the Okyeame commented.

Nana smiled, "They're young and strong. They'll be happy if they don't have to carry head loads. We elders should rest, but there isn't time."

The Okyeame chuckled. "We've done well," he said.

As the delegation approached Kumasi, Nana observed to the elders, "In the last year much of the forest here has been burned and turned into farms."

"The Asantehene has his own farms, but he expects the local farmers to raise large crops," an elder commented. "There are thousands of people here to feed, especially during the *Odwira*."

"Look at the farmers entering the road," the Okyeame said. "They're carrying huge loads."

As traffic on the great-road grew dense, the Tanoso delegation stretched out and stayed to one side. "I see more people here than I ever do in Tanoso, even on market day," Kwame said.

"Look at the head loads they're carrying," Baako remarked. "Some are full of chickens and even sheep. I don't know how they do it."

"We're almost there," Kwaku sounded relieved. "I can hardly believe it."

The delegation was energized as it approached a city gate. Sentries stopped the group to question Nana and the Okyeame. "I'm the Tanosohene, and I'm bringing my people to the *Odwira*," Nana explained. "We have machetes and spears and three guns." The sentries were satisfied and allowed the delegation to enter the city.

CHAPTER 27

Exploring Kumasi

NANA LED THE DELEGATION TO THE HOME OF HIS COUSIN, ELDER KWADWO, WHO GREETED everyone enthusiastically. "You've arrived! *Akwaaba*! Welcome!" he repeated. "You've traveled far. Put your head loads down. Take water and rest."

"*Medaase*. It's good to see you," Nana exclaimed with a broad smile. "We're finally here, and our journey was good. I hope that you and your family are well."

"We're all very well," Elder Kwadwo replied. "After everyone rests we'll settle your group. Your *nnonko* will stay with mine on my farm. Elders and headmen will go to the different homes of our clansmen and also my wife, Madam Adjowa's, family. Some will be in the city and some in villages nearby. Our people are here to show everyone the way. You and the boys will stay with my family here in Kumasi."

"*Medaase*," Nana said again. "The *nnonko* will leave my regalia in your courtyard and go to your farm with my foreman, Asare. He knows the way. The rest of us will go to our new homes."

"When everyone has prepared for dinner, they'll return here," Elder Kwadwo explained. "We'll eat together. All of you should rest well tonight. Nana, one of my sons will take care of your boys."

"*Medaase*," Nana repeated, and he asked his group to prepare for the evening. Turning to the boys, he added, "Uncle Kwadwo and Auntie Adjowa have welcomed us. You'll be comfortable here, and you'll help with the chores. Tomorrow I'll walk with you through Kumasi so you'll know your way around."

One of Elder Kwadwo's sons stepped forward. "My name is Kofi Edu, and I'm eleven years old," he said. The Tanoso boys introduced themselves.

"I'm Kwaku, and I'm eleven, like you."

"I'm Baako, and I'm thirteen."

"I'm Kwame, and I'm twelve. Your name, Edu, means the 'tenth.' Are there really ten Kofis in your family?"

"Oh, no, I was named after one of my uncles. Just call me Kofi. Come with me and I'll show you where we'll sleep tonight. We can squeeze into one hut. That's better than sleeping outside. Then I'll show you the neighborhood." The Tanoso boys followed Kofi with pleasure, eager to have a home in Kumasi.

Kofi Edu took his new friends to the home next door. "This is where my mother's mother lives. Put your things in this hut," he said, opening the door. Once outside again, he pointed to a corner of the courtyard. "We take baths over there behind the fence. I've got water for you."

"*Medaase*, Kofi. Where is the latrine?" Kwame asked.

"At the edge of town. Take your baths first, and then we'll go there and walk around before we eat."

Before long the boys ventured out to explore the neighborhood. "*Maadwo* – Good evening," Kofi Edu said many times to adults on the street, who replied. His greeting was echoed by the Tanoso boys.

"We'll stay on the narrow streets and go to the latrine first," Kofi Edu said. "The big streets are too busy. We're in the Anowo ward, not far from the market. Remember the name in case you get lost, and remember the way to the latrine."

"The houses here are tall with really steep roofs," Kwaku observed. "It would be hard to tie palm fronds on them. There are so many people in the street. Do they all fit inside at night? What do they all do? What do you do?"

"People have farms and crafts, and a lot of them serve the king," Kofi Edu explained. "My papa has a big farm and works there with people in our family and his *nnonko*. He sells a lot of food. There are thousands of people in Kumasi, and we all have to eat."

"I don't like to farm," Kofi Edu continued. "I'm apprenticed to my mother's brother as a wood carver. I help him and other carvers find good wood and carve stools and boxes and doors and tables and other furniture for rich people. I'm learning to carve umbrella frames now. I'm good at carving already."

"Will you ever have a farm?" Kwame asked.

"I don't know. Maybe not," Kofi Edu said. "Or maybe when I'm married, my wife will have a farm. Now I help my mama and papa on their farms."

Baako noticed children carrying water pots. "Where are they getting water?" he asked. "I didn't see any streams nearby."

"There's a marsh outside of the city near here," Kofi Edu said, "and the Nsuben River on the other side. My sister and I collect water from both places, and we have to make many trips. The water's heavy."

Baako reassured Kofi Edu saying, "We'll help you while we're here." Kwame and Kwaku nodded their agreement.

"*Medaase*," Kofi Edu replied. "You have an idea of my neighborhood now. Let's go home."

The boys returned to Elder Kwadwo's courtyard for a dinner of peanut soup and fufu. The group ate well and thanked their host for his hospitality. Some were curious to see Kumasi right away, and Elder Kwadwo had a suggestion.

"There's a platform nearby where the Asantehene holds court for our neighborhood. There'll be music there tonight, and people will dance the *Adowa*. We can go there."

Nana encouraged the boys to go saying, "The *Adowa* here will be more elaborate than ours in Tanoso. You should go and see it. You know the dance." Several others decided to go. Nana and the Okyeame stayed back to prepare for the work of the coming days.

Elder Kwadwo left his home with a small group shortly before sundown and walked to a wide street. The Tanoso boys were curious about the street, but it was so crowded that they could barely see anything.

They followed Elder Kwadwo to an open public space with a platform where drummers, bell ringers, and singers were gathering. Men, women, and children of all ages including babies tied to their mothers' backs filled the area in front of the platform. Before long, the drumming started. Women rang bells steadily while singers responded in a chorus. The crowd began to move.

A few dancers performed in front of the platform, moving with small steps in circles and straight lines while waving a white handkerchief. Some of them jumped several times in place to show their strength. More and more dancers joined in. Most of the Tanoso group danced.

The boys observed at first, then Kofi Edu said, "Let's dance. We can do this."

"I'm coming," Kwame replied.

"I know this dance," Kwaku added. "I'm coming, too."

"Here I go," Baako asserted.

Once dancing, the boys heard only drums, bells, and singers. They sometimes closed their eyes while moving to the music. They joined the crowd to sing a response. Being part of a crowd and mesmerized by the *Adowa* dance was the perfect beginning for their *Odwira* celebration.

The music was still lively when Elder Kwadwo tapped each boy on the shoulder. "It's time to leave now," he said. "We'll be up early in the morning." The boys knew that he was right, but left slowly. People in the street held torches to light the way. The Asantehene's guards, who protected the city at night, walked by. The boys felt certain that Kumasi was welcoming and safe.

After putting on his cloak and stretching out on his sleeping mat, Kwame thought about the sights and sounds that he had seen and heard that day. The noise of the city was unlike the noise of the forest. There were no bush babies crying or parrots squawking or even insects humming. The city sounds came from music and the talk and footsteps of people in the street. There was so much light from the torches that no stars were visible in the night sky. Seeing guards patrol the streets was new. Seeing crowds was the biggest change from life in Tanoso. Kwame already liked the big city. He thought Kwaku and Baako would agree.

Kofi Edu woke the other boys early the next morning. The Tanoso boys stretched and groaned and said that they were still tired after walking and carrying head loads for eight days. "It was worse than farm work," Baako said, "but we did it."

"You're in a big city now," Kofi Edu reminded them. "There's a lot to do, and Nana told me to wake you early. He and my papa want us to sweep the courtyard before everyone comes to eat."

The Tanoso boys stretched a little more, got up, and stepped into the courtyard. They walked to the latrine and washed with water that Kofi Edu had collected the day before. "Thanks for the water, Kofi," Kwame said. "I usually have to collect water in the morning."

"We'll have to collect more after breakfast," Kofi Edu explained.

"We know about those chores," Kwaku replied.

The boys walked next door, where they greeted Uncle Kwadwo, Auntie Adjowa, and Nana. Picking up brooms, the four worked quickly to sweep the courtyard. Other members of the Tanoso group arrived as the boys finished and put away the brooms. "We did this job just in time!" Kofi Edu said with satisfaction. "Thanks for helping."

Madam Adjowa provided her guests with sweet corn porridge, oranges, and pineapples for breakfast. She served the children last, and they greeted everyone before sitting down to eat.

After breakfast, Kwaku could not resist saying to Kwame and Baako, "What do you think of the oranges and pineapples. Aren't they great!"

"I really like them," Kwame agreed. "We usually don't see them in the Tanoso market."

"We eat them a lot," Kofi Edu explained. "They come from the coast. I like them, too."
Baako shook his head. "So many new things," he said.

Nana invited Kofi Edu to join his group and explore the market. "Why don't you take my daughter, Akosua, too?" Madam Adjowa suggested. "She knows everything about the market."

"Would you like to come, Akosua?" Nana asked. "You would be welcome. You and my daughter, Akua, are the same age, so I know that you can help us."

"Oh, yes, thank you, Nana. I want to come," Akosua replied. "I'll bring a basket."

"Then it's settled," Nana said with a grin. "I'm blessed that five children will attend me after they collect water. We'll leave while it's still cool."

Tanoso elders and headmen had their own plans for the day to sell or trade goods that they had brought to Kumasi. Nana delegated an elder to sell kola nuts and corn for him. He would need the gold dust before long.

— CHAPTER 28 —

The Asantehene's Palace

After collecting water, Akosua and the boys gathered around Nana, clapping their hands. "We're back," Akosua said. "We're ready to leave."

"Let's look at the Asantehene's palace first," Nana suggested, smiling broadly. "Elder Kwadwo told me that the Asantehene and many of his soldiers returned from Fante territory only two days ago. I'm glad that the king will be here for the *Odwira*. We'll see them all at the festival."

Adopm Street in Kumasi

"When the soldiers arrived, there was a big parade," Kofi Edu explained. "It seemed like the beginning of the *Odwira* festival. Nana, will you have an audience with the Asantehene this morning?"

181   *We Are Akan*

"Oh, no. We'll just look at the palace," Nana replied.

"Let's hurry," Kofi Edu urged. "That area gets crowded. So many people do business there."

Nana wore one of his best cloths, a gold ring on a finger of his right hand, and sandals decorated with gold ornaments. He wanted to be respected as a successful chief without being ostentatious. Around his waist he tied a leather pouch containing gold dust and weighing equipment. Akosua placed an empty basket on her head.

Nana and the children walked along narrow streets until they reached Adopm Street, which was broad and lined with elaborate one story houses. This street would take them to the Asantehene's palace. Tall trees offered a resting place to those who walked by. Chiefs were often shaded by a colorful umbrella borne by an *odonko*. "Look at this beautiful sight," Nana said. "Kumasi is famous for its broad streets and gathering places."

"Papa, why aren't you using an umbrella?" Kwame asked.

"It's not hot," Nana answered, "and I didn't want to bring an *odonko*. I just wanted to be with you children. I'll use my umbrella in the *Odwira* parade."

"I'll warn you about the king's messengers," Kofi Edu alerted the group. "When you hear drums, they're coming. Get out of the way. They travel fast, and they'll knock you down. The Asantehene wants his business done fast."

"*Medaase*, Kofi. We'll be careful," Nana said. "Look, we see people from all over the kingdom."

"There are men in long white robes," Kwaku pointed out. "Do you know who they are, Nana?"

"I don't know them, but I know they're from the savannah. Men there wear robes to protect themselves from the sun. It's hot, and there aren't many trees. We don't see those people in Tanoso because the Asantehene doesn't let them travel outside of Kumasi. Only Akans can travel freely in the forest."

"When you get close, listen to them talk," Kofi Edu told the others. "You won't understand them."

"I see people with different kinds of scars on their face," Baako said quietly to Kwame and Kwaku. "I wonder if I'll see any Gurunsi."

"We'll help you look," Kwame and Kwaku offered.

"Oh, I hear drums. Look ahead!" Kofi Edu shouted and pointed. The group barely had time to step aside before two drummers ran past them followed by two men carrying golden swords.

"Are those swords real?" Baako wanted to know.

"The tax collectors had a golden sword," Kwame remembered. "Grannie said their sword was real."

"The swords are decorated and they're real," Nana replied. "Everyone who does business for the Asantehene carries one.

"Listen to the street noise," Nana continued. "We're still in the forest, but there are more people than trees in Kumasi, and people make noise."

"That's what Mama said about Kumasi," Kwame recalled. "She didn't like the noise. I don't think that it's bad, and I see a few trees here."

"Look at the houses," Akosua said. "I love the colors. White on the top and red with decorations on the bottom. Sometimes I walk on this street just to see them. They belong to people who work for the king. Nobody else can live there."

"How do you know, Akosua?" Kwame asked.

"My papa told me. The houses have an open room in the front. Papa said that people work there so that everyone will know what's going on. You can see people working now."

"*Medaase*, Akosua. You're helping us," Nana said. "Behind the open rooms are other rooms where people work, too."

Head loads of pottery

"Look at the women with huge loads of pottery. Why don't the pots fall?" Baako asked.

"They're covered by nets," Akosua explained. "You can't see the nets from here. The women are taking the pots to the market to sell. We'll see them again."

The group walked further, and then paused under a tree. "Let's stop here," Nana said. "You see ahead a wall that surrounds many buildings. That's the palace. How many buildings can you count?"

"There are too many to count," Kwaku observed. "The palace looks like a beehive. The Asantehene must have a big family and a lot of *nnonko!*"

Nana chuckled. "You're right, and a lot of people work for him. Some of them live there. Many of the buildings inside are decorated like the houses we just passed. In the middle there is a big courtyard where the Asantehene has meetings."

"Will you go to a meeting there?" Kwaku asked.

"On Sunday the chiefs will meet with the Asantehene at the palace. For the *Odwira* parade, the Asantehene's court sits in the Place of the Cannons."

"What are cannons?" Kwame asked.

"They're big guns that whites use to protect their castles," Nana explained. "Long ago, Asantehene Osei Tutu captured these cannons from the Denkyira. Whites at Elmina Castle gave them to the Denkyira king when they were trading partners. The cannons are old and can't fire now, but Asantehenes have kept them for everyone to see."

"Why do the whites want big guns?" Kwaku asked.

"Whites fight each other from their castles and ships," Nana explained. "We've heard from traders about cannons firing balls as big as coconuts at ships, and the ships firing back. Cannons are powerful and make a lot of noise, more than our guns."

"What do the chiefs and the Asantehene talk about when they meet?" Kwame asked.

"The Asantehene will tell us about the war with the Fante and trading with whites and savannah people. We've heard that some whites don't trade for prisoners anymore. We'll want to know about that. We always need guns and ammunition from the whites.

"The chiefs will tell the Asantehene and his council what we're doing in our districts and if we want his help. We'll talk about taxes, gold mining, clearing more land to farm, and maintaining the great-roads. The meeting will take a long time because so many will be there."

"That sounds hard, Papa," Kwame said.

"It is hard, but it's important because both the king and the chiefs want a strong kingdom. Chiefs who live closer to Kumasi come for meetings more often, and those meetings are shorter. *Odwira* meetings are always long. It's the only time that all of us are together. I'll tell my council what I've learned when I'm home."

"Papa, does the Asantehene really talk to you? What is he like?" Kwame asked. "Mama said that she saw Asantehene Osei Kwame, and that he was magnificent."

"Your mother is right, and this Asantehene is magnificent too. He's new on the stool. He's done very well. He's smart and brings good people to work at the palace. He's a brave general. He led the army against the Fante. This was his first war as the Asantehene, but he says that he is a man of peace. I hope so. He usually doesn't speak directly to us, though. He talks through his *okyeame,* as I do."

"Can the Asantehene do anything that he wants to do?" Kwaku asked.

"Oh, no. No chief can. He has to follow our laws and work with a council, but he's powerful."

"How big is the kingdom?" Baako wanted to know.

"Kumasi's in the middle of the forest, and the Asantehene rules the forest all of the way to the ocean," Nana explained. "In the other direction, he rules some of the people in the savannah. They pay taxes to the kingdom.

"We know about the great-road that we call the Tano Road. There are eight great-roads to connect every part of the kingdom to Kumasi. Messengers and the army can travel to the end of each road and return to Kumasi in the time between two *Adae* ceremonies. Asantehenes believe that the kingdom is big enough to be safe and not too big for them to communicate with all of the chiefs."

"Our kingdom is so big," Kwame said. "I wonder if I can walk to every part of it. That's what traders have to do."

As the group stood near the palace wall, they heard drums again. "Get out of the way," Kofi Edu shouted. The drummers and messengers, now returning to the palace, brushed past the group again.

"That was quick work," Kwaku remarked.

"We'll watch the people here for awhile," Nana said, "but we need to drink something first. Let's go to the food vendor over there and buy coconuts. Do you want pineapple slices, too?"

"Wonderful, wonderful," Kwame said. "We don't have coconuts in Tanoso and only a few pineapples."

"Yes!" the group agreed.

Drinking coconut milk and eating pineapple slices, Nana and his group watched people coming and going through the palace gate. The Akan men wore fine cloths. Some chiefs were shaded by umbrellas. There were a few men from the savannah who wore robes and turbans. "There is a parade of visitors," Kwame observed. "Will they all talk to the Asantehene?"

"Oh, no," Nana answered. "Only a few will. There are many people just inside the gate to handle business. Most visitors will leave a gift, and some will want to talk about their taxes, getting more land or *nnonko*, whether they have to send soldiers to the next war, maybe other business."

"Do you have a gift for the Asantehene, Nana?" Baako asked.

"Yes, I brought *akpeteshie* for him. That's the usual gift. He has so many visitors that he needs a big supply. The Okyeame will take it to the palace tomorrow."

"Why are some people wearing *kente* now?" Kwaku asked. "It's too early."

"Yes, people should dress well, but not yet in a *kente*," Nana responded. "That's for the *Odwira* parade. Look, there's something surprising. I see someone coming to the palace wearing a *kente* cloth and shaded by a fancy umbrella."

"His umbrella is too fancy for now. Why is he using it?" Kwame asked. "He should wait for the parade."

"Some chiefs are proud and want everyone to notice them," Nana explained.

Nana was startled when he realized that the chief they were watching was his neighbor, Nana Somfo, surrounded by elders and *nnonko*. The group stopped at the palace gate. "My neighbor may be delivering his unusual gift," Nana thought.

Baako recognized Nana Somfo, too. "That's the chief from across the river," Baako said to Nana. "He looks proud today. I remember his *odonko* who's carrying the umbrella. Why is he here, Nana?"

"Maybe he's bringing a gift for the Asantehene," Nana replied. Nana Somfo quickly gained entrance to the palace.

"Look, horses!" Kofi Edu exclaimed. "Kwame, you wanted to see horses. Here they are."

"Oh, yes! They're big, and the men sitting on them are up so high. The horses are dancing through the crowd," Kwame observed with excitement.

"The riders wear big turbans. That makes them even taller," Akosua said. "The men are talking to their horses, and the horses understand."

"Papa, who are those men?"

"The men and their horses are from the savannah. People say they are Moors. The savannah is big, and I don't know exactly where Moors are from. Maybe we'll find out while we're here. We'll see them again."

"Horses are so beautiful, and they're smart," Akosua said. "They know what their riders want them to do."

Once the group had eaten, Nana surprised them. "Next we'll go to the foreigners' zone," he said.

"The foreigners' zone," Kofi Edu repeated. "I've never been there. I want to see it."

"I do, too," Akosua added. "Papa never takes us there."

"What is it?" Kwame asked.

"Let's find out," Nana replied, smiling.

CHAPTER 29

The Foreigners' Zone

TWO STREETS FROM THE PALACE, NANA'S GROUP ENTERED THE FOREIGNERS' ZONE where they saw small mud houses with flat roofs opening to walled courtyards. Smoke rose from hearths behind the walls. Several men, wearing white robes, walked in the streets where children also played. A few men stood under trees to feed and brush their horses. People spoke languages that Nana and the children did not understand. This was a village scene, but not an Akan village. The foreigners' zone looked like a savannah village.

Nana and the children looked around and tried to understand what they saw. The foreigners looked at them, too, but said nothing. Nana was comfortable. The children were immediately excited. "Look, look at the horses," Kwame whispered pointing to them.

Nana approached a man standing under a tree, brushing a horse that was beige with a black mane and tail.

"*Maakye*," Nana greeted the man. "I am Nana Anyensu. These are my children."

"*Salaam*," the man answered.

"Do you speak Twi?" Nana asked.

"Yes, of course," the man replied. "My name is Amir. You see my scars that look like tears falling down my cheeks. They mean that I'm Hausa but I speak Twi. I've been coming to Kumasi for a long time."

"You have a handsome horse," Nana said.

"*Medaase*," Amir replied.

"These young people would like to learn about horses. Will you help them?"

Looking at the group, Amir smiled and asked, "What would you like to know about my horse?"

"Why are you brushing your horse?"

"I'm cleaning him. He sweats a lot."

"What can a horse do?"

"I ride this one. I rode him here from my homeland, and that's a long way away. I have other horses that carry loads of cloth for me to trade in the Kumasi market. When I return home, they carry kola nuts and metal tools that I'll sell in my homeland."

Nana's group was surprised. "Here people carry cloth on their heads," Kwame said.

"Like me," Akosua added, smiling as she took the basket off of her head. "How do horses carry cloth?"

"People who have horses don't need to carry cloth on their head," Amir answered showing patience. "I tie a large pack of cloth on a horse's back."

"Do you go fast or slow?"

"Horses walk when they're carrying a load and it's hot and they're traveling a long way, but they can run if they need to. Would you like to know my horse's name?"

"Oh, he has a name! What is it?"

"I call him Doki. That's the Hausa word for horse."

"Does he know his name? Does he know other words?"

"Yes, he knows his name and a few other words in Hausa. He doesn't know Twi."

"Can we touch Doki?"

"Yes, but let me tell him first what you plan to do."

Amir faced his horse and rubbed the top of his head and neck while holding his muzzle and speaking to him quietly. Turning to the group, Amir said, "Doki's ready to greet you now. He doesn't understand Twi, but he'll know that you want to be nice to him. One at a time, rub his head or neck or side and tell him your name. Speak softly. Ask him how he is. Let the young girl be first. I'll hold Doki's muzzle."

Akosua stepped up and patted the horse's side because she couldn't reach his neck. "Hello, Doki. My name is Akosua. I live in Kumasi. I hope that you like Kumasi. You are very beautiful." Doki tossed his head and whinnied but stood still. Looking pleased, Akosua reported, "Doki likes me."

"Yes, he's happy to meet you," Amir agreed. Turning to the boys, he asked if they wanted to talk to Doki, too.

Kofi Edu rubbed Doki's side vigorously with both hands. Doki looked at him and whinnied again, pranced, and whinnied once more. The attention pleased Kofi Edu. "Doki, we're friends now," he whispered.

"He's my friend, too," Baako said after petting Doki. "Maybe because I'm tall enough to pet his head. I thought that I would be afraid of horses, but I'm not. Doki's nice."

Kwaku petted Doki and had an idea. "If horses stayed here, they could carry a chief in a chair. A horse could carry a chief fast. That would be fun." Nana shook his head at the thought.

After petting Doki, Kwame said to the group, "If we had horses in the forest, we could ride them to Kumasi. We wouldn't have to walk."

"That would be good for you," Amir agreed, "but Doki wouldn't like it. It's hot here and in the rainy season, it's too wet. I live in a hot land, but it's dry, and we don't have so many bugs. In the forest tsetse flies bite horses, and that scares them."

"Scares me, too," Kwaku admitted.

"Horses always get sick if they stay in the forest. They need grass to eat, and that doesn't grow here. My horses have to bring their own grass from the savannah to the forest. Sometimes other traders bring grass here, but I never know. You see why I can't keep Doki here for long. I return to my homeland often and bring different horses to Kumasi on my trips."

"I'LL WALK DOKI, NOW," AMIR EXPLAINED AS HE PICKED UP A THICK BLANKET AND threw it over the horse's back. Amir then placed a red leather saddle on the blanket, taking care to position it correctly and cinch the straps under the horse's belly. He strapped a stirrup to each side of the saddle. "You step in one of these when you mount a horse, and keep your feet in them when you're riding. They help you stay on, and you can squeeze your legs on the horse's belly to tell him what you want him to do.

"After I put the rest of the gear on Doki, I'll let you sit on him while I walk him. Would any of you like to do that?"

"Oh, yes," everyone replied together. They watched Amir put a bridle over Doki's head, place the bit in his mouth, and then thread the reins on each side of his head, placing them finally across the saddle. While doing this, Amir talked to Doki, and the horse nodded.

Amir named each item of gear. "There's a lot to learn about handling a horse," he explained. "Who wants to sit on Doki first?" All hands went up. Amir selected Kwaku.

"Watch me mount the horse, then I'll help you," Amir told Kwaku.

The group watched as Amir, facing Doki's side and holding onto the reins and the front of the saddle, placed his left foot in the near stirrup. He jumped slightly to swing his right leg over Doki's back and sit upright in the saddle, easing his right foot into the second stirrup. Sitting tall in the saddle, Amir looked down and said to Kwaku, "It's your turn now."

Amir dismounted and shortened the straps of the stirrups. He instructed Kwaku, "I'll lift you at first, but I have to hold the reins, too. Jump and put your left foot in the stirrup and swing your right leg across Doki's back. Ready, jump."

Kwaku jumped while Amir lifted him. Without meaning to, Kwaku pushed himself away from the horse. On the ground once more, Kwaku breathed deeply and said, "That's hard. The horse is really tall, so I need to jump higher. I want to try again."

"This time lean against the horse and hold onto the saddle tightly," Amir told Kwaku. "I'll hold you close to Doki's side." Amir and Kwaku tried a second and third time before Kwaku sat upright in the saddle.

"Here I am! Look at me!" Kwaku shouted. "I'm up high. Doki and I see far away!" The horse whinnied and backed up, but stopped when Amir held the reins tightly.

"Doki knows that you're a new person to him, and that you don't know about horses," Amir explained. "Speak calmly so that he doesn't try to throw you off. Hold the front of the saddle and keep your feet in the stirrups while I hold the reins and walk Doki along the street."

"I'm ready, Doki, are you?" Kwaku whispered, looking frightened but smiling.

"Here we go," Amir said as he walked Doki along the street with Kwaku in the saddle. Amir greeted his friends in Hausa, and they returned the greetings. Several people stopped to watch the unusual sight and seemed amused.

Kwaku rocked back and forth in the saddle even though Doki walked slowly. Kwaku hugged Doki with his legs and felt the horse move and breath deeply. Returning to his friends, he called softly to them again, "Look at me. It's really high up here. I'm moving. Doki is walking for me. I'm so happy that I don't want to get down, ever."

"Is it hard to stay on the horse?" Baako asked.

"It was hard to get on Doki, and it's bumpy up here. I'm holding the saddle so I won't fall off," Kwaku replied.

Amir was willing to take the others for a walk, too. Nana declined. The children accepted with enthusiasm. "Will you hold the reins while I lift them?" Amir asked Nana.

Nana agreed cautiously. He felt Doki's strength and was impressed. He petted Doki's muzzle and talked to him softly. "I like Doki," he told Amir. "He's smart. I wish we could have horses."

When the rides were over, Nana expressed his appreciation. This was an opportunity that he had not expected and welcomed. "Are you one of the Moors?" Nana asked Amir.

"I'm not a Moor. They ride horses like me, but they come from the big cities near the great desert, like Timbuktu and Gao. They're not Hausas. They're not traders. They come to teach us," Amir explained. "They're scholars."

"My friends and I, and maybe some Moors, will be riding our horses for the *Odwira* celebration. If you see Doki and me, come greet us!"

"We'll be there," Nana replied. "We'll wave to you." Amir smiled as the group thanked him and continued its walk.

ONLY BAAKO HAD RESERVATIONS. "MY PAPA TOLD ME THAT THE SOLDIERS WHO CAP-tured him and my mama and my grandparents rode horses."

"Baako's right," Nana said. "Armies of the savannah kingdoms ride horses, and that makes them fast and powerful. The Akan army doesn't have horses so our battles there were difficult. It's the army of the Gonja Kingdom that raids Baako's people for prisoners."

"How could Akans defeat armies that were riding horses?" Kwame asked.

"We have guns, and the savannah people don't," Nana answered. "Guns kill both soldiers and horses. Historians say that the battles were fierce."

"Can't Gonja soldiers get guns, too?" Kwaku wanted to know.

"No, Akans don't let guns go out of the forest," Nana explained. "We buy guns and ammunition from whites on the coast. We don't trade them to the savannah people, and the Asantehene doesn't allow savannah people to travel through the forest to the coast. Our kingdom is so wide that the savannah people cannot go around us.

"Baako's people don't have horses or an army. They're farmers. Soldiers with horses can capture them. That's why so many *nnonko* are Gurunsi."

"I understand better now what happened to my family," Baako said. "The army that attacked their village didn't want land. The soldiers just wanted to capture people to give to the Asantehene."

"That's right, Baako," Nana said. The Asantehene then was Osei Kwame. He gave your parents and grandparents and others to my uncle, who was the chief before me in Tanoso. I grew up with your mama and papa. They met in our *nnonko* village, and you were born there. I wanted you to grow up with Akan children so that you would look and talk like an Akan."

"I understand why I need to look Akan, but I still love my mama and papa," Baako said. "People in Kumasi know that my papa's an *odonko* because he has scars. Is he safe here?"

"Asare is safe with us," Nana assured Baako.

"Nana, riding a horse was fun," Kwaku said. "Will we see cattle here, too?"

"We'll see them in the market," Nana replied. "There's more to do here. I want to buy talismans. We have to find someone who knows Arabic."

CHAPTER 30

Arabic and Talismans

"Let's find someone who makes talismans," Nana proposed. "Amir told me where to look."

"Papa, why do you want talismans? Are you going to be a soldier?" Kwame asked.

"I have to be ready, Kwame. The Asantehene can call us for the army at any time. I inherited a war smock from my uncle. It's strong, but I want to add more talismans. They're tough. Musket balls can't go through them."

"Papa, you said that the savannah armies with horses don't have guns."

"We may have to fight the Fante again, Kwame. They have guns."

"Oh, that's not good," Kwame said.

Nana wanted to encourage the group. "Do any of you know what a book is?" he asked. No one knew. "Do any of you know that what you say can be drawn for someone else to know?" No one knew. "When someone learns what you said by looking at a drawing, the person is reading. Do any of you know what paper is?" No one knew. "Let's find someone who can teach us," Nana proposed.

The group approached a large tree where several men were sitting and drawing on white cloth with reeds. Nana greeted them, "*Mema mo akye*."

"*Salaam*," they replied.

"Does anyone speak Twi?" Nana asked.

"I do," one man replied. "*Akwaaba!*"

"*Medaase*. I am Nana Anyensu from Tanoso, near the Tano River. I want to buy talismans," Nana explained. "Do you make them?"

"My name is Abdul. I am happy to meet you. I make talismans," the man replied. "I'm Hausa, and I've been in Kumasi for a long time. I'm a trader and an imam."

"I know about traders, but what does an imam do?" Nana asked.

"When my people gather to pray, I read to them from the holy book, the Quran. It's in the Arabic language, and I can read and write Arabic. That's what an imam does, and that's why I can make talismans."

"I'm glad to meet you," Nana replied. "Before we talk about talismans, please show my family how people draw what they say so other people can know. We've never seen that. We need to learn what a book is, too."

"I will show you writing and reading," Abdul said as he placed a white cloth on a smooth board, picked up a reed to dip into a gourd full of dark liquid, and drew from right to left. Then, he said what he had drawn. "*Salaam*. That's the Arabic greeting. It means 'Peace.' To answer, you repeat, *Salaam*."

السلام

"*Salaam*," Nana said. "That's a good greeting."

"We call this kind of drawing 'writing.' May I write your names?" Abdul asked.

The group had never seen writing and stood in stunned silence at first, not knowing what to say. "We say our names in Twi," Kwame explained.

"Yes, of course," Abdul replied. "I can write your names with Arabic figures because the figures stand for sounds. We call the figures 'letters.' Your name in Arabic writing will sound the same as it does in Twi."

"I'll be first," Nana offered, and the others joined him.

"I can also write numerals," Abdul said. "I'll write a numeral in front of each name. When you look at the Arabic writing for your name and its numeral and say them, you'll be reading. I will write and you will read from right to left. Watch me."

١ - نانا

٢ - كوفي ايدو

٣ - أكوسوا

٤ - كوامي

٥ - كواكو

٦ - باكو

Abdul identified each numeral and said the sound that each letter represented as he wrote the names. "1. Nana, 2. Kofi Edu, 3. Akosua, 4. Kwame, 5. Kwaku, 6. Baako." Everyone repeated the numerals and names as Abdul wrote them and agreed that the names sounded the way they did in Twi.

"Can you write Akua and Yaw Mensah?" Kwaku asked.

"Yes, I'll add those names and give each a numeral," Abdul replied.

"And Mama and Grannie?" Kwame added.

"I'll add them, too." Abdul said each numeral and name as he wrote.

"7. Akua, 8. Yaw Mensah, 9. Mama, 10. Grannie."

٧ – أكوا

٨ – ياو مينساه

٩ – ماما

١٠ – غراني

The group was fascinated. Abdul pointed to each numeral and name and read them as the group repeated after him once more.

"Can we take the cloth home and practice reading and writing our names?" Kwaku asked. "I want to know how to read and write my name."

"Of course. I'll give the cloth to Nana Anyensu as soon as it's dry," Abdul replied with satisfaction. "Remember to read from right to left, first the numeral and then the name. I'll read everything again, and you say what I read after me."

"Writing is strange," Kwame said to the others. "How can we use it?"

"Most people won't use it much, but if you're a trader, you can keep track of what you sell and buy, and how much gold dust you have," Abdul replied.

"Suppose I had some horses," Nana said. "Can you write *three horses*?"

"Yes," Abdul said. "Here you are. I don't write the numeral for this, just the name of the numeral:"

ثلاثة خيول

"How about *four baskets*?" Kwame asked.

"Here it is," Abdul said. The group leaned close to the board to watch Abdul work.

أربع سلال

"Let's go over what I've written for you," Abdul said. "You're good apprentices." Abdul pointed to each line and read the numerals, names, and phrases once more. The group repeated the sounds, pleased to be reading.

Abdul explained more to his attentive audience. "People put words together on sheets of cloth or leather or paper in what we call a 'book.' Would you like to see a book with paper?"

"Of course," Nana replied for the group.

Abdul looked through a pouch and took out a thick leather bound object that was slightly larger than his hands. "This is a book," he said, opening it and turning a few pages. Everyone saw that the pages were filled with Arabic writing, some of it in bright colors.

"These pages are made of paper, not cloth. Paper is easier to use but much more expensive."

"What is paper made of?" Baako asked.

"Paper is made from trees and bushes in a land far away. You may all touch it but very gently. It will tear."

"It's like touching a leaf, but it's not a leaf," Nana said. "It's not cloth. It's something new."

"For a long time, people have written books about animals, trees, farming, weapons, and many other subjects," Abdul explained. "This book is different. This is the Quran. It tells us what God wants us to know. Here, look at the beginning words. I'll read them to you." Abdul read:

بسم الله الرحمن الرحيم
الحمد لله رب العالمين

"Now I'll translate the Arabic into Twi:"

> In the name of Allah,
> Most benevolent, ever merciful,
> All praise be to Allah.

"This seems like magic," Kwaku said. "Our ancestors could talk to us if what they said were in books. The historians tell us stories now, and we have to remember them. If we had books, we wouldn't have to remember. That might not be good."

"You're right, Kwaku," Nana said. "We'll always want to remember some things."

"Some of our people work for the Asantehene," Abdul added. "We write about important events in the kingdom and the taxes collected. We write messages to the Gonja kings. When they answer, we translate the messages into Twi for the Asantehene."

Hearing the name, Gonja, Baako shuddered. "The Gonja are evil. Why do you help them?" he asked.

Abdul looked sympathetic and replied carefully. "I know the Gonja hurt other people," he said, " but the Asantehene rules them. He has to talk to them. Other Asantehenes have done this, too."

"I understand," Baako said quietly.

Turning to his group, Nana said, "You see that the Asantehene is smart. He uses writing to help him rule."

*Akan war smock covered
with talismans*

"Thank you for showing us writing and a book, Abdul," Nana continued. "Now, I want to talk about talismans. What is your price?"

"For a talisman, I write the lines that I've just read from the Quran on paper. I fold the paper in a special way and put it in a small leather pouch. One talisman costs a half-ounce of gold dust."

Nana was surprised. "That's a high price. How do I know that the talismans will protect me?"

"The writing is powerful. I make talismans for soldiers in my homeland, too. They say the talismans are strong," Abdul answered. "If you sew enough of them on your war smock, no arrows or musket balls will find you."

"I'll buy three talismans even if the price is high," Nana said. "The cost of one talisman is the same as a year's tax for five men. I'll trust you to make powerful talismans."

"You will be satisfied," Abdul replied with confidence. "Watch me write on three pieces of paper. You'll see me place each paper in a leather pouch. You'll know what you have."

Nana and the children watched with fascination as Abdul wrote on three pieces of paper that were half the size of his right hand. When he finished, he read the messages and placed each on another board to dry. Abdul then opened a large leather pouch saying, "I'll take out my scales and weights now."

"I'll use my *domma* weights," Nana explained. "We'll see if our weights are equal. Five *domma* weights will equal a half-ounce. We'll weigh the gold dust separately for each talisman."

The scales attracted the attention of nearby men, who gathered around to watch. "I know the Akan way," Abdul said as he held the balance scales in his left hand between his thumb and pointer finger. On one pan of the scales, he placed a single weight made of brass in the shape of a triangle with a small hole in the middle. "This is my half-ounce weight," he said.

Nana took five weights from his leather pouch and placed them on the scales' second pan. Everyone watched to see if the second pan would lower to match the first. The second pan sank beneath the first.

"Oh," the children said.

"Nana's weights are heavier," Kwaku whispered to the others.

"Your weight is too light. You've been cheating yourself," Nana told Abdul.

"You are right," Abdul replied, looking embarrassed. "The brass caster who made this weight cheated me."

"Let me add something to your side," Nana offered, looking in his pouch for a large seed to place in the first pan. The seed's weight made the pans level.

"We can continue," Abdul said. "*Medaase.*"

Speaking in Hausa, Abdul admonished the men surrounding the group, "Stand back! Your breath will make the gold dust fly off of the pan." The men backed away, and the children did, too, because they knew that this moment was important.

Everyone watched Nana remove his weights from the scales and return them to his pouch. He took out a brass spoon and a small leather bag bound by a cord. He loosened the cord, removed a twist of cloth from the bag, opened it, and spooned out gold dust, placing it slowly and carefully on the scales' empty pan. With four scoops, the weight of the gold dust made the second pan level with the first.

"A half-ounce of gold dust," Nana said.

"Agreed," Abdul replied, taking a feather and a small brass box from his pouch. He loosened the cord around the box, removed the lid, and, with the feather, brushed the gold dust into the box. Nana and Abdul repeated this process twice more to complete the payment.

Abdul verified that the writing on the paper was dry and held it up for all to see. "I'll read the message to you again. Say the lines after me so that you'll speak Arabic once more." Abdul read, and the others repeated the message. Everyone remained quiet to be respectful of Abdul.

With Nana's approval, Abdul folded the pieces of paper and placed them in three leather pouches, tying each with a thin cord. He picked up the cloth with the names on it. "This is dry too. I'll wrap it in a leaf and give everything to Nana Anyensu."

"*Medaase*," Nana replied as he put the cloth and talismans in his pouch and added, "I have a final question for you. Who are the Moors that we saw today going into the palace? They were riding horses."

"They come from Timbuktu," Abdul explained. "That city is very far away, on the edge of the great desert. People there have many books. The Moors come here to bring us books and teach us. They are scholars."

"Thank you for the information," Nana said. "We'll go now."

"Thank you for your business. I bid you farewell," Abdul replied.

As Nana and the children walked away, Kofi Edu exclaimed, "The foreigners' zone is great. I'll tell Papa about it. I want to come back."

"The horses are the best part," Akosua said.

"I want to know more about books. Maybe I can use them if I'm a trader, or maybe I can sell them," Kwame speculated. "Maybe I can use horses, too."

"My parents came from the savannah, but they've never told me about books," Baako said. "I'll ask my papa about them."

"Where do Hausa people live?" Kwaku wondered. "I want to go there. I want to ride a horse again. Is Abdul a chief? How did he learn Arabic?"

"I don't think that Abdul's a chief," Kwame answered. "I think he's a priest. He must have learned Arabic in his training, maybe from the Moors."

"Hausas live far away but not in the desert," Nana added. "They've been coming to the forest to trade for a long time. We'll see other Hausa traders in the market. Are you ready for lunch?"

"Yes, yes, yes, yes, yes," everyone agreed.

— CHAPTER 31 —

The Kumasi Market: Crafts

THE SHORT WALK FROM THE FOREIGNERS' ZONE TO THE MARKETPLACE WAS LIKE A TRIP from the savannah to the forest. Entering the market, Nana said, "Listen to everyone speaking Twi. It sounds like a soft breeze. Smell the good food and look at the crafts. Paths are going everywhere. We're in a city, but the marketplace seems like a forest to me. We're home again."

The children had their own reactions.

"Oh, this place is big, so much bigger than our market in Tanoso," Kwame exclaimed.

"I've never seen so many people in one place. They're all busy. No savannah people are here," Baako observed.

"We'll see them later," Nana replied.

"I love the market," Akosua exclaimed, jumping up and down with excitement. "Women and children are everywhere. I didn't see any women in the foreigners' zone. Are there any?"

"Oh, yes, there are women, but they don't come out in the street. They work in their homes," Nana said.

"There's so much here," Kwaku said, looking around. "Let's start with food."

"Are you hungry?" Nana asked.

"Yes, yes, yes, yes, yes," Kofi Edu, Akosua, Baako, Kwaku, and Kwame replied as a chorus.

"What do you want to eat?"

"I want Grannie's favorite market food, smoked fish and fried plantains," Kwame said. The others laughed and quickly agreed.

"Pineapple, too" Akosua added. "It's juicy, and it will help us feel good on this hot day."

They quickly found the food they wanted, water to drink, and a corner to stand in. "Papa, why didn't you use your gold weights to buy the food?" Kwame asked.

"Oh, the price is so low that it isn't worth the trouble," Nana replied. "I don't use them much in Tanoso either because I know everyone and I trust them. Here, I'm careful if the price is high."

Nana surveyed the vast marketplace. Men, women, and children, wearing brightly colored cloths, some carrying large head loads, walked along crowded pathways to buy, sell, and trade at the stalls. Akan crafts were everywhere—pottery, baskets, wood carvings, beads, *kente*, brass castings, iron tools, and gold work. Asantehenes had supported artisans for generations, and their fine work was popular and essential for both daily life and celebrations.

Imported goods from the savannah and the coast were sold, too, including metal tools, baskets, beads, salt, guns, ammunition, many garments, and different types of cloth. Food from local farms and beef from freshly slaughtered cattle were in separate sections, and prisoners were sold in a distant area.

"What would you like to show us?" Nana asked Kofi Edu and Akosua.

"I want you to meet our Uncle Kojo, our mother's brother," Kofi Edu answered quickly. "He's a master wood carver, and I'm apprenticed to him. I'll take you to his stall."

"I have an idea, too," Akosua replied. "Our mother's sister is a potter, and Mama and I help her. I'll show you her pottery."

"Good ideas. Let's start," Nana said.

Kofi Edu guided the group along several aisles to the wood carvers' section, where he found his Uncle Kojo and introduced him to the others.

"*Maaha* – Good afternoon," Nana said.

"*Yaa. Akwaaba*," Elder Kojo replied.

"We want to see your work," Nana continued. "I understand that Kofi Edu is your apprentice."

"Yes, Kofi's working hard," Elder Kojo replied, smiling. "You'll see here the kind of carving that he's doing. I'm showing items that chiefs like since there are many here for the *Odwira*.

"There are umbrella frames that Kofi has worked on. We also carve umbrella tops, chairs, stools, staffs, and dolls that are always popular. Kofi helped on those too. Kofi, what would you like to show your family?"

"I'll show them a doll," Kofi Edu answered. "Dolls are still hard for me to carve, but I'm learning." Kofi Edu picked up one of the traditional dolls that had a large flat circle for a head and a column for a body. He showed everyone and handed the doll to Akosua.

"She's beautiful," Akosua praised her brother. The others agreed.

Akan doll

"*Medaase*," Kofi Edu said. "Nana, while you're in Kumasi, I'll carve a doll for Akua and you can take it to her. Then, Akosua, I'll carve one for you. I'm getting good enough to do this without a lot of help. Is that okay, Uncle Kojo?"

"Of course," Elder Kojo replied. "Work in my shop so I know that you're using the best wood and doing the carving right. Girls play with the dolls, but remember that they connect us to our ancestors. We color them black like the stools of our ancestor chiefs. Some women use the dolls to ask their ancestors to send a baby to carry on their families. It's very serious."

"Yes, I'll remember," Akosua said.

"Akosua doesn't have to wait," Elder Kojo said. "Let her choose a doll now, and, Kofi, you can carve another one to replace it."

"*Medaase*, Uncle Kojo," Akosua said, feeling very pleased. After looking at several dolls, she picked one out. "I'll take good care of her," she promised her uncle.

"I thank you, too, Kofi," Nana said. "I know that Akua will be thrilled to have a doll that you've carved. Our family will be honored."

Kofi Edu smiled and was embarrassed but very pleased with the response of his Uncle Kojo and Nana. "*Medaase, medaase*," he said to both. Kofi paused and then added, "What about Yaw. We need something for him."

"Yaw's never seen a horse," Kwame said. "Kofi, can you carve a small horse for Yaw to play with?"

Kofi Edu was intrigued. "I'd like to. I'm not sure if I can. Uncle Kojo, will you help me?"

"I've never tried to carve one either, but I'll try," Elder Kojo replied. "Kofi, if you work on the doll in the next three days, I'll work on the horse."

"Oh, yes, I will."

"We'll work together."

"I need a new finial for the top of my umbrella," Nana explained. "I like the one that I see here of a falcon. That's the symbol of my clan, the *Oyoko*. May I hold it?"

"Certainly. That's one of our best," Elder Kojo replied. "I carved it myself. If you have it covered with gold leaf, it will be spectacular. Goldsmiths here do that."

Nana and Elder Kojo bargained and agreed on a price. "I'll pay you now and take it to a goldsmith," Nana said to conclude his business.

"*Medaase*," Elder Kojo replied. "I'll wrap your carvings in leaves to protect them. Kofi and I will have a doll and a horse ready for you before you leave Kumasi."

"Nana, I have a question for Elder Kojo," Kwaku said.

"Please ask him."

"At council meetings the Okyeame holds a staff with a gold *Sankofa* bird on the top. Did you carve his staff?"

Elder Kojo was silent for a few moments, and then his face showed a smile of appreciation. "Staffs for an *okyeame* are elaborate and costly. We carve them here, but we didn't carve that one. At the *Odwira* celebration, you'll see an *okyeame* walking next to each chief. The Asantehene has several. Notice the beautiful staffs. We made many of them. I'm proud of our work."

"I'll look at them," Kwaku assured Elder Kojo.

Nana placed the doll and finial in Akosua's basket, and she rebalanced it on her head. Turning to Elder Kojo, Nana said, "*Medaase.*"

"Enjoy the market," Elder Kojo replied.

"Will you take us to the potters' section now, Akousa?" Nana asked.

"Follow me," Akosua answered as she led the group through the crowd. Approaching the potters, the group again saw women with nets full of pottery balanced on their heads.

"Akosua, the women with big heads look like your doll," Kwaku said.

"That's not right. My doll's pretty. Those women aren't pretty. They work too hard to be pretty," Akosua replied sharply.

Once at their destination, Akosua greeted her aunt. "*Maaha*, Auntie Yaa. I'm bringing my father's family to meet you and see your pottery."

"*Akwaaba!*" Madam Yaa replied with enthusiasm. "Women in my family have been potters for a long time. Akosua and my sister, Adjowa, help me. Adjowa makes all kinds of pots. Akosua helps shape and polish the water pots with a stone before they're fired. They must be shaped carefully, or people will have trouble balancing them. Akosua does excellent work. She might be a potter some day."

"I know about these pots," Kwame said. "Akosua, I didn't know that you helped make them. Maybe you worked on ours."

Nana picked up several pots to judge their weight and guess their purpose. He rubbed his hand over them to feel the finish. "So many designs," he said. "Where do you find new designs?"

Akan pottery

"I get ideas from other potters, and I see pots from the savannah," Madam Yaa explained. "I've been a potter since I was a child. I can copy any design, and I make new designs, too."

Nana praised her work. "Your pottery is beautiful. You and your people are very skilled. I'm glad that Akosua is helping you."

"*Medaase*," Madam Yaa replied. "Kofi, I want to send a water pot to your mother. Will you carry it home if I give it to you now? I'll make a cushion of leaves for your head."

"Yes, I can do that," Kofi Edu replied, taking the pot and leaves from his aunt. "It balances well," he said. "It'll be easy for me to carry."

"It was good to meet you," Nana said to Madam Yaa. "We need to find the metal workers. Can you please give us directions?" The group soon set off with Kofi Edu and Akosua carrying head loads.

"AKANS ARE FAMOUS FOR METAL WORK," NANA EXPLAINED TO EVERYONE. "BLACKsmiths make cauldrons and tools and repair guns. Brass casters make lamps, gold weights, balance scales, and more. We have goldsmiths for jewelry and decorations. Let's look at the brass casters' stalls first.

"The Queen Mother wants a lamp, and I want each of you to have a gold weight," Nana continued. "You'll be weighing gold dust in the market before long. Be ready to choose one."

The children were surprised and pleased. They looked at several stalls and stopped at the largest.

"*Maaha*," a senior caster greeted them.

"*Yaa*," Nana replied. "I'll look at your lamps, and these children will each select a gold weight."

"You see our products here," the caster replied.

Nana quickly found a lamp that he liked. It was as tall as half of the distance from his elbow to his wrist and had a decorative column. "Your grandmother will like the birds sitting on the rim," he said to Kwame. "The cup will hold enough oil to bring good light to her hut." Nana bargained for the price and paid.

Brass lamp for the Queen Mother

The children knew Nana's weights, which were rectangles with circles or lines for decorations. Here they found elaborate gold weights shaped as birds, fish, leopards, and even crocodiles. They liked the animals better.

"Some gold weights represent proverbs," the caster explained. "Here's one that I like. It's a *Sankofa* bird."

"Oh, we know what that means," Kwaku said. "It tells us to remember our history!"

"Good that you know," the caster complemented Kwaku. "Here's another one that's interesting. You see two crocodiles with one crossed over the other. They have separate heads, tails, and legs but only one belly. This reminds us that a family has many people who need to cooperate. There is only one belly, and all of the food goes there to be shared."

Crocodile gold weight

"I'd be scared of two crocodiles together," Baako said. "I've seen real crocodiles, and they're dangerous. I like the weight though. I choose it."

"I like the animal weights, too," Kwaku said. "Nana, your weights don't tell stories."

"That's true, Kwaku," Nana replied. "Mine are more simple, but I know many proverbs. Chiefs have to know them. Sometimes you can be more polite to people by using a proverb, so having a gold weight to remind you is a good idea."

"What does this one mean?" Kwame asked, picking up a weight of a leopard eating its prey.

"A leopard can eat any animal in the forest," the caster explained. "This gold weight warns you that a leopard is fierce."

"We know that," Kwame explained. "We've seen a leopard kill a crocodile. I'll take this one because I like leopards."

Holding a weight showing a bird caught in a trap, the caster said, "This one means 'A bird in a trap will sing the sweetest song to beg for release.' When you see this gold weight, remember that a person who makes many promises to you might want a favor."

"I'll take that one," Kwaku said. "If I'm chief some-day, I'll have to figure out if people are telling me the truth."

Leopard gold weight

"And the two of you," Nana said, looking at Akosua and Kofi Edu.

"I like drums, Nana," Kofi Edu replied. "I want the weight that shows two talking drums."

"I like the weight that shows a lamp like the one you'll give to the Queen Mother," Akosua said. "I'll take it. I'll feel closer to her."

"You've all made good choices," Nana concluded. "When we're at Elder Kwadwo's home, I'll compare your weights to mine so you'll know their value."

"I'll add one more for the chief," the caster said, looking at Nana.

"How do you know I'm a chief?" Nana asked.

"The children call you 'Nana' and it's always the chief who takes time to teach others," the caster replied. Nana smiled at the compliment.

The caster picked up a weight shaped like a chief's sword. "A chief should always have a sword with him, and this one will be easy to carry." Nana thanked the caster, and paid for the other weights.

Adding the gold weights to Akosua's basket, Nana observed. "Kofi has a head load. It's time for Kwaku to carry the basket."

"I'll do it," Baako offered immediately, reaching for the basket.

"No, Baako, the job goes to the youngest."

"I'm an *odonko*," Baako replied. "I should do it."

"No, here you're my son, and you're the oldest. Kwaku, the job goes to you."

"I'm ready," Kwaku said, placing the basket on his head. "Let's go."

CHAPTER 32

The Kumasi Market: Cattle and Cloth

"Let's find the cattle next," Nana said. Turning to the brass caster, he asked directions.

"It smells terrible over there. You won't like it," the caster warned Nana, while indicating the way.

Nana's group walked to the edge of the market to find a herd of brown and white longhorn cattle in a large field. The cattle were bony, and they bellowed loudly.

"They walk for many days to Kumasi," Nana said, "just like us. They don't get enough to eat or drink. The caster was right. It smells bad here."

"Are the cattle crying?" Akosua asked.

"They're just talking to each other," Nana answered.

"Do people ride them like horses?" Kofi Edu wanted to know.

"Cattle aren't smart like horses. People don't ride them," Nana replied.

"The people I see here are Hausas," Kwame observed.

"Hausas are big traders. They buy cattle and bring them here to sell," Nana said.

"I don't see anyone with Gurunsi scars," Baako commented.

"You won't see them here," Nana explained. "Gurunsis aren't traders. They're farmers." Baako was disappointed.

"What happens to the cattle here?" Kwaku asked.

"They're butchered," Nana replied. "The meat is expensive, and only rich people in Kumasi buy it."

"The cattle wouldn't have to walk so far if they lived in the forest," Kwaku said.

"Cattle can't live in the forest," Nana explained. "They're like horses. If they stay here for long, they'll get sick and die."

"That's sad," Kofi Edu thought.

"Look," Kwame said. "I see Amir and Doki coming toward us."

We Are Akan

Doki trotted up to the fence. Amir greeted everyone. "*Salaam*, my friends. What are you doing here?"

"*Salaam*," Nana replied.

"The cattle, we want to see them. We've never seen cattle," Kwaku explained.

"I'll show you the cattle. Who wants to ride Doki with me?" Amir asked. "We'll work with the cattle. It's easier to do that from a horse than on foot."

"I'll help," Kwaku was quick to answer.

Amir dismounted, boosted Kwaku to the saddle, and remounted, sitting behind Kwaku. "We won't be gone long. Watch what Doki can do," Amir said as he and Kwaku rode off.

"I've trained Doki to move cattle. I want him to drive one to the corral where it will be slaughtered," Amir told Kwaku.

"Oh, that's awful," Kwaku said.

"They're brought here for their meat," Amir said. "When we do this, you'll see that Doki is smart."

Amir and Kwaku circled the herd and then stopped next to it. "Hold the saddle tight. Keep your legs against Doki's side, and beware of the horns," Amir warned Kwaku.

Cattle in the Kumasi market

Pointing to a large animal nearby, Amir continued, "Doki will peel that one out of the herd." Amir took Doki through the herd to stand next to the targeted animal and push against it lightly.

"You see that Doki knows how to work with cattle," Amir told Kwaku.

Kwaku could barely speak. "Doki's smart," he said.

With Doki at his side, the animal walked slowly to the outside of the herd. "Doki will drive it toward the corral now," Amir explained. Once free of the herd, however, the animal bolted away.

"We'll chase it," Amir said, urging Doki to trot. "Hold on!"

Doki got behind the large animal once more, but it kept turning away from the horse. Doki had to walk on one side of it and then the other, back and forth. "Keep your arms and legs close to Doki and away from the horns," Amir warned Kwaku once more. The animal bolted away again, and Doki chased it.

"Hold on!" Amir told Kwaku.

"What's going to happen?" Kwaku asked.

"Our friend is getting tired. He'll slow down now. We'll get him to the corral. Hold on!"

"I like going fast," Kwaku said, releasing one hand from the saddle to wave to Nana and the others. Nana's group waved back.

"What are they doing?" Baako asked Nana.

"Doki's working the cattle. The horse is impressive. I didn't expect this. You can see why soldiers with horses are powerful."

"If Doki were chasing people, they wouldn't get away," Baako observed to the others.

Nana and the children watched as Doki drove the animal to the corral. Doki walked next to its head, guiding it and keeping it from running away.

"Do the cattle know what will happen to them?" Kwame asked.

"No, they probably just don't want to leave the safety of the herd," Nana answered.

"I feel sorry for them," Baako said. "They're just like the sheep at the *Adae*. They'll be sacrificed and sold, only the sheep wasn't sold."

"The cattle are like the duikers, too," Kwame said. "We kill duikers and eat them. The cattle are the same, but we don't hunt them."

"Cattle and sheep aren't wild animals," Nana reminded everyone. "We raise them to eat. It won't hurt our forest if we eat them. They're not like leopards. They don't help us keep the forest in balance. Let's see what Kwaku and Amir can tell us. Here they come."

"Did you watch us?" Kwaku asked when Doki brought him and Amir to the fence. "I helped Doki work the cattle. He's smart. I like to ride fast."

"Kwaku's a good rider already," Amir said. "Doki likes him."

"I want to ride a horse someday," Kwame told Amir. "Can I buy one if I go to the savannah?"

"You can, but first find someone who knows about horses to help you. Akans aren't horse people. You'll need to learn how to ride and take care of a horse. You'll have to stay in the savannah if you want to ride horses."

"That will be hard, but maybe if I'm a trader, I'll ride in the savannah, and then leave my horse with someone when I come home," Kwame said.

"I'll go back to work now," Amir explained. "It's good to see all of you. I'll wave if I see you in the *Odwira* parade."

"Thank you for helping us," Nana said to Amir. "We'll look for you in the parade."

"It's almost time for us to go home," Nana told the group. "We've been out for a long time, but I want to see the cloth before we leave. Please take us that way, Akosua."

"Follow me," Akosua said as she led the group through the market labyrinth once more.

"A little slower," Kwaku requested. "Kofi and I are carrying head loads."

"We're almost there," Akosua promised.

They soon found the weavers of *kente* cloth at their looms, moving their hands and feet with speed and precision to weave long strips of cloth from silk and cotton threads. The base threads were stretched out and held by rocks in front of the looms. As the colorful strips emerged from the weavers' hands, the rocks steadily made their way to the looms. The weavers smiled to acknowledge the audience, but didn't break their concentration.

"What beauty!" Nana exclaimed with pride. "I love the colors. There are so many designs. The Asantehene orders a new design for each *Odwira*. He'll surprise us when we see him."

"Look at the long strips of thread," Kwame observed "They look like snakes."

"Weaving is so fast and so hard," Baako said, shaking his head. "Even young men do it, and I don't see how."

"They start when they're boys," Kofi Edu explained. "Some boys my age are apprenticed to *kente* weavers. Their first job is to sew strips together to make a big cloth. Later they learn to weave the strips."

"I don't see any women or girls," Akosua said. "Where are they?"

"Only boys and men weave *kente*. Women and girls are busy doing other things," Nana explained.

"That's not fair," Akosua answered. "I would like to weave *kente*."

Kente cloth weaver in the Kumasi market

"Girls aren't weavers," Kofi Edu replied. "We can't change that."

"We love *kente* so much that it's hard to believe that the beautiful thread comes from the savannah and the whites," Nana explained. "Traders bring it to Kumasi and the weaving villages nearby. I hope that we'll always be able to get it. Kwame, if you're a trader someday, be sure to bring thread to Kumasi."

"I will," Kwame responded. "We'll always need *kente*. Are you going to buy a cloth today, Papa?"

"No, I don't have enough gold dust to buy a *kente* cloth. The price is high because it takes a long time for weavers to make even one strip. I inherited my *kente* cloth. We keep them for generations. Let's go to the stalls where *kente* is for sale. Look at the colors that make it so beautiful. See if you can find colors of the forest and our food."

"I see yellow for leaves in the dry season and bananas, plantains, corn, and pineapples," Kofi Edu said.

"I found yellow, too, and red for peppers, tomatoes, and palm nuts," Kwaku added.

"Here is green for our trees and okra. I love okra," Baako said.

"Here is purple," Akosua called out. "And orange for oranges!"

"I see black and white," Kwame contributed. "White can be for chicken eggs and garden eggs, and black can be for black stools and driver ants and cobras."

"Yams are ugly. They're only brown, but we need them to eat," Akosua said. "Brown isn't in *kente* cloth."

"Do you see blue for our beautiful sky?" Nana asked.

The children echoed, "Yes!"

"The forest is truly alive in the *kente* cloth," Nana concluded.

"Let's find the savannah cloth that Amir and Doki bring us. We'll see Hausas in those stalls." The group soon found cotton cloth woven in strips that were sewn together, like *kente*. "This cloth is strong, but it's not colorful or delicate," Nana observed. "Look at the thick threads."

Some of the savannah cloth was in large pieces for men and women to wrap around themselves. There were also tunics and robes. White, blue, and brown were the only colors. Nana and his group greeted the traders, who invited them to handle the cloth.

"Look at this tunic," Nana said as he held it up. 'It's thick and heavy. It could be a war smock, like mine."

"Savannah cloth keeps us warm at night," Baako commented. "The cloaks here are like the ones that the Queen Mother gave us."

"We use this cloth," Nana said, "but most Akans like the colors of *kente* and the cloth that comes from the whites. Their cloth is made of cotton, but the thread is very fine. It's smooth and easy to wear. Let's look at it. The traders selling it are Akan."

"The colors of this cloth are beautiful," Akosua said.

"Pick the cloth up to feel it," the trader invited.

Akosua rubbed the cloth against her face. "It's so soft," she said.

"The cloth that I'm wearing isn't colorful, but it looks like it came from here," Kwame observed.

"Your mother bought that cloth in Tanoso," Nana said. "We don't get the kind that is so colorful. It's more expensive."

"When I'm a trader, I'll bring better cloth to Tanoso," Kwame promised.

"Kwame, when you're a trader, everyone will want you to bring a lot of cloth to our marketplace. We're a long walk from Kumasi. Most people can't come this far."

"We'll go home now," Nana said with a weary smile. "I'll talk to a goldsmith tomorrow. Akosua and Kofi, please show us the way."

"You're a fine group," Nana told everyone as they walked home. "Today we saw the Asantehene's palace, the foreigners' zone, and many parts of our kingdom that are gathered together here in the marketplace. That's good, but we need to rest now."

"I want to go home, and I want to come back, too," Kwame explained. "There is so much here that we don't see in Tanoso."

"I learned more about the savannah today," Baako said. "I saw books and talismans and horses and cattle and cloth. I saw Hausas but no Gurunsis."

"When Gurunsis are in Kumasi, they're not free like Hausas," Nana explained. "They're always *nnonko* or prisoners. I'm sad about that, Baako." Baako shook his head and said nothing.

"Papa, will you go to the prisoners' part of the market?" Kwame asked.

"I don't like to, but yes, several of us will go tomorrow," Nana replied.

"You told me that you wouldn't buy more *nnonko*."

"That's right, Kwame. I don't need more *nnonko*, but your Uncle Kwasi plans to buy a man. He needs help to dig a pit mine. It's better to buy a family, but he can't afford one. He wants a Gurunsi. Others may buy prisoners, too. Asare will help us."

"I'm glad that you're not going to buy any prisoners, Papa. I think Baako is, too."

— CHAPTER 33 —

The Kumasi Market:
Prisoners and Guns

On the Tanoso group's second full day in Kumasi, Madam Adjowa took the children to her farm for the morning. They would help the *nnonko* harvest crops for the visitors' meals.

Most Tanoso travelers planned to take care of their own business that day, but Nana gathered a small group for an early breakfast. With him were his cousin, Elder Kwadwo, the Okyeame, Elder Kwasi, Elder Kofi, and Asare. Nana knew these men well and trusted them fully. He wanted their counsel before going to the prisoners' sector of the market. "Elder Kwadwo and Elder Kwasi, will you buy *nnonko* today?" he asked.

"Two of my *nnonko* are single men who need wives," Elder Kwadwo explained. "Two more women would work on my farm, and also here at home when we have visitors. I'll look for Gurunsis. They have a community on my farm already."

"I want another *odonko* to help with farming and digging a mine," Elder Kwasi said. "I'd like a family, but I have enough kola nuts for only one *odonko*. I want a Gurunsi. An *odonko* from a different group wouldn't fit in."

Nana had different plans. "You all know that I inherited *nnonko* from my uncle," he said. "They work well together, and now there are fifteen children who work on my farms and in my mines. I don't need more *nnonko*.

"Two of you want to buy Gurunsi prisoners," Nana concluded. "Kumasi has a small prisoners' market compared to the ones in Kintampo and Salaga. The Gonja bring prisoners to both of these markets. It's too far for us to go to either one, but we should find Gurunsi prisoners here."

"Asare, we'll need your help to identify Gurunsis who are willing to work," Nana said. "Talk to the prisoners. Maybe you'll find some with connections to your family."

Asare explained his feelings. "I'm sad when I see that my people are prisoners. They've done nothing wrong, and they're suffering. The Gonja raid Gurunsis to get prisoners for the Asantehene. Will that ever stop?"

"The raiding is terrible, but we can't do anything about it," Nana said. "I don't like to go to the prisoners' sector of the market because the prisoners have such sad stories. But when I'm there, I think that if the prisoners stay in the forest, we will know where they are and what they're doing. If they're sold to whites, we won't know."

"They probably work on farms where the whites live," Elder Kwadwo said.

"We'll never know what happens to the prisoners that the whites buy," Asare added. "The traders don't know the prisoners' languages. The whites don't know either. Whites don't know where prisoners come from. Whites wouldn't know where to take the prisoners if they wanted to bring them back."

"All we can do is treat our *nnonko* well," Nana replied. "We need their help, and their children will become our people."

THE PRISONERS' SECTOR OF THE MARKET WAS QUIET. NANA'S GROUP SAW AT LEAST twenty men standing and sitting in small groups, barefoot, each with a cloth tied around his waist. The men were bound together by metal collars and chains. Fear showed on their faces. They spoke to each other in low voices. In the background the faint sound of children playing and laughing could be heard.

A short distance from the men was a group of women with young children. They looked unkempt, but they were not bound. The children played. The women talked among themselves and to the children. Pots of drinking water were placed throughout the sector but there was no food. Guards with spears stood in several places.

A few Akans were looking at the prisoners, but had difficulty communicating with them. Asare had expected to see some Gurunsis, but was stunned to find so many. "These are all my people," he whispered to Nana.

"Yes, I see their scars," Nana replied.

"*Maakye*," Nana greeted the market manager, and they talked briefly. Nana turned to his group and said, "I've confirmed that the prisoners are mostly Gurunsis. They walked to Kintampo, where the Asantehene's soldiers took the younger men away. He doesn't want the ones that we see here. They're for sale."

"What is the price?" the Okyeame asked.

"For a man, two head loads of kola nuts, or 4,000 cowrie shells, or two ounces of gold dust," the manager replied. "That's a low price since this is the end of the harvest season. The price for women will be less. For children, very little. They may not live."

"Sir, I want my foreman to talk to the prisoners to learn what they know about farming and hunting, and to see if they're healthy," Nana explained. "My foreman speaks Nankane and Twi. He'll translate for us."

Prisoners in the Kumasi market

"Go ahead, but be careful. They're hungry and tired," the manager replied. "Some may be angry. It's good if you talk to them. I have only one person here who can speak the languages of the savannah. He hasn't talked to them yet."

"Why don't you feed them more?" Nana asked. "The Asantehene wants a good price for them. They need to be healthy."

"The prisoners brought some food with them, and I ordered more this morning. It will come soon. They have water."

"We'll talk to them," Nana said. "Asare, let's go."

The group followed Asare as he approached a group of male prisoners slowly and greeted them in Nankane. The prisoners returned his greeting. They recognized Asare's scars and knew that he was Gurunsi, as they were.

Asare told the prisoners that he belonged to the *Gwegene*, the lion clan. "I have survived, like a lion," he said. The prisoners understood that he was encouraging them. Asare described his ancestral village and how he was captured. He explained why he wanted to talk to them and began asking questions.

"Where are you from? What is your clan? Where is your family? How were you captured? What has happened to you since you were captured? What kind of farming can you do? What animals do you hunt? What weapons do you use?"

Prisoners eagerly told their stories. They talked so fast that Asare struggled to keep up. He translated the most important information. "They're from different villages. This man says that Gonja soldiers on horseback attacked his village at sunrise with spears and whips. Soldiers searched the huts. No one could hide, though some escaped into the grassland.

"The second prisoner said that from his district, men, women, and children were rounded up while farming. The soldiers let women keep their children, wanting as many prisoners as possible to pay taxes to the Asantehene."

Nana's group recognized the kinds of stories that they had heard before. On some raids soldiers took only young men, while at other times, they took older men, women, and children. The oldest people were left behind because they couldn't survive a long walk. Raiders could be brutal but were careful since they had to meet the Asantehene's quota for prisoners. It did them no good to injure or kill their prisoners.

Each of the six cities in the Gonja Kingdom owed the Asantehene 500 prisoners every dry season, for a total of 3,000 prisoners plus hundreds of sheep and cattle, all largely stolen from their neighbors. Knowing this, Nana felt the weight of the prisoners' stories.

The prisoners had carried food and water in head loads as they trekked to Kintampo to be turned over to the Asantehene's men. They walked for many days, crossing the savannah with few trees for shade or opportunities to escape. Prisoners and soldiers slept in the open at night with guards posted to keep animals, especially lions, away. If prisoners fell ill, they were left along the road, most likely to die.

"These men raise millet, yams, and peanuts," Asare explained. "They fish in rivers and hunt with spears, bows and arrows, and throwing sticks to kill antelopes, hyenas, snakes, and crocodiles, sometimes lions."

Asare welcomed finding members of his clan, but was disappointed that no one could give him news of his village. "I think that raiders robbed it of its young people long ago," he told Nana. "Maybe the older people moved further away from the Gonja. Maybe they joined another village."

"Thank you for translating, Asare," Nana replied. "I'm sorry that you didn't learn about your village. I think that you're right. With so many people captured, your village probably doesn't exist any more. Let's talk to the women now."

NANA'S GROUP WALKED TOWARD THE WOMEN PRISONERS, WHO WERE SEATED together, watching the children play. Two were nursing babies. Two others carried babies tied to their back. The women were not tied up or chained.

Asare introduced himself and told of his clan and village to an older woman who stepped forward to speak for the group. She greeted him and was eager to tell the story of the women's capture, and how they had worked together during their long march to carry the children, and set aside enough food and water to keep them alive. She was relieved to see them playing now. "They're hungry, but they're alive," she said with satisfaction.

Asare asked about clan and village names and crafts that the women knew. He learned that they made shea butter, wove baskets, and farmed. "They want a safe place to live with their children," Asare told Nana. "They want people to buy them and their children in Kumasi so they can stay in the forest. They don't want to be sold to whites."

One woman, who had been listening to the conversation, asked Asare for help. "My husband is your clansman. He was captured with me and our two children. He was in the group of men that you see here now, but early this morning two traders bought the younger ones to take them away to sell to the whites. Can your master buy my children and me, and look for my husband? We are hard workers and will serve him well. We want to stay together. Please help us. I beg you."

"What is your name?" Asare asked.

"My name is Apure," she replied. "I belong to the *Tugfo* clan."

Turning to Nana's group, Asare explained. "Names are important, and this woman has strong names. Her first name, Apure, means 'flower' in Nankane. Her clan name means 'eagle.' The bird is powerful, and a flower in the savannah has to struggle to survive. This is a strong woman who has already survived much."

Asare told the group what the woman had said and pleaded with them to help. "This woman looks healthy. We can look at her children later. Her husband and children belong to my clan. I'm sure that her husband is healthy since the traders chose him this morning. I believe that the woman and her husband will be strong workers, and the children will grow up to be strong also. It's unfair to break up a family. That will destroy their lives. I'm a loyal clansman. I'll train them and be responsible for them."

Nana understood the need immediately. "I want to help," he said. "It's valuable to have a good family as *nnonko*. Asare, we owe you our loyalty. Elder Kwasi and I will talk."

Nana approached the market manager. "What do you know about the traders who bought men here this morning?" he asked.

"They left right away for Elmina Castle. They didn't want to wait for the *Odwira* celebration because keeping prisoners is difficult. Some might get sick and die."

"Why aren't the traders taking them to Cape Coast Castle?" Nana asked. "It's closer."

"Whites there don't trade for prisoners anymore," the manager explained. "They want only gold and ivory. I don't know why. The Asantehene doesn't like this. Now he has to send prisoners to Elmina Castle or to the castles near Accra. Elmina's not so far away, but Accra's much farther. It's expensive to feed and take care of prisoners on such a long walk."

"We'll return this afternoon," Nana assured the manager. "We're interested in buying the woman that we were talking to. Don't let anyone buy her until you hear from us. We might buy others, too."

"I'll wait for you," the manager answered. "Be sure to come back this afternoon."

"We will," Nana replied.

Turning to his group, Nana said, "Let's look at guns and ammunition now."

Elder Kwadwo ushered the group to the gun sector of the market and introduced them to the best merchant, whom Nana greeted. "*Maakye.*"

"*Yaa.* What do you need?" the merchant asked.

"Long Dane muskets and ammunition," Nana replied.

"I have many guns. The whites use them before trading them to us, but my people have repaired, cleaned, and shot them to be certain they work well and that the ramrods are in place. I sell ammunition, too, black powder and musket balls," the merchant explained as he picked up a gun for Nana to see, pointing it to the sky.

"Do you want to see the firing mechanism?"

"Yes. I want the best locks that you have," Nana answered.

The merchant handed a gun to everyone except Asare. Merchants could sell guns only to free men. The group examined the muskets carefully, smelling and looking down the barrels, examining the firing mechanisms, removing the ramrods and inserting them into the barrels, and running their hands over the stocks and barrels to judge if they were intact.

"I bought these muskets and the ammunition from a trader who goes only to Cape Coast Castle," the merchant explained. "The whites there don't take prisoners anymore, only gold and ivory. Their prices are high, but the merchandise is better than I can find at other castles."

"I like the way you do business," Nana replied. "Show me the powder and musket balls."

The merchant pointed to several pots of black powder. "The lids are tight enough to keep the powder dry," he assured Nana, as he removed the lids from a few pots and stirred the powder with a long handled spoon. "I keep musket balls in leather pouches that you can use to carry them," he explained, opening a pouch for Nana to see. Nana was pleased with the merchant's organization and presentation of his merchandise.

"What are your prices?" Nana asked.

"My prices are high, but my merchandise is the best in the market," the merchant replied. "I sell the powder by the pot and the musket balls per pouch. Most guns cost two ounces of gold dust each. If you buy five, I'll lower the price to a total of eight ounces for five muskets."

"Before I buy guns, I'll want to shoot them outside of the city to be certain that they fire well," Nana explained.

"Of course, keep them overnight and bring them back if you don't like them," the merchant said.

"We can shoot them at my farm tomorrow," Elder Kwadwo offered.

Nana nodded slowly and said, "I'll consult with my group as we walk in the market. I'll let you know what we decide. Thank you for your help."

"You're welcome."

The group walked away slowly. They thought that the merchandise was of high quality. They had confidence in the merchant but wanted to test the guns. Elder Kwadwo assured the group that this merchant was the best but encouraged them to look at other stalls before deciding.

"I'll find a goldsmith with Elder Kwadwo while the rest of you look around," Nana said. "We won't be long. We'll find you in this sector again soon."

Elder Kwadwo took Nana to the best goldsmith, and Nana arranged have his new umbrella top covered in gold leaf. "The falcon will come alive," the goldsmith promised.

"Can you finish before I leave on Tuesday?" Nana asked.

"Yes, I work in my shop, but this stall will be open until the end of the festival. Your piece will be ready here on Sunday, I promise you." Nana agreed and paid part of the price; the rest to be paid when the job was finished.

Nana thanked his cousin. "The goldsmith will do an excellent job," Elder Kwadwo assured Nana.

Nana and Elder Kwadwo rejoined the others, and everyone advised Nana to buy guns and ammunition from the first merchant. The group returned to him, and Nana concluded the purchase of five flintlock muskets, powder, and musket balls, paying with gold dust.

Leaving the market, the Tanoso men carried the guns in their arms and wore the pouches of musket balls. Asare carried a large pot of gun powder as a head load. The group attracted attention as it walked through the marketplace. Guns always attracted attention.

CHAPTER 34

Buying Prisoners

MADAM ADJOWA AND HER SISTERS SERVED A HEARTY LUNCH. NANA ASKED HER, THE Tanoso boys, Akosua, and Kofi Edu to join him and his councilors after lunch to talk about the leopard cub and prisoners.

The group gathered around Nana as he described events of the last two days and concluded, "We need the Asantehene's help. Our neighbor, Nana Somfo, brought a leopard cub to Kumasi. I believe that he's given it to the Asantehene to gain favor."

"That was a wrong move," Elder Kwadwo asserted. "The Asantehene won't be pleased. The cub is likely to die if it's kept in a cage or be killed when it's grown. It won't know how to live in the forest."

"The cub shouldn't be a prisoner," the Okyeame insisted. "The Asantehene should give it to us to take back to the forest where it belongs. We must ask him."

"I agree," Nana said, "but I want to protect the young chief. He's an *Agona* like Madam Ama. He'll learn. I'll find him and explain what we're thinking. I'll ask the Asantehene not to punish him." The group approved of the plan. Nana turned to the boys and Akosua. "If the Asantehene gives us the cub, you'll have to take care of it."

Together they replied, "Yes!" and clapped their hands.

"Another matter," Nana continued. "This morning we learned that traders had just bought prisoners in the market to sell at Elmina Castle. A man from Asare's clan was in the group. His wife and children are still for sale. Elder Kwasi will buy them if I to try to find the man and buy him. The price for him would be a loan from me to Elder Kwasi."

"Why do you want to do this, Nana?" Elder Kofi asked.

"We know that Akan clans are strong," Nana replied. "Gurunsi clans are strong, too. We owe Asare our loyalty. I want to protect Asare's clansman and his family." Asare bowed his head in modesty. Nana continued, "With my permission the Okyeame will speak."

The Okyeame stood and began. "Nana, Elder Kofi, Asare, and I grew up together. We've been friends for most of our lives. When Asare and I were children, we lived in the

We Are Akan

nnonko village with our Gurunsi parents."

The others listened intently. The Okyeame continued with determination. "I'm Akan now, but I remember and honor my Gurunsi family. Asare, Baako, and I belong to the *Gwegene* clan, the lion clan. Our clansmen were leaders among the Gurunsi. For generations the Gonja have raided our people and broken up families. I want to protect the Gurunsi when I can.

"Let me go after the traders so that Nana can buy the prisoner who is my clansman," the Okyeame proposed. "I speak Nankane. I can talk to the traders and the prisoner and explain our purpose. I'll do all that I can to save my clansman from being sold to whites. He'll never be free, but he and his family will be safe if we take them to Tanoso. I want to protect them and we need their labor."

The group was silent for short time when Elder Kofi raised his hand to speak. "Okyeame, I've known you since we were boys and I respect your loyalty to your clan. The traders will have other Gurunsi prisoners. There are still Gurunsis for sale in the market. We can't protect them all, not even all of them from your clan."

"I know," the Okyeame replied. "We can't change this horrible trade, but we might save one family."

Baako whispered to the other boys, "The Okyeame's like me. I belong to the *Gwegene* clan."

Nana spoke to the Okyeame. "Thank you for telling us your story. It makes a difference."

"Thank you, Nana, for believing in Asare and me and our clan," the Okyeame replied.

"To overtake the traders, I would have to send a group that can travel faster than they do," Nana said. "If my group leaves tomorrow, it should catch up with the traders in three days and return. Can we do this on our own? What is the risk?"

"The traders might not sell the prisoner," Elder Kofi said.

"A bigger risk," Elder Kwasi suggested, "is that our people might have to go into Fante territory. We don't know if the Fante will keep peace with the kingdom."

"The Asantehene does frequent business with whites," Elder Kwadwo said. "He could be sending a delegation to the coast soon, even tomorrow. Maybe some of us could join it. The messengers know the road and soldiers will travel with them. Traders say that the Fante are peaceful now. The Asantehene has returned to Kumasi, so he must agree. The delegation will travel fast and should be safe."

"Roads will be busy tomorrow and the next day with so many coming to Kumasi for the *Odwira*, but travelers will stand aside for a delegation from the Asantehene. You're right, Elder Kwadwo," Nana said. "Our best hope is for our people to join such a delegation. Who's willing to go?"

Every man raised his hand saying, "I am."

Nana was relieved. "*Medaase*," he responded. "You are my trusted family and friends. You have my confidence and, I believe, I have yours."

Nana turned to the Okyeame. "You speak best for me. After we rest, go to the palace with my gift for the Asantehene. If you can see him, ask about the cub and a delegation going to the coast. If you can't see him, talk to his officials. If the answer is 'yes,' for the cub and 'yes,' for the delegation, we'll have to prepare quickly."

"Send me to the palace, too," Elder Kofi said. "With two questions, it's better if two of us go. I'll speak for the cub, and the Okyeame can speak for the prisoner. We'll take care of our business faster."

"I like that idea," the Okyeame said.

"I like it, too," Nana added. "If the Asantehene is sending a delegation to the coast and allows us to join it, the Okyeame and Elder Kwasi will go. Kwame and Baako, I'll want you to go, too. You're young and strong. You can travel fast and carry supplies. You both look Akan, and Baako speaks Nankane. That will help. You'll be safe with the Okyeame and Elder Kwasi. When you come back, you'll know your kingdom as few Akans do.

"Kwaku, I'm sorry that I can't send you, but there is a small chance that this group will travel all of the way to the coast. Royals have to be careful if we leave the forest since we don't have a scar. People outside of the forest might not recognize us as Akan."

"I understand, Nana," Kwaku said, "but I'm disappointed. I want to taste salt water."

"I hope that you and I will both see the ocean someday," Nana encouraged Kwaku. "If peace with the Fante holds, we'll both taste salt water."

"Asare, I can't send you either. You have Gurunsi scars and you might be seized and sold to whites. You'll stay with me."

"Thank you for helping my clansman," Asare replied.

Kwame and Baako encouraged Kwaku. "You'll be at the *Odwira* festival and you'll take care of the cub on the way home," Kwame said. "That's important. We'll tell you about everything we see, and you can tell us all about the *Odwira*, and the cub, and where you let the cub go. Maybe you'll see its mother."

"Akosua and I will be here with you in Kumasi. We'll play with the cub. That will be fun," Kofi Edu assured Kwaku.

"The cub will like us," Akosua added. Kwaku was still sad, and only later did he smile and talk about the cub.

The group sat in silence for a short time and then everyone applauded. "Thank you, Nana, for taking action," Elder Kwadwo said. "But, everyone, beware. The Asantehene's delegations travel fast. Traveling with them takes strength."

"If we overtake the traders in three days," Elder Kwasi suggested, "we'll return to Kumasi the same day that Nana leaves. We'll need a day to rest, but we won't be far behind him on our way home."

"I'll be happy if we save a family," Madam Adjowa encouraged everyone. "They'll be good workers for Elder Kwasi. If you buy prisoners today, I'll receive them here."

"If we give a trust payment for prisoners, it would be helpful if they stay the night here," Nana said. "We'll need to see what they're like for a day, and take them back to the market if we aren't satisfied."

"Madam Adjowa has offered to let them sleep in the courtyard tonight," Elder Kwadwo replied. "If we keep them, we can take them to my farm tomorrow. I'm already planning to take everyone there to test the guns."

"It's settled," Nana said. "I want the Tanoso boys to come to the prisoners' sector of the market with us this afternoon. They need to see what it's like. Kofi Edu, do you want to come, too? Akosua, I'm sorry but you're too young." Akosua frowned.

"We'll come," the boys answered without talking to each other.

"Good," Nana replied. "Let's rest now. We have a busy afternoon ahead. I'll join the boys so we can talk more." The group dispersed.

SITTING ON A STOOL IN THE SHADE OF A TREE WHILE THE CHILDREN STRETCHED OUT on cloths, Nana spoke frankly. "Here in Kumasi you see how our kingdom works. In the marketplace we see trade goods from all parts of our kingdom and beyond. In the foreigners' zone, we meet people with new knowledge. We cannot forget the *nnonko* who do our hardest work. We can buy them here. Soon we'll see our king. He holds all of us together.

"At the *Odwira* festival, you'll see majesty and wealth. The music of horns and drums will be loud and clear. Guns will be fired into the air, creating a blanket of white smoke. The Asantehene will be surrounded by his councilors. They'll all wear gold ornaments and *kente* cloth as they sit next to the Golden Stool, for thousands to see. The parade will bring all of the chiefs and their delegations before the Asantehene to pledge their loyalty. We are the strength of the kingdom. Over it all you'll see a sky full of umbrellas of every color. It's a fantastic scene.

"Kofi Edu and Akusoa," Nana continued, "Kwaku, and maybe Kwame and Baako, will walk with my delegation in the parade. Would you like walk with us, too?"

"Oh, yes," each answered. "We've never been in the parade."

"Now something serious," Nana said. "When we return to the market this afternoon, some of us will buy prisoners."

"Why are there so many Gurunsi prisoners?" Baako asked. "It's not fair."

"You're right, Baako. It isn't fair. It's a matter of strength," Nana answered. "Gurunsis are farmers. They don't have a king or an army, so they can't fight the Gonja soldiers. The Gonja king has to give the Asantehene taxes to buy peace. He sends prisoners and also sheep, goats, cattle, cloth, and other items, and the Asantehene gives much of this as rewards to his chiefs and generals."

"What does the Asantehene give to you, Papa?"

"Mostly sheep now. Our grandfather chiefs received prisoners and sometimes cloth and leather sandals. I give some of the sheep to the elders and headmen, and I keep a few. I won't take prisoners. I don't want more *nnonko*."

"It seems strange to buy people in a market," Kwaku said. "I'm sure they don't like it."

"My papa says that some of the people will be our clansmen," Baako explained. "What will I say to them?" Baako realized that it was rude to say this to Nana and bowed his head saying, "I'm sorry, Nana."

"It's all right, Baako," Nana replied. "Soon, you and Kwame may leave with the Okyeame and Elder Kwasi to try to find and buy a prisoner who's in your clan. You will save a man if you succeed."

"Papa, did the Okyeame break the law today?" Kwame asked. "You told me that it's against the law for anyone to reveal the origin of others or themselves."

"That's an important matter, Kwame," Nana replied. "Today we are a family group and most of us knew the Okyeame's origin. I gave him permission to talk about his Gurunsi family. His message must not be repeated outside of our family.

"Kwame and Baako, if we can join a royal delegation, Asare and I will prepare you. That will come later. Let's rest now."

— CHAPTER 35 —

Prisoners, the Cub, and a Mission

A BREEZE IN THE MID-AFTERNOON COOLED THE AIR, HINTING OF THE HARMATTAN WIND soon to arrive from the desert. Nana's group of four men and four boys made its way to the prisoners' sector of the market, welcoming the breeze while dreading the task ahead. The group was quiet, but before reaching the market, Nana spoke to the boys.

"You'll see men chained together and women with children nearby. I hope that the prisoners have had a good meal and more water since we saw them this morning."

"I've never been in this part of the market," Kofi Edu explained, "but sometimes I see prisoners chained together in the street, even children. I try to talk to them, but they don't understand me. I always feel bad for them."

Nana's group entered the prisoners' sector and stopped briefly to talk to the manager. He told them that he gave a scarf to one of the women that they had talked to earlier. "If we buy prisoners today, we'll make a trust payment in gold dust," Nana told the manager. "We can bring kolas tomorrow. Did you give the prisoners anything to eat this morning?"

"Yes, they've eaten cassava and chicken, and they've had water to drink," the manager replied. "The prisoners are healthy. I want to sell them all by tomorrow. No one will come after the festival." He waved Nana's group on.

The boys saw the men in chains. "They're my clansmen. They're being treated like animals," Baako said.

"This is terrible," Kwame replied. "We treat our *nnonko* well. They're not animals."

"I see why we're not supposed to say where people come from," Kwaku said. "Nobody wants to talk about this market."

The group continued to the women's area. Asare motioned for the woman wearing a scarf around her waist to approach them. She carried one of her children, and the other followed, holding on to his mother's cloth. Nana greeted her, "*Maakye*, Apure." Asare greeted her in Nankane. She returned the greetings in Nankane.

Asare explained Nana's plan. "Thank you," Apure replied, "for saving my life and my children's lives and my husband's life. We will work hard for you."

"Nana can't be certain if his group will find your husband, but they will try," Asare assured her.

"I will hope," Apure replied.

The four boys stood close together, staring at the children. "They're like us," Kwaku said in a soft voice.

"They're not like us," Kwame replied. "They're prisoners. They're for sale. They all look scared."

"If good families buy them, they'll be safe," Kofi Edu said. "They'll have to work, but we all work."

"They'll never be free unless a family adopts them," Baako reminded the others. "Just like me."

Elder Kwadwo spoke to Asare, "Ask Apure to tell us of two more women who would be good workers for Madam Adjowa and me, and good wives for two of my *nnonko*."

Asare translated, and Apure answered. "There are two women here that you should talk to. Each has one child. Their husbands were taken away by the Asantehene's men in Kintampo. They are strong women, and they have survived a terrible march. I'll call them."

The two women approached, each with a baby tied to her back. Asare asked them about farming and the crafts they knew, and translated their replies. They seemed healthy and told Asare the names and ages of their children. Asare asked the women what happened to them and their husbands after they were captured.

"We walked many days to Kintampo," one replied. "It's a horrible place, hot and dusty with almost no water. When we arrived we were dirty and tired and hungry. We could hardly stand."

The second woman continued, "The younger men were taken away quickly. We barely said, 'Good-bye' to them. We lost our husbands, and our children lost their fathers. We all cried."

Asare translated once more and added, "These women will be good workers. Madam Adjowa can decide if they're healthy."

"Do the children look healthy?" Nana asked.

Asare talked to the women about their children and then looked briefly at each child. "I think so," he said, "but they are frightened of me. They'll be more comfortable if Madam Adjowa looks at them."

"I have enough kola nuts to buy Apure and her children if Nana can get a good price,"

Elder Kwasi concluded.

"I'll buy the other women and their children," Elder Kwadwo decided.

"I'll bargain for a good price," Nana assured the others. "I hope the children will live. The boy can play with my son, Yaw Mensah. These children will learn Twi. They don't have Gurunsi scars, so they can become Akan. Even though they can't work yet, they're valuable to our future. Asare, explain our plans to the women."

"Nana, don't offer anything for the children," Elder Kwadwo counseled. "We shouldn't have to pay for them. They won't work for years."

"The manager wants to sell," Nana replied. "We'll pay one and a half ounces of gold dust for each woman, no more, and nothing for the children."

The manager accepted Nana's offer.

Returning to Elder Kwadwo's home, Kwame confided to the other boys, "I'm glad that Uncle Kwasi and Elder Kwadwo bought prisoners. I didn't think I would ever say that, but we treat prisoners well. Even if they're not free, they'll be safe with us."

AFTER A SUCCESSFUL VISIT TO THE ASANTEHENE'S PALACE, THE OKYEAME AND ELDER Kofi hurried to Elder Kwadwo's home. Several times they circled around travelers greeting friends and talking on the broad streets. The two men could not enjoy the leisure that the *Odwira* festival usually allowed. They had a mission.

Each had seen an official of the Asantehene. Elder Kofi won the return of the leopard cub and carried it in a large covered basket. The cub was healthy but mewing with hunger and thirst. The Okyeame gained permission for some from Nana's group to join the Asantehene's delegation leaving the next day for Elmina Castle. The privilege was an honor, and travelers had to prepare for an early morning departure.

Reaching Elder Kwadwo's home, the men found Madam Adjowa, her sisters, and Akosua making palm nut soup and pounding fufu. "Congratulations!" Madam Adjowa exclaimed when she learned of their success. "Let us see the cub! What a prize! Listen, it's hungry. I'll feed it, but first I'll tie vines around it. Hold it by the vines. It will run away if it gets loose."

Madam Adjowa cooled a small calabash of soup and offered it to the cub, which drank it and a second serving eagerly. She gave the cub raw chicken, and it ate well once more. "You see what it likes, Akosua. I'm glad it's eating. We'll try to give it more later."

Akosua and the others took turns holding the cub as it licked their hands, necks, and faces, and seemed to welcome the attention. They held tightly to the vines.

"Mama, I think the cub likes me," Akosua said.

"It's sweet now, and you can play with it, Akosua, but it will be dangerous when it's grown. The cub needs milk. Goats at our farm are still nursing. We'll get milk there tomorrow. I hope that we can keep it alive."

"What about a cage, Mama? The cub can't see anything if it's in a basket."

"Good idea! Go to the market with one of your aunties and talk to your Uncle Kojo. Tell him about the cub and that we need a cage right away. His workers can make one, and he can bring it to us tomorrow and see the cub. Be off now and tell your uncle not to say anything about the cub. Tie it in the basket. I'll watch it while you're gone."

Nana's group returned from the prisoners' market with three women and four children. Madam Adjowa and her sisters greeted the prisoners in Nankane. The prisoners returned the greeting but said nothing more. The boy seemed frightened. A baby cried.

The women carried a few supplies in head loads. "Tell them to put their head loads in the corner," Madam Adjowa told Asare. "They'll stay here tonight. My sisters and I will decide if both the women and the children are healthy."

"I'm in charge now," Madam Adjowa continued. "Kwadwo, I want water for them to bathe. Send the boys for some. I'll give them clean cloths and dinner. They'll sleep on mats in the corner. With Asare's help, my sisters and I will talk to them. Asare, explain to them what we're doing."

Nana and the other men learned of Elder Kofi and the Okyeame's successful visit to the palace with great satisfaction and immediately started planning for the trip. The Okyeame began, "We'll travel light, with extra cloths and some dried meat. Our boots should last for the trip, but we'll take sandals too. We'll need small gourds to eat and drink, and we'll take machetes and knives. The Asantehene's soldiers will carry spears and guns. Nana, you'll need to give me gold dust, your scales, and weights."

"I'll go to the market to buy dried meat. Do we need anything else?" Elder Kwasi asked.

"No, but buy a good supply of dried meat. There are villages along the way, but we don't know how long the trip will take, and many people will be gone for the *Odwira*," Nana replied.

When the boys returned with water, Nana called them together saying, "Let's look at the cub and then we'll talk about tomorrow."

"Hold onto the vines so the cub won't run away," Madam Adjowa warned. The boys spread a cloth for the cub to play on and took it out of the basket. They sat in a circle to make a human cage, watching the cub scratch the cloth. They picked it up and let it lick their faces and arms.

"I think it likes the way we taste," Baako said.

"I'll look for more things for it to play with," Kofi Edu offered. The cub soon tumbled over a coconut, sticks, and a palm frond while the boys petted it.

"The cub plays with everything," Kwaku observed. "It's almost ready to climb trees!"

Nana was intrigued. He joined the boys and took his turn to hold the cub. "I want to see more leopards like this one in our forest. They're beautiful animals, and they'll serve us well. We're fortunate. It's rare for a person to hold a leopard cub. Baako, ask the Gurunsi boy to come look at the cub. He'll like it."

Baako brought the boy over. "His name is Awane, and he wants to see the cub. Awane, look at the cub," Baako said. Awane smiled but he didn't move.

"Hello, Awane," the others greeted him in Nankane.

"He's afraid of us," Nana said, "but at least he's seen the cub. Baako, take him back to his mother."

"It's better to hold a leopard than a crocodile," Kwame said. "Even a baby crocodile wouldn't be friendly, or a python or a puff adder or a cobra."

"Or a driver ant or a tsetse fly," Kwaku added. "Maybe a monkey."

"Monkeys get into everything," Nana said, smiling. "For holding, let's stay with chicks, lambs, and leopard cubs."

WITH THE CUB RETURNED TO ITS BASKET, NANA ASKED THE CHILDREN TO STAY WITH him. "You've seen two unusual sights today," he said. "First, the prisoners' market, and now a leopard cub. The cub is doing well. What did you think of the market?"

"I don't like seeing people chained together," Kofi Edu answered. "They looked sad."

"They've been captured and taken from their families. They don't know what will happen to them or what's happening to their families," Baako replied. "I see people with the scars of other groups in Kumasi, but only the Gurunsi are prisoners. I don't like that."

"It's strange," Kwaku struggled to describe his thoughts. "We treat prisoners like they aren't real people who have feelings. We buy them in the market like cassava, but when they're *nnonko,* we treat them better. When we adopt their children, they turn into real people again."

"Everything you're saying is true," Nana replied. "After we buy prisoners, we take care of them because we need them to work for us, but being a prisoner is a cruel fate."

"Papa, you're sending some of us to find a prisoner who's going to the coast. You haven't bought him yet. Do we really have to go?" Kwame asked.

"Yes, Kwame. Tomorrow you and Baako will begin a journey to find and buy a prisoner that's in the Okyeame and Asare's clan. If you succeed, we'll save a family. That's important, and that's why I'm doing this.

"Let me tell you more about the trip. You'll travel fast on the great-road to the coast with the Asantehene's messengers, and you should catch up with the traders and prisoners in three or four days. The great-road will be busy with people still coming to Kumasi for the *Odwira* and many traders, who use the road.

"The messengers will carry a golden sword. People will stand aside for them, so you won't be delayed. A drummer will be with you to let people know when the delegation approaches a village or town or needs help. You'll travel with soldiers who will keep you safe. You'll be well received everywhere."

Kwame and Baako looked at Nana and each other and began to feel better. "We can talk to the messengers and learn what they do," Kwame suggested. "They travel to many places, just like traders."

"I'm sorry that you'll miss the *Odwira* festival," Nana sympathized. "We'll miss you, but you have an important job. You'll be with the Okyeame and Elder Kwasi. They're smart and courageous. I trust them to take care of you. Do whatever they tell you. You'll carry supplies. You'll buy food along the way and carry dried meat. You're strong. We need your help. I'll bring you back to Kumasi for the *Odwira* in the next dry season."

"I'll do my best, Papa," Kwame promised. "I'm ready for the trip now."

"Baako, Asare will talk to you more about the trip," Nana explained. "He's certain that you'll travel well. He and your mother will be proud of you."

"*Medaase*, Nana," Baako answered. "I will try."

"I'll call Asare," Nana said. "We'll help you pack. Kwaku, take care of the cub."

THE TANOSO GROUP AND ELDER KWADWO'S FAMILY ROSE EARLY THE NEXT MORNING. Shivering in the cold air, they gathered around the warm hearth while Asare held a torch. Madam Adjowa served corn porridge. After eating several helpings, the travelers were ready for the trip. They said very little, conserving their energy for the day ahead. Picking up their supplies, they made their way to the Asantehene's palace with Nana leading, and were quickly admitted to the first courtyard.

Nana, Elder Kwadwo, and Elder Kofi greeted the two messengers and introduced the Tanoso group. The messengers welcomed them and explained that they traveled with two porters who would carry supplies and spears, two soldiers with guns, and a drummer. They hoped to reach Elmina in twelve days and return to Kumasi after resting two days.

They were willing to have company but only if they were not delayed.

"We understand your plan, and we are grateful for permission to join you," the Okyeame replied. "We want to travel fast. We hope to recover a prisoner in three or four days and return to Kumasi."

"You're strong and you'll do well," Nana encouraged Kwame and Baako once more. Asare put his arm around Baako's shoulders and talked to him quietly in Nankane.

Nana, Elder Kofi, Elder Kwadwo, and Asare reassured the full group and bid everyone, "*Nanteyie.*" Elder Kwasi, the Okyeame, Kwame, and Baako left with a strong sense of purpose.

Knowing that Madam Adjowa judged the prisoners healthy, the Tanoso group spent the rest of the morning at Elder Kwadwo's farm, settling the new *nnonko* and testing the newly-purchased guns. The guns proved worthy, and Nana decided to keep them.

Returning to Kumasi in the afternoon, Nana, Elders Kwadwo and Kofi, along with Asare and five other *nnonko* carrying head loads of kola nuts proceeded to the prisoners' market. The manager received the kola nuts as payment for three women. Nana concluded the purchase, and the manager returned the gold dust left in trust. Nana's remaining task for the day was to find and talk to Nana Somfo.

— CHAPTER 36 —

Nana Somfo and the Odwira Parade

"We'll walk along Adopm Street and look for friends from the western region," Nana said to Elder Kwadwo. "We may find Nana Somfo there."

"Agreed," Elder Kwadwo replied. "I like that street. Today, it will be full of people."

The two walked slowly, occasionally stopping in the shade of trees to talk to friends. They saw Nana Somfo and his *okyeame* at a distance and signaled to them. The two chiefs soon exchanged greetings.

"I hope that you like the big city," Nana said.

"I do," Nana Somfo replied enthusiastically. "Kumasi is full of life. I've kept busy since we arrived. I'm glad to see you."

"*Medaase*," Nana replied and turned to business right away. "Nana Somfo, I think that you brought a leopard cub to Kumasi."

Shaking his head in surprise, Nana Somfo answered, "Yes, I see that you know. My *nnonko* found it in a pit trap. It wasn't injured. The elders wanted to give it to the Asantehene."

"Did you talk about releasing it? About balance in the forest?"

"Very little. They aren't interested."

"You're new on the stool, and the elders are pressuring you," Nana sympathized. "When that happens, let me help you. I know that the Asantehene wants leopards to return to the forest. He'll talk about that when the chiefs gather. You'll hear him."

"I've already taken the cub to the palace. What will the Asantehene do with it?"

"My *okyeame* asked the king's officials to give it to me. I have it now."

Nana Somfo was startled and distressed. "What will happen to me since the Asantehene doesn't like the gift?"

"He won't say anything. Nothing will happen to you. When the Asantehene talks about the forest, he'll ask the chiefs to protect leopards, parrots, and falcons. Elephants are in danger, too. Even monkeys are threatened."

"Why are so many animals in danger?"

"Our population is growing, and people often hunt with guns. Before we had guns, we didn't kill so many animals. Your elders should also decide that none of the meat or feathers or tusks of these animals can be sold in your market or to whites. If you don't do this, you may hear from the Asantehene. The elders need to know that."

"What will you do with the cub?"

"I'll take it back to our forest, although it may not survive being away from its mother for so long. If it's alive when we return to Tanoso, help us find its mother. Ask your people if they have seen her and tell me what they say. I'll want to release it as soon as I return."

"I will help you," Nana Somfo said. "I'll contact you when I'm home. I'm an *Agona*, and you are an *Oyoko*. Parrots and falcons are important to us both. I want to protect them as well as leopards. I'm glad we talked." Nana Somfo bowed his head slightly as he and his *okyeame* walked away.

EARLY THE NEXT MORNING, NANA'S PEOPLE ASSEMBLED IN ELDER KWADWO'S COURT-yard to prepare for the *Odwira* parade. They inspected and cleaned Nana's regalia of gold bracelets, anklets, rings and necklaces, elaborate sandals, velvet head band with gold ornaments, kente cloth, horse tail switch, golden swords, and finally, his stool.

Nnonko opened the large umbrella that would shade Nana and the small umbrella that would protect his stool to ensure that their framework was intact. "Nana, the green and gold of your umbrella are forest colors. A golden falcon at the top of your umbrella will feel at home," Elder Kwadwo said.

Nana smiled and replied, "*Medaase.* The *Odwira* is an adventure for all of us. I want my people around me to show our strength. Elder Kwadwo, I want you to be my *okyeame* for the *Odwira*."

"I'll be honored, Nana," Elder Kwadwo replied.

Plans were made for the drummers and horn blowers to lead Nana's delegation in the parade, with the headmen following them carrying Nana's two swords. Kwaku, Kofi Edu, and Akosua would come next, in front of Nana, waving ostrich feathers and dancing to the music.

Shaded by his umbrella, Nana would walk and wave his horse tail switch. Elder Kwadwo, carrying the Okyeame's staff, and Elder Kofi would walk on one side of Nana. The other two elders would walk on the opposite side, each carrying a new gun. Three *nnonko* would carry Nana's umbrella, his stool, and its umbrella. Other *nnonko* would walk at the back of the delegation with Asare and come forward at times to trade off the work.

Like Nana, the elders would wear *kente* cloth, gold accessories, and elaborate sandals. The musicians and headmen would be in fine cloths, but not *kente*, with some gold accessories, and boots. Wearing waist cloths and tunics, the *nnonko* would walk barefoot except for Asare who would wear sandals. The delegation was big enough for Nana to display allegiance to the Asantehene and command the respect of other chiefs, but small enough to show that he lived far from the capital.

Looking at Kwaku, Akosua, and Kofi Edu, Nana said, "You'll be in front of me in the parade. Spread out across the street. Move around and wave the ostrich feathers high over your head to attract the crowd's attention. There will be drumming and horn blowing all of the time. It will be like a dance."

"I have something to wave, too. Look at my horse tail switch," Nana said, handing it to Kwaku. "It's real horse tail hair attached to a leather strap with a handle."

"What is it for?" Kwaku asked as he, Kofi Edu, and Akosua took turns holding it.

"It carries a message," Nana explained. "Each chief who has at least a thousand people in his district may carry one. It means that I can lead fifty soldiers in the Asantehene's army. When he sees it, the king will know about my district and how much we pay in taxes. I'll wave the switch while you're waving the ostrich feathers."

"Where does the horse tail come from?" Kwaku wanted to know. "We don't have horses."

"Traders from the savannah and the whites bring horse tail hair to trade."

"That's weird. What about the ostrich feathers?" Kofi Edu asked. "I want to see an ostrich. Where do they live?"

"In the savannah," Nana answered. "I've never seen one. Traders don't bring the birds to Kumasi, just the feathers. I've been told that ostriches are as tall as a man and don't fly. They walk around on long legs like people."

"I can't even imagine a bird like that," Kofi Edu said, shaking his head.

"People will shoot guns in the air with no musket balls," Nana reminded the children. "If the noise is too loud, cover your ears with your hands."

"We won't be scared," the three agreed. "We want to be there."

"We'll be gone for a long time," Nana continued. "Eat well before we leave. We'll buy street food later. Madam Adjowa, Elder Kojo, and other people in our family will go to the Place of the Cannons to watch the parade. They'll be near the Asantehene. You can leave our delegation there and join them if you want to. They'll be home before the rest of us.

"Be sure to leave milk for the cub, close the cage, and put it in a hut. One of Madam Adjowa's sisters will stay here to watch it."

"I'll leave now and go to Uncle Kojo's to work on the doll for Akua," Kofi Edu explained. "I'll be back before you leave."

"*Medaase*, Kofi. Akua will be happy to have a doll," Nana said.

Kwaku and Akosua cared for the cub. They fed it goat milk and raw chicken. They tied fresh vines around it and carried it while skipping through the courtyard with the ostrich feathers. Occasionally the drummers and horn blowers played music. The excitement grew.

"The *Odwira* will be fun," Akosua said. "I wish we could take the cub with us. Everyone would like to see it!"

"Oh, no, Akosua," Kwaku replied. "Everyone would want to hold the cub. It would get scared and run away. We need to keep it safe. I want the *Odwira* to be perfect."

"Let's pretend that we're in the parade now," Akosua proposed. "Let's march. I'll carry the cub. Look, it likes my ostrich feather. It's trying to grab it. Look!"

"*O-dwir-a! O-dwir-a! O-dwir-a!*" Kwaku and Akosua chanted, marching and waving ostrich feathers while Nana completed preparations for the parade.

EARLY THAT AFTERNOON NANA'S DELEGATION LEFT ELDER KWADWO'S HOME TO JOIN the *Odwira* parade winding through the streets of Kumasi to the Place of the Cannons. Feelings of excitement and anticipation were high.

Every chief in the kingdom was due in Kumasi to celebrate the *Odwira*. Thousands gathered to join or watch the parade. Side streets were crowded and delegations advanced slowly as participants and spectators alike savored a view of the splendor that the chiefs brought to the city.

Umbrellas borne high to protect the chiefs and their stools stood like tall, colorful trees in an urban forest and cast cooling shadows in the afternoon sun. Bearers twirled the umbrellas and pumped them up and down to circulate the air. Drummers, horn blowers, and bell ringers played music in rhythmic and deafening sequence. Bursts of gunfire filled the sky with smoke. Women selling food circulated through the crowd, calling out to attract buyers. People talked and ate and cheered, energized by the clashing sounds.

Nana proceeded slowly, shaded by his umbrella and waving his horse tail switch. His stool and its umbrella followed him, carried by *nnonko*. The drummers and horn blowers performed. The headmen twirled Nana's swords and Kwaku, Kofi Edu, and Akosua danced. Behind Nana the *nnonko* walked under Asare's direction.

The children complained about reflections of light from Nana's swords. "Dance away from the swords," Nana counseled them while enjoying the spectacle.

As the delegation proceeded, Nana talked to the elders. "I see power and authority in every delegation. The Asantehenes have built a kingdom that is unstoppable."

"Yes, they've kept the chiefs loyal," Elder Kwadwo said. "We see that here. Osei Bonsu has brought the Fante into the kingdom. We don't have a peace treaty yet, but our traders can reach the coast now to trade directly with the whites."

"Some of the whites no longer buy prisoners. We don't know what that means yet," Nana replied. "We may have to pay higher prices for goods in the market, especially guns and ammunition. We need guns to hunt and fight in the army. If we don't have enough guns, some groups may refuse to fight."

"Akans will always need *nnonko*," Elder Kofi commented, "but the Asantehene may change the taxes on the savannah kingdoms. He could get more sheep and cloth and fewer prisoners. There may be fewer raids on the Gurunsi. That would be a good change."

"If the Asantehene has prisoners that he can't control and can't sell, he may kill them. That used to happen," Elder Kwadwo said. "I don't want to see that again. The Asantehene will have to learn what the whites are doing before he makes changes."

Nana reserved the rest of the conversation for another time. He looked for other chiefs from his region and waved when he saw them. They waved back.

Kwaku, Kofi Edu, and Akosua liked swinging the ostrich feathers in wide arcs as they danced and ran around and through the delegation. They kept time to the music while wincing at the flashing light. The elders warned them not to get tired because the wait could be long.

"We can't run slowly. This is fun," Kofi Edu exclaimed.

CHAPTER 37

The Place of the Cannons

Spectators at the Odwira parade

ENTERING THE PLACE OF THE CANNONS AT SUNSET, NANA WAS STRUCK ONCE MORE BY its enormity. It sheltered thousands. Delegations circled the Place slowly, greeting the spectators, including soldiers celebrating their victory over the Fante.

Horn blowing, drumming, and gunfire grew intense. The twirling umbrellas caught the rhythm of the music and moved the air. The urban forest danced.

"I love the bright colors of the *Odwira* umbrellas," Akosua exclaimed. "I love watching the umbrellas twirl. They hear the music."

"Listen to the elephant tusk horns," Kofi Edu shouted. "Do you hear them? They are so loud. Are real elephants this loud?"

"We hear them," both Kwaku and Akosua answered, covering their ears with their hands.

Nana's delegation passed a grand assemblage of drummers who tossed their small white drums into the air, caught them as they fell, and continued their fierce drumming.

Hausa traders and Moors, mounted on magnificent horses and wearing elaborate robes and turbans, watched the parade. Nana and the children waved to Amir and Abdul, who waved back.

The manager of the prisoners' market stood with prisoners who hadn't sold, men chained together and women holding children.

"They see the power of the kingdom that will sell them," Nana observed to Elder Kofi. "This display must frighten them."

"I hope Akans will buy them," Elder Kofi replied.

"Let us hope," Nana agreed.

Next stood Madam Adjowa, Madam Yaa, Elder Kojo, and the goldsmith, who applauded. Nana's group waved to them.

Half way around the Place of the Cannons, the chiefs of the Kumasi council were seated in elaborate chairs. The nobility of the kingdom, they were resplendent in *kente* cloths and gold adornment and looked more serious than the Asantehene himself. Nana nodded an acknowledgement to the group, and each responded with a slightly raised right hand. The chiefs smiled when the children danced before them.

Nana's delegation stopped to wait for a group of a hundred or more of the king's soldiers dancing to celebrate the military victories of all of the Asantehenes. Each soldier carried a long knife in one hand, striking it against the skull of a slain enemy held in the other hand. Inside of each skull was a stem of thyme that kept the spirits of the dead from troubling the king. The Asantehenes had long collected and displayed the skulls to show the kingdom's strength.

While waiting, the musicians of Nana's delegation performed. Elder Kofi joined the children to explain what the skulls meant. "This is awful," Kofi Edu said. "I've heard about the skulls, but I've never seen them before." The three children stood close together in silence.

Elder Kofi encouraged the children. "The skulls show the king's power, but look at his friendly smile. Asantehene Osei Bonsu is feared as a courageous general yet known for his kindness and generosity. He keeps the traditions of our people, and his rule is strong. He does business well with the foreigners who surround our kingdom. He keeps us safe."

Asantehene Osei Bonsu and the Golden Stool

Nana's delegation approached Asantehene Osei Bonsu, who was seated under a huge red umbrella topped by a golden elephant. Next to him the Golden Stool was displayed on its side in a chair.

The Asantehene wore an elaborate *kente* cloth and numerous gold ornaments on his toes, sandals, ankles, wrists, fingers, and arms, with more around his neck and on his leather headdress. "He looks rich and powerful, but it's hard for him to move with all of that weight," Nana whispered to Elder Kofi, who agreed.

"The new design of his *kente* is intricate," Elder Kofi observed. "Weavers must have spent weeks working on it. Will we see it in Tanoso some day?" Nana smiled at the question.

"The Golden Stool is magnificent," Nana observed to the elders. "I feel inspired and blessed when I see it. I serve it willingly for the peace that it brings to our forest."

"I hope that the Fante will stay in the kingdom and that peace will endure," Okyeame Kwadwo said as Nana's delegation stood at attention in front of the Asantehene.

Nana's horn blowers and drummers performed at their loudest. An *odonko* twirled Nana's large green and yellow umbrella. A second *odonko* twirled the smaller umbrella that shaded Nana's stool. The headmen waved Nana's swords. The children danced with their ostrich feathers swaying in the air.

Nana held the horse tail switch above his head, moving it back and forth slowly as the long grey horse hairs rippled in the air. The elders stood near Nana, two firing their guns and Okyeame Kwadwo displaying his staff. Asare and the other *nnonko* remained at the back, still and silent.

The musicians and headmen parted to let the children edge closer to the Asantehene whose face broadened in a welcoming smile. Seizing his time before the Asantehene, Kwaku danced faster and faster to show his energy and strength. Kofi Edu and Akosua struggled to keep up with him. With dancing, spinning umbrellas and swords, thundering music, and gun smoke rising in the air, the delegation pleased the crowd, which applauded. Nana looked proud. The Asantehene studied the group carefully.

"Tanosohene Nana Anyensu," Okyeame Kwadwo announced. Having judged Nana's status from the appearance of the delegation, and knowing no complaints against him, the Asantehene raised his hand in approval while speaking to his *okyeame,* who approached to talk to Okyeame Kwadwo, who then conferred with Nana.

With Nana's approval, Okyeame Kwadwo spoke to the children. "The Asantehene invites you to join the group of children seated in front of him. They are from his family and the families of the Kumasi chiefs. Do you want to do that?"

Kwaku, Kofi Edu, and Akosua talked briefly, and Akosua replied for them all saying enthusiastically, "Yes, we do!"

Okyeame Kwadwo conferred once more with Nana and the elders and then cautioned the children, "Keep the ostrich feathers and stay with this group. Elder Kofi will come back for you when Nana reaches the end of the parade. It's a compliment to be invited. Do whatever the Asantehene's *okyeame* asks you to do. We must leave."

Kwaku, Kofi Edu, and Akosua squeezed into the group of children. "I'm excited," Akosua said. "There's so much noise and so many people, and the Asantehene is so grand. I wonder what will happen."

"We're in a delegation of children," Kwaku said with amusement and some apprehension as he sat on the ground and held his ostrich feather high.

Turning to the girl seated next to her, Akosua said, "My name is Akosua. Please be my friend. What do we do here?"

"We'll be friends," the girl replied. "My name is Yaa. We're all waving something. Do that and cheer for the chiefs when they stop. The Asantehene usually likes them, but sometimes he doesn't. He tells his soldiers to arrest the ones he doesn't like."

"Why doesn't he like them?" Akosua asked.

"They've done something bad. I don't know what."

"Look at the Golden Stool!" Kwaku whispered and pointed. "It's on its side to keep bad spirits away just like the black stools. I know it's powerful but I'm not afraid of it. Can we get closer?"

The Golden Stool

"No! Don't try!" Yaa warned. "The people around it are guards. They have swords. They'll chop your head off."

"I'm not going to hurt it," Kwaku explained. "My papa told me that the little bells are in the shape of enemies that Asantehenes have killed, and that now the Asantehene uses the bells to call his ancestors. I want to see them better."

"Kwaku, be happy with what you can see from here. We don't want to make the Asantehene mad," Kofi Edu warned. "Look at the next delegation. Let's wave our feathers."

The group of children waved whatever they had in their hands: feathers, feather fans, and palm fronds. The objects looked like the leaves of forest trees blowing in the wind before a storm. "I wish we could make it rain," one child said, and the others laughed.

From time to time, the Asantehene sent women to the children's group with trays of coconut meat and pineapple and orange slices, which the children ate eagerly.

As the sky grew dark, men lighted torches to illuminate the Place and the parade route. The flickering light created shadows that danced among the people.

AFTER THE CHILDREN WATCHED THE ASANTEHENE APPROVE MANY DELEGATIONS, AN especially large one drew near. Kwaku counted forty drummers. Behind them came many ranks of horn blowers, swordsmen, men carrying guns, and hunters bearing spears. The chief's umbrella and his gold adornments were elaborate. His stool was ornate. The drumming, horn blowing, shooting, and dancing invited admiration. The crowd cheered. The children waved their hand-held objects wildly.

When the delegation faced the Asantehene, he looked angry, and with a wave of his hand, silenced the music. All other activity stopped immediately. Spectators fell silent. The Asantehene directed soldiers to approach the delegation. They told everyone to lay down whatever they carried. The delegation obeyed and stood perfectly still as soldiers reached the chief, seized him, and walked him quickly out of the Place while other soldiers stood guard. The crowd gasped. Members of the delegation retreated.

"That chief has been arrested," Yaa explained.

"What will happen to him?" Akosua asked.

"Maybe they'll have a trial to see if he's guilty of something. The parade will start again soon."

"This is scary," Akosua said. "Kwaku, I want to go home."

"We're okay. Just wait for awhile, Akosua," Kwaku answered.

"We have a monkey at my home," Yaa told Akosua. "You can come see it if you want to. It's cute, and you can play with it."

"Oh, I want to see it. Can I go home with you tonight?" Akosua asked.

"Yes, we can walk you to your home afterwards if it's not far away. I want to go home now, too."

"Thank you, but I have to wait for someone to come find us first. Can my brother and cousin come, too?"

"Of course. I'll go look for my papa now," Yaa explained.

Within a short time, Elder Kofi returned. "How do you like being part of the Asantehene's group?" he asked.

"It's good. We've seen a lot of chiefs," Kofi Edu replied.

"The Golden Stool is beautiful. There it is," Kwaku said, pointing.

"We saw a chief get arrested," Akosua explained. "That was scary. We don't know what he did wrong. What do you think will happen to him?"

"I don't know, Akosua," Elder Kofi replied. "All of the chiefs have to be here so that any problems can be cleared up. Getting arrested, though, is serious. There might be a trial. Are you ready to go home now? Nana and the others have returned to the Place and will stay here until the celebration is over. I'll take you home."

"Here comes my friend, Yaa, with her papa," Akosua said.

Elder Kofi greeted them, "*Mema mo adwo* – Good evening."

"*Yaa*. I am Osei Yaw, one of the Asantehene's brothers. My daughter would like your children to visit us and see our pet monkey. If you take Yaa home, I'll appreciate it. I need to stay here until the celebration's over. We live at the palace. The guards know Yaa and will let you in."

"Of course we'll take Yaa home and see her pet. I have a question. The children told me that a chief was arrested not long ago. Do you know who he is and why he was arrested?"

"Yes, that was a chief from a district near Fante territory. He's accused of helping two Fante generals escape after a battle with the Asantehene's army. It is said that he did it for a big payment in guns, and that his soldiers took the generals beyond the Tano River and released them. There will be a trial, and if he's found guilty of treason, he'll be punished severely."

Elder Kofi shook his head. "He was brave to come here but foolish to help the Fante if he did. We'll take your daughter to the palace now and see the monkey. I'm glad that we met."

The two men bowed slightly to each other and parted. Elder Kofi and the children walked around the Place of the Cannons once more to see the spectacle. Kwaku described the scene. "I hear music and I see umbrellas dancing in the torch light. I hear guns firing. I smell smoke. I feel like I'm in a forest of people, and there are hunters, but the animals are hiding. I'll never forget this. I'll tell Kwame and Baako about it. They have to know."

"I've seen the *Odwira* many times," Yaa said. "It's always big and noisy and exciting."

"I can't see the colors of the umbrellas anymore," Akosua said. "It's too dark. I miss them."

Kwaku was curious about the cannons. "Papa, this is the Place of the Cannons, but we don't see any cannons. Where are they?"

"They're here," Elder Kofi replied. "They're behind the Asantehene so you can't see them now. We'll come back and look for them."

"I want to know what they're like," Kwaku answered.

Elder Kofi and the children walked to the palace, where guards let them in. "Follow me," Yaa said. "We'll find my mama, and I'll show you the monkey." The group, accompanied by a guard, followed Yaa through a labyrinth of corridors and courtyards, greeting people along the way. "You see that not everyone's at the parade," Yaa explained.

"The palace is big," Kwaku observed. "I wonder where we're going."

Yaa found her mother with several others eating in a large dining room. Yaa introduced her new friends whom her mother greeted warmly. "I want to show them my monkey," Yaa explained.

"Of course, I'll show the way," Yaa's mother replied. Entering a courtyard, Yaa ran to pick up a small black and white monkey that seemed to greet her.

"She's beautiful, isn't she," Yaa said, petting the monkey's back. "Her name is *Kwadu* – Banana. That's her favorite food. I feed her every day and give her water. I talk to her, too, and I think she talks to me. I have to bathe her and clean up after her, but I don't mind. Do you want to hold her? Be gentle and talk to her." Yaa handed Kwadu to Akosua.

The monkey put her arms around Akosua's neck and seemed to hug her. "She's very sweet," Akosua said. "Where did she come from?"

"She's from the forest, but I don't know where. Someone gave her to the Asantehene when she was a baby. He gave her to me. I'm like her mother. We keep her on a long leash. A lot of children live here, and we all play with her."

"Kofi Edu, do you want to hold Kwadu?" Akosua asked, handing him the monkey.

"For a little while. Can we come back sometime to play with the children here?" Kofi Edu asked as he handed Kwadu to Kwaku.

"We would be happy if you visit us," Yaa's mother answered. "We welcome children."

Elder Kofi explained that he and Kwaku were visiting for the *Odwira,* and that Akosua and Kofi Edu lived nearby. "We would be happy if Kofi Edu and Akosua returned to play," Yaa's mother said. "The rest of you are welcome when you visit Kumasi."

Kwaku admired Kwadu. "I think she's smart," he said. "We know about monkeys and bananas. Yaw Mensah should meet a monkey sometime. He might learn to like them. He could make friends with Kwadu when he visits Kumasi."

After a short stay, Elder Kofi and the children thanked Yaa and her mother for showing them the monkey and inviting them to return. Yaa guided the visitors back to the entrance of the palace. "I want to see you again," she said to Akosua and Kofi Edu.

"We'll come back," Akosua promised.

— CHAPTER 38 —

Chiefs and Cannons

ODWIRA FESTIVITIES CONTINUED LATE INTO THE NIGHT. KUMASI WAS QUIET THE NEXT morning. Many slept through the morning and welcomed the ample supply of palm wine that the Asantehene distributed in the afternoon. The king conducted private rituals in the palace. In the late afternoon, he was borne by *nnonko* through the city in a palanquin, under a large umbrella, and accompanied by his councilors and musicians while guns were fired and spectators applauded.

The next day the Asantehene met with the chiefs in a palace courtyard. Elephant tusk horns and talking drums heralded the king's arrival. The chiefs stood as the Asantehene joined them and took his place in an elaborate chair. He wore an elegant *kente* cloth and gold ornaments, was shaded by a large umbrella, and surrounded by court officials. The king welcomed the chiefs and elders.

Speaking through his *okyeame*, the Asantehene immediately began by describing the war with the Fante. "The tax collectors and traders told us about the war, but I welcome hearing directly from the Asantehene," Nana said to Elders Kwadwo and Kofi as they all listened intently.

"The Fante should never have defied us," the Asantehene asserted. "They should never have blocked our pathway to the coast. They insulted us and refused diplomacy. They fought hard. We destroyed many villages and towns. I didn't want to do that."

The chiefs responded, "*Yoo.*"

"At Anomabo, I saw the ocean for the first time. It is as big as the sky. I struck it with my sword, and the water rose like that from a whale's spout. Now people are calling me Osei the Whale, Osei Bonsu. I like my new name.

"The whites at Fort Anomabo sheltered hundreds of Fante. When the whites closed the doors, more Fante crowded around the outside. We attacked, and both the Fante and the whites fired on us. After a long battle, the Fante on the beach fled, and the whites surrendered. We took half of the Fante inside the fort as prisoners. I've given some of them to my generals and sent the rest to my farms. The governor of the fort kept the others. I've learned that he sent them away on ships.

"Our soldiers were brave, but death hung heavy in the air that day. The governor of the fort came to my camp, and we made peace. In the next days, many of my soldiers became ill with small pox. I sent them home while I stayed to fight rebels. I returned to Kumasi for the *Odwira* and honored the soldiers who came with me. I left some in Fante territory to patrol.

"I'll return to the coast soon and work with Fante chiefs for a lasting peace. Our traders should be safe in Fante territory now. We are the victors, but war is always bad. I am a man of peace. I don't want to fight the Fante again." The chiefs congratulated the king and strongly supported his wish for peace.

"What is the road in Fante territory like?" a chief asked.

"There is a road that's open, but it's narrow and filled with roots. The Fante have to build a better one for our traders and our army," the *okyeame* replied. "Traders report that whites at Anomabo and Cape Coast no longer trade for prisoners."

"Why is this happening?" several chiefs asked.

"The Asantehene doesn't know why. He will find out," the *okyeame* answered. "For now, we'll trade prisoners at Elmina Castle and in Accra."

The chiefs continued to talk about the Fante and the possible continuation of the war. They were concerned that more soldiers would be called. "Who will you call? When?" They wanted to know.

The *okyeame* replied, "The Asantehene can say only that those who defeated the Fante will not be called again. Soldiers from other districts will accompany the Asantehene when he returns to Fante territory. He will leave soldiers there to ensure peace and oversee the building of a new road." It was only after some time that the chiefs were willing to turn to other subjects.

The *okyeame* reported that the annual tax had been successfully collected from all districts. "The Asantehene thanks the chiefs for their cooperation. He will share with the chiefs much of what he has received in taxes from the savannah kingdoms."

Nana raised his hand, and the *okyeame* told him to rise and speak. "I am also a man of peace," Nana began. "I seek peace in our forest. We kill animals to eat, but we are killing too many. Think of the leopards, elephants, monkeys, parrots, and falcons that you used to see. Where have they gone?"

Several chiefs showed their concern, intoning, "*Yoo*." Some added their thoughts.

"We have no leopards in my district. My father and grandfathers remembered them."

"I've never seen an elephant in my district."

"There are too many pythons and hogs. Not enough monkeys. Baboons are moving in."

"Crocodiles thrive. They are a curse."

There were no dissenting views. "I agree with you," the Asantehene replied through his *okyeame*. "Do not bring animals to Kumasi as gifts. Protect your forest animals, especially leopards. I want to welcome more elephants in the forest, too. Trading tusks to whites is not good business. When you come to the next *Odwira*, tell me how many leopards and elephants you count in your district."

Nana was pleased with the discussion and raised another matter. "I have enough stool land for more farms, and I want more people to come to my district. I invite my fellow chiefs to send people so our numbers will grow. I want more traders to follow."

The Asantehene conferred with his *okyeame* who replied, "We have heard you. We will remember you when there are people who need a new home."

Nana was satisfied with the response. He turned to Elders Kofi and Kwadwo to say, "I'll have much to talk to my council about when I'm home."

Many other topics were discussed as the meeting stretched into the mid-afternoon. At its conclusion, Nana and Elder Kwadwo walked toward the market. Elder Kofi left to find Kwaku. They all planned to meet later at the Place of the Cannons.

Nana and Elder Kwadwo walked along a broad street, greeting and talking to friends. "My children are working today," Elder Kwadwo explained. "This is a busy time in the market. We'll see Kofi Edu at his Uncle Kojo's stall. Akosua is helping her Auntie Yaa."

Nana and Elder Kwadwo soon greeted Elder Kojo. "*Maaha.*"

"*Yaa.*"

Seeing Kofi Edu at his work bench, Nana repeated, "*Maaha.*" Kofi Edu returned the greeting.

"The *Odwira* parade was magnificent. Your delegation was solid," Elder Kojo complimented Nana.

"*Medaase.* It's good for so many from Tanoso to be here," Nana replied. "I've come to pick up the doll and the horse."

"We're ready for you. Kofi Edu, bring them here."

Kofi Edu showed Nana the two carvings. "The doll is beautiful," Nana complimented him. "You've done excellent work. Akua will be pleased. *Medaase.*"

Kofi Edu bowed his head and smiled. "You're welcome," he replied.

Nana picked up the horse in both hands and turned it around and over to look at it carefully.

"This looks like a real horse," he said, "just like the ones we see here in Kumasi. Yaw Mensah will be surprised. He'll come to Kumasi with me someday and see a horse. With this one, he'll know what to look for. *Medaase*."

Carved horse for Yaw Mensah

"You're welcome," Elder Kojo replied, smiling. "You have Kofi Edu's fine work and the first horse that I've carved. I'll carve more. I think people will buy them because there aren't horses anywhere else in the kingdom."

"Thank you for making a cage for the cub, too," Nana added. "It's perfect. We'll use it to carry the cub to Tanoso."

"You'll have to work hard to care for the cub," Elder Kojo said. "I hope that it will survive the long trip. I've wrapped the doll and the horse in leaves, and I'll put them in this small basket that Elder Kwadwo can carry. You don't have helpers today."

Nana paid and said, "*Medaase*," once more. "I hope that we'll see each other at the next *Odwira*."

Elder Kojo agreed, saying, "*Nanteyie*."

"*Medaase*," Nana replied.

WALKING TO THE GOLDSMITH'S STALL, NANA EXPLAINED HIS FEELINGS TO HIS COUSIN. "I'm happy in Kumasi. I see so much that's new. I always want to come and then to leave. I miss my family, my town, and the forest, though it's good to see you and your family."

"We always welcome your visit," Elder Kwadwo replied.

Golden falcon to top Nana's umbrella

The goldsmith handed Nana the falcon, now covered with gold leaf. "It's as bright as the sun," Nana said in praise of the goldsmith's work. "It's perfect for my umbrella. *Medaase*." Handing the falcon to Elder Kwadwo, Nana paid the goldsmith.

"The falcon has come to life," Elder Kwadwo said in admiration as he placed the falcon, now wrapped in leaves, in the basket.

"I have one more stop to make," Nana said. "Let's find the looking glasses."

"Why?" Elder Kwadwo asked with surprise.

"Akosua told me about looking glasses," Nana replied. "She showed me one, and I saw my face for the first time. I didn't know how I looked. I was surprised. I want to take some home for gifts." Elder Kwadwo showed the way.

They found looking glasses in different sizes and shapes. Nana explained his interest to the trader. "Many people who come here have never seen looking glasses before," the trader replied. "They're always pleased when they see their face. These looking glasses are metal. They won't break, so you'll have them for a long time."

Nana bargained for a good price, bought several, and added them to the basket, saying, "*Medaase*," to the trader.

WHEN ELDER KOFI AND KWAKU ENTERED THE PLACE OF THE CANNONS LATE THAT afternoon, it was almost empty. "The Place was crowded and noisy just two days ago, now it's totally different," Kwaku remarked to his father. They joined Nana and Elder Kwadwo. "Where are the cannons?" Kwaku asked.

"Walk this way," Elder Kwadwo said as he led the group across the Place toward a slight rise where the Asantehene had sat during the parade. On the ground at the top of the rise lay two large, weathered cannon barrels. Everyone bent down to touch the barrels and try to move them with little success.

Kwaku rubbed his hands along each barrel. "They're rough," he said. "They look like tree branches, and they feel like bark, but they're hollow. Snakes could nest inside of them. I know they're big guns. How do whites use them?"

"We see only part of them here, so we don't know how they work," Elder Kwadwo replied. "I've heard that soldiers fire a ball as big as coconut out of them. Whites keep cannons in their castles and forts and fire them at enemy ships, and the ships fire back with their own cannons. Traders say that cannons in the castles and forts face the ocean and sound like thunder when they're fired. Whites use cannons to fight each other, not Akans. Asantehene Osei Tutu brought these cannons to Kumasi so we'll know about them."

"Will Akans ever fight the whites? Will I ever have to do that?" Kwaku asked.

Nana and the elders sighed deeply. "I hope that Akans will never fight the whites," Nana answered. "The Asantehene told us that whites in the fort at Anomabo fired at his army because he attacked the Fante soldiers who had taken refuge outside of the fort. That attack was unusual.

"Castles have been on the coast for a very long time, since before Osei Tutu created our kingdom," Nana recalled. "Whites came to the coast to trade for gold and ivory, not to fight us. Traders say that whites get sick when they leave their castles. Whites don't bring many soldiers, and soldiers can't fight when they're sick.

"You asked an important question, Kwaku," Nana continued. "I don't think that you, Kwame, or Baako will have to fight against whites. Our people may fight the Fante or kingdoms in the savannah again. I hope not, but it's possible."

"I don't want to fight anyone," Kwaku responded. "I hope that you and my papa won't have to fight in a war."

"I hope so, too," Nana replied.

Elder Kofi wanted to share his thoughts. "In the *Odwira* parade, I felt the weight of our history as the chiefs pledged loyalty to the Asantehene and honored the Golden Stool. We may see the future from here, too. If some whites stop trading for prisoners, then the Gonja may stop raiding the Gurunsi so much. Asare's people may be safer. We'll always need *nnonko* but maybe not so many."

"I'm thinking of the future, too," Elder Kwadwo said. "At the Odwira festival, we saw scholars who work for the Asantehene. If they continue to read and write for him, then other chiefs may use them. If you become a chief, Kwaku, you may need to read and write so you can send messages to other chiefs and to traders and learn new ideas. That might be in our future."

"I am the chief of a large district, but there are more powerful chiefs between the Asantehene and me," Nana interjected. "I am loyal to them, and they are loyal to me, and each of us needs the others to remain strong. Some chiefs oppose writing, but the Asantehene has shown us its value. I believe that, like wisdom, writing can spread among the chiefs and then among our people. I believe that writing and books can be important."

"How can I learn to read and write?" Kwaku asked.

"The people who can teach you are here in Kumasi," Elder Kwadwo said. "Let me find out about them."

"Learn to read and write in Kumasi, Kwaku, but you'll need to learn to be a chief from our ancestors, the elders, the Queen Mother, and me," Nana cautioned. "A chief must always talk to others and use our history and our stories. We use many words, many more than you can write. You must know what to say to reach everyone."

Part Three:

THE COAST

Cape Coast Castle

— CHAPTER 39 —

Leaving Kumasi

Two days before the Odwira festival, crowds still streamed toward Kumasi. Travelers on the great-road between Kumasi and the coast stepped aside when they saw the golden sword, identifying the Asantehene's messengers, who traveled fast. The Okyeame, Elder Kwasi, Kwame, and Baako struggled to keep up.

When the messengers came to a log barrier, tax collectors let them pass immediately. Others waited for long periods as their goods were inspected and a toll calculated. With a fast and steady pace, the messengers made good progress.

"I like to walk fast," Kwame said to Baako a few times, "but we're going so fast now that I'm breathing hard and can barely talk."

"I feel strong even though I'm breathing hard, too," Baako replied. "I like to walk fast on a wide road. I could be a messenger someday."

"So could I," Kwame said. "We could be traders, too. They don't travel so fast, and they're probably richer." Baako smiled.

The Okyeame and Elder Kwasi talked only occasionally. They were strong, but they, too, found the pace exhausting. "This trip can be so fast only in the dry season." Elder Kwasi commented several times. "Rains will make even this road muddy."

"Traders and messengers travel in rainy and dry seasons," the Okyeame replied. "This is always a trip for the strong, with hills to climb and creeks and rivers to cross. People get sick along the way, especially prisoners. I hope that our group stays healthy and the prisoners' group, too. Sick prisoners might be abandoned or worse."

"Children wouldn't survive this trip. It's too brutal," Elder Kwasi added.

"The messengers say that the Fante have been peaceful since the Asantehene defeated their army," the Okyeame recounted. "Officials at the palace said that messengers and traders get through to the castles now without being forced to pay fees or sell their goods or prisoners to the Fante."

"The only problem is the road in Fante territory. The Fante haven't built good roads,"

Elder Kwasi said. "They don't want foreigners to come into their district, even other Akans, like us. I'm glad that we have soldiers with us, but I expect the Fante to stay peaceful."

"I'm sorry that we're missing the *Odwira*," the Okyeame expressed his concern. "Seeing the other chiefs, the Asantehene, and the Golden Stool is exciting. I always find something new at the festival."

"I'll miss it, too, and I regret that Kwame and Baako won't be there," Elder Kwasi replied. "Festivals are important to celebrate and remember who we are, but this mission can make a difference for our families."

The group traveled through hilly farm land where few trees remained. *Nnonko* worked in the fields. Some of the land belonged to the Asantehene and some to farmers like Elder Kwadwo.

"Kwame, these farms look like Nana's," Baako said.

"You're right."

"Gurunsis are working here," Baako observed. "I see their scars."

"I see Gurunsis and *nnonko* from other places, too," Kwame said. "They're all working hard. They have to be strong to work like that all day."

"Can the traders sell prisoners along this road?" Baako asked.

"No, that's against the law. Do you think any prisoners will try to escape?"

"No," Baako answered. "There's no place for them to go. They don't speak Twi, and their scars show that they're foreign."

"They could hide in the day and travel at night," Kwame suggested.

"No Akans would help them. They would be captured."

"You're right," Baako. "They don't know how to find the savannah, either," Kwame said. "It's too far away."

When the messengers approached a town, the drummer announced their arrival, and the golden sword identified them. Elders offered them food and water since the chiefs were in Kumasi. The group stopped while it was still light, bathed, rested, ate dinner, and slept, preparing for an early start the next morning. The messengers did not pay for the services, but the Okyeame paid for his group.

"This trip is fast, and the road is good," Baako said to Kwame as they unrolled their sleeping mats. "We'll catch up with the traders soon."

Kwame and Baako relaxed after a day of strenuous travel, tired but no longer apprehensive.

After two days of travel, a soldier in the messengers' delegation became ill. The group stopped early that afternoon. One of the messengers explained to the

Okyeame and Elder Kwasi, "The herbalist in this town will treat the soldier, and we'll wait for a day to see if he gets better. If he's still sick tomorrow night, we'll recruit someone here to join us and carry a gun. We have to continue, and we need protection."

"I can carry a gun and shoot well. Let me take the soldier's place," Elder Kwasi offered.

"If the soldier is sick tomorrow, you can show me how well you shoot, and then I'll decide," the messenger replied. "If you replace the soldier, we'll need you for the full trip. I know that you planned to return to Kumasi after we catch up with the traders."

"We don't want to be delayed," Elder Kwasi explained. "Overtaking the traders is our greatest concern. After that, I'll continue if you need me, and the rest of my group will decide what to do separately."

The soldier was still sick the next morning, and the messenger got the approval of the town's elders to fire a gun on their land. He and Elder Kwasi walked a safe distance into the forest. With the soldier's gun and ammunition in hand, Elder Kwasi told the messenger to point to some targets.

"That tree. The one over there. The one further away. That fat raffia palm." Elder Kwasi fired and made four direct hits. The messenger observed how well and quickly Elder Kwasi loaded the gun and fired.

"You can take the soldier's place if we need you," the messenger concluded. "Like you, we don't want to be delayed. We'll leave early tomorrow morning. Thank you for your offer to help."

THE TANOSO GROUP WELCOMED A DAY OF REST AND USED IT TO TALK TO PEOPLE IN the town and explore the area. They learned that more traders had passed this way since the Asantehene defeated the Fante. Trade barriers have come down, they heard. The Fante road isn't good but it's safe, townspeople told them.

In the afternoon, the boys talked to Elder Kwasi.

"I'm confused about the Fante. Who are they?" Baako asked.

Elder Kwasi explained the complicated story. "The Fante are an Akan group that lives on the coast and that hasn't been in the kingdom before. They speak Twi with a different accent than ours and some different words, but we understand each other. They live next to the whites' fort and castle, and some of them work for the whites.

"The Fante were one of the first Akans to get guns. Their armies have always been strong, and they've always fought the kingdom. For a long time, they intercepted our traders and bought their goods, including prisoners, to sell to the whites. On the Fante part of the coast, our traders could never reach the ocean. Since the Asantehene defeated the Fante, our traders can trade directly with whites in Fante territory. The Fante still do their own trading with the whites and also work for them."

"I thought all Akans wanted to be in the kingdom," Kwame said.

"Not the Fante," Elder Kwasi replied. "We hope they have given up fighting the kingdom, and that peace will hold. The Asantehene left soldiers in Fante territory to patrol, but officials like the messengers take soldiers with them for extra protection."

"Will the Fante attack us?" Baako asked.

"I don't think so. They should respect the Asantehene's messengers. If the soldier in our delegation is sick tomorrow, I'll take his place. We'll be safe, but we might have to travel all of the way to Elmina Castle if the messengers need me."

"That's a long walk, but I want to see the castles, and I'm strong," Baako said with enthusiasm.

Kwame agreed. "We'll taste salt water and ride in a canoe in the ocean. I'm ready. I'm strong. I miss Kwaku. He would like this trip."

"We'll tell him what happens," Baako replied. "He'll tell us about the cub. I hope he's taking good care of it."

One of the messengers joined the group. "*Mema mo aha* – Good afternoon to everyone," he greeted them, and they replied.

"You're good travelers," he said. "I'm sorry that the soldier is sick. How do you feel?"

"We're well," the others answered.

"We're grateful to be in your group," Elder Kwasi added.

"There are two roads to Elmina," the messenger explained. "The other one is shorter, but the Asantehene wants us to take this one. He thinks it's better."

"We'll be two days behind the traders with prisoners," Elder Kwasi said. "We're surely traveling faster than they are. I expect that we'll overtake them in four or five days. You know the road. Do you agree?"

"You might be right, but traders with prisoners usually travel fast. It costs a lot to feed prisoners, and traders want to sell them before they get sick. I'm sure we'll overtake them in Assin Manso, if not before. Traders always let prisoners bathe and rest there so they'll bring a good price. That's seven more days of walking, and it's the beginning of Fante territory."

Elder Kwasi looked surprised. "I hope that we'll overtake them sooner," he said. "I thought they would travel much slower than we do."

"We're traveling as fast as we can," messenger replied. "Ask people about the traders and prisoners at travelers' shelters. Find out when they stayed there."

"I'll do that," Elder Kwasi replied.

"What message are you taking?" Kwame asked the messenger. Elder Kwasi looked at his nephew in surprise.

The messenger smiled. "The other messenger and I have memorized a message that we'll repeat only for the governor and his translator at Elmina Castle. Someone from the Ahanta group that lives next to the castle will translate the message into the governor's language. The governor may send a reply to the Asantehene. We would memorize that, too."

The boys were fascinated. "You have a hard job," Baako said.

"Yes, but we're trained," the messenger replied. "We're like the historians, but the messages that we carry are always changing."

"In Kumasi we saw that Hausa people can read and write Arabic," Kwame explained. "Do the whites at Elmina Castle read and write their language?"

"Yes, but no Ahantas read or write that language. No one in Kumasi does either. Ahantas only speak it."

"What do whites sound like when they talk?" Baako asked.

"They sound strange," the messenger replied. "In Elmina you'll hear them talk."

"I want to hear them," Baako said. "I want to know about them."

The messenger smiled. "If you stay with us, you'll hear them. We'll leave early in the morning. Be ready."

The soldier was still sick the next morning, and Elder Kwasi took his place. Even with the traders two days ahead now, the Okyeame and Elder Kwasi hoped to overtake them before crossing the Pra River.

THROUGH THE AFTERNOON OF NANA'S LAST DAY IN KUMASI, ASARE ORGANIZED THE *nnonko* to pack regalia, supplies, food, and water. Asare explained to Apure where they were going and what the trip would be like. He planned to carry her son on his shoulders for much of the way. He was confident that Apure and her children would do well with his help.

In the late afternoon, Kwaku, Kofi Edu, and Akosua played with the cub, keeping vines around it to hold it securely. It liked to jump and run. They fed it, and put it in the cage with fresh leaves. They practiced carrying the cage as a head load with the cub inside. The cub often moved, making the cage hard to balance. "Let's stuff more in the cage so the cub won't move so much," Kofi Edu suggested.

They tried a few items and found that chopped up banana stems were the best fillers. They experimented and found the right combination for the cub to be comfortable while confined. "We'll take the stems out when we rest so the cub can play and we can change the leaves," Kwaku told Nana.

"That should work," Nana agreed. "How will you feed the cub?"

"I know that it likes soup and milk and raw chicken and smoked fish," Kwaku replied. "We can take food with us, but it won't last more than two days. Can we buy more along the way?"

"The cub's life will depend on it," Nana answered. "We know that Nana Somfo did that on the way to Kumasi. That's our only hope."

That night's dinner was long with talk and good wishes. Nana thanked Elder Kwadwo and Madam Adjowa for their hospitality. "I hope to see you in Tanoso someday," he concluded.

"We want to come," Elder Kwadwo replied. "We need to see our family. Please give my special greeting to the Queen Mother. May our ancestors give her a long life."

Nana's party rose at dawn to an ample breakfast. The full group from Tanoso assembled, slightly altered from the time of its arrival. The Okyeame, Elder Kwasi, Kwame, and Baako were missing. Apure and her children were present.

"I appoint you as my *okyeame* for the trip," Nana said to Elder Kofi, who thanked him.

Elder Kwadwo accompanied the delegation to the city's gate, where he embraced his cousin and wished him a safe journey. "*Nanteyie*," he said several times.

"*Medaase*," Nana replied.

Hundreds were leaving Kumasi, and the great-road to the western region overflowed with traffic. Everyone walked briskly, often balancing large head loads of merchandise, purchased or traded for in Kumasi.

On his shoulders Asare carried Awane. Apure tied her baby on her back and walked with a strong pace. Kwaku struggled to balance the cage as a head load. Elder Kofi walked next to him to rebalance the cage when the cub moved, and also to help give the cub milk and broth to drink when the group stopped. Occasionally one of the *nnonko* carried the cub's cage in exchange for Kwaku's carrying his heavy, but still, load.

When the delegation stopped at the end of the first day, Nana told the group, "The Okyeame and his party should be returning to Kumasi by now. They won't be far behind us. I hope they were able to buy the prisoner that I want. Traders are usually happy to have a smaller group to maintain." The delegation agreed with Nana and shared his optimism.

CHAPTER 40

The Pra River

ON ITS SIXTH TRAVEL DAY, THE MESSENGERS' GROUP CONTINUED IN A FAMILIAR RHYTHM. "It's looking more like our forest here," Baako commented to Kwame that morning. "I hope we're going in the right direction."

"I'm sure we are," Kwame replied. "The messengers know the way. It's a hard job to be a messenger or a tax collector for the Asantehene. They walk all day. They have to find their way any place in the kingdom."

People in the towns and villages along the great-road welcomed the messengers. The travelers found comfortable shelters and an adequate food supply. They slept at sunset and rose at dawn. With the grueling pace, they made good progress, but there was little time for conversation or relaxing games in the evening.

The great-road was in good condition. Low hills were frequent. The party waded across creeks and shallow rivers. Farms and villages were further and further apart. Though often tired, Kwame and Baako gained strength and confidence in themselves.

Elder Kwasi joined the boys. "If canoes are ready, we'll cross the Pra River early this afternoon," he predicted. "The Pra is big like the Tano. It would have taken a long time for the traders with their porters and prisoners to cross. If we cross quickly, we'll gain on them."

"Are there crocodiles in the river?" Kwame asked.

"Most likely. The boatmen will tell us what to expect," Elder Kwasi replied. "We have guns."

"I remember the story you told us about Osei Tutu," Baako recalled. "Soldiers shot him when he was crossing the Pra River. Did a Fante shoot him?"

"No, he was fighting the Akyem," Elder Kwasi replied. "He thought they were weak and left his war smock at home. That was a mistake."

"Will the Fante attack us?" Baako asked.

"If the messengers think it's safe, it will be," Kwame said with emphasis. "I trust them and my papa. He said we would be safe. He's already left Kumasi."

"Nana's delegation should have a good trip home," Elder Kwasi assured the boys. "Everyone wants to be home again, but the trip is hard. The *nnonko* are carrying heavy loads, and Nana has a new *odonko* and her children to take care of. Asare will help. We'll be the last ones to return to Tanoso."

"We have so far to travel, but we're strong," Kwame said, trying to be hopeful.

THE MESSENGERS STOPPED FOR A BRIEF LUNCH. "EAT QUICKLY. WE'LL LEAVE RIGHT away," one said. The group soon set off again, almost running.

"There's a hill to climb before we reach the river. How are you doing?" the Okyeame asked the boys.

"I'm working hard," Kwame replied, his face showing strain.

"I'm used to running on the path to Tanoso," Baako answered. "That's made me strong, but this trip is harder."

"Elder Kwasi and I are working hard, too. See how the forest is growing denser. We're getting close to the river."

The Pra River came into view when the group reached the top of a low hill. Kwame and Baako saw that it was wide and shallow and rocky. Thick foliage along the river banks extended over the water. The road led to the near bank with a pier, where canoes were moored. A boat landing across the river was in sight.

"This is a big river and I don't see any crocodiles," Baako said.

"You're right," Kwame agreed. "Where are the boatmen?"

"I hope they're nearby."

Descending the hill, the messengers shouted greetings. There was no response. The group heard only the flowing water and birds in the forest, especially the parrots.

"Mema mo aha - Good afternoon, everyone," the messengers called out.

"Mema mo aha," the parrots responded.

"Mema mo aha," the messengers repeated.

"Mema mo aha," the parrots mimicked them.

"Maybe the parrots will find the boatmen," one of the messengers commented with a smile. Reaching the bank and four long dugout canoes tied to the pier, the messengers called out again and again. There was still no reply. The group found small huts with furnishings and a hearth with warm embers. "The boatmen are nearby," the messengers concluded. "Let's rest and eat a little."

The group sat near the hearth to eat bananas and dried meat. Later, some stretched out on the hard-packed ground. Others soaked their feet in the warm river. "What route do the boatmen take across river?" the Okyeame asked a messenger.

"First, the boatmen paddle hard across the current downstream from the rocks. When they've passed the rocks, they paddle across the current upstream to the landing on the other side. The river's shallow in the dry season. The current's gentle but it's hard to navigate around the rocks," the messenger replied.

"How many canoes will we need to cross?"

"Probably three. Each canoe will hold three or four passengers and two paddlers. We'll fit our baskets in and secure them."

"Are there crocodiles in the river?" Kwame asked.

"Crocodiles are always near rivers," the messenger answered. "Maybe the boatmen have killed all of them here. Pythons are a greater danger. Parrots warn us about them sometimes. We'll ask the boatmen. Don't go away from the camp. I want you here when the boatmen return."

"We'll stay," Kwame assured the messenger.

"How far ahead is Fante territory?" the Okyeame asked.

"Assin Manso is the first Fante town after we cross the river. It's a three day walk," the messenger explained. "The Asantehene's army destroyed much of the town because that's where traders from the kingdom had to sell their goods to the Fante. When the king stopped that, most people left the town, but there's still a travelers' camp there.

THE MESSENGERS GREW IMPATIENT. "WE'LL REPORT THIS DELAY TO THE ASANTEHENE," one said. "If our trip takes too long, we have to explain why." The group was restless.

Late in the afternoon, two canoes rounded a bend not far up the river and approached the camp. Six men landed the canoes and greeted the messengers. "We're the boatmen for this crossing," one explained. "We were helping fell and clean up two wawa trees to float down the river. We can wait until the logs go by or take you across now. There's a travelers' camp not far from the other bank. You can stay there tonight."

"It's good that you're here," a messenger told the boatmen. "If it's safe, we want to cross now. We want to reach the camp before dark."

"We should have enough time," the boatmen replied. "We'll be quick. Let's see what you have, eight men and two boys. Is that everyone?"

"Yes."

"Four baskets?"

"Yes. We have two guns, four spears, and four machetes."

"We'll take three canoes with two paddlers each," one boatman explained. "I'll assign each person a canoe. We'll tie down the baskets, spears, guns, and machetes in the first and third canoes because they'll have fewer passengers. Everyone agreed?"

Still looking at the group, the boatman continued, "The paddlers in the back are the pilots. They'll decide the course. The only tricky part is to avoid the rocks. Stay seated and hold on. Don't talk."

Baako was in the lead canoe. Kwame and Elder Kwasi rode in the second canoe, with the Okyeame in the third. The boys had never ridden in long canoes. They felt excited but anxious and pleased that they could see each other. The boatmen launched the first canoe.

Crossing the Pra River

Crossing to the river's midpoint, the first canoe slipped downstream of the boulders, and then traveled swiftly across the current towards the landing. The second canoe was launched. Suddenly two logs rounded the bend, a rider straddled each one. A boatman in the first canoe shouted to the boatmen in the second, "Wait! Stay behind the boulders. Let the logs go by." Boatmen in the second canoe waved a reply.

Kwame's face tightened as he gripped the sides of his canoe. Elder Kwasi said calmly, "Let's trust the boatmen." The first canoe neared the landing. The third canoe had not been launched. The boatmen in the second canoe worked hard to hold their canoe behind the boulders. The logs approached fast.

The men riding the logs kept them from rolling over by placing a pole into the water first on one side of their log and then the other. They whooped and yelled to warn of their coming. With the water so shallow, the riders were able to steer the logs, but their control was limited. The first log passed the boulders on the far side.

As the next log neared, paddlers in the second canoe couldn't keep their canoe behind the boulders. They turned downstream to avoid a collision. "We'll stay in the middle of the river until the log passes us," the pilot told his passengers. "It won't hit us."

"Hold tight, Kwame," Elder Kwasi counseled. "The water's shallow. If the canoe flips, hang on to it. I'll stay with you." Kwame gripped the sides of the canoe harder, imagining that he was a leaf carried along by the river, but fearful of the approaching log. He leaned over the far side of the canoe.

The log and the canoe soon traveled side by side. The rider on the log poled hard to stay away from the canoe, but leaned so far toward the canoe that the log rolled out from under him and sped ahead. "I'll swim to the bank," he yelled to the boatmen.

As the paddlers quickly maneuvered the canoe to stay away from the log, Kwame leaned too far and rolled out of the canoe without making a sound. Elder Kwasi grabbed Kwame's cloth, but it came off. Falling head first into the water Kwame twisted and turned until his feet touched the river bottom. He felt that he was playing in a stream once more, and he wasn't afraid. With his feet pushing against the bottom of the river, he raised his head above the water and waved one arm high to show his location. "I'm here," he yelled.

The log rider was close to Kwame and swam toward him saying, "I'm coming for you. Stay where you are. Keep your head up. Grab the pole."

Bracing himself with little jumps in the mud on the river bottom and using his hands to paddle with the current, Kwame turned to face the log rider. "I'm strong. The water won't knock me down," he said, though no one heard him.

The boatmen pivoted the canoe to paddle toward Kwame while the pilot assured Elder Kwasi, "We'll get him or the log rider will get him. We'll rescue him." Elder Kwasi watched Kwame, waving and shouting, "We're coming! We're coming!"

The log rider reached Kwame quickly, and the two used the pole as a walking stick, standing and making small jumps from the river's bottom while paddling with their hands. Slowly, they approached the bank.

Kwame had felt calm, but now he was shaking. The log rider reassured him, "It's good that the water's warm and shallow. Good, too, that your cloth came off. You're naked as a fish and that helped you. Your cloth would have dragged you down. When we reach the bank, hold on to the bushes. We'll be safe there. They're coming for us. You're doing fine."

"At first I felt like I was twisting and turning to play in the water and swim like a fish," Kwame said. "But then I got scared. I don't know how to swim. I feel better now. You saved me."

"You were strong and brave," the rider complimented Kwame. "To be safe in the water, you have to swim. You should learn."

"We live next to the Tano River and it has crocodiles. I'm afraid of them," Kwame explained.

"Crocodiles are bad," the rider sympathized. "Ask the chief to post guards so that people can use the river and learn how to swim."

"My papa's the chief," Kwame answered. "I'll ask him. He should learn to swim, too."

"You're right," the rider replied. "I hope he will."

"What will you do now?" Kwame asked the rider.

"The boatmen will take me downstream to find my log. I have to deliver it or I won't get paid. Look, the third canoe is crossing the river easily. Your canoe just had bad luck."

Boatmen in the second canoe steered it toward the bank where the current was mild. "You're good passengers," the pilot said. "It's rare for anyone to fall out of a canoe. We can thank the rider for rescuing the boy. We'll turn the canoe and pick up the rider and the boy on the way to the landing."

When the second canoe arrived, Kwame got in and the rider walked behind it. Elder Kwasi held Kwame's shoulders and said emphatically, "You showed courage and good sense. Your spirit and body are strong. I'm proud of you. Here's your cloth. It's better that it came off."

"I was scared, but I feel better now," Kwame replied. "Uncle Kwasi, I want to know how to swim. I want Papa to put more guards on the river. I want him to learn how to swim too."

"He'll have more guards there soon, Kwame. All of us need to learn to swim. If leopards can swim, people can learn."

When the second canoe reached the landing, the boatmen and passengers were greeted heartily. Baako patted Kwame's head and shoulders. "We saw the log chase you, and you and the rider fall into the river. That looked bad."

"I didn't think it would be so hard to cross the Pra," Kwame answered. "I was scared but the rider helped me. Baako, we have to learn how to swim."

"We can do it." Baako agreed.

Elder Kwasi praised the boatmen for their skill and asked, "Have you ferried a group of prisoners recently?"

"Yesterday. The crossing took a long time because the prisoners were chained together and they were slow to get in and out of the canoes. We've ferried prisoners many times. It's always hard."

"Thank you for your help today and the information," the Okyeame expressed his group's gratitude. Turning to Elder Kwasi, he said with satisfaction, "The traders were two days ahead of us, and now they're only a day ahead. We're catching up."

"I'll tell the Asantehene you work well," one of the messengers told the boatmen. To the others, he continued, "We'll stay at the next camp tonight. Assin Manso is a three-day walk. There's a steep hill just before the town, and climbing it will take time. After that we'll be in Fante territory."

Speaking to his group, the Okyeame speculated, "We should find the prisoners in Assin Manso. The traders will keep them there for a few days."

"*Yoo*," they replied with relief.

— CHAPTER 41 —

Assin Manso

Entering Assin Manso, the messengers' group found devastation. The king's army had burned the chief's palace, the marketplace, and other buildings. Few people remained in town. Those who ran the travelers' camp greeted the messengers and expressed their loyalty to the Asantehene.

"You're joining traders with prisoners here," the camp manager told the messengers. "I'll put you in a different part of the camp." The two groups settled for the evening, bathed, and ate in well-separated areas though they were aware of each other.

After the meal the Okyeame and Elder Kwasi approached the traders and introduced themselves. The two traders responded favorably. "Where did you buy your prisoners?" the Okyeame asked.

"In Kumasi. We're taking them to Elmina," one of the traders responded. "Two are sick, so we rested today and we'll stay here tomorrow. We're buying good food for them. They bathe in the river and rub their bodies with palm oil. They'll look healthy in Elmina. We want a high price when we trade them."

"Can you communicate with them?" Elder Kwasi asked.

"No," one of the traders replied. "We don't know their language. Something from the savannah. It would help if we could talk to them. Some are difficult."

"In Kumasi my chief and I saw the group that your prisoners were with," the Okyeame explained. "They were part of a tax payment that the Gonja Kingdom made to the Asantehene. When these prisoners were captured, their families were broken up. They don't know what happened to them. They don't know where they're going. Of course they're difficult, but if you want us to talk to them, we'll try."

"Do you know their language?" the trader asked.

"Scars show that the prisoners are Gurunsi. They speak Nankane as I do," the Okyeame replied.

"You look Akan and sound Akan. Why do you speak Nankane?"

We Are Akan

"I learned it as a child," the Okyeame answered.

The traders were interested. "You can tell them we're going to Elmina. They'll see the ocean. We want them to think that something good will happen to them."

Elder Kwasi replied carefully. "You'll trade them to whites. You don't know what will happen to them."

"That's right, but we can't do anything about that," one trader replied sharply. "Whites trade for prisoners. It's a business."

"We want to find a prisoner whose wife and children I bought in Kumasi," Elder Kwasi explained. "Our chief wants to buy the man and reunite the family. We can talk to all of the prisoners and then to you about buying him if he's in your group. That would make your journey easier."

"My brother and I will talk about this," one trader answered, and the two traders walked a short distance away.

When they returned, one said, "We want you to talk to the prisoners. We walked for nine days and rested here today. Tell the prisoners that we'll stay here another day and then walk for four more days. They'll see the ocean and a castle. They'll get new masters.

"The prisoners we sell usually work for local people until a ship comes to pick them up," the trader continued. "That can be a long time. If they refuse to work or try to escape, the whites will put them in the castle's prison. That's a bad place. They need to know that. Tell them, and then ask them what you want, but don't get them agitated. If you find the prisoner you're looking for, we'll talk about selling him."

The prisoners were allowed to sit and rest through the evening. They were tied together by heavy rope around their ankles and waists, and bound in two groups of four. They talked little and sang a low pitched melody. The sick prisoners were confined to a hut.

THE OKYEAME AND BAAKO APPROACHED EACH GROUP, SAYING IN NANKANE, "WE greet you as brothers." The men in the first group were startled to hear Akans speak Nankane but returned the greeting.

"We are Akan, but our origins are Gurunsi," the Okyeame explained. "Our clan is *Gwegene*. We want to learn who you are and where you are from. We bring you a message from the traders who bought you in Kumasi."

Looking at Baako, one of the prisoners asked, "Who are you? Why are you here?"

"I was born Gurunsi but in the forest," Baako explained. "My family is owned by a chief who is good to us. I think that he'll adopt me. I'm becoming Akan. I speak Twi and Nankane. The chief sent me here."

"I see in you what can happen to our children who stay in the forest," one of the prisoners said. "The traders are taking us somewhere else. If children had to walk like this, they would die. We will talk to you."

The prisoners gave their personal names and clan names, and recounted stories of their capture. Prisoners in Kumasi had told Asare such stories, but now the telling was fraught with increased fear.

"The Gonja rode horses into my family's cotton field. We ran, but the horses were faster. We couldn't escape the whips. The Gonja captured my brothers and me. We didn't see our parents again. They are old, and we took care of them. I don't know what has happened to them or my brothers."

"I'm an elder brother, and I helped my younger brothers and sisters. Our parents died when we were young. Our grandparents took care of us. They have died, too. My brothers and sisters and I were in different fields when the Gonja came. I don't know if any of them escaped. I don't know where they are or who's taking care of them."

"Gonja soldiers dragged my wife and children and me from our home. We walked to Kintampo and then Kumasi, where I was taken away. I don't know where I'm going."

After listening to the prisoners' stories and replying with sympathy, the Okyeame asked about a prisoner named Atore of the *Gwegene* clan. With more questions, he identified the prisoner and told him privately, "We are *Gwegene,* your clansmen. Elder Kwasi, my friend here, has bought your wife and children. Our chief sent us to buy you."

"My ancestors have protected me," Atore said as he knelt on the ground and covered his face with his hands.

"Say nothing more," the Okyeame instructed him. "We'll talk to the traders."

"Where are we going?" the prisoners asked the Okyeame.

The Okyeame told the group what lay ahead. "The ocean, a castle, ships that will take you away to new masters. You might work for local farmers first." The prisoners were disconsolate. Some lowered their heads to moan and wail. A few yelled defiant epithets, looking upward, raising their fists to the sky.

Two prisoners shouted, "We need to escape. Who will try?"

The Okyeame, Elder Kwasi, Kwame, and Baako watched this sad scene, feeling helpless. "While you are in the forest, may *Nyame* care for you," the Okyeame said to the prisoners. There was no response.

"Look at them," one trader said to the Okyeame. "They're angry now. We shouldn't have let you talk to them. They'll be harder to manage. They'll think they have nothing to lose if they try to escape. Only we will lose."

"They're angry because they're prisoners," the Okyeame replied tersely. "They were once free men. When they were captured, everything changed. They don't know what will happen to them."

"This business isn't easy," the trader replied.

"We identified the prisoner that we want to buy."

"Which one?"

"His name is Atore. He's in the second group, standing there quietly."

"Yes, I see him. He's been easy to manage. I'm not sure that we'll sell him to you."

"You'll sell him sometime. He told us that if he cannot see his family again, he doesn't want to live. He might not continue to be easy to manage. He looks strong enough to escape."

"Yes, that could happen. He could be harder to control now. You'll have to meet the price that I would get at Elmina Castle, and that includes the toll that I've paid on this road. The price is three ounces of gold dust."

"That's a high price," the Okyeame objected. "The whites at Anomabo and Cape Coast don't buy prisoners anymore, so there's been a big supply at Elmina. The price has gone down. If you sell this prisoner, you'll have fewer to manage. You'll be able to travel faster. It will help you to sell one early. I offer you two and a half ounces. That's higher than the price in Kumasi."

"I'll talk to my brother. We'll let you know in the morning."

"We're traveling with the Asantehene's messengers. They'll leave early in the morning. You'll have to decide tonight." The traders walked away to talk.

The Okyeame recounted the conversation to Elder Kwasi, Kwame, and Baako. "Nana gave me enough gold dust to cover the price that the trader is asking, but his price is too high."

"Are you sure you found the right man?" Elder Kwasi asked.

"Yes, Baako and I agree that his name and the clan name are right, and he gave us the right names for his wife, her clan, and their children."

"Nana and I want this prisoner. You should meet the trader's price," Elder Kwasi advised.

"The prisoner will be very sad if you don't buy him," Baako said. "I've never seen so many sad people all together. I didn't know that my parents and grandparents were like this a long time ago."

"My parents were captured, too," the Okyeame affirmed, "but our families stayed in the forest, Baako. They weren't sold to whites. This is different." Baako understood.

The traders approached. "We're ready to talk," one said.

"I'm listening," the Okyeame replied.

"We've talked about selling the prisoner and the price. We have another offer. We need the help of this young man," the trader said, pointing to Baako. "He speaks Twi and Nankane and can talk to the prisoners for us. We will trade our prisoner for him. No gold dust involved."

The Tanoso group was stunned. Baako shrank back. "No!" he yelled.

"He's not a prisoner. He's not for sale!" the Okyeame spoke emphatically.

"He's still Gurunsi. He's not old enough to be Akan," the trader replied. "You can sell him or trade him. I know the law."

"Never. Let's talk about your prisoner," the Okyeame countered. "You gave me a high price. If I meet it, I want the prisoner to join our group tonight. We'll leave early in the morning, and your group is staying here."

"We'll talk privately," one of the traders said, and the two walked away again. When they returned, one replied. "My brother and I will sell the prisoner you want for three ounces of gold dust."

"Agreed," the Okyeame answered. "I'll take out my scales. Bring the prisoner to us." When the traders returned with the prisoner, the Okyeame carefully spooned gold dust onto one of the pans of his scales, having placed his gold weights that equaled three ounces on the other. "This is the price for a life," he said. He gave a feather to the trader, who brushed the gold dust from the pan into a leather pouch. The trader tightened the top of the pouch and returned the feather. The deal was done. The traders returned to their side of the camp, leaving the prisoner with the Okyeame and Elder Kwasi.

The Okyeame reassured Atore, "Welcome to our group. You'll find your family when we return home."

Atore bowed his head. "I am grateful," he said. "I owe you my life. You and your chief will not regret this action. My family will work hard."

Kwame and Baako jumped up and down and hugged each other. "We did it! We did it," they said with both relief and elation.

Turning to Baako, the Okyeame warned, "Stay close to our camp tonight, Baako. Don't go near the traders. I don't trust them." Baako agreed.

Turning to the Okyeame, Elder Kwasi asked, "Should we start back to Tanoso tomorrow? Let's talk to the messengers."

The messengers congratulated the Okyeame and Elder Kwasi. "You saved a man's life," one said. "You accomplished your mission. You could return to Kumasi now, but we have only four travel days left to reach Elmina. We're in Fante territory, and we need two soldiers. I hope that your group will stay with us. The Asantehene left soldiers to patrol but we need more protection. I can't recruit another soldier here, and it might not be safe for you to walk back from here on your own. The new member of your group should be able to walk fast and carry supplies."

"We'll talk privately," the Okyeame replied. He and Elder Kwasi spoke together and with the boys and reached a decision. "We'll continue with you," the Okyeame told the messengers. "We understand that there are risks, but we expect that the Fante fear the Asantehene and will not attack us. We all want to see the ocean and the castles. Atore will be helpful."

"Thank you for agreeing to help us. Be ready early in the morning," the messengers confirmed their plans.

CHAPTER 42

Travelers and Rebels

WHEN NANA'S DELEGATION SET OFF ON THE SECOND DAY OF ITS RETURN TO TANOSO, THE energy of the *Odwira* celebration still propelled everyone. The morning air was cool, but when the sun rose high, the heat of the day made the walk difficult.

"I want to put the small umbrella over the cage," Kwaku said to Nana when the group stopped for lunch. "The cub will be cooler then."

"That should work well," Nana agreed. "The cub will look like a miniature chief riding high in his palanquin," he added.

"I like that idea," Kwaku responded with a smile.

The afternoon was hot enough for the men to wear their cloths around their waists, tie scarves around their heads, and chew kola nuts. Nana circulated among his people to talk to everyone. He was deeply pleased with the visit to his cousin, Elder Kwadwo, and the bond that he felt with the Asantehene and the royal court.

Asare helped Apure care for her children. He described the *nnonko* village and the women who would welcome her. "The men will build a hut for your family," he assured her.

Apure worried about her husband. Nana and Elder Kofi encouraged her, saying that Elder Kwasi and the Okyeame would do their best to find him. "If anyone can do it, they can," Elder Kofi told her several times, and Asare translated. She believed them.

"I'll tell you about the work that your family will do for Elder Kwasi," Asare said. "He is a good owner, but *nnonko* work hard. Men fell trees, clear the land, plant, weed, and harvest. Women help on farms. The hardest work is mining. Men dig the mines and bring out the soil and rocks. We crush the rocks, and women go through it all to look for gold. It's hard work, but we have our own farms, and the elders give us food from their farms, and we hunt. We have enough to eat, and we're safe from raids. Our children have the chance to be free."

"I understand that our lives will be hard," Apure replied. "My dream is that we'll be safe and that my children will be free again someday."

CARING FOR THE CUB WAS DIFFICULT. NANA BOUGHT CHICKEN THAT THE CUB ATE well, but there were few villages with a nursing goat or sheep. When there was little or no milk, Kwaku gave the cub soup. It drank often and appeared healthy though less active than it had been in Kumasi.

That evening after dinner, Kwaku took the cub out of its cage and bound it with fresh vines. Surrounded by local children and holding firmly to the vines, he watched the cub drink palm nut soup and play with palm fronds. The local elders admired the cub and supported Nana's hope for leopards' return to the forest.

"Let's make a circle and let the cub loose to play," Kwaku proposed. Inside of the circle, the cub ran from one child to the next as they picked it up by the vines and let it lick their skin.

Children commented and questioned.

"It's beautiful!"

"It's friendly."

"It doesn't seem wild."

"I want to keep it!"

"Does it like peanut soup, too?"

"How will it find its mother?"

Kwaku explained. "I'm taking it home to find its mother."

The cub suddenly leaped over a child's shoulder and sped through the courtyard. Children ran after it. "It's getting away," several yelled.

An elder stooped and caught the cub. "It will escape if you're not careful," he warned. "It runs fast. It's a wild animal."

"*Medaase*," Kwaku said with relief. "We have to hold it by the vines. I can't lose it."

"I hope that today the Okyeame, Elder Kwasi, Kwame, and Baako arrived in Kumasi with Apure's husband," Nana told his delegation that night. "They'll be only a few days behind us. We'll all feel great pleasure when we see them in Tanoso." Asare translated for Apure.

TWO DAYS LATER, AFTER DINNER, NANA TALKED TO HIS DELEGATION. THE GROUP WAS relaxed and happy, though tired. "We are halfway home," Nana said to encourage everyone. "The *Odwira* was important, but I want to be home again." Others agreed, chanting, "*Yoo*."

"This has been a long trip. I'm grateful that all of you came with me," Nana continued. "I'm satisfied with the guns and ammunition that I bought in Kumasi. I hope that the rest of you found what you needed."

"I sold palm nuts and bought tools and glass beads," one elder commented. "The beads will sell well in our market. I'll make a profit."

Another elder explained, "I sold kola nuts and bought fine cloth and hooded cloaks. I'll keep one cloak and sell everything else. I'll get high prices in Tanoso."

"I sold kola nuts and bought a lamp and gold weights. I'm satisfied," a headmen added.

"I bought gold weights. Prices in Kumasi are lower than those in Tanoso," another headman commented. "If we had a bigger market in Tanoso, the prices would be lower."

The group supported this view, again murmuring, "*Yoo.*"

"The door to your hut is only a mat. Tie it in place," Nana told Kwaku. "We saw baboons today. They would kill the cub. The headmen in your hut will use spears if baboons break in."

Before dawn, hooting baboons woke Kwaku and the headmen who shared a hut. When the baboons shook the door, one headman picked up his spear, and the other held the door. The cub curled up in Kwaku's arms. Men came out of other huts and chased the baboons away.

"Don't leave the cub alone," a headman advised Kwaku. "Baboons are all around us."

"The baboons scared the cub and me both," Kwaku said as he cradled the cub. "The cub's sleepy. Maybe it's hungry."

The road leaving Assin Manso was bad. It was narrow and frequently blocked by roots and fallen branches. The travelers followed it into the dense, shadowy forest, climbing over rolling hills, and crossing shallow streams. Walking in dim light throughout the day, the messengers' group listened to the muffled crackling of leaves moving in the wind, the squawking parrots, and the falcons' shrill cries to give them news of the forest.

Farm plots near the road were small and overgrown with weeds. Burned huts scarred the occasional village. The travelers saw few people. The area seemed almost abandoned.

One of the messengers remarked to the group, "The Asantehene will make the Fante rebuild this road. It's more of a path than a road. It's hard for us to walk. It's even harder for traders and the king's army. The Fante want it like this. They don't like strangers."

"Many men will be needed for road building. They won't be able to farm," Elder Kwasi observed. "The Fante can eat fish so they won't starve."

"The Asantehene may send *nnonko* to work on the road," the Okyeame said, "but he'll make the Fante pay."

Although the group walked fast, the Okyeame and Baako were able to talk to Atore and learn the fate of the *Gwegene* clan. Atore smiled broadly saying, "We are brothers. How life is strange! You are free, and I am a prisoner, but we are all *Gwegene,* and you are trying to save my family. I thank you."

Road from Assin Manso to the coast

"Kwame and I will teach your children how to speak Twi. They can learn to be Akan," Baako said.

Atore smiled. "My wife and I will teach them to be Gurunsi even if becoming Akan is their fate. We cannot forget our people."

"Where do most of the *Gwegene* live now?" the Okyeame asked.

"Many in our clan and in other clans moved away from the Gonja, but we have to stay near the river. It feeds us and protects us. We need it for water and fish, even crocodiles.

"When we're near the river, we can hide along the bank where horses cannot go. Some people have escaped the raids in boats. We have to act fast and often there is not enough time.

"There are antelopes in the grasslands but no place for hunters to hide, so only a few go there. Gurunsis harm no one and yet we're attacked," Atore lamented. The Okyeame translated. Elder Kwasi, Kwame, and Baako expressed their sympathy.

The group stopped twice to rest and eat during the day but took no long breaks. Just before sunset, they reached a village with a travelers' shelter. No other travelers were there.

"With the bad road, this trip is getting harder," Kwame said to Baako as they unrolled their sleeping mats. "This was our tenth travel day from Kumasi. If we were walking home, we would already be in Tanoso."

"I want to see the ocean," Baako replied. "We've walked so far. We'll finally see it."

The women preparing breakfast for the messengers' group, and the village itself, seemed unusually quiet the next morning, and the messengers spoke of this. The travelers learned why when the women left. Five men stepped out of the forest, surrounded the campsite, and pointed guns at the travelers. Wearing dirty waist cloths, the men walked in old sandals, carried leather pouches, and wore knives in holsters tied to their waists.

"Stand up! Put your hands behind your head!" their leader ordered. He spoke Fante. Baako translated for Atore. The travelers complied.

"What are you doing?" a messenger asked. "We are messengers from the Asantehene. His soldiers will protect us."

"You have only two soldiers with you. That's not enough," the leader replied.

"If you rob us or harm us, the Asantehene's patrols will come after you. You will not escape," the messenger replied. "Who are you?"

"We're Fante. We won't surrender to the Asantehene."

"You're rebelling against the Asantehene. He will hunt you down. You will not survive," the messenger spoke with authority.

"We're hungry. We need to buy food and more guns and ammunition," the rebel leader said. "We won't harm you unless we have to, but we'll take what we need. Empty your head loads."

The travelers did so. The Fante rebels gasped when they saw the Asantehene's golden sword. They were interested in the scales and the guns.

"Where is your gold dust?" a rebel asked.

"We don't carry gold dust," a messenger replied.

"I have only a little," the Okyeame explained. "I bought this prisoner yesterday."

"Put your pouch on the ground," a rebel told him.

"Stand over there," the rebel leader ordered, pointing to the side of the camp. The travelers gathered together. Three rebels looked through the items on the ground while two others continued to point guns at the messengers' group.

One of the messengers received permission to speak. "The golden sword is valuable, but you'll never sell it. Everyone knows that it belongs to the Asantehene, even the whites."

"We know that the Asantehene is powerful. We'll take the gold and the guns. We want the boys and the prisoner, too. We can trade them at Elmina Castle. The Asantehene won't care. That's what he does."

The travelers shuddered. "Don't do it!" a messenger said. "The boys are Akan. They're part of our group. They're protected by the Asantehene."

"He won't find us. The Fante always trade prisoners, even Akan prisoners. The whites don't know the difference." Looking at the boys and the prisoner, the rebel leader directed them in a loud voice, "Come with me."

Baako translated for Atore, and the three walked forward slowly. Baako and Kwame were stiff and sweating. Atore was calm.

"What are you saying?" the rebel leader asked Baako.

"I'm speaking Nankane. The prisoner doesn't speak Twi. He needs to know what to do," Baako explained.

Another rebel tied the three prisoners together with a rope that circled the waist of each and led them toward a forest path. The prisoners walked an arm's length apart with a slow and uniform pace.

Atore was familiar with this experience and tried to help Kwame and Baako. "Walk carefully," he said. "Watch the path so you don't trip. If anyone falls, he pulls the others down. We don't want to hurt each other. Don't let the rope rub against your skin. We don't know what's going to happen, but let's take care of ourselves." Baako translated for Kwame. Atore's words helped the boys stay calm.

Turning to the messengers' group, the rebel leader said, "My friend will hold you at gun point for awhile. Don't follow us. You'll get lost, and people here won't help you. Stay on the main road. You'll be safer there."

Suddenly the Okyeame called out in Nankane, "Be brave! Don't fight! Don't try to escape! We will find you!" Baako translated for Kwame.

"What did he say?" the rebel leader asked Baako in an agitated voice.

"He told us to be brave," Baako replied without emotion.

"That's good advice, but it won't help you. You're prisoners."

With the rebels gone, the messengers' group stood in stunned silence. "This is outrageous!" Elder Kwasi said to the messengers. "We traveled with you for safety and look what has happened. Our boys are in danger."

"I'm sorry that this has happened. It's very strange," a messenger replied with emotion. "The Fante rebels are desperate, not brave. They'll be caught, but we have to act fast. Our drummer will sound an alarm. Village drummers will pick up the message. Soldiers will hear the drums and look for us. They'll punish this village. The chief knew what was going to happen. That's why he's not here."

"How will we find the boys?" Elder Kwasi asked the messengers.

"We'll stay on the main road to Elmina Castle and the soldiers will go into villages to look for the rebels," one messenger explained. "People will help them. They're afraid of the soldiers. They don't want to offend the Asantehene."

"We're going to the same place," the second messenger added. "There are two castles and a fort on this part of the coast. The whites at Fort Anomabo and Cape Coast Castle don't trade for prisoners anymore. Only the whites at Elmina Castle do. I hope that the rebels will take the boys and Atore there right away. The Asantehene will get them back even if the rebels sell them. He won't let his people be kidnapped and sold."

"We have a three-day walk and we have to travel fast," the first messenger explained. "If our people are sold, a ship might come by and pick them up before we arrive. The rebels will travel on a river and then along the coast by canoe. They'll arrive at the castle first."

"Elder Kwasi and I will carry head loads since we've lost our porters," the Okyeame said. Everyone packed, feeling distress and despair at losing the boys and Atore. Drumming started, helping the group walk with determination. Village drummers soon echoed the alarm.

In the late morning the group met a small troop of the Asantehene's soldiers, responding to the drumming. When the soldiers learned what had happened, they agreed to search the villages. "The rebels will travel on water to Elmina Castle," the soldiers' spokesman said. "I'll send one of our group to alert the patrol on the beach near the castle. If we don't find them, we'll ask the governor of the castle for help. He respects the Asantehene."

CHAPTER 43

River Ride

Baako and Kwame slowly regained their sense of direction and footing. They walked cautiously on the winding, narrow path filled with tree roots. Atore encouraged them. "I know how you feel. When you're captured, you're not sure where you're going or what will happen to you. I've felt this way before, but now I can hope because your people are coming for us. Don't be afraid. Breath deeply and stay calm." Baako translated.

"We should walk carefully and not trouble the rebels," Kwame reasoned and said to the others. "I don't want them to get angry. They're dangerous, but they have to get along with the villagers. When the villagers hear drumming, maybe they'll help us. What do you think, Baako?"

"Everybody here is Fante. They won't treat us well. They don't like the Asantehene."

"I wish my papa knew what has happened to us. He would help us. He would rescue us," Kwame said.

"My papa would help, too. He can throw spears. I want him to come," Baako replied. "I used to be afraid of the Asantehene, but now I want his soldiers to find us."

"The soldiers will hear the drums. They'll find us," Kwame whispered with conviction. "Papa says that Asantehene Osei Bonsu is powerful."

"He made the same mistake that Osei Tutu did," Baako asserted. "The Asantehene looked down on the Fante. The rebels are strong. They want to fight. The Asantehene didn't stay here to fight them." Baako translated the conversation for Atore.

The rebel leader spoke briefly to the captives. "My name's Ebo. You're Akan, and the *odonko* is from the savannah. Why are you here?"

"The Asantehene gave permission for us to travel with his messengers," Kwame explained. "My father and uncle wanted us to buy this *odonko*. We found him and bought him from traders yesterday, but we had to continue because one of our elders is now a soldier for the messengers. The other soldier got sick."

"The Asantehene doesn't know that we'll still fight," Ebo said. "You will all be *nnonko* soon. We'll walk to the river and take canoes to my town. We'll spend the night there and be on the beach tomorrow afternoon, and maybe at Elmina Castle tomorrow night. We'll beat the messengers there. Keep walking. Don't stop. Don't talk."

"I'm thirsty," Kwame told Ebo after walking for some time.

"We'll stop when we come to a stream," Ebo replied.

"I need to pee," Baako said.

"We'll stop now. Step off of the path and pee. We'll find a stream soon and fill a gourd. You can drink more water."

"I'm hungry. When will we eat?" Kwame asked.

"We'll stop at the next village. Don't talk," Ebo retorted.

Late in the morning, the rebels stopped outside of a village that Ebo entered to buy kenkey and pepper soup. When he returned, he handed out the food, and the rebels ate heartily.

Kwame picked up a kenkey roll, unwrapped the corn husk, ate a little, and said, "I've never eaten kenkey before. It's sour. We sell our dried corn to the Fante to make it. Now I know what it is. I don't like it, but I'm hungry."

"I like it," Baako said. "Atore, can you eat this kenkey?"

"I eat everything."

Baako translated for Kwame and advised, "We should eat it. We might not get food tonight."

"I'll try," Kwame agreed.

The rebels knew the forest paths. When a path became too difficult, they returned to the main road for short periods, sending one of their group ahead as a scout to warn of soldiers. They saw no soldiers, but the drumming troubled them.

THE REBELS SOON APPROACHED THE RIVER AND A VILLAGE WHERE THE HEADMAN welcomed them. "Don't talk to anyone! Don't try to escape!" Ebo warned Kwame and Baako. "If you don't follow my orders, I'll kill one of your group. It doesn't matter to me which one. Tell your friend. I'll hire canoes, and we'll travel on a river from here."

Baako translated for Atore and added, "I wanted to see the ocean, but not like this."

"I don't like being a prisoner," Kwame said. "What would Papa and Mama, and Grannie and Uncle Kofi say if they knew we were prisoners? They wouldn't want us to be prisoners."

Atore counseled the group, "Stay calm and do what the rebels tell us. Soldiers will find us." Baako translated, and the boys tried to stay calm.

The headman told the rebels that because of the drum alert, he expected the Asante-hene's soldiers to search his village at any time. "Be prepared to leave quickly," he cautioned.

Kwame whispered to Baako, "Soldiers are searching for us. I think they'll find us before we get to Elmina Castle." Baako translated.

THE REBELS HAD STORED SUPPLIES IN THE VILLAGE AND LOADED TWO CANOES WITH guns and ammunition, spears, knives, extra poles and paddles, food, and water. Each canoe had two boatmen to paddle and steer. The boatmen in the back of the canoes were the pilots.

Ebo divided the rebels between the canoes, and placed Baako and Atore in one canoe, and Kwame with him in the other where they both were passengers. The rebels pushed off. The pilots steered to the deep water in the middle of the river. With the help of the strong current and prevailing wind, the canoes rode well but were slowed by their heavy loads. The canoes stayed close together so their occupants could talk. Ebo's canoe was slightly ahead.

"The forest isn't dense here," Kwame said to Ebo. "I see farms and other canoes. I think that more people live along the river than along the path."

"That's right. We trap fish in the river and travel by canoe. That's faster than walking."

"Do people float logs down the river?"

"Yes. We need wood for canoes and paddles and stools. We cut down all of the big trees near the ocean long ago. We go inland to find wood. Watch for logs. They travel faster than canoes."

"Why are you a rebel?"

"Fante people were never in the kingdom before. We have our own chiefs and our own militia – the *asafo*. We don't want to be soldiers for the Asantehene. We don't want to pay taxes to the kingdom."

"Do you trade with the whites?"

"Of course, and we work for them, too. The whites have been here in their fort and castles for many generations. We sell them fish and pineapples and coconuts and other food and water. We take supplies and everything that the whites trade for, including prisoners, from the castles to the ships in our canoes. We unload their ships, and whites pay Fante chiefs to use their land."

"Elder Kwasi told us that the Fante didn't let traders from the kingdom go all of the way to the castles. He said that the Asantehene didn't like that."

"That's right. We don't want those traders to cross our land. They're coming now. Some of us will continue to fight the kingdom. We want others to join us. We need more guns. I'll trade you and your friends for guns and ammunition."

"That's not fair."

"I have to protect my people."

Kwame said nothing more. "What if the Asantehene's soldiers don't find us?" he worried. "We'll be traded to the whites. I'm scared, but I can't say that to Ebo. I won't give up. That's what he wants me to do."

LARGE WHITE SEABIRDS FLEW OVERHEAD, SQUAWKING AS THOUGH THE CANOES WERE trespassing into their space. "I've never seen those birds before," Baako told his captors. "They're not forest birds. Why do they make so much noise?"

"That's just what they do. Maybe it's because the ocean is noisy, too," a rebel suggested.

Baako longed to see the ocean and the beach, while still hoping that the Asantehene's soldiers would find him, Kwame, and Atore. "That's our only chance," he thought. "We're getting close to the castles."

As the boats rounded a broad curve, the pilot of the second canoe pointed to the left bank. "Look, two crocs entering the water," he said in a loud voice.

"The birds were telling us about them," Baako thought.

"The crocs will catch us because were moving slowly. There's one for each of us," Ebo yelled. "Stand up when they get close." Both pilots soon stood, each holding a pole, ready to pound a beast.

One crocodile turned to swim alongside the second canoe. Its pilot beat the crocodile's tail and back with his pole. He couldn't reach the snout. Soon, the boatman in the front could no longer paddle because the crocodile was too close to him. He used a pole to steer the canoe as it slowed.

The crocodile turned to face the canoe, hissing and resting its snout on the side. Baako and Atore moved away from the snout and leaned to the canoe's opposite side. Baako was trembling. The pilot pounded the crocodile's snout, making the canoe rock back and forth. The beast tilted its head back and grabbed the pole in its teeth.

"Ahh!" the pilot yelled as he let go of the pole and sat down to restore balance. He was desperate. "Ebo, shoot and scare the croc," he shouted to the other canoe.

"I can't. It's too close to your canoe," Ebo shouted back.

Atore said calmly to Baako, "Ask him if I can use a spear. I'll kill the croc."

Baako explained to the pilot, "Savannah people kill crocs with spears. The prisoner will do that if you let him."

The pilot was unsure what to do. Baako sensed that and added, "My father is from the savannah and I've seen him kill a crocodile with a spear. We won't hurt you. We can't escape. We know that you or the crocodile would kill us if we tried."

"Tell him to spear the croc but do nothing else," the pilot said. Baako translated.

Atore picked up a spear and stood with his feet far apart. The others watched with apprehension as he drew his arm back. With great force he rammed the long spear into the beast's skull, behind its eyes. The crocodile seemed to gasp and became limp. It turned away from the canoe and sank, taking the spear with it.

"Great strength, Atore," Baako said. Atore nodded but said nothing.

"Killing the croc was worth a spear. Thank your friend," the pilot told Baako, who translated. Atore bowed his head. The boatmen began to paddle the canoe once more.

Passengers in Ebo's canoe witnessed the scene with fear, knowing that their lives were at risk if the canoes capsized. When the second crocodile approached their canoe, the pilot in the rear used his pole to beat the animal, saying to the others, "This is all I can do. I can barely reach the croc. Look, it's swimming away now."

"Why are crocodiles coming after us? Do they think we're fish?" Kwame asked Ebo.

"They steal fish from traps along the bank. We smell like fish with our food on board. They want to find out what we are. Our canoes are low and slow moving. I don't want them to tip us over. Look, the croc is coming back. I'll shoot it this time."

Ebo loaded his gun, stood, and fired. The noise startled nearby birds, which squawked as white smoke filled the air. When the smoke cleared, the crocodile was no longer visible.

"Did you kill it?" Kwame asked.

"Probably not, but it's not bothering us now. I hope we won't see it again. Good riddance."

The river trip continued, with the rebels greeting other travelers. Traveling without farming or fishing supplies or crops, the rebels' canoes looked different from the others, but no one questioned them.

In the late afternoon, Ebo told everyone, "We'll soon arrive at my town's pier. We'll build shelters in the forest nearby for tonight. I'll talk to my mother and find out what people know from the drums. Tomorrow we'll see the ocean."

CHAPTER 44

The Ocean

WHEN THE CANOES ARRIVED AT THE PIER OF EBO'S TOWN, EVERYONE GOT OUT, PICKED up gear, and dragged it and the canoes into the forest.

"Build shelters," Ebo told the others. "I'll go into town. My mother will give us food." Looking at the prisoners, he added, "I'll leave you untied so you can help us, but if one of you tries to escape, I'll kill the others."

"We won't try," Kwame assured Ebo, and Baako translated.

Ebo left carrying a loaded gun and a spear, with a knife in a holster around his waist. Entering the courtyard of his home from the back, he saw his mother and aunt preparing dinner while children played nearby. "My nieces and nephews," he thought and smiled.

From the side of a sleeping hut, he called his mother in a soft voice. She hurried to greet him, saying, "*Akwaaba*, my son!" Her sister, too, offered greetings.

"I'm going to Elmina Castle to trade prisoners," Ebo explained. "We're building shelters near the pier. They'll be well hidden. No one will see us. We need food for tonight and tomorrow. You won't see me again for a long time. Have people heard the drumming?"

"Yes, my son. I feared that the message was about you. Soldiers have searched the town already. They may come back. I cannot tell anyone that you're here, even your father. I'll bring you food tonight. You must leave now!"

At that moment they heard the town crier ringing his bell and saying that soldiers had returned. The chief was calling the townspeople to the palace.

"Someone might have reported seeing our canoes on the river today," Ebo whispered to his mother. "We didn't look like the others."

"Stay here until everyone is at the palace and then leave. I'll find you after we eat."

That evening the rebels greeted Ebo's mother warmly as she entered their camp. She talked to the prisoners and was sympathetic. "I'm glad that you're not tied up," she told them.

"What clan do you belong to?" she asked the boys.

"I'm an *Agona*," Kwame replied.

"I'm an *odonko*, but soon I'll be an *Oyoko*," Baako answered.

"I am an *Agona*, too," she told them solemnly. "We are parrots. The *Oyoko* are falcons. Together, we are the guardians of the forest."

Ebo's mother brought fried plantains and smoked fish for both dinner and food for the next day. Rebels and prisoners ate separately.

"This is Grannie's favorite market food. She'd be happy to know that we're eating it," Kwame told Baako with somber amusement. "I want to tell her sometime. I hope I'll see her again. The crocodiles were so bad on the river today, Baako. Tell Atore that he was brave. I want to learn to use a spear like he does."

Baako translated for Atore, who bowed his head. "I will teach you," he responded.

"Do you think the soldiers will look for us on the beach tomorrow?" Baako asked Kwame.

"I hope so. Maybe we can walk slowly. If people on the beach hear us talk, they'll know we're not Fante. Maybe they'll tell the soldiers."

"Can we do something so the rebels won't trade us?" Baako asked. "What can we do?"

Baako translated the conversation for Atore, who replied, "Don't try to escape. Trust the soldiers. If they don't find us soon, they'll wait for us at the castle. They need to show the Asantehene that they can protect the messengers. If they can't, there will be more rebels. The Asantehene wouldn't like that." Atore's words helped calm the boys' fear.

"The soldiers will stay in town tonight," Ebo's mother told the rebels. "They're looking for you. People reported seeing you on the river today. Chiefs know about you but not your identity. Your friends see that you're missing. They suspect what you are doing."

"I want my *asafo* – militia – to join us. I'll talk to my friends when I return."

"Do not continue, my son. One of your prisoners is an *Agona*, your clansman. Your ancestors will be angry that you've kidnapped him. If you sell him, they will punish you. If the soldiers find you, they will punish you. You will not escape. Do not bring this shame upon our family."

"Mother, I respect you, but our ancestors have not protected us from the Asantehene's army. We have to fight."

"Our priests warned us not to fight the Asantehene. We did not follow their advice, and the war has brought devastation. Do not continue to fight the kingdom, my son." Ebo said nothing and looked sad.

"Beware, you are in danger," Ebo's mother said once more. "I must go before I am missed. I hope that I'll see you again. Leave early in the morning."

The rebels took the advice seriously. Their canoes were in the middle of the river before soldiers arrived at the pier. The soldiers yelled at the rebels but didn't fire their guns.

"They won't shoot at us," Ebo said with confidence. "They don't want to hit the prisoners. They'll look for us on the beach. We have to travel fast."

The rebels steered the boats to the middle of the river where the current was the strong. They ate from their food supply and didn't stop during the morning. Everyone grew tired from the heat and later a headwind, but they continued, knowing that the soldiers would as well.

IN THE EARLY AFTERNOON, THE REBELS AND THE PRISONERS WALKED ON THE BEACH near Cape Coast Castle. Kwame, Baako, and Atore had longed to see the ocean, and the sight astonished them. They wanted to go close. Ebo cautioned them. "I'll tie you together and take you across the beach to the water. I'll be next to you. Look around but don't try to get away. You're strangers here. You wouldn't get far."

"Look, Baako, it's so big, the water, and the sand," Kwame whispered. "They look like the sky and clouds. They are that big. Big like our forest. Our rivers don't seem big anymore."

"I see. I see," Baako replied. "I can't believe it! The water makes noise and goes on forever." He translated for Atore.

"The water looks like the waving grass of the savannah," Atore marveled. "The water makes noise like the grass."

"We want to taste the water," Baako told Ebo.

"It's salty. You won't like it."

"We want to try it," Baako repeated.

"Walk slowly. Feel the dry sand under your feet," Ebo instructed. "It's hot. You'll feel the wet sand soon. It's cold, but the ocean water is warm. You don't see this in the forest."

Ebo seemed strangely kind and was willing to help his prisoners understand the new setting but reminded them, "Don't talk to anyone."

The prisoners walked slowly and carefully on the beach, first crossing the dry sand and then the wet sand. "We don't see sand on river banks. I like sand. It's better than mud," Kwame said.

When the prisoners reached the water, they watched gentle waves roll in. Standing side by side, they stooped to touch the water. They stomped and laughed as the receding waves carried sand from beneath their feet. They picked up foam and threw it at each other. They tasted the water and spit it out. "Terrible, terrible," Baako shouted while laughing.

"So strange," Kwame agreed.

Atore couldn't follow the conversation but said to Baako, "This is beautiful and mysterious. What's on the other side of the water? Where will prisoners go when they leave the beach?"

"I don't know," Baako replied. "We will never see them again."

Kwame scooped up water and splashed Baako. "Too bad that we can't jump into the ocean the way we do in the stream," he laughed. "We could if we weren't tied up."

"Maybe," Baako answered, also laughing.

Atore and the boys' attention turned to a group of men not far away, pulling in a large net. The men tied the ends of the net around the base of nearby coconut trees and lined up on each side of the net to continue to pull it in. Some men wore anklets of metal rings that clanged together to make music as they stomped their feet.

Slowly the net emerged from the ocean full of small, shiny, jumping, silver fish. Once the net was on the beach, women scooped up the fish in baskets and took them away to smoke and sell. Small children picked up a few fish by their tails and ran away with them.

For a brief time, the prisoners lost themselves in the sights and sounds of the beach and the ocean. They were cooled by the breeze, and their world seemed peaceful.

"Will we eat fish tonight?" Kwame asked Ebo.

"Fish and pineapples," Ebo answered. "That's beach food."

"We'll go to my cousin's home now," Ebo explained. "I'll leave my gear with him, and he'll help me find canoeists to take us to Cape Coast Castle. It's not far. The whites there don't trade for prisoners anymore. We'll go on to Elmina, the next castle, to trade you."

By mid-afternoon Ebo had identified canoeists for the short journey and paid them in advance. He tied a pouch containing gold dust and gold weights, along with a knife in a holster, around his waist. His men wore their knives and carried only rope. They brought cloths to protect themselves and their prisoners from wind and sun.

Ebo did not tie the prisoners together. "Don't try to escape," he warned them. "We would recapture you quickly."

"I'm worried now. We're getting close to a castle," Baako told Kwame. "I want to see my papa and mama again. I want the Asantehene's soldiers to find us. Atore thinks they will, but I'm not sure."

"I want to see my papa and mama, too," Kwame replied. "I hope we'll see soldiers before we get to Elmina Castle. If soldiers don't find us, maybe the whites will help us. They don't want the Asantehene to be angry with them."

The rebel group and their prisoners met five fishermen with two canoes on a distant part of the beach. Ocean canoes were longer and narrower than river canoes and usually carried fishing nets. These held only the fishermens' scant supplies, leaving ample room for passengers. The fishermen were muscular and spoke with strong voices. They were barefoot and wore only cloths around their waist. After greeting them, Ebo said, "Tell us what to expect."

"We'll travel on the other side of the waves to Cape Coast Castle," the canoes' owner explained. "You'll always see the beach. Crossing the surf is rough. The canoes usually rise over the waves and slam down on the backside. Sometimes we go through the waves. Stay low. You'll get wet, but we won't tip over. Hang on, so you don't fall out. The waves are loud, and we can't hear each other, so don't talk. We're used to carrying prisoners from the castles to the ships. We know how to do this."

"There'll be two oarsmen in each canoe," the owner continued. "One in front. One in back. Passengers sit in the middle. If you get sick, puke in the water, not in the canoe. After we cross the waves, the water will be calm."

The owner directed two rebels, including Ebo, to the first canoe. He placed Kwame and Baako in the back, near him and his apprentice. He sent the other rebels and Atore to the second canoe. The passengers looked at each other with apprehension. "Be brave," Atore shouted. Baako translated.

Kwame's legs trembled. He wanted to sit down. "I don't want to fall out of the canoe," he told Baako. "I would be lost. They couldn't pick me up and I can't swim."

"If we hold on tight, we won't fall," Baako encouraged Kwame.

Boatmen pushed the canoes through the breaking waves, jumped on board, and paddled hard to drive the canoes over the surf. "Hang on," the owner yelled to his passengers. He hoped they heard him. A severe up and down motion continued for several minutes. Passengers bounced while gripping the sides of the canoes hard and bowing their heads low. The ocean's roar was deafening.

Waves swept over the canoes, drenching everyone. Salt burned their eyes. The boys yelled with fright, but the canoes emerged intact and upright, though they had taken on water. The extra boatman in the second canoe and the owner's apprentice in the first canoe bailed water. One of the rebels got sick but hung on and puked in the ocean. The boatmen avoided rocks and navigated over the swells to calm water.

Crossing the surf

"I'm scared, but this is exciting. Harder than crossing the Pra," Kwame whispered to Baako.

"I feel like I'm sitting in a tree that's blowing in the wind," Baako whispered back, "like a bird in a storm."

"I'm Kobe," the apprentice told Kwame and Baako. "My uncle's teaching me to be an oarsman. I bail water now. It's always rough to go through the waves, but I'm used to it. I like to do it. We'll all be fine."

"I'm Baako. My friend is Kwame. We're prisoners. We won't be fine."

"I'm sorry," Kobe replied. "I meant that the canoe ride will be fine. You can relax."

On course to Cape Coast Castle, the canoes maintained speed against the headwind. The boys and Atore eased their grip on the sides of the canoes, and welcomed the cooling wind in their faces, though the rays of the western sun were bright. Kwame and Baako began to enjoy the ride.

CHAPTER 45

Cape Coast Castle and Tanoso

Cape Coast Castle

THE BOATMEN CONFERRED IN SIGN LANGUAGE AND ONE OF THEM IN EACH CANOE TOLD his passengers that the trip to Cape Coast Castle was going well.

"This is the ride that prisoners sold to the whites take," Baako said to Kwame. "I'm scared. They must be scared, too."

"I'm scared. I don't like being a prisoner, but I wanted to see the ocean," Kwame replied. "That's why I want to be a trader."

"Traders have to walk a long way," Baako reminded his friend. "It would be better to be fishermen if the Fante would let us."

"The Fante don't want us here. I've begged my ancestors to stay with us even if we're not in the forest," Kwame answered. "I told them that we'll go back to the forest. I think they still see us. I told them that you'll be adopted. I hope they believe me. I asked *Nyame* to help us, too. When prisoners are traded, do their ancestors follow them?"

"My papa says that our Gurunsi ancestors followed us into the forest. I think they know where I am now. I hope they follow the Gurunsis who are traded to whites."

The boatmen paddled vigorously. "This is hard work," the canoe owner told the boys. "Here is where we earn our gold. Are you scared? My nephew used to be scared, but he's not anymore."

The boys looked at each other. "We aren't scared of the ocean, but we're scared of castles and ships," Kwame replied. "Will we see any ships?"

"Yes, there's a ship anchored at Cape Coast. Fante unloaded it and took everything to the castle. I worked on that job."

"I did, too," Kobe added. "I helped carry crates of cloth. They were heavy."

"What do ships bring here besides cloth?" Kwame asked.

"They bring metal tools like hoes, knives, and machetes, guns and ammunition, and some special items like beads and looking glasses. Traders take the goods everywhere."

"All of those things were in the Kumasi market," Baako recalled.

Fante canoeists loading a ship at Cape Coast Castle

"Now our people are loading the ship with the gold, elephant tusks, and pepper that the whites traded for," the canoe owner continued. "We also load supplies for the crews like water casks, firewood, and all kinds of food. Crews need to eat well."

"We used to load prisoners, but ships here don't take them anymore," he continued. "I didn't like carrying prisoners. I couldn't talk to them. They were afraid. Some fought me. Children cried. A few prisoners jumped out of canoes or off of ships and drowned. It was bad. I didn't want Kobe to see it."

"Do Fante work for the whites all of the time?" Kwame asked.

"Some, like me, work when whites need us. Other Fante trade with them. A few Fante work in the castles, but we're farmers and fishermen most of the time. Look at the castle when you're close," the canoe owner suggested. "There's a lot going on there."

The boys smiled. "More time for the soldiers to find us," Kwame whispered to Baako.

"You boys have Akan scars, but you aren't Fante. What are you doing here?" the canoe owner asked.

Kwame and Baako looked at each other and then at the canoe owner. They shook their heads and said nothing. The owner nodded.

The passengers and boatmen soon saw the outline of a white castle at the end of a narrow point of land protecting a bay. "That's Cape Coast Castle," Kobe said with excitement. "We're close. It's so big. You have to go see it."

"It looks like a cloud," Kwame observed. "It doesn't look real."

"There are many castles on the coast," the owner explained. "They don't look real, but they are. They're made of stone and bricks. They've been here for a long time. Fante built some of them for the whites. Whites come and go. They don't stay long. A lot of them get fevers and die here. There are never many in the castles."

Baako waved to Atore and pointed to the castle. Atore waved back, and the three prisoners stared ahead, eager to see more. As the canoes approached the castle, the boys saw the ship anchored beyond the surf. "It looks like a giant canoe," Baako gasped. "Why is it so far away?"

"The ship needs a lot of water to float. The water near the castle is too shallow for it," the canoe owner replied. "You see the wood on top that looks like the frame of a hut. The whites hang cloth from there to make sails. The wind pushes the sails to move the ship. Fantes use sail canoes when we fish far out in the ocean. Our canoes have only one sail, and boatmen still paddle. You turn the sails to make a ship or a canoe turn. It's beautiful to watch."

"Wind is powerful," Kwame agreed. "In the forest, it moves fire."

The owner signaled to the boatmen in the other canoe. "We'll land before we get to the castle," he said. The canoes rode the surf onto the beach, and everyone got out to drag the canoes across the beach and tie them to coconut trees.

"That was a good ride," Ebo said to the canoe owner. "What's going on at the castle? Will we find canoeists there to take us to Elmina Castle?"

"The fishermen are out. Boatmen at the castle are loading the ship. That's many days of work," the canoe owner replied. "Elmina Castle isn't in Fante territory. People there are Ahanta, and they aren't always friendly to us. Some boatmen won't go there."

"Stay on the beach," the canoe owner warned. "Drums have told us of danger and the Asantehene's soldiers are everywhere. If they see you, they'll want to talk to you. Good-bye and good luck."

"Good-bye and good luck," Kobe repeated to Kwame and Baako and waved. Kwame and Baako waved back.

THE MEN OF NANA'S DELEGATION TALKED AND LAUGHED AS THEY ATE BREAKFAST ON the seventh day of their travel to Tanoso. "We'll be home tomorrow," Nana said to the group with deep satisfaction. "We'll expect the Okyeame, Elder Kwasi, the boys, and Atore in five more days. Soon after, we'll celebrate our own *Odwira* in Tanoso and welcome the new year." Murmurs of satisfaction spread through the group.

"You'll be in your new home before long," Asare assured Apure. "Our village will welcome you."

"I'm grateful that my children have survived this trip," Apure replied. "Thank you for carrying my son. He will respect you. I will welcome a new home among Gurunsi people if we are safe. I want my husband to come."

"We all want to see him," Asare sympathized with her. "Nana and I want to see our sons, too. We all must wait and hope."

"Nana, the cub won't eat. He just wants to lie down." Kwaku was anxious. "What can we do?"

"Bring him to us," Nana replied. "Asare and I will look at him."

Kwaku lifted the cub from its cage and took it to the hearth where Nana and Asare waited. Nana held the cub and passed it to Asare. Others looked at it, too.

The cub lay still with its eyes open but made no sound. It let Nana pick up each of its paws. It did not get up. Asare held it with similar results.

"What did you give it to eat this morning?" Nana asked Kwaku.

"This town has no milk, so I tried to give it some palm nut soup and smoked fish. It didn't eat or drink."

"Did it drink soup last night?"

"Yes, it drank a little, but it wasn't active like it used to be."

"It's hard to raise a wild animal in a cage," Asare said. "They're not like chickens or sheep. They're not used to taking food from people. I've tried to raise duiker fawns. They didn't survive."

"Kwaku, you have cared for the cub well," Nana said. "You've done everything possible for it. Try to give it soup and fish and water again today. We might find milk for it tonight. We can do nothing more. It needs its mother."

Kwaku thanked Nana and Asare and took the cub to its cage. He cleaned the cage and added fresh leaves while talking to the cub. "I'm your senior brother. I'll take care of you. I won't put you on my back, but I'll stay near you. We're almost home. We'll look for your mother soon."

Nana's group set off quickly. An *odonko* carried the cub in its cage as a head load shaded by an umbrella. Kwaku walked next to him, carrying a basket as a head load and a calabash of soup in one hand. He and the *odonko* stopped frequently, and Kwaku offered soup to the cub. There was little response.

THE PIERCING SOUND OF HORNS AND THE STEADY BEAT OF DRUMS SIGNALED THE return of Nana's delegation to Tanoso on its eighth day of travel. Townspeople lined the main road to applaud. Cries of "*Akwaaba! Akwaaba!*" rang out.

In the palace courtyard, the travelers put down their head loads to greet family members and friends. Nana quickly retired to the family courtyard to embrace the Queen Mother, Madam Ama, Akua, and Yaw Mensah, who saw that he was well. They immediately asked about Kwame, Baako, the Okyeame, and Elder Kwasi. Nana explained where the missing people were and that he had sent messengers to tell their families.

"*Akwaaba*, Nana," Madam Adjowa greeted her brother as she entered the family courtyard. "I'm glad you've returned. My husband told us about your trip, but I want to hear about the leopard cub from you. Kwaku brought it home. It looks sick, and Kwaku's crying. What has happened?"

"I'm glad that you are here, my daughter," the Queen Mother said. "We have much to learn."

"So much has happened," Nana replied shaking his head. "The cub is from here. Nana Samfo's *nnonko* found it in a pit trap. He took it to Kumasi and gave it to the Asantehene."

"He didn't want to protect leopards after you talked to him?" Madam Ama questioned.

"His council wouldn't agree," Nana explained. "The Okyeame and Elder Kofi went to the Asantehene's palace to ask for the cub so that we could return it to our forest. They received it, and the cub was well in Kumasi. Kwaku and his cousins cared for it there, and Kwaku has cared for it on our journey home.

"Kwaku did his work well, but he's found very little milk for the cub. He's given it soup and water and meat. Now it will drink very little. I fear it will die before we find its mother. If that happens, we'll bury it here in the palace. I don't want anyone to dig it up for its skin."

"I understand why Kwaku's crying," Madam Adjowa said. "He doesn't want the cub to die."

"The leopard mother may be crying, too," the Queen Mother commented. "Since you left, Nana, no one has seen the leopards."

Nana looked uneasy. "I wonder where they've gone," he said. "Asare is settling the new *nnonko* in their village. I must talk to others now. Tell Kwaku to bring the cub to me later." Nana returned to the main courtyard.

"YAW MENSAH AND I WANT TO GO HOME WITH YOU TO SEE THE CUB. WILL YOU TAKE us?" Akua asked her aunt.

"Of course. All of you come. Kwaku needs company," Madam Adjowa answered. They found Kwaku sitting under a tree in the courtyard of his home, holding the cub in his lap.

"*Akwaaba*, Kwaku. We have missed you," both the Queen Mother and Madam Ama said.

"Thank you for taking care of the cub," the Queen Mother continued. "What is it doing now?"

"The cub's sleeping," Kwaku explained without looking up. "I told it that we're home. When it's strong, I'll look for its mother. It's weak now. I don't know if it will be strong again. It was well until a few days ago. I thought it would be happy to come home."

"I want to touch the cub. I'll be very gentle," Akua said.

"Let me touch it, too," Yaw Mensah said. "I saw it run down the path when it was strong and I couldn't catch it."

"Be careful," Kwaku directed. "Don't wake it up." Akua and Yaw Mensah each petted the cub with one finger.

"It's so soft," Akua said. "Will you give it something to drink soon?"

"I want to. Grannie, can we find milk for the cub?" Kwaku asked.

"I'll ask in town if there is any milk," the Queen Mother offered. "Let's try giving it water first. I'll get some."

"*Medaase*, Grannie," Kwaku replied.

A short time later, the leopard cub died peacefully in Kwaku's lap with Akua and Yaw Mensah nearby. "It's gone to sleep forever," Kwaku told them.

"I want to touch the cub one more time," Akua said. "I'm sad that it's gone."

"Can I touch it, too?" Yaw Mensah asked. "I'll remember when it ran on the path to the stream, just like me."

"Yes, touch it gently. We'll miss it, and its family will miss it," Kwaku said. "Kofi Edu and Akosua will miss it. We all played with it in Kumasi, but I wanted it to live in our forest again. Call Mama. I'll give the cub to her."

THAT EVENING NANA TOLD HIS FAMILY OF ELDER KWADWO AND MADAM ADJOWA's generous hospitality in Kumasi. "They send all of you greetings and promise to come to Tanoso. I hope to see them here with Kofi Edu and Akosua, who welcomed their cousins and Baako. We were honored."

"Elder Kwadwo's mother was my younger sister," the Queen Mother said. "I miss her, and I want to see Kwadwo and his family again. My family is precious."

"They will try to come," Nana assured his mother.

Nana continued, "The boys and I, along with Kofi Edu, and Akosua explored the market and the foreigners' zone in Kumasi. The market is immense, with so much for sale from our kingdom and beyond."

"I've seen the market but not the foreigners' zone. What did you find there?" the Queen Mother asked.

"The boys will tell you details. I'll say that we learned about a horse called Doki and how imams write words in a language called Arabic. For my war smock, I bought three talismans with Arabic writing inside. When the boys are here, I'll show them to you. Kwame will teach you how to write your names in Arabic."

"Oh, I want to do that!" Akua said clapping her hands.

"Yes!" Yaw Mensah exclaimed.

"I'm sorry that the cub has died," the Queen Mother said in a regretful voice. "I'm certain that Kwaku did his best to save it, but keeping a wild animal alive in a cage is almost impossible. I'm disappointed that Nana Somfo took the cub to Kumasi. He was foolish to do that. I want to speak to him."

"*Medaase*," Nana replied. "I'm sorry for the cub, too. I talked to Nana Somfo in Kumasi and I'll talk to him again soon. I want to persuade him to help me protect leopards. I don't want a palaver with him. Let me talk to him."

"I'll respect your wishes, but be strict with him, my son. He has much to learn."

The following day Nana and members of the *Odwira* delegation informed the council about their trip and distributed the new guns and ammunition. The elders were pleased but concerned about continued conflict with the Fante. Nana told them what he had learned. "We may hear more from the Okyeame and Elder Kwasi when they return," he added. "After that, we'll depend on traders to inform us."

Four days later, the Okyeame, Elder Kwasi, and the boys had not returned. With the immediate families, Nana speculated that the travelers had stayed with the messengers to travel to the coast. "They won't be home for a long time, maybe thirty days," he told the group. "We'll help your families until they return. We must be hopeful. If there are difficulties, the Asantehene will send messengers to tell us."

— CHAPTER 46 —

Approaching the Castles

Women on the beach carried machetes and head loads of coconuts and pine-apples. Ebo signaled to a woman, who put her tray down and with her machete cut both fruits open and offered slices to the group. "They're delicious," she said, smiling. Ebo paid her as everyone savored the fruit.

Ebo looked worried as he conferred with his men. He told the prisoners, "We'll walk toward the castle now. I'll look for canoeists to take us on to Elmina Castle this afternoon. It's not far.

"I won't tie you together because I don't want to attract attention, but don't try to escape. We can easily overpower you. You boys don't sound like Fante, so don't talk. Men from the savannah are always prisoners," he said looking at Atore. Baako translated. Everyone carried the extra cloths as head loads. The rebels carried their ropes and wore knives in their waist holsters. Ebo wore his pouch for gold dust and gold weights.

The rebels responded to greetings from people they met on the beach. The prisoners nodded. Nearing the castle, the boys saw the immense height of its solid white walls. Beyond the walls were taller buildings with windows. The group approached a seaside corner of the castle and came upon a work site of intense activity. Balancing towering head loads, porters streamed out of the castle's huge beach-level doorway to deposit their loads in waiting canoes, which took them to the ship.

The prisoners were stunned. "The porters look like driver ants at work," Kwame whispered to Baako, beyond the rebels' hearing. Baako nodded to agree. Frantically busy, the canoeists and porters failed to greet the rebels.

Beyond the worksite, the rebels and prisoners saw a lower castle wall where ten cannons rested, facing the ocean, prepared for combat. "The big guns tell us where the danger is," Baako whispered as he nudged Kwame and pointed to the cannons. "It's from ships."

While intrigued with the worksite, Ebo was frustrated. "I won't find anyone here to help us," he told his group. "Everyone's busy. The beach behind the castle is narrow and

We Are Akan

rocky, so we can't walk there. We'll turn around and go back the way we came, and then walk around the town before we return to the beach. We'll walk to Elmina. We can't take the main road. Soldiers will be patrolling it."

Away from the castle, there were few people on the beach, and the prisoners talked to each other while walking ahead of the rebels. "What do you think of the cannons?" Kwame asked Baako.

"I couldn't see much of them, but they looked big, like the ones we heard about in Kumasi," Baako answered. "It would be hard to carry cannons from the ocean all the way to Kumasi. No one could carry a cannon on his head. Porters must have used hammocks."

"Imagine launching a canoe loaded with cassava, yams, and plantains," Baako said. "That would be hard. I wouldn't want to try it, but the Fante are really good boatmen."

Kwame agreed. "I wouldn't want to launch a canoe full of prisoners either. I hope we don't end up in one. I want to believe that Atore is right and that the Asantehene's soldiers will find us. Atore's smart."

"Where do you think Kwaku is now? Kwame asked.

Baako shook his head and spoke in a low voice. "Maybe he's in Tanoso already. I hope that he can find the cub's mother. I hope we'll tell Kwaku about this trip sometime. He wouldn't like it now.

"Kwame, I've been thinking that we could run away from the rebels when we're near Cape Coast town. We can run fast, and people there might help us. We might find the soldiers."

"What about Atore?" Kwame asked in surprise. "We came so far to find him. We can't desert him. The rebels would sell him. The Okyeame told us that he and Elder Kwasi would find us. He told us to be brave."

"Atore can come with us," Baako answered. "I want to be brave, but I'm afraid."

Ebo pointed down the beach and warned, "Soldiers! Quick, into the coconut grove. Prisoners, don't talk!"

"Someone reported us, maybe the canoeists who brought us here," Ebo said. "We'll walk in the grove until we're on the other side of the town. We'll break up now. I'll take two men and the boys. The rest of you walk separately. It's legal to have a savannah person as a prisoner. If you're stopped, the soldiers will respect that. Put a rope around his waist. The soldiers are looking for a group with three prisoners, and Atore can't tell them anything.

"When we're past the town, go back to the beach and walk to Abura. It's the next fishing village. We'll sleep on the beach tonight. If we don't see each other, we'll meet in the morning on the beach near Elmina Castle," Ebo concluded his plan. The other rebels agreed. Baako translated for Atore.

Atore replied in whispered tones, "Be brave! The soldiers will find us. I'll see you again tonight. Don't try to escape. The rebels don't want to hurt us because they want to sell us. Don't give them a reason to hurt us."

Ebo left with his group first. He had a determined look and voice. "If we're stopped," he told the boys, "answer questions but don't give any hint that you're prisoners. If one of you does, I'll kill the other. I have my knife. I may die, too, but I'll kill one of you first." The boys were stiff with fright. Ebo had never been so threatening.

Both rebel groups navigated the coconut grove skillfully as they walked inland. They greeted farmers. "We don't have tools or crops. We don't look like farmers," Baako whispered to Kwame.

"You're right. I hope that someone will tell the soldiers," Kwame answered.

"Don't talk. That slows you down," Ebo said in a menacing voice. "Walk faster." The boys complied. The group traveled rapidly and soon returned to the beach to walk on wet sand. Farmers, fishermen, and women carrying baskets of fish as head loads populated the beach. They greeted Ebo, who nodded in reply.

"It's so much easier to walk here," Baako told Ebo.

"Walk faster," Ebo responded.

One of the rebels tapped Ebo on the shoulder and pointed to the ocean. "Look!" he said. "Look, another ship!"

Everyone turned to see a second ship sailing toward the castle. "It's sails are open," Baako observed. "The wind is pushing them. The ship is moving. It's coming to see us!"

"We'll hear a cannon blast," Ebo warned. "That's how the whites welcome a ship and call the canoeists to work. For a welcome, they don't use cannon balls. They don't want to waste them or hit the ship. They just use powder."

"I hope that we'll hear a blast even if we can't see the cannons," Kwame said.

"We will," Ebo confirmed. "The blasts are louder than thunder."

Four soldiers approached the group. It was too late to leave the beach. "Walk slowly," Ebo said. "Don't say anything."

One of the soldiers signaled the group to stop. "We're from the Asantehene's army," he said. "You're strangers here. Who are you? Where are you from?"

Ebo remained calm and replied, "We're from Assin Manso, and we're going to Elmina."

"Why aren't you using the main road?" the soldier asked.

"We came to Cape Coast by canoe and couldn't bring our weapons," Ebo replied.

"There are rebel groups in the area, and so we're walking on the beach where there are many people. I want my nephews to be safe."

The soldiers looked at the group and seemed convinced by the story. "You may continue," one said as they walked away.

"I hope they believed me," Ebo told his group. "We need to hurry."

There was a loud explosion. People on the beach froze. The noise frightened birds into silence and stole words from people. The boys curled up on the sand, hands over their heads.

Gradually birds resumed their flight, and people talked once more. "Cannon blasts scare everyone," Ebo said. "Fantes hate them. Be prepared for more."

"The noise was so loud. We had thunder but no rain," Baako said. "It scared me even when I knew it was coming."

"My ears have never heard such a noise," Kwame said as he uncurled his body and stood once more. "What would happen if a cannon shot a ball? Would a cannonball destroy a ship?"

"I'm not sure what would happen," Ebo answered. "Cannons are powerful and can probably damage a ship. I'm glad that I don't live near the cannons."

Two more cannon blasts tore through the air as the group continued walking. Each time, people on the beach stopped, stood still, and covered their ears with their hands.

"Does Elmina Castle have cannons?" Kwame asked.

"All the castles do," Ebo replied. "It's good that the cannons point toward the ocean, not at us."

As the sun set, the group approached Abura. They saw fishermen dragging nets in from the ocean and women loading baskets with fish, all working to the music of the fishermen's anklets.

A path through a coconut grove gave easy access to the town. While Ebo bought food for dinner and the next day's breakfast, his companions looked for a place to build a shelter. The second group joined them. They drew drinking water from a nearby stream, where they also bathed. Over dinner they made plans for the next day.

THE MESSENGERS' GROUP REACHED CAPE COAST TOWN WELL BEFORE SUNSET AND settled at the travelers' shelter. The Okyeame and Elder Kwasi walked to the beach. "This is truly another land," Elder Kwasi said. "The ocean, the castle, and the ship are beyond what I could ever have imagined."

"The ocean brings us ships, and the savannah bring us camel caravans," the Okyeame replied. "We feel alone in the forest, but we're connected to distant places. The kingdom protects us, but we have to fight. The Asantehene will return to defeat the rebels. He won't tolerate them."

"We'll arrive at our destination tomorrow afternoon," Elder Kwasi said. "We don't know if soldiers have found our boys and Atore yet. The messengers believe that the Asantehene's soldiers are following the rebels, and that we'll see them in Elmina. I hope they're right."

CHAPTER 47

Elmina Castle

THE BOYS AWOKE ON THE BEACH IN AN EARLY MORNING FOG TO SEE FISHERMEN, SOME bearing torches, loading nets into their canoes. "Look at their torches," Kwame told Baako. "Fishermen can't take torches with them. They won't see anything after they launch their canoes."

"They're brave," Baako said. "They know the stars, but in the fog, they can't even see the stars."

"Maybe they just go straight out but not far," Kwame answered. "Even that's dangerous. I couldn't be a fisherman. I can't swim, and I don't know the stars, and I don't like the fog."

"You could learn about those things," Baako replied. "I could, too."

The group ate a good breakfast. Ebo wanted everyone to eat well, especially the prisoners, whom he planned to trade that day. "Healthy prisoners bring a good price," he believed.

Both rebels and prisoners wrapped themselves in cloths to stay warm in the cool morning air. "I won't tie you together because I want to move fast," Ebo told the prisoners. "Don't try to escape. We would catch you. We'll be at Elmina Castle before the sun is high."

Ebo was in a good mood, looking forward to the end of the long journey. "I'll trade the prisoners for guns and ammunition," he recalled to his men. "We'll get a good price. We need more fire power. The Asantehene has attacked twice. When he comes back, we'll be prepared." Fellow rebels nodded with approval. Baako translated for Atore. The prisoners shuddered.

Atore seldom started a conversation, but now he said to Baako, "I'm certain that the soldiers are waiting for us in Elmina. They've seen us on the beach. They want to capture the rebels. It will be easier to do that in or near the castle. Stay calm. We'll be rescued. Tell Kwame what I've said."

When they were a safe distance from the rebels, Baako translated for Kwame, who replied, "I hope that Atore's right. He's trying to help us. We have to stay calm, but the rebels are dangerous even if they're nice to us sometimes. They might fight the soldiers. They might hold us as hostages."

"Atore doesn't think they will. He says the soldiers will be stronger than the rebels, especially if we are all in the castle."

When the rising sun burned away the fog, a beautiful setting emerged. The shoreline curved gently. Deep green coconut trees lined a beach of shimmering white sand. Coconut fronds swayed in a light wind. The ocean glistened like dew on forest trees. Waves crashed onto the beach with musical rhythm and receded, leaving white foam.

"The foam looks like clouds," Baako said. "We see clouds in the sky and on the beach." White sea gulls squawked loudly and flew close to the group before settling on boulders or in the water. The fishing canoes were no longer in sight.

"We see green trees and red paths in our forest," Kwame said quietly to Baako. "We see green here, too, but there is so much white and blue. It's totally different."

"It's different and it's dangerous," Baako replied. "The sound of the waves and the birds scare me now. It's not safe on the beach. We're safer in the forest."

"There are snakes in the forest and crocodiles and other animals, too," Kwame reminded Baako.

"We know about them. Here I don't know what will happen," Baako declared. "I'm scared of what I don't know. I want to run away when we're in Elmina town. The Ahanta people in the town might help us."

"Don't do it, Baako," Kwame pleaded. "You'll be stabbed, maybe killed. I think Atore is right. The Asantehene's soldiers probably know where we are. They'll probably help us. They probably want to capture the rebels when they're in the castle. Then they'll free us." Baako didn't reply.

Following the curve of the beach and going inland at times to avoid boulders, the group soon approached the white cloud that was Elmina Castle. The boys looked at each other and pointed. They tapped Atore on his shoulder and pointed. "There it is," Baako whispered.

"There is a castle behind us and a castle in front of us," Kwame said. "We're prisoners between them. We're like birds flying from one boulder to another, but inside of a cage."

"I wish I could fly," Baako answered. "I would fly into the forest."

As the group trekked further, the outline of Elmina castle emerged. Next to the ocean, it consisted of several large, white buildings surrounded by a high wall. Between the travelers and the castle, the narrow Benya River flowed into the ocean. Fishing canoes were visible once more. A few fishermen worked on canoes and nets along the river banks. "It looks like Cape Coast Castle but quieter," Kwame said to Baako. "No ships are here."

Elmina Castle

Elmina town hugged the bank of the river's near side. "We'll go into town, follow the road to the castle, and cross a bridge," Ebo told the boys. Kwame thought Ebo sounded anxious. "Prisoners, keep your heads down and don't say anything. I want to get into the castle fast.

"There's a rest house in town next to the chief's palace. That's where the messengers will go. On water we stayed ahead of them. We were delayed in Cape Coast, but we're still ahead. After the messengers arrive, everyone will be looking for you. We need to move fast."

"Didn't the drums tell people about us already?" Kwame asked.

"The drums told people about danger, not about you," Ebo replied. "I know that you're good people and that you boys are young. After I trade you, I think that you'll be *nnonko* for whites. I hope that you'll get good masters. I'm trading a clansman, and I want my ancestors to forgive me, but they haven't protected my people. I'm doing that." Baako and Kwame looked at each other in fear. Baako translated for Atore.

Atore spoke again, "Stay calm. I believe that the soldiers are waiting for us." Baako translated.

Ebo was annoyed. "Don't talk," he ordered.

The group soon left the beach to walk into Elmina town, where they followed well-ordered streets lined with vegetable stalls and busy with shoppers. As the group approached the bridge, Baako suddenly broke away, pushed shoppers aside, and ran between stalls toward the river. Atore chased and tackled him. Ebo grabbed Kwame's shoulder.

"Don't try to escape," Atore told Baako harshly. "Your Gurunsi ancestors fought lions. Be brave like they were. Come back to the group or you'll be killed."

"I'm afraid," Baako answered, getting up slowly.

"Be brave!" Atore repeated, pulling Baako to standing and holding his arm to walk him back to the group. The shoppers remained silent witnesses to the incident. They had seen such before.

"Thank your friend for stopping you. I won't kill you now. I'll trade you," Ebo told Baako in a harsh voice, grabbing him firmly by an arm.

The group crossed the bridge and approached the castle. The drawbridge to the castle was raised. Pointing to the moat on three sides of the castle, Kwame asked, "What is it? Are crocodiles in there?"

"It's a moat with ocean water. No crocodiles are there. Moats keep people away from the castle," Ebo explained, and called, "*Agoo,*" to ask permission to enter.

"*Amee,*" came an affirmative reply from an Ahanta guard stationed at the moat. The drawbridge was lowered.

The group crossed the bridge, and another exchange took place at the castle door.

"*Agoo.*"

"*Amee.*"

"I have prisoners to trade for guns and ammunition," Ebo said to a guard through a small window in the door.

"I'll open the door and call the governor. Leave your weapons at the door," the guard replied.

The rebels were uncomfortable but complied with the order and walked through an enormous door to enter the courtyard. The guard raised the drawbridge, its chains rattling as it slammed shut. He closed the door. Rebels and prisoners alike were alarmed. "We close the door for safety," the guard explained.

The group stood in a large courtyard where several guards were stationed. The surrounding walls were three and four stories high, with windows facing the courtyard, and outside stairways providing access to upper floors. The group heard cries of distress from behind a massive nearby door fitted with a small opening that was covered by bars. "That's the prison," a guard said. Everyone moved away from the door.

Courtyard at Elmina Castle

Near the wall on the ocean side of the castle, a group of prisoners, both men and boys, stood naked, pouring water over their bodies from large gourds and scrubbing themselves with leaves. With their ankles hobbled by chains, they moved haltingly. They were too far away for the boys to see their scars.

Above the courtyard on the castle's ramparts were prisoners carrying head loads, working for the castle. Other prisoners were being exercised there. At one end of the walkway, firewood and casks of water, destined for ships, were stacked. Only male prisoners were visible. The lamentations from the prison joined the surf's roar to create a mournful background noise. The castle's atmosphere was tense, unlike that of an energetic beach or marketplace.

"This castle's bigger than the Asantehene's palace. Where do you think the cannons are?" Kwame said to Baako, who shook his head.

"I see many people, but no one is talking," Baako replied. "They're all sad."

The uniformed governor of Elmina Castle, accompanied by an interpreter, descended one of the stairways. He greeted Ebo and asked his business.

"I have three prisoners to trade for guns, gunpowder, and musket balls. I want Long Dane guns and high quality ammunition."

"Why have you come here?" the governor asked.

"You're trading prisoners, and I live nearby," Ebo explained. "The whites at Cape Coast Castle don't take prisoners anymore."

"Yes, we are Dutch, and we trade for prisoners. The English no longer take them. Your prisoners are young and look healthy. I see from their scars that two are Akan and one is from the savannah. How did you get them?"

"They were traveling with the Asantehene's army. They weren't armed. We captured them as the army was leaving." Kwame and Baako looked at each other, wondering if the governor would believe the lie.

"Where have these prisoners been since the Asantehene's army left?"

"They've been working on my family's farm near Assin Manso."

Addressing Kwame and Baako, the governor asked, "Prisoners, is this true?"

Kwame and Baako looked at the each other, the rebel leader, and Atore, deciding how to respond, and knowing that they might risk their lives if they told the truth. They said nothing.

"I see that you don't want to talk. You may need to protect yourselves," the governor said.

"When I hear the *oburoni* talk, I can't understand him. The words are strange," Baako whispered to Kwame. The interpreter smiled.

"Patrols of the Asantehene's army have warned us of danger," the governor explained. "I agreed to let a patrol see any prisoners brought here. If I don't do this, there will be a palaver. Guard, call the soldiers." The rebels stiffened. The boys became hopeful.

Four soldiers descended a stairway. The rebels and boys recognized them as the ones they had met on the beach the day before. The soldiers' spokesman asked the prisoners to tell him who they were and how they were captured. Feeling safer now, the boys and Atore told their stories. Baako translated for Atore.

"These are the prisoners that we're looking for," the soldiers' spokesman told the governor. "They were traveling with the Asantehene's messengers, and these Fante rebels kidnapped them. The Fante are guilty of treason against the Asantehene. Hold them in your prison."

"You can trade the rebels here," the governor told the soldiers. "Five healthy prisoners will bring a good price."

The rebels pleaded, "No, don't trade us. Don't trade us. We don't deserve that! We didn't harm our prisoners. We fed them well. We didn't beat them. Let our chief handle this. Let our *asafo* handle this. We beg you!"

"We follow Akan law," the soldiers' spokesman told the governor. "Hold the rebels until the king's messengers arrive and identify them for certain. We'll take the prisoners to the rest house and wait for the messengers. They'll be grateful for your help."

The governor called for leg irons. "I'll keep them until I hear from you," he told the soldiers. The rebels begged for their lives as guards clamped irons around their ankles and led them to the prison.

Baako, Atore, and Kwame were thrilled to be free and safe once more, but alarmed to see the rebels in danger. "Be fair to them," Kwame said to the soldiers. "They didn't hurt us." The boys thanked the governor for his help. He replied favorably and ordered the drawbridge lowered for the boys, Atore, and the soldiers.

— CHAPTER 48 —

Castle and Cannons

Reaching the rest house, Kwame and Baako collapsed on the floor and cried out in relief. "Thank you for this miracle. I was afraid that our ancestors could not reach us," Kwame said to the soldiers as his tears flowed. "I want to go back to the forest where I'm safe. I want to go home."

Baako, too, was emotional. "I've never been so scared. We walked for many, many days, and now I want to tell my mama and papa what happened. How did you find us?"

Atore expressed his gratitude and asked Baako to translate. "Thank you for saving us. I want to see my family again. Soldiers tore us apart for the Asantehene, but now his soldiers have saved me. How life can be strange."

The soldiers were sympathetic. They called for food and water, and their spokesman explained, "Drums alerted us to danger. A patrol met the messengers on the main road and learned what happened. People saw you and told their chiefs, who let us and other patrols know.

"We were certain that the rebels planned to trade you at Elmina Castle and hoped that they would bring you here right away. We watched and saw you and followed and waited. You and your elders took risks coming to the coast. The Asantehene rules here, but some Fante rebels haven't surrendered."

"We heard them talk about getting more guns and fighting," Baako said.

"They want to fight, but the Asantehene is too strong for them," another soldier asserted. "We'll capture the other rebels, too. They won't escape."

The messengers' group arrived in Elmina town that afternoon and greeted the boys and Atore with great happiness and feelings of relief. "We were worried about you," the Okyeame confessed. "I know that the drums send a powerful message, and I hoped that the soldiers would find you, but I couldn't be certain. I thank our ancestors for your safety."

Elder Kwasi had a similar message. "I, too, thank our ancestors. The *Oyoko* and *Agona* clans are powerful, and our ancestors watch over us. We must honor them."

"The *Gwegene* clan is strong, too," the Okyeame added. "We were all in danger, and our ancestors protected us. I'll pour a libation for them." Everyone stepped outside to pray with the Okyeame as he poured a libation thanking the ancestors in three clans.

"If Nana traveled well, his delegation arrived in Tanoso today," Elder Kwasi said. "He'll tell our families what we're doing, but he doesn't know that we've come to the coast. He'll be concerned about us when he sees that we are delayed, but he has confidence in us. He'll reassure our families and care for them."

"I'm happy that you're safe," a messenger explained. "We'll rest here for the next two days and then return to Kumasi. A patrol of soldiers will accompany us to Assin Manso, where we leave Fante territory. We'll be safe."

"When will the traders with prisoners from Kumasi arrive?" Baako asked. "We're safe, but what about them? They're suffering."

"We may see them here soon," the Okyeame replied. "I wish that we could help them. Trading prisoners is a terrible business. It will go on as long as whites want prisoners. The Asantehene won't stop the trade. It helps him."

The soldiers' spokesman addressed the messengers. "Come with us to the castle to see the men we've arrested. Tell us if they're the ones who robbed you and kidnapped the boys and the prisoner."

The messengers wanted first to greet the Elmina chief and deliver their message to the governor of the castle. The soldiers' spokesman accompanied them. The chief welcomed the messengers and invited them to return to the palace later that day. He wanted the Asantehene's soldiers to stay nearby since he feared a Fante attack on his people, who were loyal to the king. He asked the messengers to tell the Asantehene.

The messengers presented their golden sword to the guards at the castle's moat and drawbridge and were escorted to the governor's office, where they were welcomed as representatives of the Asantehene. They took turns repeating their message in short segments, giving the interpreter time to translate the Twi into Dutch.

The governor listened carefully and nodded to indicate that he understood, occasionally asking a question for clarification. He immediately dictated a reply. "The guns and ammunition that the Asantehene requests for payment of rent for Elmina Castle will be ready when he returns. The Ahanta remain loyal to the kingdom. They will defend Elmina if the Fante attack. Send more soldiers to guarantee the peace." Knowing now the Asantehene's plans, the soldiers' spokesman asked the governor to turn the rebel prisoners over to the Asantehene directly when he returned.

"I want to hear the messengers' account of what happened and see if they identify the men that I'm holding," the governor replied. The messengers soon identified the rebels, and the governor agreed to hold them for the Asantehene and not to sell them. The soldiers were satisfied with the resolution.

The next day the Okyeame and Elder Kwasi with Kwame, Baako, and Atore explored Elmina town with a local elder. They admired the orderly town and watched with fascination as canoes returned from the ocean and moored on the river banks with nets full of fish. "They must go far away to catch so many fish," Kwame speculated. "Look how women unload the canoes and take the fish to ovens."

"We could eat fish here forever!" Baako said with pleasure.

The group requested and received a limited tour of the castle by an Ahanta guard. They were fascinated to hear whites speak to each other and the guard speak to them in Dutch. One of the whites greeted the group, "*Guedenmidtag* – Good afternoon," he said, and the guard responded.

"Will you show us the cannons?" Kwame asked the guard, who agreed and led the way.

Cannons at Elmina Castle

After climbing a stairway to the ramparts that supported the cannons, the group approached them and even touched and tried to move them to feel their weight. They saw the cannon balls stacked in containers.

"The cannons are gigantic," Elder Kwasi remarked to the group. "I didn't know that they're so much bigger than our guns."

"The cannon balls are huge," the Okyeame added. "It's good that the cannons point to the ocean."

"The cannons in Kumasi came from here long ago," Baako remembered. "Now I know why the Asantehenes want us to see them. They want us to know about the castles. We have to tell Kwaku about the cannons and how they are loud when they're fired."

The Okyeame expressed the sentiments of everyone, "The cannons show us strength. Look, we can see Cape Coast Castle from here. It's close."

"The people in these castles aren't friends. That's why they need cannons," Kwame said. "Maybe they fight a lot."

"We see that they're prepared to fight," Elder Kwasi replied, "but cannons only shoot at ships, not at other castles. The danger comes from ships."

"It's all so new," Kwame said, "the idea of fighting from ships. Do Akans ever fight from canoes?"

"Our armies almost always fight on land," Elder Kwasi answered. "It would be hard to use our weapons from canoes. Akan soldiers always travel by walking, sometimes through the forest for protection."

"We've heard many languages," Baako said. "Everyone speaks Twi. The Okyeame, Atore, my papa, and I speak Nankane. There was Hausa and Arabic in Kumasi, and now Dutch at Elmina Castle. The people at Cape Coast Castle are different from the Dutch. What language do they speak?"

"They speak English," the guard explained. Ahantas don't speak that language, but many Fante do. They learn it when they work for the whites."

When the group crossed the drawbridge to leave the castle, they found the traders with prisoners from Kumasi waiting to enter. The prisoners were tied together with rope that circled the waist of each and a second rope that circled one ankle of each. One trader carried a machete and spear. The other carried a gun. Two porters carried spears. The prisoners looked frightened.

The Okyeame greeted them. They bowed their heads slightly to acknowledge him but said nothing. "Baako, these are our people. May our ancestors protect them," the Okyeame declared.

Atore acknowledged his friends and uttered greetings in a low tone as he touched each one on his shoulder while passing by.

On their second day in Elmina, the Okyeame and Elder Kwasi talked at length with Kwame and Baako. "We know that your trip was difficult, and we imagine that you were worried much of the time," Elder Kwasi said. "The Okyeame encouraged you to be brave when the rebels took you away. We think that you survived because you were brave and didn't resist. The rebels wanted to trade you, not injure you, but they might have hurt you if you had resisted."

"When we were afraid, Atore helped us," Kwame explained. "He knows how to be a prisoner. He said to stay calm and eat well and do what the rebels wanted. Baako translated so we could talk to each other. The rebels said they would kill one of us if we didn't follow their orders."

"Thank you, Atore, for helping our boys," the Okyeame said in Nankane. Atore bowed his head to show respect.

"When I speak for Nana," the Okyeame continued, "I use many proverbs to help everyone understand. Elders say, 'Two light leaves combine to become heavy.' We see that in the brooms we make to sweep our courtyards. Many light leaves make a strong broom. Kwame and Baako, together you were strong, and you accepted Atore's advice. You didn't look down on him. You were wise, and that gave you strength."

"I tried to escape when we were in Elmina town," Baako confessed. "Atore chased me and tackled me, and brought me back to the rebels. He told me that my ancestors fought lions and that I should be brave like them, but my body was shaking."

"I will thank Atore, again," the Okyeame responded. "Perhaps our ancestors sent him to protect you and Kwame. We will never know, but do not be ashamed. You were strong for this difficult trip. You wanted to survive, and you did. I believe that our ancestors are pleased. I'll tell Nana what happened with both of you, and I believe that he will be pleased, too."

"Kwame, I'm your senior uncle, and later I'll be responsible for you," Elder Kwasi said. "You will move to my home when you become a young man. I'm very sorry that you were kidnapped, but you did well.

"We see your character in your friends. It is good that you, Baako, and Kwaku are friends. I'm certain that Kwaku has worked hard to care for the cub. The three of you strengthen each other, just as our elders work to strengthen Nana, and Akan chiefs work to strengthen the Asantehene. We are never alone. We are all in the broom together."

Kwame and Baako were grateful for this recognition and thanked the Okyeame and Elder Kwasi. "A broom made of palm leaves is strong," Kwame said. "I know because when I'm home, I sweep with a broom everyday."

"The *nnonko* make brooms," Baako added. "I know how to put the leaves together to make a broom strong."

— CHAPTER 49 —

Elmina to Kumasi

After two days in Elmina, the Asantehene's messengers prepared to return to Kumasi, accompanied by a patrol of four soldiers. Addressing the full group on the morning of their departure, a messenger explained, "We have a message from the castle for the Asantehene. We're a big group, but we have to travel fast because the Asantehene needs to hear the message before he returns to the coast. We're carrying food and water so we can eat during the day, taking little time. Four soldiers will be with us until we reach Assin Manso and leave Fante territory.

"Along the way people will ask what happened with the rebels. We'll tell them what the rebels did and their fate. I hope that will convince more Fante to stay loyal to the Asantehene.

"Our travel time to Elmina was thirteen days, but we were delayed at the Pra River and when one of our soldiers became sick. We want to return to Kumasi in twelve days, seven days to the Pra River, then five more days to Kumasi. Are you ready?" The group murmured assent.

"Look at Elmina Castle one more time," Kwame urged Baako as the group departed. "It's huge and scary. The whites look strange, but they were nice to us."

"I wanted to see whites, but now I want to leave," Baako said. "I was scared when we came. I'm glad Atore stopped me when I tried to run away, but I want the king to stop trading prisoners. The Gurunsi suffer too much."

Kwame agreed. "I didn't want Papa to buy another prisoner," he said, "but it's good that he bought Atore. I want this trade to stop, too. We have enough people to do our work in the forest, and I don't want anymore prisoners to come to the castles."

"We'll see Cape Coast Castle again today," Kwame continued, now eager for the trip. "I want to see the ships again. Maybe we'll hear cannons, too. I want to know where the whites come from and how they make all that we trade for. If I'm a trader, I have to know about that."

"You said that you didn't like to travel so far."

"I think now that I will be a trader, but only in the dry season when it's easy to walk, even if I have to walk a long way. I'll stay home in the rainy season. Then I can be with my family. I'll sell things in the marketplace and work on our farm. If we don't have *nnonko* when I'm a trader, who will be my porters? I'll have to find people in my family who want to be traders like me and work with me."

"I want to see the fishermen again. I want to go fishing in the ocean," Baako said. "The fishermen are brave and smart. We could come back and find Kobe. I think he would help us."

"I like hearing the whites talk and the guards talk to the whites," Kwame said. "The whites' language sounds strange. Do you think we could learn it?"

"I think so, but no Ahantas read or write Dutch, so the Asantehene doesn't write messages to Elmina Castle. That's strange because the castle has been here for a long time. It must be hard for the messengers to memorize the king's messages," Baako answered. "It would be easier to write and read messages."

"I hope we go to the next *Odwira* in Kumasi," Kwame said. "We missed the festival this time. Maybe we can be apprentices in Kumasi like Kofi Edu. He's learning to carve. I could learn to be a trader, and you could learn to write. Or maybe we could both learn to write. That would help me be a trader."

"I want to see an *Odwira* festival, too," Baako replied. "If you're a trader, maybe I would go with you to the savannah someday. I want to see it and find the Gurunsi people. We would have to find out where they live. Maybe Atore could show us. Kwaku might want to come, too."

"Most of all, I want to be free," Baako stated firmly. "I have to be free to do all of these things."

"I think my papa will adopt you," Kwame was encouraging. "He'll learn about this trip when we're home again. He'll know you did well."

"I tried to escape," Baako said.

"Not until the end, and that was really scary. I was afraid, too," Kwame consoled Baako.

"Seven days to the Pra River, and five days from there to Kumasi. That's our plan," the Okyeame repeated to the boys. "We'll find little hills and a poor road to Assin Manso, but the soldiers will pace us. After that we'll be on a great-road again. Even the big hills near Kumasi won't slow us down."

Others shared the Okyeame's enthusiasm. "I want us to be in Kumasi soon, and then in Tanoso again," Elder Kwasi added. "Our families need us."

Baako translated for Atore, who replied, "My family is safe. I want to see them again. Tanoso will be my new home."

O NCE IN THE FOREST, THE GROUP WELCOMED THE FAMILIAR SOUNDS OF SQUAWKING parrots, screeching falcons, hissing boars and grasscutters, and crying bush babies.

"When I hear forest sounds, I know where I am and what to expect," Kwame told the Okyeame on the second evening of their return journey. "I feel safe."

"Even if we have snakes and ants and mosquitoes?" the Okyeame asked.

"Even with tsetse flies and crocodiles," Kwame replied, smiling.

The group was startled during the night by a growling sound that persisted for several minutes. The boys couldn't identify the sound and stayed inside of their hut. At breakfast a soldier explained. "That was a leopard. They usually hunt at night. We've heard them, but we've never seen one. Local people know about them."

"I didn't know there were leopards here," Kwame exclaimed. "My papa said that they were all killed near Tanoso, but we saw some. He wants them to stay near us."

"Your papa is brave," the soldier replied. "Leopards are dangerous, and most have been killed. Your people will have to be careful if leopards return to your area."

"Some may have been killed here in the fighting," Elder Kwasi suggested.

"Some may have left the area because of the fighting," the Okyeame speculated. "Perhaps the ones we saw near Tanoso came from here."

"Just like the baboons. I hope the baboons come back to the coast," Baako said, "but I want the leopards to stay with us. Kwaku's taking the cub home. Its mama will be happy to see it. I want to see it again, too."

T HE GROUP ARRIVED IN A SSIN M ANSO IN FOUR DAYS. "Y OU KEPT US SAFE. W E ARE grateful. Protect the traders. We wish you success," the messengers told the soldiers.

The soldiers spokesman replied, "*Medaase*. We're pleased that we rescued the captives and arrested the rebels. The Asantehene will return soon with his army. There is much work to do here. You'll travel now on a great-road. Two men with guns are with you. You'll be safe."

Three more days took the group to the Pra River and a swift crossing. At the end of five more days of strenuous travel, the group arrived in Kumasi. With the drummer beating his drum furiously, they entered the city, and the messengers ran to the palace with the others trailing behind.

The messengers were granted an immediate audience with the Asantehene. They delivered the message from the governor of Elmina Castle and reported on their trip with details about the robbery, kidnapping, and arrest of the Fante rebels.

The Asantehene thanked the messengers and told them to rest. Planning a return to the coast, he was sending messengers to call new groups of soldiers to join him or meet him in Fante territory. He was pleased to learn that more guns and ammunition would be waiting for him at Elmina Castle. Alarmed about the robbery and kidnapping, he summoned the other travelers to the palace.

Elder Kwadwo led the group to the Asantehene's palace. They were ushered into a courtyard, where one of the Asantehene's brothers met them. "*Akwaaba*. I am Osei Yaw," he said. "Meet our pet monkey, Kwadu. She'll greet you, too."

"We learned about Kwadu from my children, who came here during the *Odwira*," Elder Kwadwo explained.

"Then I met your family. I'm glad to meet you now," the host replied. "The Asantehene wants me to learn what happened with your group and the Fante rebels. I'm sorry about the trouble but happy to see that you returned safely."

The Okyeame told of finding Atore, the robbery, and the kidnapping of Kwame, Baako, and Atore. He asked the boys to explain what happened to them.

"So many things in a short time," Kwame answered, and he and Baako described their kidnapping and captivity, and how the soldiers rescued them.

"That's quite an adventure," their host said with interest and sympathy. "How did the rebels treat you?"

"They kept us tied together most of the time, and the leader didn't want us to talk," Baako answered. "He fed us well, and he didn't beat us. Sometimes he was nice. He wants to fight the Asantehene. He wants the Fante to be free again, but he and his friends are in prison now."

"The rebels committed treason," Elder Osei Yaw stated affirmatively. "They will never be free again. The Asantehene wants your family to know that he regrets this incident. The Fante will be punished. He will replace the gold dust that was stolen."

Turning to Elder Kwadwo, Elder Osei Yaw continued, "The Asantehene will send new yams to your home to compensate for your family's suffering."

"We thank you and the Asantehene for your concern," Elder Kwadwo replied.

"May I ask you a question?" Baako said to their host.

"Please go ahead."

"We learned in the foreigners' zone that the Asantehene sends messages to the Gonja kings in Arabic, but the messengers to Elmina Castle memorized their message and said it to an interpreter. Why doesn't the Asantehene find people to write the whites' language?"

"Why can't we learn to write in Twi?" Kwame asked. "Abdul in the foreigners' zone wrote our names in Twi with Arabic letters. Writing in Twi would be the best."

"You ask important questions," Elder Osei Yaw replied. "I'll try to answer you. The imams brought writing to us long ago. They came with books written in Arabic. Asantehenes have used their knowledge to exchange messages with the savannah kingdoms that have imams. At our court imams keep records for the Asantehene. Some traders keep records in Arabic, too.

"There are no imams on the coast. Asantehenes sent children to the castles to learn the whites' languages long ago, but nothing came of it. The Kumasi chiefs are suspicious now and don't want to do that again. If we trade directly with more castles, I think that the Asantehene will want our children to learn the whites' languages. Writing in Twi, I don't know about that. I'll tell my son to ask the imam."

"Thank you for your patient answer," Elder Kwasi said immediately.

"*Medaase*," Baako and Kofi repeated.

"I want to learn to write Arabic. Can I learn here in Kumasi?" Baako asked.

"Muhammad al-Ghamba is the senior imam in the foreigners' zone," Elder Osei Yaw explained. "He sometimes comes to our court, and we call him Baba. He's teaching seventy boys in the foreigners' zone how to read and write in Arabic. The Asantehene sends some children to him, including one of my sons. While you're here, go with my son to the imam. See what he's like."

"*Medaase*. I want to do that," Baako replied with enthusiasm.

"I want to learn how to be a trader. Can I do that in Kumasi?" Kwame asked.

Elder Osei Yaw nodded. "There are so many traders in Kumasi. If you stay here, you can be an apprentice to one of them."

"*Medaase*," Kwame responded. "I'll ask my mama and papa if I can do that. I might want to learn Arabic, too. Traders use that language. May I go with your son tomorrow?"

"Yes. If you boys come in the morning, you can go with my son to learn Arabic."

"Kwame and Baako, if you return to Kumasi, Madam Adjowa and I will welcome you to our home," Elder Kwadwo offered.

"That will be prefect," Elder Osei Yaw said. "Come see us in the morning. Thank you for telling me your story. I'll talk to the Asantehene. I wish you a safe journey home. *Nanteyie*."

— CHAPTER 50 —

The New Year

IN THE LATE AFTERNOON OF THEIR EIGHTH DAY OF TRAVEL, THE OKYEAME, ELDER KWASI, Kwame, Baako, and Atore entered Tanoso. People on the main street applauded. Nana received the delegation at the palace with great warmth. "*Akwaaba!*" he said over and over to his son and friends. "I'm pleased they found you," he told Atore, who bowed his head.

The Queen Mother, Madam Ama, Akua, and Yaw Mensah soon joined everyone repeating, "*Akwaaba*," as their tears flowed. The travelers smiled with pleasure, but their faces showed fatigue.

"Okyeame and Elder Kwasi, go home to your families," Nana instructed. "Baako and Atore, stay here. I'll send a messenger to tell Asare to come for you. The town crier will tell everyone that the full *Odwira* delegation is home again. Tomorrow, the Okyeame and Elder Kwasi will tell the council about their trip. Tomorrow night, our family will gather to celebrate."

Kwaku burst into the courtyard and ran to his friends. The boys huddled together, jumping up and down and yelling, "We did it! We did it! We did it!"

THE NEXT MORNING ASARE BROUGHT ATORE, APURE, AND THEIR CHILDREN TO THE palace. Asare translated as Nana spoke to them. "You are safe here. You have a village here. Asare will train you, and you will work for Elder Kwasi. He will talk to you soon."

"For us to be together again is more than I thought possible," Atore explained. "I thank my wife for asking for your help, and you for helping. There was danger, but your people succeeded. We respect you and the Asantehene, even though it is the Asantehene who causes the Gonja to raid us."

"Our children will grow up in peace," Apure added. "*Medaase.*"

Nana acknowledged the tribute and concluded the audience. Atore and Apure repeated, "*Medaase.*"

Nana was jovial that night. With the return of his full delegation from Kumasi, he and the council were preparing for the *Odwira* celebration in Tanoso. "We'll remember our ancestors, celebrate our yam harvest, and mark the beginning of the new year. We'll eat yams again soon," he assured his family.

The Okyeame, Elder Kwasi, Elder Kofi, Madam Adjowa, and Kwaku arrived, as did Asare and Baako to join Nana's family around the hearth. "I'll share some of Kumasi with you," Nana said, bringing out two pouches. "First though, I want the boys to tell you what they learned on their trip." The audience paid close attention.

"I cannot say at one time all that I learned," Kwame began. "The kingdom is big, and I saw the different lives of Akans. I know forest life. I saw city life and life on the coast. There were craftsmen, traders, fishermen, soldiers, and messengers for the king, working in ways that I didn't know about.

"Whites bring us tools and cloth. Other foreigners bring us books and can teach us to read and write. I met my cousins, Kofi Edu and Akousa. I missed the *Odwira* festival. I fell into the Pra River, and I know I must learn to swim. I walked for more days than I can count. I saw the ocean and castles and heard a leopard growl. I'm happy to be home, but I want to do it all again." Kwame's audience applauded.

Baako continued the story. "The Okyeame, Elder Kwasi, Kwame, and I traveled with the king's messengers and found the prisoner that Nana wanted to buy. Fante rebels kidnapped him, Kwame, and me. His name is Atore, and he helped us. He told us what prisoners do to stay safe and he tackled me when I tried to escape. He told me to be brave like my ancestors who hunted lions.

"The rebels took us to the ocean where we tasted salt water and rode in a canoe. We heard an *oburoni* talk, and the Asantehene's soldiers rescued us. In Kumasi we saw books. There are many new things, but this one is the best. I want to read and write." The audience applauded once more.

"I returned from Kumasi with a leopard cub taken from our forest," Nana recounted. "The Asantehene gave it to me to bring home. He will help us protect leopards, as well as elephants, monkeys, parrots, and falcons. We want our forest to be whole again. The cub was well in Kumasi, and Kwaku cared for it on our return trip. He did all that he could for the cub before it died. I hope that the rest of its family has survived. Kwaku took part in the *Odwira* festival, and I want him to tell you what he saw and heard."

"I'm happy that Kwame and Baako are home again," Kwaku began. "I missed them in Kumasi. The *Odwira* parade was grand with the Golden Stool, big umbrellas, loud music, gunshots, and all of the people. I saw the Asantehene, and I know he is powerful. I want our

Odwira festival to be big and noisy like the one in Kumasi. I want to read and write, too."

"*Medaase*, Kwame, Baako, and Kwaku," Nana thanked the boys. "I'm pleased that you came with my delegation to Kumasi, and I'm deeply grateful that you have returned safely. I thank our ancestors for protecting you. I'll ask the Okyeame, Elder Kwasi, and Asare to speak now."

"It was an honor to travel with the Asantehene's messengers," the Okyeame spoke first. "We needed their help to find Atore. Our trip to the coast was difficult. Kwame and Baako remained strong when we crossed the Pra River and entered Fante territory. Baako helped me talk to prisoners. He respected Atore after we purchased him."

"I took the place of one of the messengers' soldiers, but I couldn't protect us from the rebels," Elder Kwasi explained. "They are dangerous. The boys were brave when they were kidnapped. Baako translated so Kwame and Atore could talk. The boys took advice from the *odonko*. The three of them helped each other and survived."

Asare spoke, "I know Kwame, Kwaku, and my son well. I see them work hard on Nana's farms and help each other. They're learning to throw spears and will soon learn to hunt. I'm pleased that Baako translated for Atore. The boys needed his help and accepted it."

Nana concluded, "Kwame, Kwaku, and Baako, you walked a great distance and carried supplies. You followed the direction of your elders. You were brave when you faced the unknown. You sought counsel when you had questions, and you helped others when they needed you. You have proven yourselves worthy to become leaders of our people. I will adopt Baako." The boys maintained a respectful silence but smiled with great pleasure and satisfaction. The audience applauded.

"I will share more of Kumasi," Nana said to the group as he opened the pouches. "From the brass smith, there is more light for our Queen Mother. I've brought a brass lamp for her with an oil cup that has birds sitting on its rim. Perhaps they will sing to her."

"*Medaase*, my son. You are generous," the Queen Mother responded with delight.

"For Yaw Mensah, I have a carving of a horse that's like the real horses we saw in Kumasi." Nana handed the carving to his son. "You see what a horse looks like, Yaw Mensah. It's big enough for a person to ride on its back."

Yaw Mensah held the horse with curiosity. "Oh, I like it," he said. "*Medaase*, Papa."

"This is the first horse that Madam Adjowa's brother, Elder Kojo, has carved," Nana explained. "He did it for you, Yaw." The others admired the horse, too, especially those who had never seen a real one.

"In Kumasi I rode fast on a horse called Doki," Kwaku recalled. "He knew how to make cattle move. His owner talked to him in Hausa, and he understood."

"I want to see a real horse, Papa," Yaw Mensah said.

"In time, Yaw Mensah, in time," Nana answered.

"Akua, your cousin, Kofi Edu, carved a doll for you," Nana explained as he handed the gift to Akua, who held the doll carefully.

"*Medaase*, Papa. I'll thank Kofi Edu when I see him. The doll is beautiful." Others agreed.

"For the boys, there are gold weights that they selected." Nana named the weights and passed them to everyone to see the fine work.

The boys replied, "*Medaase.*"

"As for me," Nana said smiling, "the brass smith gave me a gold weight in the shape of a sword so I may always carry a sword." Nana passed the gold weight, and the others smiled, too. "We saw looking glasses in the Kumasi market, and Akosua wanted all of us to have one," Nana told the group. "Many people in Kumasi use them. They come from the whites. We've heard of them, but no traders have brought them here. I'll give each of you a looking glass so you'll see your face." Everyone was fascinated and spent time looking at their own face and the faces of others. Some laughed. Some frowned while others squealed with pleasure.

"Let us return to reading and writing," Nana continued. "You know that I inherited my uncle's war smock. It has many talismans, but I wanted more to be prepared if the Asantehene calls us to fight the Fante. I took the boys to the foreigners' zone in Kumasi to find someone who makes them. We met an imam, a priest, a Hausa named Abdul who can read and write Arabic. I bought talismans from him. He assured me that they are strong." The group murmured with discomfort.

"I asked Abdul to tell us about writing. He showed us how he draws pictures for sounds and how he writes on both cloth and paper. We saw Abdul write on paper to make talismans. He read to us what he had written and translated the message into Twi.

"Abdul told us that imams write messages to Gonja kings for the Asantehene. He showed us many papers with writing put together to make a book. We saw him write our names on cloth. Baako, show everyone our names." Baako unrolled the cloth and held it up for everyone to see. Some gasped. No one spoke.

١ - نانا

٢ - كوفي ايدو

٣ - أكوسوا

٤ - كوامي

٥ - كواكو

٦ - باكو

٧ - أكوا

٨ - ياو مينساه

٩ - ماما

١٠ - غراني

"Tell us what is on the cloth," Madam Ama directed.

"Here are our names," Baako replied. "Abdul wrote them in Arabic letters." Holding a finger under each numeral and name, Baako read from right to left, "1. Nana; 2. Kofi Edu; 3. Akosua; 4. Kwame; 5. Kwaku; 6. Baako; 7. Akua; 8. Yaw Mensah; 9. Mama; 10. Grannie."

The group looked and listened, fascinated and suspicious. "This is new. What does it mean for us? What will we do with writing?" the Queen Mother asked.

"There's more," Kwame answered immediately. "When Baako and I returned to Kumasi from the coast, we went to the foreigners' zone with a nephew of the Asantehene. A different imam teaches boys how to read and write. We practiced with them. If Baako, Kwaku, and I learn to read and write, we'll write what we learn. We'll read to people. We won't have to remember everything."

"We could write the names of our ancestors. We could write what the talking drums tell us. We could write Ananse stories. We could write the names of our crops and how much we harvest," Kwaku suggested. Adults shook their heads at these ideas.

"What does a book look like?" Madam Adjowa asked.

"We saw a book that is as big as a man's hand. Abdul said that some books are bigger," Baako explained. "A book has many pages. It has front and back covers made of leather to keep it safe. Covers can be brown or black or red or green. Abdul said there are books about food, cloth, gold, horses, armies, so many things."

"With the other boys in Kumasi, Baako and I wrote more words on cloth," Kwame continued. "We'll show you and read the words."

Kwame, Kwaku, and Baako reading Arabic

The group was quiet and appreciative as Kwame read some of the words, "Monday, Tuesday, Wednesday."

"Kwame, my son, this is so very new to us," Madam Ama said softly. "I'm proud of you."

"Kwame, Kwaku, and Baako have learned of new possibilities for their lives and ours," Nana said to the group. "Reading and writing and books may become important. Change will come, even if slowly. We look for leaders who can prepare us." The audience applauded once more.

"We want to teach you writing," Kwame said to Akua and Yaw Mensah. "We'll help you." Akua and Yaw Mensah with the older boys broke off twigs from pieces of firewood and retreated to a corner of the courtyard to write their names in the dirt.

"You are my family and my close friends," Nana concluded. "Your presence in my life is a gift from *Nyame* and my ancestors. I am blessed. With the *Odwira*, we will join together to honor our ancestors, celebrate the yam harvest, and welcome a new year."

"Our ancestors are watching and listening," the Queen Mother told the group. "My brother is smiling."

A SHORT TIME LATER, THE *ODWIRA* CELEBRATION IN TANOSO BEGAN EARLY ONE morning when Nana, the Okyeame, and several elders walked to a sacred place on the bank of the Tano River to pour a libation to the ancestor chiefs and the spirits of the river and the forest. A sheep was sacrificed and a gun fired. When the group returned to the palace, the talking drums called everyone together for a parade.

Musicians led the parade with the music of elephant tusk horns, ringing bells, and drumming. The blacksmith, the potters, and other craftsmen and women, traders, hunters, and farmers took part and showed their role in the community by carrying items that they had made or used in their work. The market manager led several women bearing head loads of crops from their farms. Headmen from nearby villages walked. Children danced.

Elders and clan heads joined, wearing their finest cloths and jewelry, with some walking under colorful umbrellas. A few fired muskets into the air using gunpowder but no musket balls. Asare was permitted to bring several *nnonko*, including the newly arrived family into town. They watched with curiosity. The long parade wound through town several times.

*Borne in his palanquin under a colorful umbrella topped by a golden
falcon, Nana celebrates the Odwira festival in Tanoso.*

Shaded by his colorful umbrella bearing the finial of a golden falcon and wearing *kente* cloth and gold adornment while waving his horse tail switch, Nana was borne high in his palanquin by four *nnonko*. An *odonko* followed carrying Nana's stool, also protected by an umbrella. Nana's elegant appearance and ready smile brought cheers and applause from his people.

Everyone living in Tanoso and nearby villages was in the parade or watching or doing something of each while cheering. Standing on the side of the main street, Kwame, Kwaku, and Baako held palm fronds.

"Let's go," Kwaku urged. "We'll celebrate that Nana is going to adopt Baako."

"Yes," Kwame affirmed. "Soon, we'll all be Akan." Baako smiled with pride.

"I'll show you how we danced in Kumasi," Kwaku offered. Stepping into the parade, he twirled, stomped his feet, and waved palm fronds. Kwame, Baako, Akua, and Yaw Mensah joined him. The Queen Mother and Madam Ama waved.

The parade concluded when Nana returned to the palace. Sitting in his royal chair with the Queen Mother, the Okyeame, and elders on either side, Nana received each elder and headman, who pledged his loyalty. When the Odwira celebration concluded, Nana and his people ate newly-harvested yams. The edges of two years had met.

INTRODUCTION TO THE AKAN PEOPLE

THE AKAN PEOPLE HAVE LIVED IN THE RAINFOREST AND ON THE COASTAL PLAINS OF Ghana for over a thousand years. They are divided into many groups that have different names, but share a core culture, and speak the same language, Twi. Akan culture remains vibrant today, with over seventeen million Akan people living in Ghana, and thousands more living in other countries.

For two hundred years, 1701-1900, most Akan were united in the Asante Kingdom that governed much of the area that is now Ghana. By 1800, the kingdom, known for its complex culture, extensive trade network, and courageous army was the most powerful of its time in West Africa.

At the time of the kingdom, most Akans lived in villages and towns governed by clans, elders, and chiefs. The capital, Kumasi, was a major city. The Akan extended family structure was strong, providing for cooperative work to clear land, farm, hunt, fish, and mine for gold. Seeking a greater labor supply, Akans used prisoners of war and foreign people as slaves, who were protected by Akan law and whose descendants were adopted by Akan families.

For centuries, forest-dwelling Akans traded food crops with coastal Akans for salt and smoked fish. They traded gold and kola nuts, products of the forest, with people of the savannah to their north for cattle, cloth, salt, shea butter, and slaves, as well as luxury goods brought by camel caravan across the Sahara Desert from North Africa and Europe.

Europeans sailed to Akan territory on the Atlantic coast in the late 1400s. Trading companies from the modern countries of Portugal, Holland, Great Britain, France, Denmark, Sweden, and Germany built forts and castles as trade depots on the Akan coast. Europeans exchanged manufactured goods, especially cloth, metal tools, and later, guns and ammunition, for gold, ivory, and pepper. By the mid-1600s, Akans traded prisoners to Europeans as well, thus entering the Atlantic slave trade to the Americas.

The year of the story, 1807, was pivotal for Akans. In March, the British parliament outlawed British participation in the slave trade. With this, the Asante Kingdom lost a major buyer of its prisoners. In June, the kingdom's army defeated the Fante, an Akan group on the coast, giving the kingdom greater access to coastal trading and more power but peace with the Fante was years to come.

Throughout the 1800s, the Asante Kingdom grappled with the changing economics of its trade, as Europeans, with the exception of the British, gradually abandoned or sold their trade depots in Akan territory. The kingdom engaged in diplomacy, compromise, and conflict with British traders and the British government. A British army defeated the Asante Kingdom in 1900 and the kingdom, with surrounding areas, became the British colony called the Gold Coast. In 1957 the Gold Coast gained independence as the nation of Ghana.

MANY READERS KNOW ASPECTS OF AKAN CULTURE. SOME READ AND TELL STORIES about Ananse, the clever spider. Akan music and dance are familiar. Strips of intricately woven *kente* cloth enhance graduation robes. The Akan names, Kwame and Kofi, are well known. Many African-Americans trace their history to the Akan people. Millions have toured the trading forts and castles on the Ghanaian coast which are now museums.

Fewer readers, however, know Twi, the Akan language. Words and phrases for greetings and familiar items in Twi are included in the story along with their English translations. The Twi word for slave, *odonko*, and the plural, *nnonko*, are also used. Recordings of these words and a conversation in Twi may be heard at **www.dorothybrownsoper.com**.

Akan history, religion, oral traditions, rituals, celebrations, stories, music, dance, crafts, and art have been studied and described by many scholars. Their work is the basis of *We Are Akan*, and several of their publications are listed in the bibliography. For those who want to know more, these and other publications are available in research and some public libraries. Despite this scholarship, there are few works of fiction or non-fiction for the general public that include the history of the Akan people or the Asante Kingdom. *We Are Akan* is fiction, but it will introduce readers to both.

For reference, the glossary includes the names of individuals in the story, a listing of the Twi words and phrases used and their translation into English, and further information about the Akan culture and the sites visited or mentioned in the story.

The author's website includes resource materials for educators. The book's illustrations may also be downloaded for educational purposes. Please visit **www.dorothybrownsoper.com**.

GLOSSARY

INDIVIDUALS IN THE STORY

Abdul: Hausa trader and imam in the foreigners' sector of Kumasi. He reads and writes Arabic and makes and sells talismans.

Adjowa: Baby girl born on Monday

Akosua: Daughter of Elder Kwadwo and Madam Adjowa; lives in Kumasi; 8 years old

Akua Anane: Daughter of Nana Anyensu and Madam Ama; lives in Tanoso; 8 years old

Amir: Hausa trader in Kumasi with the horse named Doki

Anyetata: *Odonko* belonging to Nana Anyensu; Asare's wife and Baako's mother; of the Gurunsi people; speaks Twi

Apure: Gurunsi prisoner whom Elder Kwasi bought with her two children in Kumasi; wife of Atore

Asa: Child of an *odonko* belonging to Elder Kwasi and Madam Ama

Asantehene Osei Bonsu: King of the Asante Kingdom; ruled 1800-1823

Asantehene Osei Tutu: Founder of the Asante Kingdom in 1701; died c. 1717

Asantehene Osei Kwame: King of the Asante Kingdom; ruled 1777-1798

Asare: *Odonko* belonging to Nana Anyensu; foreman of Nana's *nnonko*; Anyetata's husband; Baako's father; of the Gurunsi people; speaks Twi

Atore: Gurunsi prisoner bought from the traders taking him to Elmina Castle; husband of Apure

Atta: Akua's friend

Atoyene: Asare and Anyetata's daughter; Baako's sister

Awane: Gurunsi boy; son of Apure and Atore

Baako: *Odonko*; Asare and Anyetata's son and eldest child; friend of Kwame and Kwaku; 13 years old

Ebo: Fante rebel whose group kidnapped Baako, Kwame, and Atore

Elder Kofi: Nana Anyensu's brother-in-law; married to Nana's senior sister, Madam Adjowa; Kwaku's father

Elder Kojo: Brother of Madam Adjowa in Kumasi; wood carver; called 'Uncle Kojo' by Kofi Edu and Akosua. Kojo is one of the day names for a boy born on Monday.

Elder Kwadwo: Nana Anyensu's cousin in Kumasi. His mother was a younger sister of the Queen Mother.

Elder Kwasi: Madam Ama's senior brother

who will be responsible for her children when they are grown; called 'Uncle Kwasi' by Kwame, Akua, and Yaw Mensah

Elder Osei Yaw: Brother of the Asantehene; lives at the palace in Kumasi

Kofi Edu: Son of Elder Kwadwo and Madam Adjowa; lives in Kumasi; 10 years old

Kobe: Fante boy who rode in a canoe with Kwame and Baako; apprenticed to the canoe owner who is his uncle; 12 years old

Kwabena: Son of Madam Afua who goes to the stream to collect water with her, his sister, Yaa, Akua and Yaw Mensah

Kwaku: Son of Elder Kofi and Nana's senior sister, Madam Adjowa; friend of Kwame and Baako; possible heir to the chieftaincy in Tanoso; 11 years old

Kwame Okoto: Elder son of Nana Anyensu and Madam Ama; friend of Kwaku and Baako; 12 years old

Madam Abena: Madam Ama's senior sister; called 'Auntie Abena' by Kwame, Akua, Yaw Mensah and other children

Madam Adjowa: Nana's senior sister; called 'Auntie Adjowa' by Kwame, Akua, and Yaw Mensah and other children

Madam Adjowa: Wife of Elder Kwadwo; mother of Kofi Edu and Adjowa; lives in Kumasi

Madam Afua: Woman in Tanoso who takes Akua, Yaw Mensah and her children, Kwabena and Yaa, to the stream to collect water

Madam Ama: Wife of Nana Anyensu; mother of Kwame, Akua, and Yaw Mensah; her children call her 'Mama'

Madam Yaa: Potter in Kumasi; sister of Madam Adjowa in Kumasi

Muhammad al-Ghamba: Senior imam in Kumasi who founded a school and taught Arabic to boys; called Baba in the Asantehene's court

Nana Akomea: Eldest of the grandfather chiefs of the black stools

Nana Anyensu: Tanosohene, chief of the Tanoso district; called 'Nana' by townspeople and 'Papa' by his children, Kwame, Akua, and Yaw Mensah; husband of Madam Ama

Nana Somfo: Young chief of the Akan district across the Tano River from Tanoso

Okomfo Anokye: Priest of Osei Tutu who commanded the descent of the Golden Stool from the sky

Okyeame: Spokesman for Nana Anyensu; occupies a high ranking position

Queen Mother: Mother of Nana Anyensu and Madam Adjowa; holds a high office; a counselor to Nana; called 'Grannie' by Kwame, Akua, Yaw Mensah, and other children

Tawia: Akua's friend

Yaa: Daughter of Madam Afua who goes to the stream to collect water with

Akua and Yaw Mensah; name of one of the Asantehene's nieces who lives at the palace in Kumasi

Yaw Mensah: third child of Nana Anyensu and Madam Ama; 6 years old

AKAN NAMES GIVEN ACCORDING THE DAY OF THE WEEK THAT A CHILD IS BORN; BOY/GIRL

Monday: Kwadwo—Adjowa
Tuesday: Kwabena—Abena
Wednesday: Kwaku—Akua
Thursday: Yaw—Yaa

Friday: Kofi—Afua
Saturday: Kwame—Ama
Sunday: Kwasi—Akosua

AKAN DEITIES

Asase Yaa: Goddess of the Earth. Akan people honor her and give her a day of rest on Thursdays by pouring a libation to her and refraining from tilling the soil.

Nyame: Akan supreme being who created heaven and earth.

FOLK HERO

Kwaku Ananse: The clever and sometimes troublesome spider or spider/man who is a central figure in many Akan folk tales.

PLACE NAMES

Introduction: With the exception of the fictional town of Tanoso in *We Are Akan*, place names refer to authentic sites.

Two castles and one fort of the numerous trading depots built by Europeans on the Atlantic coast of Ghana beginning in 1482 figure in the story and are listed below.

Most castles and forts were built for legitimate trade in which Europeans offered manufactured goods such as cloth and metal tools and later guns and ammunition in exchange for gold, ivory, and pepper. In the early1600s, the forts and castles became trading depots for the Atlantic slave trade while legitimate trade continued.

Trading companies from the modern countries of Portugal, Spain, Holland, Sweden, Denmark, Germany, France, and Great Britain built and governed castles and forts at different times over three centuries, and often fought one another over them.

A limited number of European traders lived and worked in the castles and forts and paid local chiefs for the use of their land. Local people were hired to work for the traders, transferring goods and prisoners by canoe between the trading ships and the shore.

During the slave trade, prisoners worked on nearby farms or were held in prisons in the forts and castles until ships arrived to take them to the Americas.

At the time of the story, a British trading company governed Fort Anomabo and Cape Coast Castle, and a Dutch trading company governed Elmina Castle.

Abura: Coastal fishing village between Cape Coast and Elmina.

Accra: In 1807, the site of three trading depots governed by traders from Denmark, Holland, and Great Britain; now the capital of Ghana.

Assin Manso: Trading town in Fante territory where prisoners bathed and covered their bodies with palm oil as they approached the castles to be sold to the Atlantic slave trade.

Benya River: Located in southwestern Ghana; flows into the Atlantic Ocean in Elmina, just east of the castle.

Cape Coast Castle: Large stone castle on the Atlantic coast of Ghana. The Portuguese built a fort on this site in 1555. Traders from Sweden, Denmark,

Holland and Great Britain governed the site and the structure gradually became a castle. British traders governed the castle after 1665.

Elmina Castle: Large stone castle on the Atlantic coast of Ghana built by the Portuguese beginning in 1482. This was the first such structure on the Ghanaian coast. In 1637 the castle was captured by a Dutch trading company that governed it at the time of the story.

Fort Anomabo: Stone fort on the Atlantic coast of Ghana. This trading site was established in 1640 and governed by trading companies from several countries until it was captured by the British in 1753.

The fort was the site of a major battle between the Asante Kingdom and the Fante in June, 1807.

Gonja lands: Located in the savannah of north-central Ghana. The Gonja Kingdom became subject to the Asante Kingdom in the mid-1700s.

Traditional leaders continued to govern but paid taxes to the Asante Kingdom in prisoners, livestock, cloth, shea butter, and luxury goods such as leather, ostrich feathers, and beads.

Gurunsi lands: Located in northwestern Ghana and southwestern Burkina Faso. The Gurunsi were farmers, hunters, and fishermen who had neither a central government nor an army. They were frequently raided and captured by the Gonja and given as tax payments to the Asante Kingdom.

Kintampo: Trading town in the Asante Kingdom about 100 miles northwest of Kumasi; located on a great-road; site of a major slave market.

Kulpawn River: Located in northwestern Ghana in the homeland of the Gurunsi people.

Kumasi: Capital of the Asante Kingdom,1701-1900; centrally located in the rainforest approximately 100 miles north of the Atlantic coast. Kumasi remains a large city and trading hub in Ghana.

Nsuben River: Once flowed on the east side of Kumasi and created a nearby marsh. The river and marsh were sources of water for the city at the time of the story. The river no longer exists.

Ofin River: Flows west of Kumasi; a tributary of the Pra River.

Pra River: Flows south of Kumasi to the Atlantic Ocean.

Salaga: Trading town in the savannah of northeastern Ghana about 150 miles from Kumasi; located on a great-road; controlled by the Asante Kingdom from the mid 1700s through the late 1800s.

The city was a major trading site for forest and savannah products and also for prisoners captured further north and given to the Asantehene as tax payments or sold to private traders.

Savannah: Grasslands with rolling hills and few trees north of the rainforest in Ghana.

Tano River: Major river in southwestern Ghana; flows to the Atlantic Ocean.

Tanoso: Fictional town in *We Are Akan*; capital of a district within the Asante Kingdom; located in the southwest of the kingdom next to both the Tano River and a great-road; about 100 miles or an eight day walk from Kumasi.

ETHNIC GROUPS

Ahanta: Akan group that lives in Elmina.

Akan: Group speaking Twi, and sharing a matrilineal culture. Akan people live primarily in the rainforest of Ghana and the Ivory Coast.

In 1807 the Akan were organized in geographical subgroups with separate names and most were incorporated into the Asante Kingdom.

Akwamu: Akan group that hid Osei Tutu and his servants when they escaped

from the Denkyira.

Akyem: Akan group whose soldiers killed Asantehene Osei Tutu.

Asante: Akan group whose chief in the late 1680s, Osei Tutu, united other Akan groups to form the Asante Kingdom.

Denkyira: Akan group living inland in central Ghana. In the 1600s the Denkyira had an independent kingdom.

Europeans: Dutch and British

Ewe: Ethnic group living in the Accra area and further east. They are not Akan but were incorporated into the Asante Kingdom.

Fante: Akan group that lives on the coast of central Ghana. The Fante successfully resisted incorporation into the Asante Kingdom until 1807, when their army was defeated at Fort Anomabo.

Ga: Ethnic group living in the Accra area and further east. They are not Akan but were incorporated into the Asante Kingdom.

Gonja: Ethnic group that lives in the savannah of north central Ghana. The Gonja Kingdom was ruled by the Asante Kingdom from the mid-1700s until 1898.

Gurunsi: An agricultural people, speaking Nankane, who live in northwestern Ghana.

Hausa: People from what is now northern Nigeria.

Moor: Scholar from the savannah cities.

Wassa: An Akan group living in south-western Ghana.

AKAN REFERENCES

African yam: A large brown oval shaped tuber with a tough skin, native to West Africa that is peeled and cooked before being eaten.

Akan clans: *Aduana, Agona, Asinie, Asokore, Asona, Beretuo, Ekuana, Oyoko*

Akan stool: A wooden stool carved from a tree trunk and measuring approximately 12 inches high, 18 inches wide, and 10 inches in depth. The seat is usually slightly curved.

Stools were the basic furniture of an Akan courtyard. They were usually left outdoors and replaced frequently. Stools with an elaborate base were carved for royal or wealthy people and kept indoors.

Each chief has a stool that is the symbol of his chieftaincy. The Golden Stool is the symbol of the Asante Kingdom.

Akpeteshie: Locally made alcoholic beverage.

Asantehene: The king of the Asante Kingdom; the title means 'chief of the Asante' in Twi.

Bushbaby: A small nocturnal primate that lives in trees. Its cries sound like those of human baby. Also called a galago.

Cassava: Small shrub native to Brazil but widely grown in the Akan rainforest at the time of the story.

Its large white root, one to two feet long, and up to six inches in diameter, is peeled and boiled and eaten pounded in fufu or ground and used in a dish called *gari*.

Cloth: Traditional Akan dress consisting of a single cloth that a person wraps around him/herself at the waist, across the chest, or around the body and over one shoulder. The plural is "cloths."

Cowrie shells: Shells of small to large ocean snails that are abundant in the Indian Ocean. Cowrie shells were frequently used as currency in African trade networks.

Dry season: In the rainforest of Ghana, the dry season, meaning no or few rains, is from November until March. The Harmattan wind blows during much of this period. Yams are typically harvested at the beginning of the dry season. Temperatures are cool.

Duiker: Antelope of moderate size. Several species live in Ghana. Their favored habitat is an old growth forest. Leopards are their main predator.

Fufu: A paste made from African yams and/or cassava and/or plantains that are boiled and then pounded in a mortar by a pestle until they form a thick paste that's eaten with soup. Fufu is a major delicacy.

Gold weights: Small brass weights made in many designs; used to weigh gold dust on a balance scale.

Golden stool: The symbol of the Asante Kingdom. In a traditional story Okomfo Anokye, the priest of Asantehene Osei Tutu, calls the stool from the sky and explains that it contains the soul of the Asante Kingdom.

Grasscutter: a large rodent that lives near water in tropical areas. It is nocturnal and lives in small groups. It's hunted for food and is considered a pest because it eats agricultural products. Also called a cane rat. If frightened it will grunt and run toward water.

Great-road: The Asantehenes paid to have district chiefs build and maintain eight wide and largely straight roads radiating from Kumasi to all parts of the kingdom. They were the main trading routes that also allowed swift passage of the king's representatives and the army.

Harmattan wind: Blows off of the Sahara Desert over West Africa at the end of the dry season. The wind typically begins in December and continues until March.

Gurunsi clans: *Gwegene, Tugfo*

Kenkey: Staple food among coastal people in Ghana made from milled dried corn kernels formed into a ball and wrapped with a corn husk or dry plantain leaves.

Kente cloth: The Akan and Ewe people practice a complex form of weaving to create *kente* cloth. The cloth is woven in strips about four inches wide. Strips are sewn together to make large cloths worn on festive occasions.

Kente cloth originally was woven with cotton and silk threads. Now rayon threads are used. The cloth is colorful, expensive, typically shared in a family, and can serve multiple generations.

Libation: The pouring of a drink on the ground while a prayer is said. Akans poured libations to honor their ancestors and also *Nyame, Asase Yaa,* and other spirits.

Long Dane musket: From 1750 through the early 1800s the most popular gun among the Akan was the long Dane flintlock musket, originally introduced by Danish traders and later offered by English and French traders.

Odwira festival: Annual festival held during the dry season to celebrate the African yam harvest and the beginning of the new year. Purification rites to honor ancestors are also performed.

District chiefs were required to attend the festival in Kumasi to pledge loyalty to the Asantehene. Chiefs also met with the Asantehene to discuss business and settle outstanding disputes.

Chiefs held an *Odwira* festival in their own districts after returning from the *Odwira* festival in Kumasi.

Oil palm tree: Native to the rainforest. Oil from its fruit is used as a cooking oil, an ingredient in palm nut soup, and as a body lotion. The fruit and oil are red in color.

Okyeame: Spokesman for a chief. Each chief has one or more to speak for him at official meetings

Those addressing a chief talk to the *okyeame,* who conveys a message to the chief even while he is sitting nearby. This practice saves the chief from having to handle difficult people who might embarrass him. The chief also addresses people through his *okyeame.*

An *okyeame* is a high ranking official who is respected for his knowledge of stories, legends, and proverbs that he uses to enhance the speech of a chief.

Outdooring: Ceremony held on a child's eighth day of life to celebrate that he or she "has come to stay."

A child receives a day name at birth. At his/her outdooring the father gives one or more additional names to his child.

Oware: Traditional game of stones played on a carved board or in holes dug in the ground.

Palanquin: Elaborate hammock carried on poles by four to six men. The rider sits with his legs stretched out and leans against a backrest. He can be seen from ground level.

A chief is carried in his palanquin in a celebration only before his subjects and subordinate chiefs, never before a chief of higher rank. The chief is shaded by a large umbrella topped with an elaborate finial.

Palm wine: Traditional alcoholic beverage obtained from a felled palm tree.

Raffia palm tree: Native to tropical areas. Its fronds were trimmed and tied to a wooden framework to construct a roof.

Rainforest: Dense, evergreen forest with tall trees in a tropical weather zone.

Rainy season: In the rainforest of Ghana, substantial rains fall from March until October. Temperatures are warm. Food crops are raised during this period.

Sankofa bird: Mythical bird whose feet face forward while it looks backward to illustrate the belief that people must learn from their history.

Shea tree: Native to the savannah areas of West Africa. Oil is extracted from the shea nut to make shea butter which is used as a body lotion and cooking oil.

Stool house: A room or a hut in the courtyard of a chief's palace where the black stools of ancestor chiefs are kept.

A blackened stool signifies that the owner has died. Stools of deceased successful chiefs are blackened and kept in a stool house to be venerated at *Adae* ceremonies.

Tsetse fly: A large biting fly native to the rainforest. It lives on the blood of vertebrate animals, including humans, and can carry a sleeping sickness parasite. The disease can be fatal to humans, horses, and cattle.

Wawa tree: A tree native to the rainforest whose trunk was used to carve dugout canoes and for construction.

TWI WORDS AND PHRASES

The following Twi words and phrases are used in *We Are Akan*. They are recorded along with a conversation in Twi at **dorothybrownsoper.com**.

Adae: /ah-DIE/; Ceremony to praise accomplished ancestor chiefs whose stools were turned black and preserved in a stool house or stool room

The *Adae* was celebrated every forty-two days. No work was done on the day of an *Adae*.

Adaepa: /ah-die-PA/; the day of preparation before the *Adae* celebration

Adowa: /ah-JO-wa/; Festive dance accompanied by singers

Agoo: /ah-GO/; May I come in?

Ahena: /eh-HE-na/; water pot

Akan: /ah-KAN/; ethnic group in Ghana that speaks Twi

Akwaaba: /ah-KWAA-ba/; Welcome!

Amee: /ah-MEEH/; I'm coming

Ampe: /am-PEY/; girls' game of clapping and jumping

Asafo: /ah-SA-fo/; local militia

Asante: /AH-san-ti/; Akan group centered in Kumasi

Asantehene: /AH-san-ti-he-ni/; king of the Asante Kingdom

Aso: /ah-SOH/; hoe used on farms

Bra aha: /BRA-ha/; Come here!

Dayie: /DA-yi-eh/; Good night

Domma: /DOH-ma/; a gold weight for one-tenth of an ounce

Dua: /dju-ah/; tree

Fie: /fi-eh/; home

Kwadu: /kwey-DU/; banana

Maadwo: /maah-JO/; Good evening to one person

Maaha: /maah-HA/; Good afternoon to one person

Maakye: /maah-CHI/; Good morning to one person

Medaase: /mi-DAA-si/; Thank you

Me ko fie: /meh-KO-fi-eh/; I'll go home.

Mema mo adwo: /meh-ma-mow-AJO/; Good evening to more than one person

Mema mo aha: /meh-ma-mow-AHA/; Good afternoon to more than one person

Mema mo akye: /meh-ma-mow-ACHI/; Good morning to more than one person

Nana: /naNA/; Chiefs and other respected elders are addressed as Nana.

Nanteyie: /nan-ti-YI-eh/; Good-bye or safe journey

Nkruma: /n-KRU-ma/; okra or okro

Nnonko: /non-KOH/; slaves

Nnwira: /n-WI-rah/; weeds

Nsuo: /n-SU-oh/;water

Nyadoa: /NYAA-do-wa/; garden egg, eggplant

Oburoni: /oh-BRO-ni/; caucasian person

Odonko: /oh-don-KOH/; slave

Odwira: /o-DWI-rah/; annual festival to celebrate the yam harvest and pledge loyalty to a chief

Okyeame: /oh-chi-AH-mi/; a chief's spokesman who is a person of high rank

Oware: /oh-WA-ri/; traditional game of stones

Tie: /ti-eh/; listen

Twi: /chwee/; language spoken by the Akan people

Wassa: /wa-SA/; Akan group that lives in the southwest of Ghana near the Tano River

Yaa: /yaah/; Generic response to a greeting

BIBLIOGRAPHY

Anquandah, Kwesi J. 1999. *Castles and Forts of Ghana.* Atalante and Paris: Ghana Museums and Monuments.

Appiah, Kwame Anthony. 2018. *The Lies that Bind: Rethinking Identity, Creed, Country, Color.* New York: Liveright Publishing Corporation.

Appiah, Peggy. 1989. *Tales of an Ashanti Father.* Boston, MA: Beacon Press Books.

Bowdich, T. Edward. 1966. *Mission from Cape Coast Castle to Ashantee.* Third Edition. London: Frank Cass and Co., Ltd.

Dupuis, Joseph. 1966. *Journal of a Residence in Ashantee.* Second Edition. London: Frank Cass and Co., Ltd.

Edgerton, Robert B. 1995. *The Fall of the Asante Empire, The Hundred-Year War for Africa's Gold Coast.* New York: The Free Press.

Fynn, J.K. 1975. *A Junior History of Ghana.* London: Prentice Hall Press.

—. 1971. *Asante and Its Neighbours 1700-1807.* Legon History Series. Evanston, IL: Longman.

Getz, Trevor R. 2018. *Primer for Teaching African History: Ten Design Principles.* Design Principles for Teaching History. Durham and London: Duke University Press.

Getz, Trevor R., and Rebecca Shumway, eds. 2017. *Slavery and Its Legacy in Ghana and the Diaspora.* London, New York: Bloomsbury Academic.

Kea, R.A. 1971. "Firearms and Warfare on the Gold and Slave Coasts from the Sixteenth to the Nineteenth Century." *The Journal of African History* 12 (2): 185-213.

Kimmel, Eric A. 1994. *Anansi and the Talking Melon.* Anansi the Trickster Series. New York: Holiday House.

Konadu, Kwasi, and Clifford C. Campbell, eds. 2016. *The Ghana Reader: History, Culture, and Politics.* Durham and London: Duke University Press.

Koslow, Philip. 1996. *Asante: The Gold Coast.* The Kingdoms of Africa. New York: Chelsea House Publishers.

Manning, Patrick. 1990. *Slavery and African Life, Occidental, Oriental, and African Slave*

We Are Akan

Trades. Cambridge: Cambridge University Press

McCaskie, T.C. 1995. *State and Society in Pre-colonial Asante.* African Studies. Cambridge: Cambridge University Press.

McLeod, M.D. 1981. *The Asante.* London: British Museum Publications, Ltd.

Nketia, J.H.K. n.d. *The Role of Traditional Festivals in Community Life.* Legon,Ghana: University of Ghana, Institute of African Studies, Education and Culture Series.

O'Grady, Alice O. 2008. *Ashanti Saga: The Fort.* Bloomington, IN: iUniverse.

Perbi, Akosua Adoma. 2007. *A History of Indigenous Slavery in Ghana from the 15th to the 19th Century.* Revised edition. Accra, Ghana: Sub-Saharan Publishers.

Rattray, R. S. 1930. *Akan-Ashanti Folk-Tales.* Oxford: Clarendon Press.

—. 1923. *Ashanti.* Oxford: Clarendon Press.

—. 1929. *Ashanti Law and Constitution.* Oxford: Clarendon Press.

—. 1927. *Religion and Art in Ashanti.* Oxford: Clarendon Press.

Shumway, Rebecca. 2011. *The Fante and the Transatlantic Slave Trade.* Rochester, NY: University of Rochester Press.

Smallwood, Stephanie. 2007. *Saltwater Slavery: A Middle Passage from Africa to American Diaspora.* Cambridge, MA: Harvard University Press.

St. Clair, William. 2007. *The Door of No Return: The History of Cape Coast Castle and the Atlantic Slave Trade.* New York: Blue Bridge.

Vogt, John. 1979. *Portuguese Rule on the Gold Coast, 1469-1682.* Athens: University of Georgia Press.

Wilks, Ivor. 1975. *Asante in the Nineteenth Century: The Structure and Evolution of a Political Order.* Cambridge: Cambridge University Press.

—. 1993. *Forests of Gold: Essays on the Akan and the Kingdom of Asante.* Athens: Ohio University Press.

Yarak, Larry W. 1990. *Asante and the Dutch, 1744-1873.* Oxford Studies in African Affairs. Oxford: Clarendon Press.

ONLINE RESOURCES

Numerous websites can be found for topics relating to the Akan people. Searchable topics include the following:

Accra
Adae festival
Adrinkra symbols
Adowa dance
Akan people
Akan palanquin
Akan stool
Ampe
Asante Kingdom
Asante people
Asantehene Osei Tutu I
Asantehene Osei Tutu II
Assin Manso
Bushbaby
Cape Coast Castle
Castles in Ghana
Driver ant
Duiker
Elmina Castle
Ewe people
Fante people
Fort Anomabo
Ga people

Gold weights
Golden stool
Grasscutter
Gurunsi people
Harmattan wind
Kente cloth
Kola tree
Kumasi
Long Dane flintlock musket
Nankane language
Odwira festival
Oil palm tree
Okomfo Anokye
Oware
Pra River
Puff adder
Python
Raffia palm tree
Sankofa bird
Shea tree
Tano River
Tsetse fly
Twi language

We Are Akan

ACKNOWLEDGEMENTS

My husband, Dave, and our children, Emmett and Margaret, have given me love and support in my work for many years, including joining me on trips to Ghana. *We Are Akan* is partly theirs.

Writing *We Are Akan* has been like taking a long trip on an Akan great-road. The destination was known, but the way was filled with new people, new information, surprising curves and bumps, and unexpected events. The journey has enriched me.

It all started during my two years in Ghana as a Peace Corps volunteer. I taught French in a rural, boarding high school, Asankrangwa Secondary School, where I was the first and, at the time, only female teacher. The school was in its third year and had admitted girls for the first time. I was placed in charge of the girls' dormitory. My students, colleagues, and friends taught me my school duties and about Akan life. I'll always be grateful.

After returning to the US, I earned a master's degree in African history and have taught African history and culture in several public school settings. Writing *We Are Akan* was a destination point on my personal great-road journey. I hope that readers will feel welcome in a culture that may be new to them.

My Akan friends have inspired and informed me and made this work possible. I owe a special tribute to my former student, Agnes Oppong, her late husband, John Bissah, and their daughters, Matilda and Abigail Bissah. They were generous hosts and helpful informants to my family and me during our visits to Ghana.

Several people informed me on specific topics. The late John Bissah and I conferred in letters and by phone for several years. John taught me about the Akan culture that he lived, as well as that of his parents and grandparents. I worked with Alberta Boakye and the late Thomas Kobina Doughan, who advised me on Twi vocabulary and Akan traditions. Emmanuel Attah Poku, Master Drummer at the Centre for National Culture in Kumasi, told me of the role of talking drums in Akan ceremonies.

Hanan Elsherif, Arabic Studies Coordinator, University of Oregon, provided the Arabic included in the story.

Elinam Kwabena Amevor, Twi instructor and graduate student in the School of Journalism and Communication, University of Oregon, recorded the Twi words and phrases used in the book and listed in the glossary. Vivian Akua Koomson and Paul Kofi Koomson, recorded the Twi conversations and advised me about Twi pronunciation. Mrs. Koomson teaches English in Ghana. Mr. Koomson is a graduate student in the School of Journalism and Communication and also an instructor in Twi at the University of Oregon. Mark Stafford of Stafford Video Productions in Eugene, OR recorded and edited the conversations. To listen to the recordings, please visit my website at **www.dorothybrownsoper.com**.

Kathryn Polansky, an award-winning javelin thrower, described the mechanics of throwing javelins to me. We generalized from that to spear throwing. My cousin, Johnny Kemp, a lifelong Texan, talked to me about handling cattle and the vocabulary to describe the job.

I thank others who helped with research, writing, and publishing. The knowledgeable research librarians at the Knight Library of the University of Oregon were generous with their time. Several friends from my Peace Corps group encouraged me. I especially appreciate the efforts of Saundra Gourley to read and comment on an early draft. I am deeply grateful to the Creative Writing group at the Osher Lifelong Learning Institute of the University of Oregon in Eugene. Members listened to me read excerpts of my work for over four years and offered thoughtful comments to guide me. I'm indebted to Pat Edwards of Groundwaters Publishing for editing early drafts and publishing excerpts from the book in three issues of the *Groundwaters' Anthology, 2017-19*. *We Are Akan* came to life with the gifted and inspirational staff of Luminare Press in Eugene, OR, who put it all together to make it shine.

I reserve special recognition for James Cloutier, the book's illustrator, who is a well known artist in Oregon. I was familiar with James' paintings of Maasai people in Kenya, where he worked as a Peace Corps volunteer. I knew that he could create illustrations to illuminate my work and originally suggested a dozen or so. We worked for four years, with James' doing significant research, to develop a pictorial message that has extended to over ninety illustrations. I'm deeply grateful for his contributions. They add more than words can convey.

ABOUT THE AUTHOR

DOROTHY BROWN SOPER grew up in Bakersfield,California. She graduated from Bakersfield High School and received a scholarship to Stanford University, where she majored in French. Her first experience living outside the US was studying for six months at the Stanford campus in France.

When she applied to the Peace Corps, she was invited to teach high school French for two years in Ghana. Assigned to a rural boarding high school and being the school's only female teacher at the time, she was placed in charge of the girls' dormitory. She credits her students and colleagues with teaching her about Akan culture and her school duties.

Returning to the US with plans to tell Americans about Africa, she earned a master's degree in African history at UCLA. As an elementary school teacher in the Eugene, Oregon public schools, she developed and taught many units on African history and culture.

Knowing that there is little for young people to read about Africa, she wrote *We Are Akan* in response. It is a work of historical fiction that is also an introduction to African history.

The author lives with her family in Eugene, Oregon. Please visit her at **www.dorothy-brownsoper.com**.

ABOUT THE ILLUSTRATOR

JAMES CLOUTIER was born and raised in Oregon and graduated from high school in Portland. He received a baseball scholarship to the University of Oregon, where he majored in art education. While in college, he took part in a Crossroads Africa program in Ethiopia.

After two years in the Navy, James joined the Peace Corps and worked in Kenya for two years in the land resettlement program, creating audio-visual materials to train land recipients to become cash crop farmers. Returning to the US, he received an MFA in photography at the University of Oregon and has pursued a career as a freelance illustrator/cartoonist/graphic designer. He founded Image West Press and has published several books of photography and cartoons about Oregon.

James specializes in drawing portraits of Oregon athletes, as well as creating cartoon maps of Eugene and Oregon. His painting of the American flag that first appeared in the children's book *14 Cows for America* by Carmen Agra Deedy is now displayed in the 9/11 Memorial Museum in New York City. Its caption reads: *To the People of America with Compassion from the Maasi.* James lives with his wife and grandson in Eugene, Oregon.

Made in the USA
Monee, IL
02 November 2020

46589578R00197